Volume 26

Satisfy your desire for more.

Secret Rendezvous by Calista Fox

Conservative McCarthy Portman is the maven behind the successful Manhattan dating service, Rendezvous. She's seen enough happily-ever-afters to long for one of her own, but when her renowned matchmaking software pairs her with the wild and wicked nightclub owner Josh Kensington, everything she's always believed about love is turned upside down.

Enchanted Spell by Rachel Carrington

Witches and wizards don't mix. Every magical being knows that. Yet, when a little mischievous magic thrusts Ella and Kevlin together, they do so much more than mix—they combust. But not everyone in Wizard Country is excited about Ella's appearance, especially once it becomes apparent her presence could very well kill a masterful wizard.

Exes and Ahhhs by Kate St. James

Former lovers Risa Haber and Eric Lange are partners in a catering business, but Eric can't seem to remain a silent partner. Risa offers one night of carnal delights if he'll sell her his share then disappear forever. Eric figures he has to play along—or does he?

The Spy's Surrender by Juliet Burns

The famous courtesan Eva Werner is the perfect double agent, England's secret weapon against Napoleon. Her orders are to attend a sadistic marquis' depraved house party and rescue a British spy being held prisoner. As the weekend orgy begins, she's forced to make the spy her love slave for the marquis' pleasure. But who is slave and who is master?

Calista Fox

Rachel Carrington

Kate St. James

Juliet Burns

Volume 26

Secrets

Satisfy your desire for more.

SECRETS Volume 26
This is an original publication of Red Sage Publishing and each individual story herein has never before appeared in print. These stories are a collection of fiction and any similarity to actual persons or events is purely coincidental.

Red Sage Publishing, Inc.
P.O. Box 4844
Seminole, FL 33775
727-391-3847
www.redsagepub.com

SECRETS Volume 26
A Red Sage Publishing book
All Rights Reserved/December 2008
Copyright © 2008 by Red Sage Publishing, Inc.

ISBN: 1-60310-005-9 / ISBN 13: 978-1-60310-005-2

Published by arrangement with the authors and copyright holders of the individual works as follows:

SECRET RENDEZVOUS
Copyright © 2008 by Calista Fox

ENCHANTED SPELL
Copyright © 2008 by Rachel Carrington

EXES AND AHHHS
Copyright © 2008 by Kate St. James

THE SPY'S SURRENDER
Copyright © 2008 by Juliet Burns

Photographs:
Cover © 2008 by Tara Kearney; www.tarakearney.com
Cover Models: Reby Sky and Jimmy Thomas
Setback cover © 2000 by Greg P. Willis; GgnYbr@aol.com

Printed in the U.S.A.

Book typesetting by:
Quill & Mouse Studios, Inc.
www.quillandmouse.com

Contents

Secret Rendezvous

by Calista Fox

To My Reader:

I have a soft spot for bad boys with big hearts. I love a tough exterior, but even more compelling is the mushy heart that lies beneath it. Josh Kensington is a fun hero—he's smart, he's successful and he's a wild-child at heart. But when Josh loves, he does it for keeps.

I first introduced Josh in *Intimate Rendezvous* (*Secrets, Volume 17*), and though I had not initially intended a story for him in the Rendezvous trilogy, by the time I reached the third story, I knew he was going to be my hero. I hope you find his fun-loving, big-hearted ways as endearing as I do. And what better heroine to match him with than Rendezvous' very own dating guru, McCarthy Portman? Fire and ice? Oil and water? I think not. These two know how to set the sheets ablaze!

Chapter 1

"Now this is a perfect gift!" Cat Hewitt let out a little squeal of delight as she lifted the black patent leather, thigh-high boots with five-inch heels out of the gift bag McCarthy Portman had just handed her. "These babies will inspire a whole new batch of erotic fantasies for David. He's going to love them!"

A pang of regret speared McCarthy's insides as Cat and the other women who'd gathered after-hours at Rendezvous for Cat's bachelorette party admired the gorgeous boots McCarthy had spent weeks searching for. They were incredibly sexy. So much so, she'd been shocked to find that she'd wanted a pair for herself when she was purchasing Cat's. Despite the lofty price tag and the fact that she'd never, ever worn anything quite so daring.

But splurging on erotic items when you had no one to share them with was just, well, pointless.

As she'd done while buying Cat's gift, McCarthy forced herself to ignore the twinge of envy that suddenly crept up on her. Last year, Cat had joined Rendezvous, the exclusive dating service McCarthy worked for, in hopes of finding a soul mate. She'd succeeded.

Just one more happily-ever-after to add to the growing list.

As pleased as McCarthy was by the impressive number of perfect matches made by her state-of-the-art software, and her diligence, she was disappointed she was unable to find her own match.

Frustrated that she had yet to meet a man with whom she was compatible, McCarthy had finally broken down and entered her profile into her dating system this very afternoon. But even that last-resort tactic had yielded unsatisfactory results. The last name she'd ever expected to see in conjunction with hers had appeared on her screen as her top match.

Josh Kensington.

For a split second, excitement had speared her insides. She'd literally gotten the jolt of a lifetime. But her euphoria had been short-lived. Confusion had quickly set in. McCarthy had stared at the computer screen for a good five minutes, wondering how on earth her matchmaking software had connected her to Josh Kensington, the owner of The Rage, the rowdy nightclub housed in the same building as Rendezvous.

Josh was the hunkiest man she'd ever laid eyes on. Definitely not what she was looking for in a match. McCarthy didn't want the hottest thing since Brad Pitt as a boyfriend. Talk about pressure.

Plus, Josh was a party animal. McCarthy was a computer geek. Josh soaked up the wild, pulsating MTV-video scene, for which his club was famous, like the parched earth after a severe drought. McCarthy preferred the cozy atmosphere of Rendezvous. She liked the jazz music that filled the club, loved to hear the soft laughter that drifted on the sexually charged air. The intimate club was infinitely more stimulating than the Head-Banger's Ball that took place downstairs every night.

Reasons number one and two why she and Josh were not simpatico.

Still….

As she'd continued to stare at her laptop, she'd been forced to admit there was something thrilling about seeing Josh's name pop up on the screen when she'd searched for a match.

That his profile had made it into her golden database at all was a bit of a shock. He'd never expressed interest in finding a girlfriend and had never sought McCarthy's help in hooking him up with the many beautiful, successful women who belonged to the exclusive dating service.

Obviously his cousin, Cassandra, had entered his information into the computer. Cass owned Rendezvous and she'd mentioned a time or two that she wished Josh would consider finding a nice girl to settle down with.

McCarthy was certainly that.

Well, actually, she wasn't just a nice girl. She was a good girl. Which made her completely unsuitable for bad boy Josh Kensington.

Strike three.

She should have just turned the computer off right then and there.

She hadn't. Clearly a glutton for punishment, she'd pulled up his photo and gazed at it with a bizarre mixture of desire and dread. Josh was simply too gorgeous for words. McCarthy had never known a man who could be considered breathtaking, but Josh stole hers with ease. He exuded raw sexuality and intense heat. Everything about the man screamed hot sex. From his silky blonde hair, to his mesmerizing ice-blue eyes, to his bulging biceps, to his long, sinewy legs, Josh Kensington was a sexual fantasy waiting to happen.

Which was all bad and wrong in her mind—and where the dread came into play. McCarthy wasn't into perfection. She preferred her men to have a flaw or two. That made her much less self-conscious of her own shortcomings. Having three beautiful sisters, not to mention a best friend like Cass—who was not only beautiful but who, like Josh, also radiated sensuality in the most irresistible way—tended to make McCarthy feel like a wallflower.

But, given her optimistic nature, she was certain her Mr. Right was out there somewhere. And she hoped to find him soon. In fact, her cutting-edge software should have had her on the road to romance this very night.

Unfortunately, there seemed to be a glitch in the program.

Something had gone seriously awry, because there was no way on God's green earth she and Josh Kensington could be a match.

No. Way.

But, McCarthy reminded herself, tonight wasn't about her. It was about Cat. She and her fiancé, David Essex, intended to elope at the end of the week. Following the phenomenally extravagant affair the Hewitts had just hosted in honor of their son's marriage to Cass, Cat thought New York society could do without another elaborate Hewitt event.

Unfortunately, she and David would be running off to Bali for their elopement while Cass and Dean were honeymooning in Tuscany. Cat had insisted they simply couldn't wait any longer to get married.

McCarthy thought the couple's impatience was romantic. And she was pleased to be able to throw Cat's bachelorette party after-hours at Rendezvous, complete with a bottomless pitcher of Cosmopolitans and some very erotic gifts.

"This is for you." Cat passed a large red gift bag to McCarthy. Her grin was positively wicked. "It's a goody bag." She gave McCarthy a conspiratorial wink.

"For me? Why on earth...?"

Cat smiled brightly at her. "For doing all of this for me," she said as she made a wide sweep with her hand, encompassing Cat's group of girlfriends that were gathered on the crimson-colored, crescent-shaped sofas that filled the cozy lounge. "I know you're up to your eyeballs managing the club while Cass is on her honeymoon, and yet you found the time to pull together a girls' night out. It's fabulous, Mac." Cat scooted across the velvet-upholstered sofa she sat on and gave McCarthy a quick hug. "You're a wonderful friend. And this is the best bachelorette party a girl could ask for."

The others agreed, raising their cocktail glasses to toast McCarthy.

"This is nothing," she said. "The male strippers haven't even arrived."

"Strippers? Plural?" Cat clasped her hands together and let out another squeal of delight. "See? Best bachelorette party ever!"

Chapter 2

"What the hell is going on upstairs?"

Josh Kensington glanced up from the batch of martinis he was making. He could barely hear his bar manager, Clint, over the raucous din that filled the nightclub. A Springsteen cover band rocked the joint, and the hypnotic flashing of strobe lights made it difficult for his eyes to focus. Regardless, Josh felt perfectly at home.

The Manhattan-chic club boasted two long, stainless steel bars, black leather furniture and glowing sapphire accents. It was also home to some of the hottest bands on the circuit. The Rage was Josh's idea of heaven.

"What's with the mop?" he asked.

"Rendezvous sprang a leak. It's trickling down into the men's john. What are those girls doing up there?"

"Aw, shit." Josh dropped toothpicks with large olives into the martinis he'd poured out of the shaker. He wiped his hands on a towel and said, "Make sure these get delivered to the table up front. VIPs. I'll take care of Rendezvous."

He came round the bar and worked his way through the tight throng of people that packed The Rage. When he made it to the dimly lit foyer, he took the spiral wrought iron staircase up to the second floor and let himself into Rendezvous, his cousin's club, with his key. He secured the door behind him, mindful of the break-in that had occurred here last year. Then he crossed the hardwood floor of the foyer.

The bacholerette party had obviously adjourned. But McCarthy was still at the club, sitting at her desk up front, her fingers clicking away on the keyboard of her laptop. She wore a white Oxford shirt over a white tank top and jeans. Soft blonde curls sat on her shoulders and framed her pretty face. The trendy black frames perched on her pert nose made her look studious and seductive at the same time.

Whenever she wore them, Billy Idol's *Rock the Cradle of Love* suddenly played in Josh's head, and his otherwise sensible brain was infiltrated by the vivid image of McCarthy dancing on top of her mahogany desk, hair flying in all directions as she carelessly tossed aside her reading glasses and slowly unbuttoned her blouse to reveal a lacy bra and the rounded tops of her full breasts.

A classic conservative-executive-by-day, hot-stripper-by-night fantasy. It made the adrenaline pump in his veins, and it also caused Josh to wonder what kind of lingerie McCarthy hid beneath her neatly pressed Ralph Lauren clothing.

His groin tightened at the thought of McCarthy in sexy underwear. Ignoring the heat that suddenly flooded his body, he walked farther into the dimly lit club. McCarthy didn't even notice, so engrossed was she with her work.

Josh couldn't help but let out a soft laugh as he shook his head. McCarthy epitomized the word tenacious. She'd go to the ends of the earth to ensure the singletons—as Cass called her dating service members— found their perfect match.

"Give it a rest, Mac. It's late. You've had a busy day, plus you hosted a bachelorette party," he said. "Your clients are content for the evening. Go home."

McCarthy glanced up from her laptop, clearly not surprised to see him because he dropped in to visit her a few times a night. Just to see if she needed anything. And well, too, because he enjoyed spending time with her.

"Not all of them are content. Most of them are still looking for...." Her voice trailed off and a frown canted her glossy lips. Her blonde brows knitted together. "Hell. Sometimes even I don't know what they're looking for." She slid the glasses down her cute nose and off her face.

She sat back in her chair, looking contemplative. And tired.

Josh knew she'd been putting in a lot of hours lately. He was concerned that she wasn't getting enough sleep, but he didn't mention his suspicion.

Instead, he planted his palms on the edge of her desk and leaned toward her. "They're looking for a hot hook-up, McCarthy."

She grinned and a little twinkle flickered in her emerald-colored eyes. "You are so cynical. Not everyone is looking for simple, no-strings-attached sex, Josh. A lot of our clients want to fall in love. And I want to help them."

Josh considered this for a moment, but he wasn't so sure he bought into the computerized compatibility fairytale. It was a little too neat and tidy and sticky sweet for him. Josh was a man who thrived on sexual stimulation. Details like someone's occupation or their five-year plan didn't mean squat to him. It was chemistry—on a physical and emotional level—that connected people. Not the answers they left on a ten-page questionnaire.

He straightened, shrugged his shoulder and said, "Whatever."

He moved away from her desk.

"Where are you going?" She pushed her chair back and stood. Following him through the lounge, the soles of her loafers making soft, wispy sounds on the polished hardwood floor, she traipsed after him as he made his way to the back of the club. "Josh?"

He waved a hand in the air. "Don't worry about it. You sprang a leak in one of the bathrooms. I'll fix it."

The wispy noise turned to solid thumps. "What?" Her voice kicked up an octave or two. "What do you mean, I 'sprang a leak?' Oh, God! Is something wrong with the club?"

Josh held his chuckle in check. Cass had left McCarthy in charge of Rendezvous while on her honeymoon. Though Josh believed her to be up to the challenge, clearly McCarthy wasn't so sure she could handle the responsibility. "Nothing's wrong with the club. Just the bathroom. I told you, I'll take care of it."

She continued to pursue him down the long corridor that led to the restrooms. As they approached the ladies' room, water began to flow toward them on the tiled floor, seeping from under the door.

Behind him, Josh heard McCarthy gasp. "Holy shit. If I flood the club, Cass will never forgive me!"

Josh shot her a look over his shoulder. "Chill, sweetheart. You're not gonna flood Rendezvous." He smiled at her, hoping to reassure her. Josh liked McCarthy. She was smart and pretty and down-to-earth. So unlike the pretentious, overly made-up women who frequented his club, vying for his attention. McCarthy was a rare breed—soft, sweet and genuine. He liked her smile and her creative mind. He also liked that she was always lost in thought.

Unfortunately, she was a tad on the insecure side when it came to managing the club. That wasn't Josh's problem and he wasn't inclined to help cure her of the misguided shortcoming.

He had his own issues.

Mainly, his nightclub. The Rage had become just that—all the rage in New York. It was now the ultimate Manhattan hot-spot, having hit the radar screen of New York's elite party-goers. He was now in competition with Bungalow 8 and Bed, the two hottest clubs in town. Celebrities occupied his VIP room and the line outside the club circled the block, reminiscent of Studio 54 in its heyday.

It was everything Josh ever dreamed of. Yet, he had to admit, there was a lot more pressure on him these days. Luckily, he'd had the good sense to hire Clint. Otherwise, Josh wouldn't have time to breathe. Or keep an eye on McCarthy.

Flinging open the door to the ladies' bathroom, he stepped inside the large room. A fountain of water shot out of a broken pipe under the sink, spewing water in all directions, instantly drenching his hair and his black T-shirt.

"Oh, hell," he grumbled.

McCarthy pulled up short in the doorway and let out a little squeak. He glanced at her over his shoulder and found that her bright green eyes had widened and her mouth gaped open.

"Don't freak on me, sweetheart."

"Oh, my God! What are we going to do? There's, like, two inches of water on the floor! And now the hallway is getting flooded. Josh!"

"First, we're gonna turn the water off." He crouched down low beside the sink and twisted the silver knob on the wall. The fountain died. "Second, we're gonna get a mop and clean up this mess. And then we're gonna call a plumber."

He looked at McCarthy over his shoulder again. She stood in the doorway, her jaw still slack, her eyes still bulging in their sockets.

Damn, she was even prettier when she was in distress.

His gaze remained on her as he shoved a hand through his hair, which was soaked from roots to ends. He pushed long bangs off his face, but the wet strands clung to his neck. He felt drops of water trickle down his cheeks and pool under his chin before falling to the floor. He was dripping wet.

As he stood to his full six-foot-two-inch height, McCarthy's gaze slowly swept over him from head to toe. A curious look flashed in her vibrant eyes, and he saw her suck in a sharp breath. The look she gave him was intense, sensual. It was the kind of look Josh had been the recipient of many times before. But never from her. He and McCarthy had flirted and teased each other for years, but never once had she looked at him with blatant lust in her eyes.

It excited Josh more than anything had in years.

Unfortunately, just as the hint of sexual awareness entered her eyes, it vanished. But the heated moment lingered between them.

McCarthy backed away from him. "You're soaked. I have towels. I'll be back." She disappeared down the hall.

Josh stared after her. What, exactly, had McCarthy been thinking about just then?

He stood in the shallow pool of water, quickly ruining his black leather boots. He didn't care. All that registered in his mind was that something had just happened between him and McCarthy. What was it?

She returned a few minutes later, looking less flustered, though her cheeks were still a bit flushed. Thrusting a towel at him, she said, "Here. Sorry about your clothes."

Josh frowned. She didn't even make eye contact with him. "They're just jeans and a T-shirt, Mac. No big deal."

Her gaze dropped to the floor. She visibly cringed. "Oh, shit. Your boots."

"They'll dry. Just like the rest of me."

He wished like hell she'd look at him. He wanted to see that flicker of awareness again. He wanted to know if McCarthy's feelings toward him had somehow morphed from close friends to potential lovers.

Was McCarthy attracted to him? Did she want him the way he'd wanted her for the past few years?

He couldn't tell—and she sure as hell wasn't inclined to confirm his suspicions. Instead, she started to push the mop she'd brought with her around the bathroom floor.

Josh reached a hand out and clasped the wooden handle. "Let me do this. Your shoes are a hell of a lot more expensive than mine. No sense in ruining them."

"Josh." Her gaze finally lifted to his face and she gave him a challenging look. All traces of lust had disappeared. She was back to being a businesswoman, not a woman who might have needs Josh was more than willing to satisfy. "Rendezvous is my responsibility while Cass is gone. I apologize for my temporary hysterics, but I'm fine now. I can handle this."

"I know you can." He actually had to force the strained tone from his voice. He didn't want to talk about Rendezvous. He wanted to talk about what had just happened between them. He wanted to know what she'd been thinking when she'd looked at him earlier. But McCarthy seemed to have quickly moved past her indiscreet moment. What choice did Josh have but to move past it as well?

"I'm already drenched," he told her. "So you may as well let me clean up. Why don't you go shut down your computer and take care of whatever else needs to be done. I'll give you a ride home."

"What about The Rage?"

Josh pried the mop from her hands. "I pay Clint good money for a reason. He can handle the club on his own. Now get out of here before you lose the chance to salvage those shoes."

Her hand shook as one manicured finger depressed the power button on her computer. McCarthy's body seemed to vibrate with an unfamiliar energy. She'd tried to be cool with Josh, but damn it. His name just kept flashing in her mind the way it had on her screen. And when they were in the bathroom together, all she could focus on was his soaked clothes clinging to his hunky body.

The long strands of his hair had been plastered to his neck, which was lightly corded with a thick vein running its length and pulsing steadily with life. His biceps had strained against the hem of the short sleeves of his T-shirt. The wet material had been pulled tight against his well-defined pectoral muscles, showing off the hard ledge of his chest. Not to mention the ridges of his six-pack abs.

And his jeans—they'd been plastered to his long, sinewy legs, his perfectly sculpted ass, his pelvis, his—

Oh, God. She let out a soft moan. Okay, yes, she'd looked. The bulge between his legs had drawn her attention and held it. And then something had happened to her. Erotic visions had danced in her head, unbidden.

Josh reaching out to her, pulling her against his hard, wet body. Pushing her down onto the tiled floor, pulling her blouse open with impatience, the buttons popping all over the place. Water rushing all around them as his hands cupped her breasts and his lips and tongue sought her nipples and teased them endlessly. His erection pressed against the juncture of her legs, rubbing against her, making her restless. Soft moans escaping her lips that turned into desperate pleas.

Take me, Josh. Thrust that hard cock into me. Make me come. Please, please, please.

McCarthy snapped the laptop closed. What the hell was she doing entertaining erotic fantasies about Josh? Granted, it wasn't the first time, but it was definitely the first time since his name had been associated with hers in her database. Now it seemed all she could think about was sex with Josh.

There are worse things to be obsessed with.

She laughed, despite herself. Okay, so there was nothing wrong with fantasizing about the guy. She just needed to keep a firm grip on reality. She and Josh were not compatible.

The smartest thing she'd done over the past few years was ignore the sexual pull she felt when he flirted with her or when she caught him staring at her.

So, like many times before, she pushed thoughts of Josh Kensington from her mind. Instead, she focused on the closing tasks she'd put off in order to host Cat's bachelorette party. Counting cash drawers, filling out paperwork, stocking the bar—they were chores that preoccupied her mind while Josh cleaned the mess in the bathroom.

She could handle this minor catastrophe, she told herself. Everything was okay with the club. She'd get a plumber to come in first thing tomorrow morning and everything would be fine when she opened for business that night.

As for Josh, well, a girl could have her fantasies. But McCarthy would ignore the fact that he'd appeared at the top of her "ideal match" list.

Yes, that was the smart, sensible thing to do.

Resolved to keep her strange matchmaking revelation to herself—no one needed to know Josh's profile had been linked to hers—she turned off the stereo and collected her purse and house keys from the office. As she made her way back into the lounge, a loud thud echoed in the room.

"What the hell...?" Josh's deep voice seemed to fill the entire club. Or maybe it just filled all the cracks and hollow spaces inside her.

McCarthy drew up short as Josh stared at the toppled gift bag Cat had given her and the vast array of sexually oriented items that had spilled out when he'd knocked it over. She gasped.

Josh picked up the elaborate vibrator, still in its packaging. He inspected the erotic toy for a moment before turning his attention to her. Holding the package in his hand, he gave her a scorching hot look.

"McCarthy Portman. You wicked, wicked girl."

Chapter 3

Her jaw fell slack. McCarthy stared at the offending sex toy with a mixture of dread and excitement.

First of all, how positively mortifying that Josh thought it belonged to her! Well, okay. It did belong to her. But it wasn't like she'd actually purchased it. The vibrator was a gift. As were the nipple gel and the fur-lined handcuffs and the black satin blindfold—

Oh, for the love of God.

Letting out a slow sigh, she wondered how the hell she was going to escape this nightmare.

She could feel the heat flood her cheeks and creep down her neck. Rendered speechless by her extreme embarrassment, she simply stared at Josh and the vibrator.

Somehow the sex toy, which had seemed perfectly innocent when Cat had given it to her because McCarthy knew it would never be removed from its packaging, now seemed decadent. Sexy. Erotic.

Which was why excitement registered deep within her.

Flashes of Josh watching her as she pleasured herself with the pretty pink phallic toy filled her mind. For a moment, she was overcome with the intense—albeit insane—desire to partake in some shameless, naughty fun with Josh.

But, of course, that was absurd. She couldn't. They couldn't. It would be all bad and wrong because… because…

Because?

McCarthy frowned.

Why, exactly, would it be wrong to have one wild night with Josh?

Because you are a good girl and he will break your heart.

Not if I don't let him.

Get a grip! You can't date him! No matter what your incredibly ac-

curate matchmaking program says!

McCarthy sighed. Her internal debate was pointless. She knew she couldn't date Josh. She'd never make it out of the encounter emotionally unscathed.

But could she sleep with him?

Just once.

Her gaze shifted from the vibrator he held to his handsome face. Josh continued to eye her speculatively, a sexy grin playing on his lips.

Lips she suddenly longed to feel on every inch of her body.

She found it interesting that she couldn't admit to him that the sex toys he'd discovered weren't anything she'd ever used before. And that she had no intention of ever using them. Because, quite frankly, Josh's smoldering gaze told her he found this little discovery titillating. And that made McCarthy feel deliciously wicked.

Knowing she had to speak—to salvage the moment and her pride—but not wanting to spoil the fantasy he was obviously weaving, she said, "It's not polite to rifle through a woman's private possessions, Josh."

His grin was positively devilish. "Bag fell, babe. I'm just recovering the contents for you."

His ice-blue eyes sparkled with mischief, making McCarthy all the more aware of his raw sexuality. Suddenly, her nipples felt a bit tighter behind her sensible cotton bra. And a curious samba beat started to play between her legs, making that most intimate part of her pulse and thrum in time with her pounding heartbeat.

"Although," Josh continued on, his sexy voice increasing the desire that now flooded her veins. "I must say, I am a bit confused."

Having no idea what possessed her to flirt, she said, "It's called a vibrator, Josh. Surely you've seen one before?"

He chuckled. "I know what it is, Mac."

"Then you know its purpose. So would you be so kind as to put it back in the bag?"

He stared at her a moment longer, the curiosity in his eyes turning to something darker. Something much more evocative. It stole her breath. Her body instantly became a reed in the wind, bending toward him of its own volition. The inner vixen Josh's heated gaze awoke coaxed her to cross the room. To get a bit closer to Josh.

McCarthy stayed rooted where she was, doing her absolute best to ignore the dangerous, wanton vixen within.

It was no easy feat. But she reminded herself that Josh was a heartbreaker. And McCarthy couldn't afford to take a chance that he'd trample hers.

Endless moments ticked by, until Josh finally turned the bag upright and returned all the contents to it. Save for one little "goody."

McCarthy caught her lower lip between her teeth when he scooped up the two-piece lingerie set that had spilled out of the toppled bag. Holding up the miniscule panties and the barely-able-to-contain-her-breasts demi-bra, both red lacy garments, he eyed her once again. The lingerie dangled from his long fingers.

"This just keeps getting better and better," he said.

Crossing her arms over her chest, she gave Josh a stern look. "Back in the bag."

Josh shook his head.

"Now."

"Oh, no." His beautiful blue eyes glowed in the candlelight that illuminated the intimate lounge. "This is way too good to pass up."

"They're not mine, Josh," she finally said, unable to maintain the farce. "None of those things are mine."

He crooked a blonde eyebrow at her, challenging her.

"Okay. Yes, they're mine," she admitted. McCarthy never could tell a lie. "But they're not *really* mine. I mean, I didn't buy any of that stuff. Cat gave me the goody bag."

"I always did like that girl." His gaze shifted to the lacy outfit he held. "She's got good taste in lingerie, that's for damn sure."

McCarthy fought back a smile at his cavalier attitude. "Fun's over. Put it back."

He shook his head again. Unexpectedly, he crossed the lounge in several long strides, stalking toward her until their bodies nearly touched. "I'm having a thought," he said, a wicked glint in his eyes. "An inkling, actually."

McCarthy's heart slammed against her chest. Damn it. Why'd he have to be so gorgeous? So charismatic? So magnetic? She felt helpless against his sexual allure.

Stay focused. He's just a man. Let it go.

"You've had your fun, Josh. Give 'em back." She reached for the lingerie but he lifted his powerful arm and held the lacy garments just out of her reach. Damn him for being six-two!

"Not so fast."

She suppressed the smile that threatened her lips. No need to add fuel to the fire. Still, she had to admit, getting Josh a little hot and bothered was the most excitement she'd had in… hmm. Much longer than she cared to admit.

Her hands, seemingly of their own volition—or perhaps that of the vixen—reached out and grasped his still-wet T-shirt, which clung to his sculpted chest and corrugated abdomen. She could see the grooves through the thin material and it did a wicked number on her senses. Holding fistfuls of his shirt, she yanked him toward her and stared deep into his mesmerizing eyes.

"Give. Them. Back."

His gaze was much too hot, much too mischievous as he uttered his reply. "No."

"I could hurt you," she said.

"Give it your best shot, sweetheart."

She tried to stare him down. It didn't work. His gaze was a scorcher and it set every nerve-ending ablaze.

She should know better than to play games with Josh Kensington. He was way out of her league.

"Okay, fine," she said. "Keep them."

She released his shirt and turned to slip away. But his free hand reached out and snaked around her waist, pulling her up tight against his body. With her back pressed to his front, he held her captive. And she could feel every hard, tense muscle pressed against her. In fact, if she wasn't mistaken—

McCarthy gasped. "Josh Kensington!"

He had a hard-on!

A. Hard. On.

Holy shit!

He chuckled, low and deep. The sound tickled her ear then reverberated deep inside her, making her stomach flutter and her pussy throb with excitement.

McCarthy shot him what was surely a scathing look over her shoulder. But the way his eyes lit with fire and his blonde brow crooked, she was pretty damn certain she'd only managed to spur him on.

He didn't release her. In fact, his grip on her didn't loosen at all. Mc-Carthy's backside was pressed to Josh's front and the fire that roared through her body was a five-alarm rager.

"Wanna hear about my inkling?" he asked in a low, husky tone.

"Not really," she replied on a shaky breath.

Ignoring her, he said, "It's really more of a proposition. You're curious to hear it, right?"

"I said no."

But she knew she was lying to him—and to herself. Of course she wanted to hear what he had to say. In fact, she was dying to find out what wickedly fabulous thoughts he was having about this bizarre encounter.

But to admit it aloud?

McCarthy didn't think she could go there. No matter how much the inner vixen prodded her.

"Let me go," she finally said. Although, even she had to admit that her words and her tone weren't the least bit convincing.

"Are you sure? Because you just might like this." His suggestive tone was enough to make her toes curl in her soggy loafers.

"You've had your fun," she repeated, although the erection that continued to press against her suggested he was still looking for a little action.

Oh, Goddamn it.

It wasn't like McCarthy wasn't interested in what he had to offer. Truth be told, she'd never been more interested in a man in her life!

But, he was Josh.

She was almost unable to disassociate herself from the friend she'd always been to him and the lover she could be. Wanted to be. Yet his damned erection kept her in a constant state of arousal and all McCarthy could really think of was sex.

Sex. With. Josh.

She let out a low sigh. No. It wouldn't just be sex with Josh.

It would be really hot sex with Josh.

Oh, hell. There was no getting around it. She wanted him. Badly. And he seemed inclined to… accommodate her? Okay. It was more than that. He wasn't just trying to accommodate. He was initiating!

Oh. My. God.

The vixen within suddenly took over. As if she'd clubbed sensible McCarthy over the head and commandeered her mental faculties.

Well. Not so much her mental faculties. The inner vixen was focused solely on McCarthy's very lonely, desperate-for-attention pussy. The dull ache between her legs was interspersed with sharp stabs that made her breath catch every time the erotic pangs shot straight to the heart of her. The curious sensations ruled her body, overpowering McCarthy's common sense. She could no longer remember why, exactly, she shouldn't engage in some decadent fun with Josh Kensington.

He was, after all, the star of her most sensual fantasies. And she had no doubt that he knew how to please a woman.

And, well, quite frankly, McCarthy could use a little pleasure in her life.

How long had it been since she'd had sex? A year and a half? Two years? Shit. She couldn't even pinpoint the date or a decent time frame, it had been so long.

She groaned inwardly. Her life was consumed with matching up Manhattan's hottest singles. Somewhere along the way, McCarthy had forgotten about her own needs.

But now, here was a man who was interested in satisfying some of those needs.

"So what do you say?" said man asked in his low, sexy tone. Josh knew her internal debate because he knew her so well.

Admittedly, only a fool would turn down an opportunity like this.

Still. Flirting with Josh was like playing with fire. At the moment, however, she was feeling just restless—and reckless—enough to risk getting burned.

"Mac." His head was close enough to hers that his lips brushed her neck, just below her ear, as he spoke. "I've had some really great orgasms because of you. But those were just fantasies. The real thing will be infinitely better."

McCarthy's nipples tightened. Oh, Christ. The man even talked sexy. Every fiber of her being stood up and took notice. She wanted to turn in his arms and press her breasts to his chest. She wanted to feel his hands on her body, impatient and insistent.

"You're acting very strange tonight, Josh." Her voice sounded full of lust, even to her. Deep and throaty and provocative.

"I want to see you in this lingerie," he told her, ignoring her statement. "What do you say? Will you model this sexy red outfit for me?"

She gulped.

Prance around in lacy underwear? In front of him? While he… what? Drooled? Got even harder?

Laughed?

She groaned. "Be serious," she said. "Wasn't one of your recent conquests a lingerie model?"

"Victoria's Secret. Skin and bones, though. No curves whatsoever. You, on the other hand." His grip on her waist tightened, pressing her even more against his rock-hard body. And that erection that still enticed her. Tempted her. She wanted desperately to reach behind her and cup the length of him. Rub his hard cock until he forgot all about the lingerie and instead begged her to get naked with him.

She would.

So why wouldn't she model the outfit Cat had given her?

Because this can't seriously be happening. He can't seriously want to see me in those itty bitty scraps of lace.

"You," he continued. "Have the kind of curves that inspire fantasies. The really dirty kind, Mac."

She wilted a little in his arms.

"Tell you what. We'll make this a mutually beneficial deal. We'll make a bet."

She laughed. This was how they managed to settle all disputes in their friendship. "What can you possibly bring to the table that will make this a 'mutually beneficial' wager?"

Suddenly, he released her. Spinning her around, his strong hands gripped her upper arms and he stared deep into her eyes. His intensity startled her, even more so than his abrupt movements.

"You know what I want," he said in his soul-stirring voice. "What do you want, Mac?"

She opened her mouth to speak, but her tongue suddenly felt swollen and weighted. Her pulse kicked up a notch and her heart leapt into her throat. Breathing became an unnatural challenge.

"Okay," he said, letting her off the hook. "I'll make the wager. One game of pool. If I win, you show me how sexy these lacy things look on that gorgeous body of yours. If you win, I'll give Clint my tickets for Sunday afternoon's game, and I'll come over and install the surround sound for your new big screen TV."

McCarthy's eyes widened. She'd been waiting for a break in Josh's overly busy schedule for the past few weeks. He'd promised to set up the complicated sound system, but hadn't found the time. Considering she was a huge movie buff, having the full effect of the big screen TV with the surround sound was a very big deal to McCarthy.

So much so that she seriously considered his proposition. Actually, it was sort of a no-brainer. She eyed him with suspicion. "In the entire five years I've known you, you've only beat me at pool twice."

"So you'll have to give me a handicap."

"No way."

His grin was mischievous and downright sexy. "Come on. Gimme a break."

"You still won't beat me." Her competitive nature overruled the vixen and Miss Sensible.

"Try me."

"Fine." Supremely confident she'd win this bet—and have her surround sound installed this very weekend—McCarthy found it impossible not to take him up on his offer. "I'll play you. But there will be no handicap. You challenged me, so you'll have to accept the consequences."

Josh released her. The mischievous glint in his mesmerizing eyes should have given her pause, but the odds were in her favor. And she was damn sure she had nothing to worry about.

The cocky grin on Josh's face didn't faze her at all.

She pushed past him and marched into the pool room where two ornately designed pool tables, gifts from Cass's uncle, were situated. She selected a stick while Josh mixed a batch of his famous martinis.

When he joined her, she mused, "I can't decide which movie to watch first. Something with a lot of action and noise, I think."

Josh handed her a cocktail. "You haven't won anything yet, sweetheart."

She flashed him what she knew to be a confident grin. "Oh, but I'm just one game of pool away from adding the finishing touch to my theater room. Four oversized recliners were delivered last week. The big screen is connected to a state-of-the-art DVD player. The thick, chocolate-colored velvet drapes I hung in the room block out all the light from outside. I even have my old-fashioned popcorn cart set up. Once you hook up the surround sound and strategically place my eight—count 'em, eight—speakers, it's bye-bye to Harkins and hello to McCarthy's Private Entertainment Room."

Josh laughed. "If you lose this game, sweetheart, I won't give Clint my tickets and I won't have a free day for another month. Which means bye-bye to your entertainment room."

"I won't lose."

"We'll see about that." Josh picked a stick and then propped his hip against the edge of one of the tables. "What do you say we up the stakes?"

She narrowed her eyes at him. "You just love losing to me, don't you?"

His grin was slow and sexy. The sight of it did the craziest damned things to her insides. "I just like to keep things interesting. So, let's say, for every ball I drop, you remove an article of clothing. And vice versa."

McCarthy's jaw dropped, but she recovered quickly. "Feeling particularly lonely tonight, Josh?"

He continued to grin at her. "Not lonely. Horny." His ice-blue eyes twinkled in the seductive glow of the wall sconces and chandeliers. His gaze swept over her body from head to toe, pausing for an indiscreet amount of time at her breasts. "The thought of you in that sexy red outfit is doing a wicked number on my libido, Mac. And all those toys you bought." He whistled under his breath. "We could put them to good use, sweetheart. Real good use."

"I didn't buy them," she reminded him. Her voice came out as a mere squeak. It was a wonder he'd even heard her.

But he had. His grin widened. "Whatever. So, how about it?"

"You live dangerously," she managed to croak out.

"Let's just say I'm feeling confident about my ability to win this game. I have incentive, after all. The best kind." He wagged his brows at her.

McCarthy's palms began to sweat, but she maintained her composure. "Suit yourself. But for the record, this was your idea."

"One of my best." He held out the two swaths of red lace he'd carried over to the table. "I want to see these on you. So. You go put them on under your clothes and I'll rack the balls."

His audacity was astounding. So, too, was his confidence. If he'd been any other man, she would have told him to go to hell ten minutes ago. But this was Josh. The sexiest man she'd ever met with a wicked charm that stirred her soul. And commanded her passion.

But McCarthy was feeling pretty confident herself, so she snatched the lingerie from his hand and sauntered off. Over her shoulder, she said, "You'd get a better view of these off of me than on. There's no way in hell you're going to drop enough balls to see what my underwear looks like."

He snorted. "We'll see about that."

Chapter 4

Josh watched her go, enjoying the tantalizing view. She had a great ass, even in loose-fitting jeans.

He wasn't quite sure what had come over him tonight, but the events of the evening were leading him down an enjoyable path. The look Mc-Carthy had given him in the bathroom had sparked his interest. Then the discovery of her erotic toys and that too-hot lingerie—Christ, it was a wonder he was able to work this slow seduction. When all he really wanted to do was strip her down and make love to her. In every way possible.

His fantasies were one thing. The reality of the situation was that it didn't matter what she wore or where they were or what position in which they made love. He wanted her. Plain and simple. Naked beneath him or on top of him. It didn't matter. Josh just wanted to feel her soft skin against his, explore her gentle, feminine curves, listen to her moan in ecstasy. He had the insatiable desire to bring her endless hours of pleasure.

Something about McCarthy Portman stirred his senses on a level he couldn't even begin to explain. She always had. So far, he'd kept his distance. She was too into her work and, quite frankly, so was he. As much as Josh had always wanted to explore the chemistry between them, the timing had never been right.

Until tonight.

Right now, there wasn't anywhere else he wanted to be. There wasn't any other woman he wanted to be with.

Cass would claim kismet if she were here. She'd say something about the stars and the moon being in perfect alignment. That's when two souls connected, she always said.

Josh didn't believe in all the cosmic mumbo jumbo his cousin spewed.

But he did have to admit, there was something perfect about this evening. About this unexpected opportunity that had magically presented itself.

He sipped his martini while he waited for McCarthy to return from the ladies' room, which he'd managed to put back in order. The fact that he so rarely—okay, next to never—beat her at pool didn't faze him in the least. He intended to have his cake and eat it, too. Dropping a few balls would let him get a glimpse of McCarthy in that incredibly sexy lingerie. He was dying to see her in nothing but the red lace bra and panty set.

But really, the pool game bought him some time. Whether he won or lost the game, he'd win the ultimate battle—seducing McCarthy.

He took another sip of his cocktail then set the glass on the pub table next to hers. He returned to the pool table and racked the balls, a smile on his face that he knew was cocky.

Although he didn't suck at pool, McCarthy was infinitely more skilled. He may not beat her, but he certainly had the incentive to try.

When she returned, they did their typical routine of determining who would break. For once, his ball made it to the end of the table and back, rolling to a stop mere millimeters from the lip of the table. Hers was an inch away. He grinned at her. He was off to a good start.

Josh leaned over the table, lined up the cue ball and broke the conglomeration of balls at the opposite end. Two balls dropped into the far pockets. He turned back to McCarthy and grinned at her.

"Looks like I'm stripes." He eyed her from head to toe, debating his options. Finally, he said, "Let's start slow. Your shoes and your shirt."

Her jaw clenched. She didn't reach for either. "Who said you get to decide?"

"Oh, for Christ's sake, McCarthy. You're wearing a tank top under your shirt."

Looking a little disgruntled, she toed off her wet loafers and then removed the Oxford shirt that had hung open over her white tank top. "Happy?"

"Not yet." Seeing the hint of red lace—both color and texture— through the thin material of her tank top spurred him on. He eyed his options on the table, lined up another shot. He missed. "Shit," he grumbled.

The smile on McCarthy's pretty face indicated she felt supremely confident he wouldn't be removing any more of her clothing.

"Well, all I can say is that this had better be worth my time." She eyed him with a hint of lasciviousness mingled with a coy smile. She was teasing him.

Josh smirked at her. "You haven't won squat yet."

"Oh, but that big screen TV is going to sound so great in my apartment. Especially with those high ceilings. The acoustics are fantastic in the room I've converted into a home-theater."

She surveyed the table. Josh brought her martini to her and offered her the glass while she assessed her first shot. Taking several small sips, she finally decided on her plan of attack and handed over the glass so she could take aim. As she bent over the table, concentrating on lining up her shot, Josh moved behind her.

"You've got a great ass, Mac. I've admired it every day for five long years."

She eyed him over her shoulder. "You can't throw me off with cheap flattery, so don't even try."

"This isn't cheap flattery, babe. This is genuine appreciation of your considerable assets." His gaze locked with hers. "And let me tell you, thinking about that perfect ass just barely covered with red lace is making me even harder."

Her lips pursed together. He'd stunned her into silence. She opened her mouth to speak, but no words came out. Josh fought the natural desire to chuckle at her prudence. McCarthy was a good girl through and through.

Or so she thought.

Josh, however, thought different. In fact, he suspected McCarthy was a powder keg of passion waiting to be ignited.

And tonight, he had the overwhelming desire to light the fuse.

"Tell me," he said in a low tone as he reached a hand out to her and placed it on the small of her back. He leaned forward and rested the other palm on the red velvet felt that covered the table. His body practically curled around hers, his erection pressing against her hip. His head dipped so he merely had to whisper in her ear. "How do you like to be touched, sweetheart? Do you like a man to touch you softly, gently? Or do you like it a little rough?"

"I can't shoot while you're hovering over me, Josh," she said in a sharp tone. One that held a distinct sexual edge to it. He was turning her on, whether she'd admit to it or not. "Give me some breathing room for Christ's sake."

Josh's head dipped just a bit lower, so his lips brushed the shell of her ear. "I think you like it a little rough," he whispered. "I think you'd like a man to be so overcome with desire he just has to have you. Up against a wall. Bent over a table. Wherever, whenever the mood strikes. I think," he said as his mouth moved to the thin lobe devoid of an earring. "You like explosive passion. The kind that consumes you and makes you lose all control."

His teeth playfully nipped her bare lobe and she gasped. Her elbow dropped to the table, as though her knees had just buckled and she needed something else to stabilize her.

Josh bit back a triumphant grin. He'd hit the nail on the head this time. Mac liked it dirty. Whether she knew it, though, remained to be seen. But he could prove it to her. He sensed she clung to the good girl principles that ruled her sensible brain. But buried deep within her was a bad girl. He could tell. In fact, McCarthy's passion called to his, practically begging him to free her from her conventional, conservative bonds.

He would do just that.

"You're not playing fair," she said in a breathy tone.

"Never said I would."

"Just back up a few feet so I can make this shot."

"Make it now," he said. His hand slipped beneath the hem of her tank top and slid slowly up her spine. She shivered and he felt goose bumps beneath his fingertips.

"Josh, I can't concentrate." Her gaze remained on the cue ball in front of her, though he was fairly certain she didn't see it.

No. If Josh was working the kind of magic on her that he thought he was, McCarthy's mind wasn't on pool. It was on sex.

His fingers grazed the clasp of the red lace bra she wore. More than anything, Josh wanted to unfasten the sexy piece of lingerie. But he resisted.

For the moment.

"I propose an amendment to our wager," he said as his mouth moved lower still, grazing her long neck.

"I'm gonna hit you over the head with this stick if you don't stop."

He chuckled. "Let's say we forget the game. I undress you. You undress me. I kiss you. We lose ourselves in the moment, and we see what happens."

"No thanks," she said in a tight voice. "I want my surround sound more than I want you."

"Liar."

She repositioned her arm and lined up her shot again. In a swift, fluid motion, she hit the cue ball, sending it careening across the table. She dropped the six ball in the far corner pocket. She straightened, forcing Josh to do the same. She shot him a shit-eating-grin over her slender shoulder.

"You didn't seriously think you could distract me with your sex talk, did you?"

Chapter 5

It almost worked.

The truth was, McCarthy almost threw all caution to the wind and took Josh up on his offer.

Holy shit! The man infiltrated her senses on every level! His warm breath tickling her skin, his teeth teasing her earlobe, his fingers grazing her skin. It was a wonder she hadn't come right then and there!

No two ways about it, Josh was lethal. The man knew how to seduce her, body, heart and soul.

She needed to put some distance between them, so she crossed to the bistro table where Josh had left her martini. She took one long gulp and then another.

And then, just because the internal fire still raged, she drained the remainder of the glass.

She fished out the toothpick and bit an olive off the end.

Goddamn it. Her body hummed with a curious sexual vibration that left her seriously off-kilter. How she'd managed to block out Josh for the two seconds it took to sink the six ball was beyond her.

Calm down, she told herself.

It was still her turn and now was the time to run the table. If she could just get through this game and emerge the victor—in short order, *oh, please God!*—then she could gracefully extract herself from this situation, in a dignified fashion, and skip on out of Rendezvous without revealing a hint of flesh or red lace.

Josh would hook up her surround sound system then go back to chasing his chippies, and they could pretend their heated game of strip pool never happened.

Except….

She wasn't all that eager to wrap up the fun in such neat, tidy order.

She slid the last olive off the end of the toothpick and popped it into her mouth. As she chewed, she gave serious consideration to Josh's overactive libido. He'd told her straight out that he was horny. Looking for a little action.

Why on earth had he chosen her? Why was he wasting his time trying to seduce her when, downstairs, there were a hundred beautiful girls dying to get their shot at him?

McCarthy had seen for herself—on numerous occasions—the way the women who frequented The Rage vied for Josh's attention. Their scantily clad bodies practically dripped over the two long bars Josh bounced back and forth between. Some nights, when the crowd got particularly rowdy, girls would climb on top of the bars and dance. It wasn't uncommon for tops and bras to come off. That was generally about the time McCarthy slipped out and caught a cab home.

So. If Josh was in need of relieving some sexual tension, he didn't have to waste his time trying to sneak a peek at McCarthy's lingerie. He had a bevy of beauties lined up around the corner.

All sure things.

Why was he here with her tonight?

Lost in thought, she didn't hear Josh approach the table. When he reached around her and poured another martini in her glass from the stainless steel shaker he held, she jumped.

He grinned at her, his blue eyes twinkling with mischief. And promises of wicked things to come.

McCarthy sucked in a breath. Her nipples tightened behind the flimsy swath of red lace that barely covered her breasts.

Admittedly, she'd been impressed by the way the demi-bra plumped up her breasts, but seriously… who the hell could wear a bra like this in real-life situations? She felt like she was spilling out of it… bursting at the seams. And the panties! Christ, there was barely anything to them, and most of the material was wedged up her ass.

Needing further fortification before she turned and faced Josh, she reached for her glass and took a sip.

Focus on the game.

She eyed the table over her shoulder. She'd left herself with a good setup. Three balls were in perfect alignment. The game was practically hers.

Steadfast determination returned to her. She moved past Josh, who was oh-so-casually leaning against the wall next to her table, sipping his own martini and eyeing her with a lascivious look that made her wet. Her Kegel muscles tightened.

And that's when McCarthy knew she wasn't getting out of this bizarre sexual encounter with Josh quite as easily as she'd anticipated.

While she tried to mentally steel herself for what lay ahead, Josh said, "So what's it gonna be, sweetheart? My shirt or my jeans?"

She turned and stared at him, dumbfounded. She'd completely forgotten that dropping that first ball meant Josh lost an article of clothing.

McCarthy knew she should be pleased about this. Excited, even. But those emotions didn't register. Instead, heat crept up her neck and tinged her cheeks.

She really hadn't seen this game as the double-edged sword it was.

If she didn't run the table and beat Josh, she'd lose her clothes. She'd have to stand here in front of him in nothing but the tiny strips of red lace that barely even constituted underwear.

Yet, if she did take the table, that would mean Josh would be standing here in nothing but…?

His boxers?

Less?

She groaned. He chuckled.

He knew exactly what she was thinking. The cad.

"What's it gonna be, Mac?" he asked again. He moved away from the wall and walked slowly toward her, his fingers toying with the top button of his faded Levi's. Jeans that fit him sinfully well. Plus, they were still wet, so they were still plastered to his powerful legs and perfect ass.

McCarthy's mouth practically watered at the sight before her. She didn't think it was possible, but Josh looked even better when he was wet. Long, damp strands of blonde hair still clung to his neck. His bangs were pushed back, giving him a messy, unkempt look. A sexy look. Like he'd just stepped out of the shower and raked a hand through his hair.

He really was a walking fantasy. And although she'd convinced herself a long time ago that he wasn't the sort of man she should get involved with, McCarthy was suddenly having trouble remembering the reasons why it was such a bad idea to fall into bed with Josh Kensington.

Especially when his gaze dropped to her chest, which rose and fell quick enough to reveal her arousal, damn it. The look of longing—

wanting—that played on his chiseled features made her insides clench. A dull, achy feeling settled into her most intimate area, making her painfully aware of the lack of attention that particular part of her body had received over the past couple of years.

"How about I help you decide?" Josh finally said, a teasing smile playing on his lips. He clenched fists full of black cotton in his hands and tugged the hem of his T-shirt from the waist of his jeans.

McCarthy's gaze dropped to his abdomen as he peeled the wet material from his body, exposing a wide expanse of rippled muscle and tanned skin.

An unbidden sigh escaped her parted lips. The dull, achy feeling intensified into sharp, uncomfortable stabs as her vagina now insistently demanded attention.

Satisfaction, actually.

That's what it longed for—a sated feeling only Josh could help her achieve.

Oh, but Goddamn it. He was Josh Kensington. Bad Boy.

And she was McCarthy Portman. Good Girl.

And everyone knew what happened to good girls who fell for bad boys. She'd get her heart trampled for sure.

And yet… Some mystical inner force—perhaps the vixen he'd awoken earlier—made McCarthy reach a hand out to Josh. Her fingers just barely skimmed the ridges of his well-defined abs. They itched—burned, really—to move higher, over the swells of his pectoral muscles. His chest was wide and perfectly sculpted. His skin was smooth and warm. The muscles tightened beneath her light touch, and his innate response to her made McCarthy want him all the more.

Her heart rate accelerated and her pulse raced. When her gaze lifted and locked with Josh's, she could see—plain as day—that he was equally enrapt.

He liked the way she touched him.

Her hand moved up to his chest. The pad of one finger just barely skimmed a nipple and Josh's jaw clenched. The heat that lit his eyes darkened the irises to a deep blue hue that was mesmerizing.

Josh took hold of the pool cue she held in her other hand and pried it from her. He tossed it on the pool table, then said, "Touch me with both hands, sweetheart."

She didn't want to. She knew if she did, she wouldn't stop there. She wouldn't be able to stop what would inevitably happen next between them. But common sense had long since abandoned her and now what ruled McCarthy's usually sensible brain was passion.

Taking one small step forward, she closed the gap between them. Their thighs brushed, their torsos slowly melded together. The hand that had previously held the pool stick now rested on Josh's thick forearm as his own hand gripped her hip and he pulled her that much closer to him.

The breath escaped her body. His gaze was smoldering, yet not the least bit intimidating. He wanted her, but he didn't unnerve her with the intensity of his desire. Her hand moved up his arm to his rock-hard bicep and then his broad shoulder, her fingers gliding over his smooth, hot skin. Her other hand remained pressed to his chest, the only barrier, other than her clothes, between their upper bodies.

Josh's head dipped and his warm lips brushed her forehead, her temple. "Let's say we're both winners tonight," he suggested in a low, intimate tone. "I'll hook up your sound system. You'll show me your lingerie. We both win."

"And that's all you want?" she asked in a breathy voice. "To see my lingerie?"

His lips grazed her cheek, her jaw. His warm breath tickled her skin and teased her senses. The hand on her hip slid back and down. The other one joined it until he cupped her ass in both hands. "I think you already know the answer to that question."

"Maybe you should spell it out. Just so I'm clear on what it is you want here, Josh."

It was a wonder she could speak, let alone think straight. But apparently her sensible brain hadn't taken full leave. McCarthy was smart enough to determine what she was getting herself into before she got in too deep.

Josh kissed her jaw, then moved lower, his lips brushing her throat.

"I want you," he said.

It seemed like such a simple statement, yet his deep, intimate tone packed one hell of an erotic punch, leaving her speechless.

Chapter 6

To Josh, it really was as simple as that. He wanted McCarthy.

Yet Josh knew she would need more of an explanation. And, quite frankly, she deserved it. The last thing he wanted to do was hurt her or lead her down a path he might be incapable of traveling with her.

But she knew that already, right? After all, they'd been friends for five years. She knew he wasn't into commitment, that he didn't whole-heartedly believe in the sappy happily-ever-after she and Cass touted to their clients.

Not to say Josh wasn't into monogamy—he could do that. For a short time. But, admittedly, his interest waned after a while.

Yet, he couldn't deny the fact that he'd wanted McCarthy for several years. He'd lusted after her longer than any other woman he'd known. But was that just because he'd never had her?

Josh didn't have an answer, so instead, he focused on the moment. He said, "Look, I don't want to tempt you to do something you don't really want to do, Mac. But you've got to admit that, tonight, this feels right."

Her eyelids fluttered closed and her forehead pressed to his chest. She gave a slight nod and whispered, "I could do this. With you. I could completely give myself over to this moment. But then what, Josh?"

His jaw clenched. He'd known she'd ask that. "I can't answer that anymore than you can, sweetheart. I don't know what this is," he said as one hand moved up her spine. He held her close to him. "All I know is that I've wanted you for a long, long time. And now here we are, in each other's arms. Doesn't that mean something to you, Mac?"

"Of course it does. But—"

"So let's start with this. Maybe it's just sex. Maybe we're just extremely hot for each other tonight. Then again, maybe it's more. I don't know."

Her head lifted suddenly and she stared up at him. Her large green eyes were compelling and full of questions. "Make me a promise. If this is just about sex, then it's a one-time thing only. Don't try to seduce me or sway me when you're horny or lonely or in-between bedmates. If this is just meant to be a one-night stand, Josh, promise me you'll keep it that way."

The look on her face was so intense, her need to have certainty in her life was so absolute, that it suddenly occurred to Josh he couldn't do this. He couldn't put one of his best friends in this position. Disentangling himself from her, he stepped away. He reached for his martini and gulped it down.

McCarthy propped a hip against the edge of the pool table and stared at him. She pushed a fat blonde curl behind her ear and then crossed her arms over her chest. "What's with the guilty conscience? I thought this was what you wanted."

His gaze locked with hers, steady and sure. "It is. But what if this really is just a one-time thing? What will that do to our friendship?"

"I don't know," she said as she shook her head.

She seemed to give it serious consideration, though. Endless moments stretched out between them until, suddenly, she glanced back up at him and smiled. A soft, sweet smile that warmed his insides.

"I'm a big girl, Josh. And I'm a dating specialist, for God's sake. I know more about one-time hookups than most of the singles that come here looking for love. I've seen every side of love and sex. I've seen hopes of love dashed. I've seen players played by another. And I've seen the most incompatible of couples discover the one thing about the other that makes them fall in love." She shook her head, as though she'd just had some sort of revelation or epiphany.

She continued on, saying, "I have no delusions about anything, Josh. I can't afford to. My job at Rendezvous is to help people see past physical attraction and find something solid to hang on to. Starting a relationship is simple. Easy. But maintaining one? Well. That's a horse of a different color."

Josh shook his head. His cock pulsed and throbbed in wicked beats and he wanted nothing more than to get naked with McCarthy and do the most decadent, hedonistic things with her. Things that would leave her blushing for a month.

But damn it. What if he didn't want her after tonight?

He scowled.

No, that really wasn't the issue at hand. If he were honest with himself, he'd have to admit that the true concern was the direct opposite.

What if one night wasn't enough? What if he wanted her tomorrow? And the next day and the next?

Knowing she deserved as much honesty as he could stomach dishing out, he said, "Let's just say, for argument's sake, that we did sleep together. You'd want to try to turn it into a relationship, wouldn't you?"

She nodded. "It's a natural desire. I believe in romance and relationships."

He considered this a moment, then said, "I don't know that I believe in the same things you do, Mac." Damn it. He could drive himself crazy thinking about this—thinking about McCarthy. Wanting McCarthy.

Or he could take the chance of a lifetime. Jump in feet first and see if he sank or swam.

Suddenly, he reached for her and pulled her to him again. With their bodies melded together, he knew he was doing the right thing. To deny himself the pleasure of her body would be regrettable. And Josh didn't do things he regretted.

He'd worry about tomorrow when the sun came up.

Right now, all he could think about was making love to McCarthy.

She looked a little shocked by his abrupt move, but he could also see relief in her eyes. She was just as torn as he was, and something told him she needed him to make a move. To make a decision. Whether it was a good one or a bad one. Right or wrong. She needed him to take the lead.

"Here's my promise," he said as his hands slid up her sides. "I swear I want you right now more than I've ever wanted anyone. What that means, I can't tell you. All I can say is that I'll be honest. If it's just a one-time thing, I'll be man enough to admit it. And that will be that, Mac. You have my word."

She nodded her head. "I trust you," she said in a soft voice. "More than anyone else." She closed her eyes and let out a long breath. "It's been a really long time for me, Josh. And you're the one I want to end the dry spell with."

His groin tightened as her hands eased around to his back. Her fingertips pressed into his muscles as her head lifted and tilted to the side.

Josh suddenly needed to kiss her more than he needed to breathe. His head bent to hers and his lips just barely grazed hers. An electrifying jolt registered for a brief moment before he claimed her mouth. McCarthy's soft lips parted and Josh's tongue eased past them, seeking hers. Her arms tightened around him and she let out a low, throaty moan that was nearly his undoing.

Sure, they hadn't resolved squat. What this might or might not mean. But that no longer mattered to Josh. All that mattered to him, all that consumed his mind, was making love to McCarthy. Pleasing her, driving her wild. Making her moan and beg for more.

Making her come.

Repeatedly.

The desire gripping him intensified. An insatiable hunger tore through his body. One hand plowed through her hair, holding her head in place as he deepened the kiss. Maybe it was the martinis. Maybe it was McCarthy. But Josh had never felt so enrapt before, so lost in the moment. His muscles tensed and bunched, his cock throbbed. He wanted, more than anything, to be buried deep within McCarthy's warm, wet depths.

Suddenly, the need to feel her skin against his took hold of him. His hands shifted and he clasped the hem of her tank top in his fists. Pulling the soft material upward, he broke their kiss so he could haul the top over her head and toss it on the pool table.

"Oh, God," she gasped. "Here? You want to have sex here?"

Josh grinned down at her, knowing it was a wicked one. He backed her up against the far wall of the pool room. When she was trapped between him and the rack hanging on the wall, he said, "We'll never make it to my place. And yours is even farther away."

He pried her hands from his back, where they'd returned after he'd removed her shirt, and lifted them high above her head. Wrapping her fingers around the top of the pool rack, he then slid his hands oh-so-slowly down her arms, along the outer swells of her breasts and over her ribcage. The lacy bra she wore drove him wild. It sat low on her full breasts, causing the plump flesh to rise above the scalloped edges.

Josh let out a low groan. "Red is definitely your color, sweetheart." His eyes feasted on the milky white flesh that bulged over the top of the red bra. Her areolas and nipples, small and an enticing shade of dusty rose, were just barely concealed by the lace. The pebbled centers of her breasts pushed against the thin fabric, begging for his touch.

Josh wanted nothing more than to take each delectable bud into his mouth and lavish it with the teasing pressure of his tongue. But he knew McCarthy well, and he knew his seduction of her had to be a subtle one until she felt as comfortable with their secret rendezvous as he did.

His head bent again, his lips seeking the warmth and suppleness of hers. She let out a soft whimper as his mouth sealed to hers and he engaged her in another slow, sensuous kiss. He pressed his body against the length of her. His hands eased over her bare skin. He could feel her stomach quiver beneath his fingertips, felt her chest rise and fall against his. As he moved his hands higher, she sucked in a breath.

Cupping her lace-covered breasts, he gave them a gentle squeeze. McCarthy's soft, lusty moans and her slow surrender wreaked havoc on his insides, making him harder than ever before. At the same time, his heart wrenched a little, knowing how much she trusted him. Knowing how much she wanted him.

"I'll give you everything you want, sweetheart," he whispered in her ear. "Everything you need."

He felt her body tremble, heard her breath catch. He leaned just a tiny bit closer to her, pressing his body to hers. One leg wedged between hers, forcing them further apart. His hands moved over her ribcage and to her back. Her breasts flattened against him, just below his pecs. Josh let out another low groan as lace and silky skin stroked his bare flesh with every brush of McCarthy's chest against his.

God, she felt good. And he'd barely even touched her yet!

But the night was still young. And Josh intended to make the most of every minute he had with her.

Chapter 7

What was most stunning to McCarthy wasn't how incredible Josh's hands felt on her body. She'd known that he'd overwhelm her senses and drive her crazy with wanting him. But what surprised her most was how wantonly she responded to him. All inhibition seemed to melt away as Josh's fingers eased over her burning flesh.

As his lips grazed her neck, she came just a little more undone. His strong hands on her body, his tongue gently teasing her skin, the crisp smell of his cologne, mixed with his male heat, turned her on more than anything she'd ever experienced before.

True, McCarthy hadn't engaged in such a primal, heated encounter before, but she was savvy enough to recognize the intense chemistry that existed between her and Josh. The air around them was sexually charged. And with every breath she took, he infiltrated her senses all the more, seducing and tempting her and making her so very excited. And wet.

Her fingers gripped the wooden rack they were wrapped around as Josh's mouth blazed a trail down to her breasts. His soft lips swept over the top of one globe, then inched lower to her nipple, which begged for his touch.

Swiping the hard center with his tongue elicited a sharp cry from her. Her eyelids fluttered closed. The combination of his warm breath, the rough lace that still covered her breasts, and his talented tongue pressing against the sensitive bud made McCarthy's pulse race and her insides seize up. The throbbing between her legs intensified.

Oh, but what sweet torture it was!

A passion-induced haze rolled into her head, shadowing all doubt and uncertainty. All reservation slipped away. Maybe she wasn't Josh's type and maybe this wasn't anything more than a wild impulse brought on by the impending full moon or, more realistically, basic physical needs and desires. But she intended to indulge in the moment. McCarthy was smart enough to know what an amazing sexual opportunity she had at this very moment. She knew Josh would fulfill her deepest, darkest fantasies.

Only he could.

When his fingers pushed aside the lace of her bra and his tongue laved her pebbled nipple, she knew Josh would pull out all the stops to heighten her arousal, and then he'd exhaust himself pleasing and satiating her. He was that type of man. Built for this type of sensual activity. Wired internally to know instinctively how to pleasure a woman.

Josh would know how to turn her inside out. He'd know exactly what she wanted—what she needed—better than she probably knew it herself.

In fact, she suspected she wouldn't even have to tell him what erotically wicked things she longed for him to do to her. He'd know.

Men like Josh were just that way. Intuitive and incredibly resourceful. Skilled in the ways of pleasing women. Innately talented at fulfilling needs and desires women themselves didn't even know they had.

Josh would do more than awaken her passion. He would command it.

A jolt of excitement hit her hard at the impending pleasurefest she was about to engage in.

Josh glanced up at her from his bent position, where he'd been attending to her nipple.

A trace of triumph—and knowing—flickered in his beautiful blue eyes. He knew he had her hooked on sexual desire. He knew she was caught in his web.

"Stay here, sweetheart," he said in a low, intimate voice. He stepped away from her and disappeared into the lounge.

With every second that slipped by, McCarthy grew more curious at what he was up to. She also grew more aroused as the anticipation welled within her. When Josh returned with the goody bag Cat had given her, a wicked thrill shot through McCarthy from head to toe. She'd known Josh was a bad boy. And sinful beyond her wildest imagination. But what she hadn't expected was that his daring, adventurous side called to hers.

In fact, McCarthy hadn't realized she even had an adventurous side—until Josh dumped the contents of the bag on the pool table and reached for the fur-lined handcuffs.

But the excitement that washed over her, consuming every inch of her and driving out all safe, sensible instincts, told her she was about to learn her true nature.

And Josh Kensington would be the one to show it to her.

As he looped the chain connecting each cuff over the rack and gently secured her wrists above her head, McCarthy's heart rate accelerated. Breathing became a difficult task. Josh stared down at her, and the heat that lit his now-dark gaze made her painfully aware of his erotic intentions.

But oh, what exquisite pain it was! Even as her pussy throbbed in sharp beats and her breasts ached for his hands or his mouth to pleasure them, she reveled in this slow, sensuous torture. Every fiber of her being cried out for his touch. Every nerve-ending danced and sizzled, set ablaze by the scorching hot look Josh gave her and the knowledge that he intended to do things to her no other man had ever done.

Truly decadent things that ought to make her blush just thinking about them. But no. McCarthy wasn't the least bit ashamed. She was entranced. Excited. Enveloped in sheer ecstasy.

As though Josh had read her wicked thoughts, he said, "I'm going to show you what it's like to have every inch of your gorgeous body worshipped." His hands slid down her arms once more, his fingertips lightly grazing her skin in a touch that was both erotic and tender. She shivered with anticipation of everything he intended to do to her.

Josh's fingers whisked away the lacy cups of her bra. Tucking the material under her full breasts, he then paid them homage by sliding his palms over them, teasing her nipples and making her die a slow death while she waited for him to suckle each erect tip.

He gave her breasts a not-so-gentle, but not quite rough, squeeze, then slid his hands down her stomach. His fingers deftly worked the button and zipper on her jeans. He then eased the denim over her hips and down her legs. She stepped out of the thick material and he tossed her jeans aside. His hands went on a loving exploration of her legs, starting with her calves. His fingers grazed the backs of her knees, teasing the sensitive flesh, before his hands moved higher, up to her now quivering thighs.

Josh grinned up at her, giving her a sweet, yet oh-so-sexy look that made her insides burn and her heart soar. "You're trembling."

She sucked in a sharp breath, nodded her head.

Josh's seductive look was enough to make her heart melt.

"Don't worry, sweetheart. You're going to enjoy every second of this."

That wasn't at all what she was worried about. Neither did she doubt that she was going to enjoy every glorious moment of whatever Josh did to her. She knew every touch would be more sensuous, more stirring, more arousing than the last.

"I'm not trembling because I'm nervous," she said in a voice she barely recognized as her own. It was low and throaty and full of desire. "It's just you," she said simply. "The way you touch me. The way you look at me. It makes me feel…" She searched her jumbled brain for the right words. "Sexy," she said in a quiet voice.

Josh stared up at her. "You are sexy, babe. Damned sexy."

McCarthy had never thought of herself that way. But tonight she felt provocative and desirable.

All because of Josh.

She grinned at him and shook her head. "I can't even think straight right now."

"Maybe," he began as his fingers slid inward to caress the sensitive flesh of her inner thighs. "It's time you stop thinking so damned much." His hands moved further upward to the juncture between her legs. His thumbs skimmed the scalloped edges of the red lace panties she wore.

McCarthy gasped.

Josh winked at her. "Stop thinking, sweetheart. Just feel."

His gaze remained locked with hers as he gently stroked her swollen folds with his thumbs, the lace providing absolutely no barrier from his heat and electrifying touch.

McCarthy felt her composure slip. When Josh's thumbs slipped beneath the edge of the panties and his flesh connected with hers, she could no longer hold his gaze. Her eyelids dipped and she let out a soft whimper of need.

Nothing had ever felt quite so exquisite, quite so erotic. The pads of his thumbs glided over her wet, highly sensitized lips, making McCarthy hotter. And wetter. The juices seeped through the opening of her vagina like warm honey, teasing her further.

Then Josh's thumbs parted her, pulling the dewy folds open just as his mouth pressed to the heart of her. Through the thin lacy panties, she felt the heat of his breath and the pressure of his lips on her.

McCarthy moaned.

The tip of Josh's tongue teased and tormented her, a preview of wicked things to come.

Her fingers gripped the ledge of the pool rack again. She wasn't going anywhere because her wrists were restrained, but McCarthy still felt the need to hold on, knowing she was in for one wild, outrageous ride.

Admittedly, the handcuffs added an element of excitement she'd never expected. McCarthy felt as though her good girl sensibility had been hit head-on by an eighteen-wheeler. The last vestiges of prudence lay scattered at her feet, sexual road kill.

What emerged in its wake was a wanton, adventurous spirit that longed to experience all the erotically delicious sensations only Josh could evoke. She wanted him to devour every inch of her and take her places she'd never been before.

His hands slid away for just a moment before his fingers curled around the waist of her panties and he dragged the skimpy material down her legs and off of her. Her eyes were still closed, but she could feel his gaze on her, feasting on her bare flesh.

"Goddamn," he whispered. "You are one hell of a sight, McCarthy." His hands roamed her body, gliding over her belly to her hips and then back and down to her ass. He cupped her cheeks and said, "You're beautiful. Absolutely perfect."

"Hardly," she managed to say.

"Oh, yeah," he said. "Totally perfect. You have the kind of body men fantasize about, sweetheart. Long and luscious, with soft curves and creamy skin." He groaned, low and deep.

Then his hands moved from her ass to her pelvis. Inward and down until the heel of one hand covered her mound. He applied just the right amount of pressure to make her whimper in need as he massaged the sensitive area.

Ribbons of desire caressed her insides, her heart, her soul. Her toes curled, pressing into the hardwood floor.

Josh's hand slid lower, his fingers spreading her lips. His head bent forward and his tongue took one long swipe over her, culminating in a sharp flick of her sensitive clit. She cried out from the intense sensations that rocketed through her body.

"Oh, God." She gasped. Her grip tightened on the rack.

McCarthy had never known such intense pleasure. No man had ever made love to her with his mouth. And she innately knew no other man would ever make her this hot, this restless, this in need of release.

Josh lifted one of her legs and draped it over his broad shoulder. His mouth covered her and he alternated between stroking her with his tongue and suckling the swollen nubbin between her legs. McCarthy rushed toward what was sure to be a powerful orgasm. Her heart thundered in her chest and she panted softly. Desire coursed through her now, hot and bright.

What Josh did to her body was more explosive than she'd dreamed possible. His mouth on her, pleasuring her in a way that made her lose all control, sent her careening toward a release she was suddenly desperate to experience. Intense sensations consumed her, heightening her arousal to a nearly unbearable degree.

"More," she whispered on a sharp breath. "Oh, God, please don't stop." She whimpered and whispered encouragement, wanting Josh to know how much she loved his intimate touch. Wanting him to know how crazy with desire he made her.

And then he pushed a finger deep into her core and she was done for. Her climax tore through her. The sensations were electric, intensifying to an overwhelming degree before the fiery heat and pleasure consumed every fiber of her being.

"Josh!" she cried out. Little bursts of light flashed behind her closed lids. Her heart slammed against her chest and her entire being tensed as she embraced the erotic sensations that pulsed and surged inside her.

She held onto the endless moments of rapture, squeezing her inner walls tight around Josh's long finger, holding him captive as she clung to the delicious sensations that prickled her nerve-endings and set her insides on fire.

She could have stayed in this glorious place forever. Nothing had ever felt quite so wonderful. So right. McCarthy had never luxuriated in such a beautiful, all-consuming, decadent moment of pleasure.

Her breath came in shallow pants, but she managed a smile for Josh. Staring down at him, her eyelids heavy and her mouth quivering at the corners, she said, "Promise me you'll do that again before the night's over."

Chapter 8

Josh couldn't help but grin at her. "You are a vixen, sweetheart." He winked at her. Then he hauled himself up and extracted the key to the handcuffs from his back pocket. Releasing her wrists, he rubbed them gently, then did the same with her arms. He hadn't meant to leave her hanging there for so long; nor had he wanted to rush the experience of tasting and pleasing McCarthy.

"Circulation okay?" he asked.

She nodded as she melded to him. Josh wrapped his arms around her and held her tight, feeling the vibration of her body against his.

"I had no idea that would be so incredible," she whispered, her warm breath teasing his nipple.

Josh dropped a kiss on the top of her head. "That wasn't your first time, was it?"

She nodded again.

Josh was stunned into silence. Although, knowing he was the first man to pleasure McCarthy in that way not only stroked his ego, it also made him insanely relieved. He couldn't say why, for sure, but it made him happy to know he'd been McCarthy's first in some respect. He'd been the first to show her how much she could enjoy his touch and his mouth on such an intimate, private part of her body.

But Josh wasn't done loving her. The night was young and he had a head full of fantasies to explore and desires to fulfill.

His lips grazed her forehead and her temple. When she tilted her head to meet his, his mouth covered hers in a possessive kiss. Something stirred deep inside him, making him want to claim her. He wanted McCarthy to belong to him. He didn't want any other man to touch her, to kiss her, to make love to her.

Suddenly, Josh felt the overwhelming urge to be the only one.

The emotion confused him and he tried to skirt around it, unsure of its origin or meaning.

Her fingers pressed into the muscles of his back as she held him to her, in a territorial way that matched his own. His hands plowed through her silky hair as he kissed her, long and deep and with all the passion that ruled his body. Despite his confusion over the intensity of his emotions, Josh refused to hold himself in check. He held nothing back. He felt a natural desire to give McCarthy everything he had... and take everything she had to offer.

When their heated kiss ended, he was short of breath. His lips skimmed her jaw, her throat, her collarbone. It seemed to take an absurd amount of time for his senses to return to him. They never really did. He was totally off-kilter and feeling something he'd never felt before.

At least, this was something he'd never felt with another woman. But if Josh were honest with himself, he'd have to face the fact that he had always been protective and territorial where McCarthy was concerned. And he'd always felt immense relief that she hadn't been involved with any other man all this time.

Again, he wasn't quite sure what all of that meant. He only knew that, when he'd touched her and made her come, he'd wanted to hold onto the erotic moment as much as she had. Pleasing McCarthy, Josh realized, was infinitely more arousing than anything he'd ever known. Deeply, emotionally stirring, actually.

A little shaken by the depth of his feelings, but not unnerved by them, he gathered her in his arms again and said, "I've changed my mind about tonight."

McCarthy looked at him with wide, questioning eyes. The pain of rejection was stamped all over her beautiful face.

Josh groaned. "No, no. Sweetheart, that's not what I meant." He hated that he'd hurt her feelings—it hadn't been his intention at all. "What I mean is, I don't want to do this here. No, it's more than that. I don't want to fuck you at Rendezvous, Mac. I want to take you to my apartment and make love to you."

Her stunned expression really shouldn't have surprised him. But it did. She stepped out of his embrace and crossed her arms over her chest. Not in a defensive way, Josh noted. But in a self-conscious way.

Her eyes narrowed on him as she said, "You don't take women to your place, Josh. And you sure as hell don't make love to them."

He eyed her curiously. "How do you know that?"

Her dark green eyes rolled in the sockets and she let out a puff of air. "You have a reputation, Josh. Everyone in the neighborhood knows it. You're the love 'em and leave 'em type, and the only way to leave 'em is if you have sex at their apartments. Not yours. Besides," she said as her arms moved away from her chest and her hands set on her shapely hips. "Who said you get to call all the shots tonight?"

He grinned at her, despite the little fight she was putting up. Josh had known her for five years. They were practically best friends. He could see right through her, whether she knew it or not. She was trying to retain some control over the situation. She didn't want to get hurt, and that was understandable. Lord knew he didn't want to hurt her. Not ever.

McCarthy was simply shielding herself from him. He could tell by the way she stared skeptically at him. There was a glimmer of hope in her eyes that told him she wanted this evening to be more than just a hot, one-night hook up. But she doubted the possibility.

But Josh no longer did.

Sure, at first, he'd been looking for sex. Or so he'd thought initially. He'd suspected the sparks would fly with McCarthy and they'd singe the sheets together. But somewhere along the way, he'd given into the beauty and the mystery of McCarthy, and he'd fallen under her spell. Perhaps he'd always been under it. Wasn't he the one who came upstairs five, six times a night just to get a glimpse of her? Wasn't he the one who always offered to stop by her apartment to help with her latest project, knowing she'd cook lunch or dinner for him and he'd get to spend some private, alone time with her?

He'd been chasing her all this time. In a very subtle, measured way. In the interim, he'd sampled a variety of women and, as a result, had gotten the natural urge to roam out of his system.

Josh didn't want anyone else. He wanted McCarthy. More than he'd ever wanted any woman.

He knew it deep in his bones. And the challenging jut of her perfect chin, which made him want her all the more, confirmed that she was the one.

The sudden realization should have jolted him to the core.

It should have knocked him on his ass.

It should have made him bolt for the door.

It didn't.

She stood before him—her bra tucked under her full, tempting breasts, the centers of which were still tight with her arousal. She didn't look the least bit intimidated by him. Rather, she appeared ready to call "bullshit" at a moment's notice because she wasn't about to let him get away with deceiving her. Just looking at her, and knowing how she'd hold him to his word and to the highest of her standards, had his pulse racing.

She did the craziest things to his heart.

McCarthy was so unlike the women he'd dated—slept with, rather—in the past. She was true to herself, and she wouldn't allow her emotions to let her get swept away. She would challenge him every step of the way and hold him accountable for every action.

She would keep him on the straight and narrow.

She was the only woman who could.

Reaching for her, Josh drew McCarthy back into his arms, though she was a wee bit reluctant to come.

His grin widened. "You're a hard ass," he said. "I'll give you that. I know better than to fuck with you, Mac. You'll never let me get away with anything. Not even the most minor of infractions."

"That's because I know you so well. You're a little boy who likes to be bad, Josh."

He knew his grin had just turned wicked—and a bit lascivious. "So be bad with me, baby."

McCarthy laughed. She relaxed a little in his arms, he noticed. "I just was."

"Felt good, didn't it?" he murmured. His lips brushed over her temple. "And you want more, don't you?"

She let out a long sigh. "You are addictive," she whispered.

Her eyelids fluttered closed as he continued to drop kisses on her face. His lips swept over her cheek before his mouth pressed to hers again. He kissed her slowly this time, as though they had all the time in the world to enjoy each other. When her lips parted, welcoming him inside, Josh's tongue tangled with hers. He kissed her long and tenderly, knowing he conveyed the emotions that had sprung forth this evening.

He couldn't explain what the hell had just happened between them. What had transpired to make him suddenly realize he wanted McCarthy more than he'd ever wanted any other woman. And not on a temporary basis.

Luckily, he was man enough to recognize and accept the revelation.

Now, all he had to do was convince McCarthy that he wasn't just looking for a hot hook-up.

Which was incredibly ironic, he had to admit.

As he pulled away from her, he cupped her face in his hands and said, "I've reconsidered my position on commitment. I'm ready to give it a try."

Chapter 9

McCarthy couldn't stop her jaw from dropping. She stared at Josh, quite certain she'd heard him—or interpreted his words—wrong.

Way wrong.

Yet the way he stared down at her, with such intensity and certainty in his eyes gave her the niggling suspicion that perhaps he'd had an epiphany tonight.

But holy hell! What was she supposed to do with this new information? This new Josh?

He couldn't be serious.

Surely he was just toying with her. Luring her deeper into his seductive web.

And if she didn't get out now, she knew she'd never escape unscathed.

Extracting herself from him, she crossed the room to where her Oxford lay on the floor. Pulling the lace cups of her bra back into place and then tugging her shirt on, she quickly buttoned it and searched for her jeans.

Ah, over there.

She stalked across the room and gathered her pants and her panties up. Josh, however, reached for her wrist, stopping her from dressing.

"Unless you're putting your clothes on so we can go back to my place, I think we ought to sit down and talk about this."

"What's to talk about?" she demanded as she yanked her wrist free of his loose grip. She bent at the waist and stepped into the red lace panties she was loath to wear again because they'd make her think of what Josh had done to her tonight. But what choice did she have? Her sensible cotton underwear and bra—both in boring white—were tucked neatly in the tote bag in her office, where she'd stashed them after changing into the lingerie Cat had bought her.

Thinking of the way this evening had started out and how it was ending, made McCarthy groan.

What the hell had happened? One minute, she was enjoying the most erotic, decadent orgasm of her life, and the next, Josh was acting all lovey dovey and… weird.

So un-Josh-like.

"Mac," he said as he propped a hip against the edge of the pool table and crossed his massive arms over his perfectly sculpted chest. A chest she was better off not looking at. She turned away. "Goddamn it," he said under his breath.

"Look, I don't know what kind of game you're playing here, Josh, but it's time to put an end to it." She searched for her loafers, found them, and slipped into each soggy one. Spying her tank top on the table, which she'd completely forgotten about, she snatched it up with a hand and stalked out of the pool room. She didn't care that she'd left a bag full of goodies on the pool table. She'd gather up all that naughty and not-so-her stuff tomorrow and toss it in the trash.

So much for her Good Girl Gone Wild experience. She should have known better. Hadn't she reminded herself earlier that Josh was way out of her league? And that playing with him was a dangerous, risky business?

What on earth had made her think they could just have sex and be done with it?

Then again, what on earth had possessed Josh to turn the tables on her and make this more complicated than it was?

Shouldn't she be the one flooded with emotions? Shouldn't she be the one falling all over herself with mushy feelings?

Not Josh. Never in a million years should Josh say to her the things he just had.

Collecting her black leather tote bag and pulling on her full-length wool coat, in a sensible shade of winter white, she couldn't help but note in disgust, she walked briskly toward the entrance to Rendezvous.

Sensible was suddenly a characteristic that tore her apart. It was a natural trait, one she'd been perfectly content with the whole of her life. Well, until tonight, that was. Somewhere along the way, as Josh had seduced her, she'd discovered she liked throwing caution to the wind.

She liked standing on the ledge and teetering there, wondering what would happen next.

But then her sensibility warred with her reckless behavior, reminding her that living on the edge brought with it uncertainties she couldn't handle.

Like Josh's peculiar, unexpected, heart-wrenching revelation.

She'd been right all along. He was going to stomp all over her heart.

But damn it. For the briefest period of time, Josh had helped to unleash her deepest desires, and McCarthy had felt freed of her uptight constraints. She'd felt liberated.

And then Josh had ruined everything.

He'd gone too far.

Who did he think she was? One of his barflies who waited with bated breath for him to notice them? One of his many lovers who didn't mind being toyed with, as long as they could have just one night with the notorious Josh Kensington?

Shit. Who had she been fooling? She could no more have a one-night stand than Josh could keep from having yet another conquest fall in love with him.

He was a womanizer. A rake. A chauvinistic—

No, wait. He wasn't that. He didn't have a chauvinistic bone in his body.

He was just, well, Josh.

Fun-loving. Free-spirited. Adventurous. Lover of the female form.

And a confirmed, eternal bachelor.

To the best of her knowledge—and the Manhattan grapevine—he'd never led any woman to believe she had a shot at a long-term commitment with him. So what was with his strange behavior tonight?

McCarthy drew up short at the door. Josh's back was braced against the red velvet, tufted material that covered the double doors at the entrance of the club. He'd put his shirt back on and his arms were crossed over his chest, his booted feet crossed at the ankles. His jaw was set in a hard line. He was pissed.

"So that's it?" he asked. "I was honest with you and now you're blowing me off?"

"I'm not blowing you off," she said in her defense. "I'm maintaining my dignity. A shred of sanity."

"Oh, cut the crap, Mac." He moved away from the door and gripped her upper arms in his hands. "You're the one who's always spouting the cheesy B.S. about soul mates and destiny and true love. And yet, here you are. Running from it."

Her mind simply couldn't process his words. Her eyes bulged in their sockets and her head shook of its own volition. "I can't even begin to fathom what's come over you," she all but sputtered.

Suddenly, Josh grinned at her. His eyes lit with a vibrancy that left her breathless. "I'm shocked, Mac. Really, I am. Here you are, renowned dating guru, and yet you can't tell when a man has fallen in love with you?"

He truly couldn't have said anything more shocking to her. She wrested her arms from his grip and literally staggered toward her desk and dropped her tote bag on top of it. She closed her eyes, tried to reconcile Josh's words. And all the questions they evoked.

How was it possible?

When had it happened?

Why her?

McCarthy was vexed to the very core of her being. And completely lost in thought. So when Josh's hands rested gently on her shoulders, she jumped. But Josh was right there to hold her steady. His body pressed to hers, his front to her back.

His soft voice filled her ear as he said, "It took me by surprise, too. But damn it. I feel like I've always known we'd end up together. Deep in my heart. And I guess—I mean, I think—I just wasn't ready to admit how I felt. Until tonight. Everything is just so different between us now."

His lips grazed her cheekbone and McCarthy's eyelids closed. "I don't understand."

"I know. And I'm sorry I can't give you a better explanation. I can't really figure it out myself, Mac, except I just realized that I've always loved you."

Tears suddenly built behind her closed lids and seeped out of the corners of her eyes. "Josh," she whispered. If he was leading her on, toying with her emotions and her affection, she'd kill him. "Don't say things you don't mean," she warned him.

"I wouldn't," he said in an adamant tone. "You know I wouldn't. You're one of my closest friends. I'd never lie to you or hurt you. Maybe that's why I waited so long to let these feelings out. Because I wanted to be sure—one hundred percent sure—before I said anything. But damn it, Mac. Tonight I just—I don't know." He let out a sharp breath. "I saw you and I touched you, and I made you come. And all I could think was, 'I want to make her feel this good, this desirable, every day for the rest of her life.'"

"Oh, God." She choked back a sob. "You can't seriously be saying this to me!"

"I am." His arms wrapped around her waist and he held her tightly. "I'm not trying to fuck with you. I'm trying to tell you that I love you."

She shook her head in denial, yet she knew Josh. He'd never spout lines like this—

Unless he meant them.

McCarthy gasped. Her eyes flew open and she reached for his hands, locked at her waist, and pulled them apart. She turned in his loose embrace and stared up at him, desperate to see the look in his eyes.

"You love me?" she demanded.

Josh grinned his usual sweet, sexy grin. The one that made her heart melt. "Yeah. And I think you love me, too."

Her chin hitched up a notch. "What makes you so sure?"

He gave a quick shrug of one broad shoulder. "For one thing, you wouldn't have played strip pool with me. It's not your style. Nor would you have let me touch you—make love to you—the way I did."

She gnawed her lower lip for a moment, then said, "Perhaps."

"You need further proof? I can give it to you."

McCarthy eyed him with mounting curiosity. "Oh, really?"

He nodded. His cockiness was part of his charm, she had to admit. "You wouldn't have gotten so upset with me tonight if you didn't love me. If you didn't want everything I said to you to be true."

It didn't take a rocket scientist to know he was right.

Shit.

She was in love with Josh Kensington.

Renowned womanizer. Sexy playboy. The ultimate bad boy.

But the feeling was mutual.

He was in love with her.

"Josh," she suddenly said on the hard rush of air that escaped her.

"Yeah, babe?"

She smiled, despite herself. Despite this completely bizarre experience. This unexpected turn of events. "I do love you."

He winked at her. "I know."

She laughed and swatted at him. "You're damned arrogant."

Reaching a hand up to her face, he brushed away a tear that rolled down her cheek. "Yeah, I'll have to work on that."

"No," came her vehement response. "Don't. I love who you are right this very minute. Don't change a thing."

"You're the first woman who's ever said that to me. Everyone else, Cass included, treats me like a fixer-upper. A man to mold into what they want."

His hand cupped her face and he stared deep into her eyes. Every shred of doubt she'd had previously slipped away. What she saw in Josh's eyes was passion, lust and love. Perhaps those things had always been there, and she'd just been too blind or too scared to see them. But McCarthy knew, in her heart, that what they shared was real. And lasting.

"You're not a fixer-upper. You're unique."

"And smart enough to know this is a good thing between us. I won't fuck it up, McCarthy."

Her heart swelled. Emotion gripped her. Suddenly, all she could think about was being naked with Josh. She wanted no barriers between them. She wanted him to love her and hold her close. She wanted to share every minute of the rest of her life with him.

"Take me home," she suddenly said. Every second without him inside of her was more painful than the last.

She wanted him. She needed him.

Desperately.

"Josh," she continued in an insistent voice, the urgency—the hunger— rushing through her like a raging fire. "Make love to me."

Chapter 10

Josh had never brought a woman back to his apartment, as McCarthy had so astutely pointed out. He stepped aside after unlocking the door and pushing it open and let her enter his domain. He was curious to see her reaction.

He was, by all counts, the quintessential bachelor. Not to mention a fan of rock and roll and a fairly decent guitar player and drummer. He didn't cook—he ordered in or ate out. He didn't do such a hot job keeping the place in order, so he hired someone to do it for him three days a week. His house manager, as Mrs. Agatha James preferred to be called, did his laundry and ran his errands. Josh paid her well to keep his life organized so that he could focus his sole attention on running The Rage.

Usually, he didn't think twice about the state of his prime Westside pad that boasted an awesome view of Central Park. Since no one visited, he didn't have to worry about whether it was in shambles. Thank God Agatha had been in today, though. She'd tidied the place up and, as was her custom of late, she'd added another item to the mantel over his fireplace. This time, it was a square-columned ivory candle resting on a squat black marble holder.

Josh eyed the new addition with curiosity.

"What are you staring at?" McCarthy asked as she roamed the open great room and then came to a standstill next to him.

"That candle on the mantle."

Her gaze followed his. "It's nice. And that holder... Josh, it's gorgeous." She crossed to the fireplace and eyed it more closely. "Where'd you get it?"

"Agatha," he said. McCarthy would know of whom he spoke. That was another thing that had convinced him they'd been leading up to the explosive revelations of the evening—McCarthy was the only woman, aside from his cousin, who knew every minute detail of his life. She was the only one he shared his secrets and dreams with. The only one he considered calling on Sunday morning to recap the week and look toward the future with.

"She has great taste," McCarthy mused. "The set goes perfectly with your apartment. She must really like you, bringing you gifts like this." She raised an eyebrow at him suggestively.

He laughed. "My guess is, she's trying to soften the place up. Make it more chick friendly in hopes I'll bring one home."

McCarthy tried to stifle a grin, but it played on her soft lips anyway. Her gaze scanned the vast room once more. "It is a little… manly. I can honestly say I've never seen someone take their love of music and turn it into a design element in quite this fashion."

Josh eyed the large black leather sectional in the center of the room, the only traditional piece of furniture he owned. In front of the sofa sat a custom-made coffee table that had a glass top and two small flying V guitars that comprised the legs. The end tables matched, and lamps with tall, slim glass-columned bases and white shades adorned them. Five electric guitars and one twelve-string acoustic guitar lined the far wall with specially designed mounts. Personalized, autographed posters of rock legends hung on the other walls, which were painted a sharp dove-gray color that looked sleek and modern against the thick white baseboards and crown molding. A stack of amps flanked the tall marble fireplace.

Admittedly, it looked more like a music studio than a living room, but it was home to Josh.

"I suppose we both have our fetishes," Josh said as he wagged his brow at her. Of course, he was speaking of her love of movies, but Josh couldn't help but tease her by hoisting her goody bag in the air. "Exhibit A."

Splashes of pink tinged her otherwise perfect complexion. "I can't believe you brought that here." She rolled her eyes.

He set the bag on the coffee table and crossed to where she stood in front of the fireplace. Josh's arms slipped around her waist, and he whispered in her ear, "We could get pretty wild with all of that stuff."

She laughed, albeit nervously. Josh felt her tighten in his loose embrace. "I seriously wouldn't know what to do with half of it."

"You'll just have to let your imagination run free, sweetheart. I can help you with that."

McCarthy all but buried her face in his chest, but Josh wasn't about to let her off the hook so easily. Maybe it was because he'd tapped into his inner emotions that he wanted McCarthy to step beyond her perceived limits as well. There was something liberating about this entire evening—about the unexpected release of feelings he'd felt brewing for so long, but which he'd not had an outlet for. Because he hadn't really known, until tonight, that all of his desire and passion and love was for McCarthy.

His hands skimmed over her hips, down to her ass, and it he gave it a gentle squeeze. "What do you say, Mac? Wanna walk on the wild side with me?"

She practically melted in his arms. He could feel her body go limp as she all but slumped against him. And that now-familiar tremble of her legs, the vibration in her entire body, gave him the answer he sought.

Much to his delight, she had the verve to lift her head and meet his gaze. She said, "Show me how to be a bad girl, Josh."

He let out a low groan. "Gladly, sweetheart."

His mouth crushed over hers and he kissed her with all the passion and love he felt for her. McCarthy's arms snaked around his neck and she pressed herself against him until their limbs were twisted and every inch of their bodies were melded together. That overwhelming desire took hold of Josh once again, making him feel as though he'd never get enough of her. He wanted her in every way possible. He wanted to brand her with his mouth and his hands. He wanted to take her to dizzying heights with the kind of hedonistic lovemaking her luscious body inspired.

Suddenly, Josh couldn't stand another moment with the barrier of their clothing between them. His fingers worked the buttons on her Oxford, then the fastening of her jeans. He pushed her clothes and shoes off her body and went to work on the sexy lingerie she wore. When she was completely naked, he scooped her up in his arms and carried her down the hall to his bedroom.

He set her gently on the bed, then held a finger up in the air. "Don't move," he said.

He rushed out of the room and retrieved the goody bag from the coffee table. When he returned, he dropped the bag on the floor beside the bed. Some of those toys may come in handy later in the evening, or early in the morning. But for now, he just wanted to feel McCarthy's soft, silky skin against his and explore every pleasurable gift she had to offer.

This was all very new to Josh, and yet… As he stripped off his clothes and stepped between McCarthy's parted legs, forcing her to lie back on the bed as he settled on top of her, he could honestly say there was something so right about the moment that it felt familiar. Comfortable. Yet extremely exciting at the same time.

Making love to McCarthy for the first time would be incredible— he had no doubt. But making love to her after all that had transpired between them this evening would be mind-blowing. She wasn't one of his typical conquests. She had absolutely nothing in common with those other women—except that she was beautiful and desirable.

But as Josh's hands roamed her body and she moaned softly and writhed beneath him while his fingers and mouth teased her skin and explored her body, Josh knew that he'd been working his way to this moment. He'd sown his wild oats. He'd engaged in empty affairs and heated moments that were fleeting. All of which had left him hungry for something more.

And that something more was McCarthy Portman.

He kissed her again, long and deep. He palmed her breasts, then played with the hard nipples, the pads of his thumbs flicking across them. He broke their kiss and dropped his head to the center of her breasts, desperate to lave and suck them.

McCarthy's back arched, thrusting her breasts upward. Josh slipped a hand around to the small of her back, keeping that portion of her body elevated and pressed to him as he continued to tease one tight nipple with his mouth. Her fingers wove through his hair and she let out a throaty moan that spiked his arousal.

Just knowing how hot he could get her, how wet she would be when he finally slid his fingers or his cock inside her drove Josh to the edge of sanity.

"God, I want you," he whispered against her plump breast.

"Make love to me, Josh," she said in a breathless tone.

His hand skimmed down her stomach to her nearly bare mound. Warm, dewy flesh met his fingers. He slowly rubbed her swollen clit with the pad of one finger.

"Oh," she whispered on a sharp breath.

Josh's tongue curled around her nipple as his finger moved lower. He traced her opening, then dipped his finger inside. Slowly. Her upper body bowed even further off the bed, as though demanding more of his intimate touch. Josh was happy to oblige. He worked two fingers into her tight canal and stroked the core of her.

McCarthy's fingers gripped his biceps. He felt her muscles tense, but she didn't stop him. She gave herself over to the moment, allowing him to bring her the kind of pleasure he longed to.

Josh wanted her to be free of all inhibition. He wanted to make her feel sexy and cherished.

He wanted to drive her wild with desire.

Increasing the tempo so his fingers pumped in and out of her, he pushed her right to the edge. He could feel the pressure build inside her as her inner walls clenched his fingers. Her breathing grew shallow until she panted in little breathy gasps that made him even hotter.

"Come for me, sweetheart," he whispered before his mouth seized her nipple once more and sucked it.

McCarthy's fingers dug into his arms. Her back arched and her head fell back on the pillow. "Oh, God," she whimpered. "I want you so much."

And then he felt her entire body tighten. She let out an erotic cry of pleasure as she came. Her body vibrated and she gasped for air.

Josh grinned. This was just his warm-up act.

Chapter 11

She would never, ever be the same.

McCarthy knew that what was happening to her tonight—what Josh was doing to her body and her heart—was a once in a lifetime experience. He had the ability to turn her completely inside out, heightening the sensitivity of all her erogenous zones and making her feel intensely aware of every single touch, every single breath that caressed her.

But there was so much more to the rare, exquisite pleasure he brought her. Not only did Josh arouse her more than anything she'd ever experienced before, but he also touched her heart with his tenderness. It was as though he knew she needed to be loved slowly at first. She needed the chance to get acclimated to this new, wanton side of her.

And then taking a walk on the wild side was exactly what she intended to do!

McCarthy could not deny that Josh had sparked deep desires she'd never known existed. She wanted him more than she'd ever wanted anything. He made her feel hot and restless and in terrible need of the pleasure only he could bring her.

As her hands slid over his powerful arms, then down his chest to his rigid abdomen, a sharp thrill of excitement targeted her most intimate area.

"You are built so perfectly," she whispered as her fingers grazed his hot flesh.

Josh smiled down at her. "Keep going, sweetheart."

Her hand flattened against his belly, then moved lower. The tips of her fingers glided over the head of his penis and her body jerked in response to the erotic touch as much as his did. Josh let out a low growl that made her womb tighten. His eyelids dipped and his breathing grew ragged as her hand eased over his hard cock. Her fingers wrapped around the shaft.

The width of him was startling, yet oh-so-tantalizing. A wicked thrill shimmied up her spine at the thought of how incredible Josh would feel inside her. Thick, hard and hot. She knew he'd fill her tight canal and make her feel whole. Complete.

Excitement gripped her, chasing out the nervousness that danced through her. She wanted to bring Josh immense pleasure, as he'd done to her. This first time with him was monumentally important and she wanted to touch him the way he liked to be touched. Yet McCarthy didn't have a hell of a lot of experience with this.

Fortunately, as she slid her hand up and down his shaft, then glided her palm over the head, he responded so vehemently, she felt certain she was doing this right.

Spurred on by Josh's deep moan of pleasure, McCarthy shifted on the bed and bent her head to him. Her tongue whisked over his hard cock, from base to tip. Josh's fingers plowed through her hair, pushing the long strands away from her face. She took this as a good sign, and continued on, her actions growing bolder as Josh groaned and gasped and his fingers tightened in her hair.

"Oh, yeah, sweetheart," he said in a low, sexy voice. "You're right on the money."

As though he'd known she had reservations. She couldn't help but smile, loving the fact that Josh was always on the same wavelength, that he intuitively knew what she was feeling. What she was thinking.

Feeling particularly brazen, she closed her mouth over his tip. Josh sucked in a sharp breath. She drew him deeper into her mouth.

"That's it, baby," he whispered. "Oh, God. Mac, you make me so hot."

Her insides coiled tight with desire. McCarthy's head bobbed up and down as she worked his cock, drawing it almost out of her mouth, then pulling it back in. Slow at first, then a bit faster. When she pulled away and merely licked the length of him, she felt Josh's muscles tense.

"You could make me come, sweetheart. In a heartbeat."

A curious sense of power took hold of her. Knowing she pleased him and took him to the brink empowered McCarthy like nothing else. It liberated her, in fact. She suddenly felt raw with need, desperately wanting to feel him inside her. Desperately wanting to make him come.

She glanced up at him, found him staring intently at her. The look he gave her was a scorcher. Wild and passionate. He wasn't the least bit wary about showing the true breadth of his emotions—they were there in his beautiful blue eyes for her to see.

"I need you inside of me, Josh," she said in a quiet voice.

He gripped her upper arms and pulled her against his body. Rolling onto his back, he took her with him so she was settled on top of him. One long arm stretched toward the nightstand and he rummaged around for a moment before extracting a foil packet that shimmered in the moonlight seeping through the narrow opening of the drapes. Once he was sheathed, McCarthy straddled his lap as Josh's hands clasped her hips. The tip of his cock pushed against her opening, making her gasp with anticipation and excitement.

She eased downward, feeling her body's resistance at the sweet invasion.

"Slow," he whispered in a tight voice.

McCarthy nodded, though she didn't think she could manage slow at the moment. With every breath she took, she wanted him more. Josh's hands tightened on her hips, forcing her to hold steadily above him.

"Josh." She gasped. "I'm not fragile. I'm not going to break."

His jaw clenched for a moment. "You're damn tight, baby. I don't want to hurt you."

"You won't. Trust me. I know my body. I'm ready for you, Josh. I'm ready to feel you fully inside me."

He let out a low growl. "Goddamn it, Mac. I don't want to lose control."

"Why the hell not?" She pushed against him, forcing him to penetrate her aching vagina. She sucked in a breath. "Oh, yes," she whispered.

And she pushed further down onto him, unable to stop herself or take it slow, as he'd suggested. Every moment without him inside her was a moment of senseless torture. She knew he wanted her as much as she wanted him. Why bother fighting it? Why hold back?

Why not lose control?

"Josh," she coaxed in a sultry voice. "Walk on the wild side with me."

Chapter 12

He couldn't hold back another second. Josh thrust up into her and she let out a sharp cry of pleasure. She settled over him, taking him all the way in, though it was a damned tight fit. So tight it was nearly painful. But it was a good kind of pain. The kind that would have him howling in pleasure if she moved even the tiniest little—

"Oh, Christ. Mac!"

She rocked against him, her inner walls squeezing him tight, holding him in a vice grip as her pelvis moved back and forth in a slow sensuous rhythm.

"You're gonna be the death of me, babe."

She grinned down at him. Her hands were splayed over his chest and her thick curls bounced on her slender shoulders. The look in her eyes was priceless. Feminine power reigned. She knew she was driving him wild, and it clearly pleased her. Made her feel uninhibited. Which was fine with him. He didn't want her to hold back. Not an ounce.

"You feel good inside of me, Josh." Her voice was soft and tinged with desire. A bit throaty and sensual.

"Feels damned good to be here, sweetheart." He pushed up into her, making her moan. Her warm, wet pussy sheathed him, encasing him fully. Driving him completely out of his mind.

Josh could come right here and now. It took so little effort on her part.

It was more than just the way her body fit so perfectly with his. No, Josh felt more than sexual desire, more than lust. Yes, she was beautiful, and the way she rode him, her hair swaying on her shoulders, her breasts rising and falling with every breath she took and thrust he made, was enough to send him into a tailspin.

But the prevailing emotion that gripped him was love.

This was something he'd never experienced before. And he had to admit, he liked the way his feelings for McCarthy intensified his desire for her.

Holding her tight, he increased the tempo, rocking her against him, pushing deep inside her until her eyelids fluttered closed, her mouth quivered and her body trembled. Her sharp gasps mingled with soft moans of pleasure.

A myriad of fantasies flitted through his mind—the numerous ways he wanted to take her. All the wild and wicked things he wanted to do to her.

He thrust deep into her and she cried out as she came, clutching at him. It was all Josh could do not to come right then.

McCarthy wanted this intensely erotic, overwhelming sensation to go on and on. She held her breath as she allowed every fiery feeling that blazed inside her to rage for as long as possible before the sensations began to ebb. Still, her skin tingled, her nerve-endings seemed to crackle and sizzle. Her orgasm abated, but left in its wake a peculiar residual effect—as though Josh had branded her.

His heat, his touch, his love for her was emblazoned on her heart and at the core of her.

This, she suddenly realized, was the elusive element—the mysterious, life-altering experience so many of the single women who were members of Rendezvous sought.

Unexpectedly, McCarthy had found it. With Josh.

Her matchmaking software had been right after all.

She smiled suddenly, and Josh crooked a blonde eyebrow at her. "What?"

McCarthy shook her head, fighting back the tears of joy that threatened her eyes. When the wave of emotion subsided, she said, "I want this moment to last forever. It's just so perfect. So right. So wonderful."

"Trust me, sweetheart. It gets better." And in one fluid movement, he flipped her onto her back, while still inside her. McCarthy moaned as he settled between her legs. One large hand moved up her thigh as Josh wrapped her leg around his waist. Then, oh-so-slowly, he began to move inside her.

She clutched at his biceps as he skillfully heightened her arousal, taking her to that beautiful place she was now addicted to. Her eyes shut and she let out a soft gasp as Josh loved her.

When she felt the tightening in her womb and the rush of sensations at her core, she whispered, "Come with me."

Josh groaned. He picked up the pace, pumping in and out of her with the kind of vigor that drove her right to the brink. She felt overcome with emotions. Drowning in sensations that were so incredibly amazing. Her head thrashed back and forth on the pillow. Her fingertips pressed into his hard muscles.

"Josh." She gasped for air. "Oh, God. You feel so good. This is so... Oh, God!"

Her orgasm hit her hard and fast. All the erotic sensations Josh evoked welled inside her and converged, until an explosive eruption made her cry his name.

But just as fabulous as her own orgasm was, she derived equal pleasure from the way Josh convulsed and surged inside her as he came.

Holding him tight, she savored every last moment of the breathtaking experience.

Chapter 13

He'd loved her in ways she'd only fantasized about. When morning dawned and a thin strip of sunlight filtered in through the narrow crack of the heavy, burgundy drapes, McCarthy's eyes drifted open.

Her body felt used and sore, but in such a fabulous way she certainly couldn't complain. Josh had one hell of a repertoire. She smiled as she thought of the incredibly wicked ways he'd touched her and made love to her. Four times. He'd even dipped into the goody bag.

She should be ashamed of herself for all the things she let him do to her, and the things she'd done to him. But she wasn't. Not the least little bit.

Stifling a giggle, she rolled onto her side and reached for him. Josh had held her until she'd heard his soft snoring, then she'd scooted over to her side of the bed, uncertain as to how long he'd be interested in holding her. And she'd feared his arm, which had been draped around her shoulders as her head had rested on his chest, would fall asleep if she lingered too long.

He'd let out a soft protest as she'd inched away, but had quickly drifted back to sleep. McCarthy had watched him for a while, snuggled close to him, burrowing deep under the thick, burgundy duvet and the crisp white sheets.

The satisfaction she'd felt had come not only from being loved so thoroughly, but from knowing she was the first woman to share Josh's bed. She was the first woman he'd let into his life and his heart in this way.

She'd stared at him for a while longer, loving the peaceful look on his handsome face and the rise and fall of his muscular chest as he breathed steadily, easily.

And then she'd closed her eyes and listened to the faint yet reassuring sound of his snoring, and that had lulled her to sleep.

Being physically exhausted and sexually satisfied, not to mention emotionally sated, she'd slept late into the morning. Now, as her fingers skimmed over the rumpled sheets at her side, up and over until she found warm flesh, she sighed contently.

It was more than that, actually. For the first time in her life, McCarthy was deliriously happy. Also, for the first time in her life, she felt perfectly at home. She knew she belonged with Josh.

And that revelation was as exciting and heart-warming to her as all of the others that had occurred over the past ten hours.

"What are you smiling about?" he asked in a lazy tone. He sounded as satiated and content as she felt.

"You. This. Us." She moved closer to him as he reached for her and draped his arm around her shoulders. Snuggling against his side and resting a hand on his chest, she said, "I woke up once and thought I'd dreamt the whole evening. And then I felt you beside me and I knew it wasn't a dream."

He groaned as he stretched his other arm over his head and rested his hand on the pillow beneath his head. His grip on her shoulders tightened for a moment, and then his fingers began to lightly stroke her bare flesh, making her tingle from head to toe.

She loved how he touched her with such familiarity. And a comfortable intimacy that spoke volumes. There was an innate connection between them, and she could tell Josh felt it as strongly as she did.

"So why'd you slip away last night?" he asked. His tone was still low and sexy, raspy with sleep, but she didn't miss the note of concern he projected.

McCarthy smiled again. "I wasn't sure. I mean, I just… you know." She let out a soft, nervous laugh.

Josh shifted on the bed, rolling onto his side until they were face to face. "You just didn't know if I could handle the intimacy."

She grinned at him. "How do you always know what I'm thinking?"

His grin, in return, was slow and sexy. "Because I know you." He was quiet for a moment, as though lost in thought. Then he added in a serious tone, "I kept reaching for you, but you weren't there."

"I was," she assured him. "I was just giving you your space."

Josh's chiseled features seemed to harden before her eyes. "Mac," he said in a reasonable tone as he propped himself on one elbow. "I need you to know something."

Her insides tightened in anticipation.

Please, God, don't let him tell me he just got carried away last night and he didn't mean anything he said.

But as she looked deep into Josh's eyes, she knew better. And so her insides uncoiled as she asked, "What?"

Josh stared at her a moment, his gaze deep and full of passion. "I've never done any of this before. I've never felt this way about a woman. I've never made love to a woman the way I did you, and I sure as hell never wanted to stay with one all night. Nor have I ever wanted to hold one all night. But I wanted to hold you last night. All night."

McCarthy felt the tears well in her eyes. She closed her lids, fighting back the emotion that overcame her.

Josh continued on. "I honestly felt like I couldn't be close enough to you. I wanted to feel your skin on mine. I just wanted to hold you close."

She nodded, unable to speak. This romantic side of Josh was even more emotionally stirring than the erotic side of him.

It seemed to take an absurd amount of time for her to find her voice, but when she finally did, all she could manage was a simple, "I didn't know."

His fingers swept over her cheek, brushing away a few wayward strands of hair. "Now you do." His head dipped and he kissed the tip of her nose.

McCarthy had to squeeze her eyes shut again, to stave off the flow of emotion that threatened to turn her into a weeping willow.

Josh said, "Baby, things are different for me now." His fingers skimmed lower, over her jaw, down her throat, across her collarbone. "I want to hold you at night and make love to you in the morning." He chuckled suddenly. "Oh, hell. I want to make love to you morning, noon and night."

McCarthy laughed, too. She swiped at a wayward tear that seeped out of the corner of her eye when she opened it. She said, "Never in a million years would I have guessed you had such a soft heart."

He grinned at her in the way that made her heart soar. "You've always known it. Otherwise, you never would have given me the time of day."

McCarthy eyed him for a moment, knowing deep in her bones he spoke the truth. She never would have let things go as far as they had—starting with the friendly teasing before the pool game—if she'd doubted Josh's sincerity, good intentions and true heart.

"I'm astounded by how well you know me."

Josh's head dipped and his lips brushed hers. "Ditto." He kissed her, long and deep and with all the passion he'd exhibited last night. When he drew away from her, he said, "Why don't you get a little more sleep? I have a quick errand to run, and then…" He wagged a brow at her.

McCarthy giggled, then stifled a yawn. She'd been putting in a vast amount of hours the past few months. With Cass planning her wedding and then taking three weeks off to honeymoon in Tuscany, McCarthy had stepped in and taken over a huge amount of responsibility at Rendezvous.

It was what she'd always wanted, really. Cass treated her and compensated her as a partner. Thus, it was monumentally important to McCarthy that her friend and partner be able to trust her to take care of the club and their members and Cass' investment.

She settled comfortably in the plush bedding as Josh slipped from the bed. She suspected he was headed to the gym. She knew he worked out religiously.

"Come back soon," she whispered before sleep descended upon her once again.

The next time McCarthy awoke, she peered at the alarm clock on the nightstand and was surprised by the large digitized numbers staring back at her. She'd slept until nine-thirty. Granted, she felt refreshed and relaxed, but it was surprising that she'd slept so soundly away from home.

Thinking of Josh brought a smile to McCarthy's face. She slipped from the bed and traipsed through his apartment, in search of him. When she didn't find him, she decided to step into the shower. Afterward, she used his hairdryer and then applied a little bit of makeup that she kept in her purse. Since she didn't have any clean clothes with her, she took one of Josh's white button-down shirts from the closet and put it on.

By the time she wandered back out to the living room, Josh returned. He came through the door toting a bag from the bakery around the corner from Rendezvous and The Rage. McCarthy's stomach suddenly growled as the smell of coffee and fresh bagels wafted under her nose.

Josh settled next to her on the sofa and set the goodies on the table.

Then he reached for McCarthy. One hand pushed through her hair, whisking the strands away from her face. Then his mouth was on her and she lost all coherent thought. Even food and coffee lost its appeal.

When Josh pulled away, her eyes remained closed. She knew her smile was dreamy and sappy. "You kiss me like you've been doing it for years."

"I have," he said. "In my fantasies."

McCarthy's eyes fluttered opened. Her fingers skimmed over Josh's chiseled cheekbone and she said, "You say the damnedest things."

Josh let out a soft chuckle. "Just speaking the truth, babe." He eased away from her and reached for the bag of bagels.

She watched him spread out the feast on the glass top. Dressed in a tight-fitting navy-colored T-shirt and faded Levi's, he looked delicious. She wanted very much to fall back into bed with him. Last night had been the most incredible night of her life. She could think of nothing more physically satisfying or emotionally stirring than having Josh make love to her.

Thinking about last night reminded her that she needed to call a plumber to fix the pipe in the woman's restroom before she opened for business at six that evening.

"I need to use your phone book to call a plumber," she said.

"Already taken care of," Josh said as he handed over a tall to-go cup of coffee.

"What do you mean?"

Josh took a sip of his own coffee, then said, "I phoned a friend of mine first thing this morning and met him over at Rendezvous. It was a quick fix."

"Josh." McCarthy returned her coffee to the table. "That was my responsibility."

"Well, it's one less thing you have to worry about today."

She couldn't say for sure why his helping her at the club rubbed her the wrong way. But it did. "Josh, you have your hands full with The Rage. You don't have time to help me with my problems at Rendezvous. And, quite frankly, you shouldn't. Cass left me in charge. I'm the one who's responsible for what happens at the club."

He stared at her, dumbfounded. "Mac, I called a plumber and let him into the club. Big fucking deal. You're the one who's kept everything running smoothly all this time. I just did you a small favor so you could sleep in this morning. I know the insane hours you've been keeping and—"

"Oh, shit." She groaned, suddenly feeling even worse. "You keep the same hours. And you got up early this morning to do something that I was supposed to do so that I could sleep?" She cringed, feeling like the ultimate slacker. Here she was, trying to prove to herself and to Cass and to everyone else that she was capable of managing Rendezvous— particularly so Cass could have a life, without constantly worrying about the club—and she'd completely blown it.

Hadn't Josh been the one to save the club from flooding last night? She wouldn't have even known the woman's bathroom had sprung a leak were it not for him. And, in her panicked state, how long would it have taken her to turn the water off? How much damage would have been done?

And then, as if all that wasn't enough, he'd been the one to clean the mess. He hadn't wanted her to ruin her shoes.

"Babe, I don't see what the problem is."

She shook her head and sighed. "The problem, Josh, is that you have your own worries. You don't need mine heaped on top of them. And— well, damn it. With you stepping in all the time to save the day, how I'm ever going to prove I can handle running Rendezvous?"

"Who the hell are you trying to prove it to?" he suddenly demanded. "Do you honestly think Cass would have turned over half of the respon- sibilities to you when she started planning her wedding if she didn't trust you? Do you really think she would leave the country for three whole weeks if she doubted your competence or had concerns about you being in charge?"

Springing from the couch, she planted her hands on her hips and said, "Maybe the only reason she felt comfortable leaving was because she knew you'd be downstairs. She knew you'd take care of everything." Damn it! Why hadn't she seen it before? "I can do more than just match up singles, for Christ's sake."

Josh let out what sounded to be a long-suffering sigh. "I know that, Mac. Cass knows that. Everybody knows that. So why do you feel like you have something to prove?"

"Because I—" She glared at him. She really didn't know why his helping her at the club pushed her over the edge of sanity.

It didn't bug her when he helped out at her apartment. When he came over to help her install decorative rods for her window treatments or fix a running toilet or whatever other home repair or improvement came up, she didn't mind his assistance and good intentions.

Hell, she'd been waiting for him to hook up her surround sound for two months! Sure, she could've had the techs from the electronics store install the system. She could even figure it out for herself, considering her strong technology background.

But she'd waited for Josh. Probably because it was the only time she ever got to spend time with him alone. When he came over to her apartment for one chore or another, she usually cooked him dinner and they hung out. Those were private moments she'd always cherished.

Taking all of that into consideration, she knew it was irrational to get so upset over his helping her out at the club. But it did upset her. In fact, it made her feel… like a child. Ridiculously so.

"I don't understand what you're getting so worked up about," he finally said. He reached for a bagel and took a bite of it.

It occurred to McCarthy that there was more to her rant than just the fact that he was doing tasks she ought to take care of—that he'd gone out for coffee and bagels while she'd slept.

Shaking her head because she really wasn't sure why she was so annoyed, she turned on her bare heels and stalked off. Once inside Josh's bedroom, she stripped off his shirt and slipped into her own clothing. Scooping up her purse and her jacket, she headed toward the front door.

"So that's it?" he asked as her hand closed over the doorknob. "You're just going to leave, mid-fight?"

"We're not fighting," she said over her shoulder. "We're setting boundaries."

"Fuck the boundaries," he said as he rose from the sofa. "I'll help you whenever I damn well feel like it. That's part of being in a relationship, Mac. Christ." He shook his head. "You're the expert in this field. Why the hell am I the one to see things so clearly while you're in the dark?"

"I'm not in the dark." Frustration mounted. "I just don't want you doing things that Cass relies on me to handle."

"Oh, hell, McCarthy." She could tell he was getting pissed because he only ever used her full name when he was deathly serious. "If you want to run off, then fine. Run off. But if I want to help you with something, you can be damned sure I'm going to. Whether you like it or not."

She ground her teeth together. Why had she never seen before how truly obstinate he was? So stubborn and pigheaded and…

Helpful. Concerned. Gracious.

Ugh.

Letting out a low groan, she turned away and yanked open the door.

Chapter 14

For a moment, Josh wondered what the hell had just happened. But then, as he settled back on the leather sofa and sipped his coffee, he suspected he already knew the answer to that question.

He'd scared the shit out of McCarthy.

It occurred to him that he'd pushed too fast, too soon last night. What with the seduction and the declaration of love and the determination he had to help her at Rendezvous, he'd likely overwhelmed her.

Sometimes, Josh wasn't so smart about people's reactions to him. He'd learned over the years that women latched onto every crumb he tossed their way, so he'd adjusted his generous nature to accommodate for the trouble he sometimes caused. He'd never intentionally misled anyone. Occasionally, though, he'd come on a bit too strong or shared too much of his interest in a woman without explaining that it was a caught-up-in-the-moment sort of thing, not a permanent affliction.

But what he felt for McCarthy was so much stronger, so much more powerful and emotionally gripping than anything he'd ever experienced before. And he wanted her to know it. For once, he'd found exactly what he was looking for and he desperately wanted to prove to her that he was serious about her. That these feelings were true and lasting.

In doing so, he'd pushed her right out the door.

Cursing himself for being three kinds of fool, he rose from the sofa and restlessly paced in front of the tall fireplace. Hadn't he reminded himself last night that McCarthy had uncertainties about her ability to run Rendezvous on her own? Sure, she was damned smart, not to mention an incredibly talented computer programmer. He knew she'd been offered a king's ransom to sell her matchmaking software to other dating services. But McCarthy had always claimed her trade secrets were for Rendezvous clients only.

Josh knew the success rate of Rendezvous hook-ups wasn't just due to McCarthy's dating program. It was her personal interest in the clients, her desire to help them find their match that made Rendezvous the most popular dating service in New York. And it was quickly gaining a reputation around the world with its online version.

When McCarthy was making matches, she was the epitome of self-confidence. But when it came to running the club, she wasn't quite so sure of herself.

And Josh hadn't done her any favors by pushing her aside and playing the He-Man Hero.

Damn it. He was the reason she felt incompetent. Why the hell hadn't he realized, before he'd stepped all over her toes, that swooping in to save the day wasn't heroic? It was detrimental to her confidence.

He'd just wanted to help. But she just wanted to prove she was capable of running the club so Cass could go on her honeymoon.

Josh feared he was the catalyst to a major confidence setback.

What the hell had he been thinking?

She was being ridiculous.

As McCarthy slid into the chair behind her desk and powered up her laptop, she scolded herself for being so touchy with Josh this morning.

What on earth had gotten into her?

Here he was, trying to help her and how had she responded? By biting his head off and turning her back on him.

Fully disgusted with herself, she lifted her gaze from the computer and scanned the crowd that had filed in. The intimate lounge, softly lit with candlelight and small table lamps, was filled with hopeful singles. All of them were looking for the one thing McCarthy had found last night.

And given up this morning.

Shame and grief swept over her. She'd totally overreacted, she knew it. But why?

As she watched the dating rituals unfold in the club—ranging from first-time conversations to renewals of past interest—she could have kicked herself for being so foolish.

Hadn't her software, which had an astronomical success rate, matched her perfectly with Josh? And then he'd admitted his feelings for her. He was a confirmed bachelor turned loving boyfriend. Why had she blown it with him?

The answer took a while to come to her, but when it did, she cringed.

Sabotage. That's what it was. Plain and simple. She'd purposely extracted herself from the budding relationship with Josh because she was scared to death of what had happened between them last night.

She was afraid to let him love her.

All of her nonsense about not wanting him to help her at Rendezvous was, quite simply, bullshit. In truth, she was deeply grateful that he owned the club downstairs and was always close at hand for whatever crisis arose. Besides, he was Cass' cousin. Of course he was going to take a personal interest in seeing that everything ran smoothly whether Cass was in town or not.

And, quite frankly, that provided McCarthy a measure of comfort.

Josh had never intentionally done something to make her feel incompetent. He'd always been helpful, as a friend. This morning, he'd tried to help her as a boyfriend would. He obviously knew how exhausted she was because of the excess hours she'd been putting in—of her own volition.

Cass had discussed with her the possibility of hiring a part-time bar manager, but McCarthy had insisted she could juggle making matches and running Rendezvous. And so far, she'd done a great job. With the exception of last night's little blip, everything was under control.

Frowning, she pushed aside her computer. Resting her elbows on her desk, she pressed her fingertips together and set her chin on the steeple. She gazed out at all the activity unfolding before her.

Millions of people all over the world were looking for love.

She'd found it.

How could she have been so stupid to throw it away? Why was she so afraid of Josh's love?

Unfortunately, she didn't have any answers to those questions. She knew the problem. She just wasn't so sure of the solution.

Josh debated going upstairs to see McCarthy before he opened The Rage for the evening. If he barged in and demanded she accept his love, wouldn't that, in theory, be the same thing as commandeering her responsibilities at Rendezvous and trying to solve her problems for her?

As he stewed over the right way to handle the situation, he worried about whether McCarthy was slipping away from him. With every minute that passed—with him not going to her and her not coming to him—he feared he was losing her.

But Josh wasn't exactly skilled in this area. He could woo a woman, no sweat. But to convince one he loved her and would do anything for her was another matter. Clearly, he didn't know how to finesse McCarthy romantically.

Seducing her was no problem. But making a relationship work and creating harmony was clearly not his forte. It was, as she'd said last night, a horse of a different color.

As he prepped the bar for the evening crowd, he wondered if their affair had been brief and fleeting. Or if McCarthy would give him a second chance.

Slicing a lime open, he scowled deeply as he worried over his romantic *faux pas*.

"If you're gonna butcher the fruit," one of his cocktail waitresses said, "Let me cut it up."

He eyed the lime he'd slaughtered. Scooping up the mess in his hand, he tossed the mutilated pieces into the trash. He handed over the knife to Heather and said, "Thanks. I'm a little preoccupied."

"Obviously. I'd ask if it's woman problems you're suffering from, but I've seen you operate. You clearly don't have issues in that area."

Josh eyed her curiously. "Meaning?"

She shrugged. "Meaning, you're very up front about your intentions. Any woman who falls for you or reads more into your passing interest is her own brand of fool."

Josh's scowl deepened.

Heather laughed. "That was a compliment, Josh. I just mean that you don't lead women on. They know what they're getting themselves into. I think that's cool. As a woman, I respect that you don't play games."

And that's when it dawned on Josh.

He'd told McCarthy he loved her. But had he really divulged his true intentions to her?

Chapter 15

She was behind the bar when Josh sauntered into Rendezvous. It was a bit surprising to see McCarthy making martinis rather than matches, but the club was slammed with patrons and she was clearly doing what she could to help the two bartenders keep up.

Josh fought every natural instinct to slip behind the bar and take the shaker from her small hands. She was concentrating so hard she didn't even see him, and all he could think was, "Let me help you!"

Josh was a martini master. McCarthy was a dating guru. She ought to be doling out romance tips, not serving up cocktails. But stepping into all roles at Rendezvous was her responsibility while Cass was away, and Josh knew he had to respect that. He knew he had to let her do all of the things she felt accountable for right now.

But that didn't mean he couldn't let her know that he was always close at hand.

"Hey," he said as he slid onto the only empty barstool.

She glanced up at him and a soft *oh* escaped her lips. "Didn't see you come in."

"Yeah, you're pretty busy. I won't keep you. I just wanted to tell you…" He shook his head. His eyes scanned the crowd. He seemed to have drawn quite a bit of interest.

"Yeah?" she said as she struggled to get the top off the stainless steel shaker without spilling the contents all over the bar. Finally successful at her task, she poured the martinis and placed them on a tray for one of her waitresses to deliver.

Josh smiled at her. "You're doing a great job."

Surprise registered on her pretty face. But the expression quickly morphed to concern and confusion.

"What are you doing here, Josh?"

His smile widened. "I just came here to tell you I love you, babe."

Her jaw fell slack. So, too, did that of the people around them, some of whom he recognized. Josh let out a soft chuckle. So he'd just blown his bad boy, eternal bachelor reputation to hell. He didn't care.

In fact, Josh only cared about one thing. And she was standing in front of him with a bewildered look on her face.

"Look," he said. "I know you want to do things your way and you don't want any help. But you've got to understand something about me, Mac. I'm not a sit-back-and-put-my-feet-up kind of guy." He gave a nonchalant shrug of one shoulder. Then he reached for the short cup filled with toothpicks and selected two. He pierced the olives in the container next to him and handed the toothpicks to McCarthy. "For your martinis."

Her jaw clenched for a moment. Josh wondered if she'd pitch a fit that he'd helped her.

She didn't. So he continued on. "When you need help or if there's some way I can pitch in—no matter how big or small the task—I'm going to do what I can. Because I love you. And because I want to be with you. And because I want to share things with you. Everything, really. I want to be there for you, Mac. Always. I mean, that's what being in love and being in a relationship is all about, right?"

McCarthy's hand slipped and she dropped the martini shaker. It clamored to the floor. She whispered, "I don't know." She glanced around the club, as though taking in the singles mingling about and sitting at the bar in front of her. A fine mist clouded her eyes and the corners of her mouth quivered. She said, "I'm a total fake."

It was Josh's turn to be taken aback. "What are you talking about?"

She lifted her hands in the air and said, "I spew all this crap about how to make a romance work. What to say, what to do. I fix people up and I give them advice, but what the hell do I really know about love and romance? How the hell did I become the premier dating guru of Manhattan when I haven't had a successful relationship in my entire life?"

Josh couldn't help but grin. "Just because you haven't been in love before—"

"It's more than that, Josh."

"No, it's not." He reached across the bar and grasped her hand in his. Staring deep into her eyes, he said, "You do know what the hell you're talking about. Look at all of the matches you've made so far. Just because we have one little fight doesn't mean you don't know what the hell you're talking about."

"I did it on purpose," she said. "I picked that fight with you on purpose."

"You think I don't know that?"

She stared at him in surprise.

Josh rushed on. "We're both freaking out here because neither one of us has felt this way before. Neither one of us has ever been in love. But here's the thing, sweetheart. We are in love. And that means I'm going to do whatever I can, whenever I can, to help make your life a little easier, to make you happier, to give you everything I think you deserve." His heart suddenly leapt into his chest as he continued on. "And you're just going have to deal with it, babe. I'm not threatening your independence or compromising your competence. I'm sharing my life and my love with you."

Fat tears formed in her pretty green eyes and slid over the rims. But she didn't say anything, so Josh finished.

"I love you. And that means I'm going to do everything in my power to protect you and please you and cherish you. Got it?"

Tears streamed down her cheeks. Her teeth clamped down on her lower lip. She shook her head as though trying to find the right words. The entire lounge fell silent and Josh realized he'd made a scene. Quite a scene. But he didn't care.

"Now," he said. "Tell all of these people you love me." Her mouth gaped open at his audacity. He crooked a brow at her. "Tell them."

McCarthy laughed. She lifted her hands in the air as though in surrender and announced, "I'm in love with Josh Kensington." She eyed him with a curious mixture of shock and happiness. Then she said, "And Josh Kensington is in love with me. Sorry ladies, but he's officially off the market. For good."

A loud round of applause broke out. McCarthy leaned toward him and whispered, "We've broken a few hearts tonight. But you're not the man for those ladies. I'll help them find their match, but you're mine."

Josh reached for her and gave her a long kiss.

When he released her, she said, "I need two things from you."

"Name it. I would do anything for you."

She nodded. "First, I need you to promise that you'll tell me every single day how much you love me."

Josh couldn't contain the grin that spread across his lips. "That's an easy one, babe."

"And second," she said. "I need you to teach me how to make a martini because mine taste like shit."

Epilogue

The wedding was another wild fantasy brought to life.

They waited for Cass and Dean and Cat and David to return from their respective honeymoons. Then they all flew to Vegas for a rock-n-roll themed wedding at the Hard Rock Café Hotel and Casino.

McCarthy wore a pair of white leather pants paired with a white satin button-down blouse. She carried a single red rose down the aisle before she stood with Josh—looking devastatingly handsome in black leather pants, boots and shirt.

Following a night of dancing, celebrating and VIP treatment at the ultra-hip Body English nightclub, where Josh was not only recognized by the manager but also by the band playing there, they retired to their suite. McCarthy slipped into a sexy patent-leather outfit and the thigh high boots she'd splurged on. Holding a riding crop in one hand and dangling her fur-lined handcuffs from the fingers of her other hand, she stood at the foot of the bed and said, "I'm a good girl gone bad."

Josh, who was lying naked before her, grinned in his wickedly decadent way. "The wild side suits you, baby."

About the Author:

Award-winning author Calista Fox began her professional fiction-writing career in 2004, following an exciting career in PR, where she specialized in writing speeches and Congressional testimonies. Her books have received rave reviews and she is also the recipient of a Reviewer's Choice Award for Best Erotic Sci-Fi Novella.

Calista attended college on a Journalism scholarship and has worked on newspapers as an editor and reporter. She holds degrees in General Studies and Communications. Calista divides her time between Arizona, San Diego and various other locales in the U.S. and abroad. She has traveled the country several times over by Lear Jet, always with her laptop in tow, and is a spa aficionado. Visit the author at www.calistafox.com.

Enchanted Spell

by Rachel Carrington

To My Reader:

My fascination with wizards continues in *Enchanted Spell*. Of course, in my fantasy worlds, wizards and witches don't mix. That could be a problem considering the heroine is a witch, and she just happens to find herself right in the center of Wizard Country looking up at a very angry wizard. Let the fun begin!

I want to thank each and every one of you who have purchased this book and invested your time in reading it. Your support means a lot, and I wish you all the best life has to offer!

To my special readers, Michelle, Debbie, Jennifer, and Rene—a simple thank you could never be enough to express how grateful for each of you!

Chapter 1

The skies over the city of Betony split open, and Ella, who'd been pacing the narrow halls of the city's Great Room, shrieked as the floor tumbled out from beneath her. Free-falling through space, she desperately clawed the air for a handhold. As the ground rushed up to greet her, she could only close her eyes and brace for an impact that never came.

She landed in muscular arms with a solid thump. Ella cracked open one eye and surveyed her savior. She smiled brightly.

"Well, hello, there."

Ice blue eyes raked her face before the man dumped her to the ground. "Who in the hell are you and what have you done with my brother?"

"Your brother? I don't know your brother, and I don't know what you're talking about!" She tossed a quick glance around. "Or where I am."

One large hand grasped the corner of her robe and hauled her to her feet. "Before you continue lying, let me warn you. My temper is very short right now, and I'm in no mood for games."

Ella tried to free her collar, but the man held on. Giving up, she clamped her hands on her hips and stood on tiptoes to give herself more height. "You don't know what you've just taken hold of, mister, so unless you have a wish to spend the rest of your days as a chameleon, you'll let me go."

Instead of releasing her as she'd hoped, the man leaned down to peer into her face. "Are you fucking kidding me?"

No time for nerves. She shook her head. "No. I'm a witch."

"Then, lady, you're in a helluva lot of trouble because you just landed in Wizard Country."

Ella's mouth fell open. Wizard Country? Oh. My. God. A witch in Wizard Country. The two definitely didn't mix. She managed to paste a sweet smile on her face in spite of the turmoil in the pit of her stomach. "Well, in that case, I'll just be leaving then. I didn't mean to intrude."

The wizard's eyes darkened. "You're not going anywhere. In fact, I think your arrival could work out very nicely for us, most definitely for me."

"Wait a second. Am I really in Wizard Country?" Ella pursed her lips and assessed the man-wizard whose silver eyes zeroed in on her face with unwavering clarity. "I mean, as far as I know, this could be my cousin's way of fucking with me."

His muscles bulged as he crossed his arms over his chest, finally releasing her. She did give him points for the easy way he let her go. Although he didn't look any happier than he had when he held onto her.

"Which part are you having difficulty understanding?"

She tipped her head back to get a better view of his face. He was extraordinarily attractive, and Ella had a soft spot for good-looking men. Too bad this one was a wizard. They were notorious for hating witches. Although she'd fucked other enemies before, so this certainly wouldn't be the first.

He towered over her, and with that height, it was only natural she should look at his feet. Hmmm. Rather large. She licked her lips in anticipation. And big hands. Her breasts would fit perfectly in those palms.

"So do you have a name?" She leaned into him, giving him a peek at her cleavage. At least she was wearing something mildly attractive when her pissed-off cousin decided to retaliate. Ordinarily, she didn't like the robes of her coven, but this particular one had a vee-shaped neckline which draped low over her breasts. Perfect for a man with an appetite.

His fingers dug into her arm. "You should be more concerned about your own well-being than the name of your captor." He began to tow her forward.

Ella didn't bother to struggle. In all truth, she was more than a little intrigued and excited. Her aunts would probably be horrified at her thoughts, but now that she'd had time to consider her options, she wasn't about to even try to leave Wizard Country without finding out if this man at her side tasted as good as he looked.

The wizard's shoulder-length black hair glistened in the sun, a stunning complement to his perfectly chiseled features. Ella's heart rate sped into dangerous territory. Perhaps she should thank her cousin, Noelle, instead of complaining about this inconvenient interruption of her life.

With her free hand, she tested the strength of the wizard's bulging biceps and tautness of his skin. He really was as hard as he looked. She couldn't resist a low, throaty purr, which brought him to an abrupt halt.

"What was that?"

Ella sent him a provocative smile. "That was just my inner whore expressing approval."

He stared at her, his expression wavering between disbelief and confusion. "You do realize you are in a very precarious situation. Why aren't you concerned for your life?"

"Honey, if I worried every time my life was in danger, I wouldn't get anything done. And I definitely have plans to get something done this evening, provided I can interest you in some nocturnal activity."

"Kevlin."

"Excuse me?"

"You asked me my name."

Ella smiled her enticing invitation for the evening. "Well, Kevlin, it's very nice to meet you."

Another stare was his only response, but the fingers on her arm loosened.

She slid up next to him to allow her breast to brush against his arm. His nostrils flared, and her smile broadened. "I believe you were saying something about how this could work out nicely for you."

The moment the words left her mouth, his blue eyes darkened, as stormy as hurricane-tossed seas. The grip on her arm tightened. "Possibly, but only if you have the common sense to tell me where my brother is."

"Are we back to that again?" Ella tapped her mouth with her hand to fake a yawn. "What part of my response do you have difficulty understanding?"

Her paraphrase of his earlier question made his jaw tighten.

"I would be very careful if I were you."

"Yeah, well, since you don't know me, I'll give you a tip. Careful isn't in my vocabulary." Fuck it. If he was going to kill her, there wasn't anything she could do to stop him. As sharp as she was with a spell, she couldn't hold a candle to a wizard's powers. Every witch in Betony knew better than to cross one, which was precisely why Ella was beginning to believe Noelle didn't intend to send her here.

As mad as her cousin might have been for Ella's past sins, Noelle wasn't the type to deliberately put anyone in harm's way. She was too careful. Hell, the woman practically had the word careful tattooed on her ass.

"Are you listening to me?" Kevlin's dark inquiry brought a frown to Ella's face.

"Are you growling at me?"

For a moment, the captor and the captive squared off, face to face, gazes locked, each seeming to dare the other to move or even breathe.

The wizard broke first, his lips tipping upwards into a crooked smile. "If you won't tell me where my brother is, I'm going to have to result to drastic measures."

Ella's heart pumped furiously. "What kind of drastic measures?" If he was into a little bondage, she could handle that, but if he was talking about whips and chains, they were both going to have a serious problem.

Snagging her around the waist, Kevlin held her tight against his chest. "Just wait and see."

The air contorted around her, and Ella's curse was lost in the whipping winds.

Kevlin held the witch in his arms for longer than he should, but her soft, supple body felt too damned good to release. She was all curves and perfect, glowing skin. His imagination was far too poor to even contemplate the beauty beneath the robe.

But she was a witch. That would definitely be a problem. He didn't doubt his father would order her thrown into the dungeon when her presence was discovered, which was precisely why he couldn't take the witch anywhere near the palace gates. At least not now. No, better to keep her to himself.

His cock twitched at the idea. All to himself. Infinite possibilities. The witch had practically thrown herself at him moments ago. Would it be so bad to accept her offer?

As he slowed their descent from high above the grounds of his homeland, Kevlin allowed his hands the luxury of drifting lower to cup the fullness of her ass. Instead of protesting, the witch looked up at him with a sultry smile. Damn. Was she unmovable? Did she think she was invincible? She'd barely flinched when he'd told her where she was, but maybe that was just part of her ploy.

Their feet touched the soft, green grass of Shiloh, the place he called his own. Far away from the palace, Shiloh offered Kevlin the solitude he needed to recover from the constant demands placed on his time. As the next in line to ascend to Master Wizard, he spent most of his days in continuous tests of his skill, knowledge, and magic. But here he could forget about everything and everyone. So why exactly had he chosen to bring this witch here?

"Excuse me. I hate to interrupt your musings, but it's getting difficult to breathe."

Kevlin relinquished his hold and allowed her to take a step out of his embrace. He wanted the space to take a good long look at this visitor to his country. "My apologies."

"And you sound so sincere."

She circled him, giving him ample opportunity to view the merchandise. Good thing he had limitless supplies of cash at his disposal because there was no doubt he'd be buying. The woman was a stunning display of perfection from head to toe. With hair as dark as his own, eyes like twin onyxes, and skin that practically screamed *touch me*, she was an invitation to cross boundaries.

"You're beautiful."

Those large almond-shaped eyes blinked at him. "You're very astute. I like that in a man."

"Wizard," he corrected.

"Ah, yes. Wizard. Lest I forget."

"What's your name?" It shouldn't matter, but he wanted to know more about her.

"Ella." Her lips parted in a smile. "And now that we've introduced ourselves, I'd like to leave. Eventually."

He watched her tongue moisten her lower lip, and his cock grew another inch, pressing against the black slacks he wore. "Are you always so brazen?"

Ella lifted her shoulders in a shrug, which drew his attention to her breasts. "I find it saves time."

"You should be scared."

"Of what?"

"Where you are." He approached her. "Who you're with." His knuckles grazed her cheek. "What you're with. Everything. You should be scared of everything."

Something flared in her eyes, perhaps a momentary flash of fear, but she quickly banked it. The look she gave him was one of challenge, as if she dared him to scare her. "Why? Do you intend to hurt me?"

"Not if you tell me where my brother is." Her lips pursed, and the sight conjured an image of those same lips sucking the head of his cock. For a brief moment, Kevlin forgot to think.

"What makes you so sure I know where your brother is?"

Damn. Her voice was as sinful as her body. He could close his eyes and picture her whispering to him in the dark. He cleared his throat, more unsettled than he had been in a long, long time. "Because you arrived just as he was taken away."

Ella frowned, nibbled on her lower lip, and then let out a groan. "Oh, for the love of the goddesses, Noelle, could you please, just once, pay attention in one of your classes? Transportation would be an excellent place to start!"

Kevlin tensed. What trickery was this witch up to? "Who is this Noelle, and how is she involved?"

"Noelle is my cousin. She sent me here."

"Why would your own flesh and blood send you to Wizard Country?"

An audible breath escaped from between full, plum-colored lips. "Because she has no business being a witch."

More confused than ever, Kevlin took hold of Ella's arm. He needed more information, but mostly, he didn't want his entire family to come looking for him when he didn't show up for the evening meal, which was due to start in less than a half hour. "Come. We'll discuss this inside."

Ella began to meticulously peel his fingers away, and because the action amused him, he let her.

"Actually, I think I'm just going to head on home. I have a score to settle, and it looks like you're not interested in the same thing I am. I'm not a big believer in wasting my time."

He lifted his hands up and let them fall to his side. "Very well."

She stared at him, her eyes narrowed. "That's it then? You're not going to try to stop me from leaving again?"

"It's apparent you have no knowledge of my brother's whereabouts. You're free to do whatever you please."

"Great. Well, it was nice to meet you, Kevlin, but it would have been a helluva lot nicer if you were a witch instead of a wizard." Ella gave him what he could only deduce was a regretful smile before she closed her eyes, drew in a deep breath, and swept her arms wide.

Kevlin grinned when she opened dark orbs moments later. The look on her face was priceless.

"Did I forget to mention that witches have no magic in our country?"

No magic? Okay, perhaps it was time to panic now. She couldn't be without her magic. She'd always had her magic. It was her security net.

Her pulse beat a hasty rhythm, and she clasped one hand to her throat. "This is impossible."

"Apparently, someone else wasn't paying attention in class. Or didn't your fellow witches feel it was important to discuss us wizards? If they had, they might have mentioned that we have no magic in your homeland, either. Perhaps that is why we don't usually visit one another."

He was smiling at her! Damn him. Having a good laugh at her expense. Well, she might not have her magic, but there were a few things she did still have. "If memory serves me, wizards do have balls, don't they?"

That wiped the smile from his face. He took a step back to put enough distance between his crotch and her knee. "Not a good idea, witch."

"Neither is this conversation, and from the way you keep looking at your watch, it's not the right time, either."

"Unfortunately, I have other obligations which preclude me from continuing this conversation."

Ella wrinkled her nose. "Well, I'm certainly not going to stay here."

Kevlin chuckled, the sound deep and almost hypnotic. "You don't have a choice, love. Come on. Let me show you inside my home. I can assure you, you'll be quite comfortable."

He held out one hand, which she ignored.

"You'll forgive me if I don't trust this sudden change of approach."

"I'm sure learning you have no magic here is quite traumatic." The wizard's smile was lethal, but Ella wasn't as impressed now that she knew she couldn't just poof away from his charm.

"So you're feeling the need to reassure me?" One corner of her mouth turned upwards, and she whispered a curse at the bright blue sky.

With a sweep of his hand, he opened the door at the end of a cobblestoned path. "I'd like to make sure you're settled before I leave you."

Her shoulders squared. "I'm not an invalid. I'm fully capable of taking care of myself." Well, not fully capable, at least not at this point, but Ella never gave up. It was one quality her family liked about her. Probably the only one.

His hand at the small of her back, Kevlin guided her up the walk as casually as if they were old friends. The threshold glittered with some type of golden substance, and once Ella walked inside, her mouth fell open.

While the witches of Betony had all the accoutrements of wealth, they didn't choose to use their magic as part of their every day life. The wizards, however, flaunted theirs, if Kevlin's house was anything to go by.

Her head whipping back and forth, Ella took in every aspect of the magical wonderland. From the glass orbs filled with scenes of life to the floating chaise lounge, the room was awash in a golden glow. The walls seemed to disappear as she neared them, easily giving way to each room beyond.

"Make yourself at home."

Ella jumped, having almost forgotten she wasn't alone. She whirled to face him and sucked in a sharp breath. How in the hell had he gotten so close? Were her senses gone along with her magic? "Oh, yeah, I'll feel quite comfortable here. This is more like a sideshow than a home. Don't you know anything about décor? And how is one supposed to feel at ease when furniture is floating around the room like dead fish in a pond?"

Did the man ever stop smiling? The sensual tilt of his lips was doing funny things to her insides, things she wasn't used to feeling. Being a sexually liberated witch, she was accustomed to desire and carnal lust, but this was different. Too different.

"My apologies if my home has offended you." Holding his hand palm outward toward the center of the room, he began to lower his arm, bringing the chaise lounge down with it. "Better now?"

She heard the amusement in his voice and wondered if wizards really were immortal as she'd heard. This one was cocky enough to be an immortal. Her aunts certainly believed it, and even went so far as to say a prayer to the goddesses each evening to protect them from the eternal sorcerers.

Kevlin's hand touched her shoulder, and she shivered. "Are you cold?"

"No. I'm spooked. And it's not easy to spook a witch." This wasn't good. This wasn't good at all. She was getting the hell out of here no matter how she had to do it. Right now, she could only think of one way.

With the idea firmly in place, she lowered her lids to half-mast and traced her lips with her tongue. The wizard's eyes followed the brief movement, and Ella resisted the urge to smile. He might be a powerful sorcerer, but he was still every bit a man.

"What are you doing?" He sounded on edge, suspicious even.

"What do you think I'm doing?"

"Treading on extremely unsafe ground."

The husky tone of his voice told her she'd hooked him. Time to reel him in. "Really? Didn't I mention I never have been the careful type?" She tiptoed her fingers up his arm. "I'll make a deal with you."

He watched the dance of her fingertips. "I'm listening."

"I'll give you whatever you want, but in turn, you have to give me something."

"And what would that be?"

Her gaze dropped. Oh, yes. She definitely had his attention. "You have to send me back to Betony."

Kevlin moved even closer to her, if that was possible. The sheer breadth of his shoulder obliterated her view of anything but the man. His warm breath swept over her face, pleasantly minty.

"Interesting proposition, but you've forgotten one thing, Ella."

Her head tipped back, and her lips flirted with a smile. "What's that?"

"I don't have to make a deal with you to get what I want."

A man playing hard to get. This was different. Always up to a challenge, she slid her palm over his chest. "What is it you want then?"

Running his thumb over her lower lip, he grinned. "I want my brother back, but in the interim, I'll take what you're offering. After all, I have to do something to keep my mind off my grief." He leaned in and pressed his lips to hers.

Before Ella's temper could explode, she found herself kissing air. The wizard had disappeared.

Chapter 2

Damn. He couldn't focus, at least not on this speech. His father's voice droned on, but Kevlin didn't hear a word. In his mind, he still felt the curves of the witch he'd held in his arms, smelled her rain-scented hair, and saw her small pink tongue caressing her full lips.

His cock surged upward, a hard press against his trousers. He cursed silently again and shifted in his chair, while ignoring the frowning glances of the other wizards in the room.

This was one of the most important meetings of the season. On the autumnal equinox another Master Wizard would be appointed, and he would be it. The Master Wizards served as the Wizard Country's governing board and were headed by the Grand Master. After six long years of training, Kevlin would now take his place on the board under his father's lead. The only problem was, Kevlin wasn't as interested in politics now.

"Kevlin." The sharpness in Oriel's voice brought Kevlin to attention. Rarely did his father use such a tone with his family.

Clearing his throat, Kevlin responded. "Father."

"It seems I have lost your attention." The reprimand couldn't be missed.

Keeping his irritation in check, Kevlin inclined his head. "My apologies." He kept silent on the details, but the look on his father's face told him he wouldn't let this pass so easily.

As the discussion resumed, Kevlin struggled to stay connected, but Ella's face danced in front of his eyes, her taunting beauty stiffening his cock further. By Merlin, he'd never be able to walk out of this room upright.

"And that concludes our meeting. We shall resume session in two fortnights at midnight. Hopefully, by that time, Kevlin will be rid of this insidious drain on his focus." Oriel waved one hand toward the door of the meeting room, and the heavy wood flew open, allowing the wizards to file out one by one.

The door slammed shut before Kevlin could make his escape. He rubbed one hand across the back of his neck and tipped his head upwards slightly to see his father's disapproving expression. "I think the public reprimand should be enough for this evening."

Oriel tented his fingers and strolled around the rectangular table as if he were out for an evening walk around the gardens. Only the tightness of his jaw belied his relaxed posture. "I disagree. What could be more important than the discussion of your future? How could you not pay attention?"

Kevlin pushed himself to his feet, clearing his father's height by several inches. "I could describe the ceremony in my sleep and quote the decree as well. You have no need to worry. I won't disappoint you."

"Recall who you are speaking to, young man."

How could he forget? Oriel reminded his offspring constantly of their station in life, of his own position of leadership. One could never forget that the family of Oriel was an impressive lot.

One lip curled up at the corner, Kevlin walked around behind his father. "If that is all, I've got business to attend to."

"What sort of business would that be?" More than mere interest colored Oriel's tone.

Three steps carried Kevlin to the door. "The sort which does not concern you."

"Stop."

The whip of that one word, honed by centuries of honor and obedience, brought Kevlin to a halt. He didn't turn around, but simply waited for his father's condemnation.

"You know, don't you?"

His muscles tense, Kevlin looked over his shoulder. "What is it that I'm supposed to know?"

Oriel chuckled, a rare sound. "Do you think me a fool?"

Kevlin did turn then, but only to see his father's face and try to read what he really didn't know. He crossed the room, lifted one hand, and rested it on Oriel's shoulder. "You wanted me to stay behind because there's something you're trying to tell me, isn't there?"

Vivid blue eyes fixed on Kevlin's face. "I thought your mother would have already told you." He smiled a little. "She always was the talkative sort."

Kevlin chuckled at the understatement. Describing his mother as the talkative sort was akin to calling Oriel a calming influence. "So what was Mother supposed to have told me?"

The look on Oriel's face created a knot in the pit of Kevlin's stomach. The next words his father spoke weren't ones he'd ever thought he'd hear.

"I'm dying, my son."

His blood ran cold. "How is this possible? You've been alive for eight hundred years. Our guild is immortal."

"That is true, but unfortunately, there are ways to eliminate even a wizard if one is truly determined."

"And how is this done?" Kevlin's hands fisted at his sides as his mind spun with the impossibility of this discussion. Oriel was the most respected wizard in the country. No member would dare harm him, much less make the attempt—at least, that had always been Kevlin's assumption.

Oriel held up one hand which shook a little. "No one here. It was one of our enemies. A witch."

Ella paced around the amusement park Kevlin called home, alternately cursing her cousin and the wizard who brought her here. "If you're going to use a transport spell, Noelle, learn the fucking words. How could you send me here knowing I'd be about as welcome as crabs at a swingers' convention? This son-of-a-bitch could kill me."

She shook her head, pushing her hair back over her shoulder. No, this wizard had no intentions of killing her. She'd seen that look in his eyes. He had one thing on his mind, and though she wasn't opposed, she certainly wouldn't become someone's sexual slave simply because her magic had momentarily departed.

There had to be a reason why she couldn't use even the slightest of spells. Ella considered this a challenge, a puzzle she'd solve. If there was one thing a witch needed, it was her magic. Otherwise, she was just another woman, and Ella was not, nor would she ever be, just another woman.

Walking to the center of what she assumed was the living room, she drew a circle with her foot and stepped inside. Her hands came together, palms touching. Closing her eyes, she cleared her mind, allowing the stresses of the day to dissolve beneath the calming feel of the goddesses.

"Get out of the fucking circle."

The harsh command snapped her eyes open, and Ella hissed out a long breath as she turned. "It's not nice to interrupt a witch's centering."

Kevlin strode forward and clamped one hand around her wrist, yanking her hard against his chest. "Why have you done this?"

She looked up into silver eyes slitted like a cat's. "I've not done anything. I'm the victim here, or weren't you listening when I told you my cousin sent me to this hellhole?" She smacked at the hand imprisoning her wrist. "That hurts."

"Your cousin didn't send you here." Kevlin pulled her down a narrow, dark hall.

Ella would have kicked him if they hadn't been moving so fast. "Oh, so now I'm a liar. Great. Well, I've got news for you, Mr. Pain-in-the-Ass. I don't want to be here any more than you want me here. So send me home!" She ended the last word on a shriek.

The wizard kicked open a door at the end of the hallway and shoved her inside. "No fucking way. If my father dies, so do you."

"Father? Die? What in the hell are you talking about?" Ella brushed a hand down the front of her robe in an attempt to restore her dignity. She'd never been treated so ruthlessly in her life. Not that she minded a little rough play, but she preferred to be the one doling out the harshness. Oh, if only she had the use of her magic. She'd shrink this wizard to the size of a fly's balls.

The door slammed shut, and Kevlin leaned against it, preventing even an attempt at escape. "Let me explain this in simple terms, so you can keep up. My brother disappears, and my father is suddenly dying. They both coincide with your arrival. Are you following me now?"

She was starting to, and she didn't like the path ahead. Did this wizard actually think she was responsible for whatever was happening to his father? And what was it he'd said again? *If my father dies, you die.* Oh, hell. This had the makings of a really bad soap opera plot.

"Let me clarify a few things for you. I didn't arrive here. I was sent against my will. I don't know where your brother is, and I couldn't pick your father out in a crowd. Assassins generally tend to know their targets. Plus, you seem to be forgetting that my magic doesn't work here in Bumfuck."

His chest lifted and fell in time with angry breaths, and for a long moment, Kevlin only stared at her. Then he moved so fast she didn't have time to avoid him. His hands tangled in her hair, tugging so hard her scalp tingled.

"You're going to have to do a lot better than that to convince me, witch."

Okay, now she was really getting pissed. Question her morality, sure, but question her integrity? Hell, no. Glaring up at him, she held his gaze until she was sure she was the center of his attention.

Then she brought her knee up, crashing it into his balls. Kevlin let out a yelp of pain and doubled over. With a satisfied smirk, she stood back to survey the damage. Oh, yeah. Her memory was just fine. Wizards did have gonads.

Throwing him a scathing look, she swept past him and took hold of the door knob. She barely had one foot out into the hallway when a solid, all too familiar, muscular body blocked her path.

"Shit."

Wizards also recovered a lot faster from a debilitating injury.

"Going somewhere?"

Though the pain still blazed through his body, Kevlin managed to stand upright without needing to hold onto something. He wouldn't allow the witch to take the upper hand. What in the bloody hell was taking so long to block the agony? He'd healed a broken bone quicker than this.

Eyes blazing, Ella tossed her hair back. "I'd planned to."

Finally, the feeling was returning to his balls. He could breathe again, and he realized just how pissed he was. Grabbing hold of both of her wrists with one hand, he shackled her arms over her head against the door jamb.

"That wasn't a very smart move."

She bucked against him, the move shoving her breasts against his chest. "No, but it was a desperate one."

"Desperate? Is that what you are?" Surprised his cock was actually able to stand after the brutality of Ella's knee, he took a step forward, pushing his erection into her abdomen. "And just what are you desperate for?"

Her pupils dilated. "Forget about it, wizard. I might have been interested when we first met, but now, I'd rather eat a pot full of live lizards."

"Unfortunately for you, that's not one of your choices." The scent of her skin inflamed his senses. Were it not for her lack of magic, he would swear she'd bewitched him. He lifted a lock of her hair and curled it around one finger. "You're a very beautiful woman, Ella."

Her warm breath brushed over his cheek. "Is that supposed to be an apology?"

He chuckled. "Wizards never apologize." His cock pushed against her, and she swallowed hard.

"It's not going to happen." The challenge in her voice intrigued him.

"You think not?" He cupped one hand around the back of her neck before releasing her hands.

"No." Her pupils dilated, and her one word response was breathy and hesitant.

Kevlin smiled. "Though you want it to happen?" His fingers massaged her skin, and she sighed, rolling her head forward in invitation.

"Yes. I mean, no." She lifted her head and glared at him. "Stop trying to confuse me. I'm not interested in having sex with you."

He lowered his lips to her clavicle and kissed the sensitive skin. Ella shivered beneath his mouth, and he suckled his way up to her jaw line. His hands dropped to cup her ass while he feasted on her scented flesh.

Ella pressed her breasts against his chest, and the friction of her nipples against him sent his body into overdrive. With a muttered curse, he yanked at the flimsy robe she wore, rending it in two. The pieces fell to the floor, leaving behind the perfect curves of her full, golden breasts. His eyes dropped lower. Flawless.

Clothed, she'd driven him mad with each move of her hips. Naked, she drained every ounce of blood from his head and sent it rushing to his cock. He stared at her for a long time, sliding his gaze over her from head to toe, lingering on the glistening lips of her pussy.

Her mound was bare, and no doubt, silky soft to the touch. Heat roared through him like an inferno, searing everything in its path. He couldn't catch his breath.

"Are you just going to stand there staring at me?" Ella kicked off her wickedly high heels and leaned back against the wall, her hands on her hips. Put on display, she'd allowed him the freedom to look, and now gave him an invitation to touch.

"I've made you wet?" He already knew the answer to his question, but he wanted to see the fire in her eyes. There it was. A spark of energy, a realization he was going to fuck her.

"Have you?" She licked her lips with a slow sweep of her tongue, lowering her arms to her sides. "Why don't you find out for yourself?"

"I do believe you said you weren't interested in having sex with me."

Her nostrils flared. "Having sex isn't what I do, wizard." She yanked hold of his collar. "I prefer to fuck."

Thanking Merlin and all the wizards who'd gone before him, Kevlin removed his clothing with a sweep of his hand. His cock pounded almost painfully, desperately seeking the wetness between her toned thighs. But he would wait. This wasn't a time to rush. He wanted to taste every inch of her, explore each curve, and touch all the places that would make her cry out with pleasure.

Taking hold of her hands, he held them over her head and pushed her hard against the wall. His chest crushed her breasts, and his cock nestled between their bodies. His mind whirling with possibilities, he secured her wrists with handcuffs he'd summoned. As her eyes flared with defiance, he smiled.

It was going to be a long, wild ride.

As the cold metal clamped around her wrists, Ella's temperature spiked a notch. The goddesses had smiled upon her in spite of her cousin's inability to work with the magic she'd been given.

Closing her eyes, she reveled in the feel of the wizard's body against her own. His chest hair scraped her nipples, sending electrical shocks down the center of her body. His cock surged hard against her stomach, and were her hands free, she'd touch it, close her palm around its smoothness.

She twisted her hips to test the width and smiled her satisfaction. Her pussy quivered, and when Kevlin fisted his hand in her hair and yanked her head back, she came alive. This was what she'd been looking for but had never found on her own home planet. No male witch could dominate her like this, could satisfy this overpowering need to fuck with animalistic intensity.

But this wizard knew what she wanted. His lips, savage and wild, crushed hers. Their tongues met and mated, thrusted back and forth. Kevlin whirled, taking her with him, whipping through the air until they crashed against the far wall.

Ella didn't feel any pain, though her senses were heightened. She wrapped one leg around his, jutting her hips upwards to rub her damp pussy against his thigh. It was a blatant invitation, but he was taking too damned long to touch her where she wanted him most of all.

"Touch me," she commanded, arching her back.

Kevlin stepped back and lifted one finger. "You don't call the shots here, witch. This is my game." He trailed the backs of his fingers down over her breasts, traveling lower to tickle her stomach, hesitating just above her mound.

She lowered her bound hands, but in a flash, the wizard captured them again, thrusting them up over her head. She murmured a protest which he ignored.

Keeping her wrists secured with one hand, he sucked one finger of his free hand into his mouth, and Ella began to pant. The damp fingertip circled her aureole on one breast then the other before he returned the finger to his mouth. She couldn't take her eyes off his mouth sucking that one digit.

"Spread your legs," he demanded in such a low voice the words vibrated.

Tingling and shaking with anticipation, Ella obeyed, shifting her stance. Her gaze dropped to his hard cock, and she licked her lips.

"Ella, look at me."

Her eyes locked with his, and then he withdrew his finger, slipped it between the pulsing lips of her pussy, and plunged it deep within her channel. She cried out, a mixture of shock and pleasure. A second finger, then another, joined the first, stretching her channel. Moaning, she tried to lower her hips, seeking the invasion.

"Not yet." Kevlin denied her unspoken request, and she mentally cursed him.

How long had it been since she'd been the one to lose control? She couldn't think of even one time. She always remained in control, always held the upper hand, and now this wizard held her captive, taking what he wanted… giving what she wanted in pieces.

He nipped her ear, and an electrical charge shot straight to her clit. His lips moved to her neck where more nibbles followed. His fingers began a slow, torturous thrusting in and out of her slick pussy, but he kept his distance from the bundle of nerves which would bring her the most pleasure.

Goddess, she wanted him to touch her there, desperately needed to feel the slide of his fingertip over her most sensitive spot. Her imagination wasn't good enough to tell her how it would be. She'd been touched there before, but this time would be different. It had to be. This was no mortal man tantalizing her.

Kevlin withdrew his fingers, and Ella gave a moan of protest. He shushed her by pressing a light kiss against her lips. "Are you in such a hurry that you would deny yourself every essence of pleasure I can give you?"

Well, spoken like that, no. "I want to touch you." The words had a mind of their own, slipping past her panting lips in a tumble of syllables.

"Do you now?" He glided his damp hand up over her stomach, circling one finger around her belly button while his gaze locked with hers. "What would you like to touch first?"

She really had to pick a spot? Her brows dipped. "Everywhere."

"It's impossible to touch me everywhere at one time, witch. You'll have to be more specific."

She ground her teeth together, both infuriated and electrified. "If I had my magic, it wouldn't be so impossible."

He arched one eyebrow. "No? Hmmm. That has definite possibilities, but I think, for now, we'll leave you neutralized. Now, where was I?" Releasing her arms, he brought them lower. "Hold your lips open."

The sensual demand nearly made her knees buckle, but her fingers followed his every word, parting the throbbing lips of her pussy with eager anticipation. Her engorged clit ached for his touch. On fire, she couldn't battle her own desire. She wasn't so sure the wizard hadn't used his magic to ignite her.

Kevlin knelt in front of her, his head level with her exposed vulva. For a long moment, he simply breathed, drawing in her scent. His action enhanced her pleasure, and Ella's head bumped against the wall as she leaned back, breathlessly waiting for…

The touch of his tongue.

"Oh, yes!" She screamed the words and arched forward.

He didn't look up or acknowledge her approval as his tongue began to circle around her clit, teasing the bundle of nerves until each stroke became a masterful tease. He took his time, bathing the plump fleshy lips of her pussy before diving inside to taste more of her juices.

In full pant now, Ella opened her eyes and watched his dark head move ever so slightly as he feasted on her woman flesh. Tingling from the tips of her fingers to the soles of her feet, she widened her stance and dug her fingertips deeper into her pussy, opening more for him.

Chuckling low, Kevlin moved his lips across hers, stopping to suck her clit into his mouth, allowing his tongue to rub back and forth across the nub.

She was going to come, and not like ever before. This would be a powerful orgasm. The tension mounted, and her legs began to shake. A fine sheen of perspiration coated her skin. She was close. So close.

"Yes," she hissed.

He grabbed the cheeks of her ass and dug in, shoving his face so deep into her pussy, he seemed to meld with her flesh. Animal noises sounded in the back of his throat, proof he was enjoying his meal.

Warmth swelled over her and enveloped her in a cocoon of blissful heat. Her hips began to rock back and forth, and the gentle tingles she'd grown accustomed to over the years became a sizzle, singeing her skin from the inside out.

Kevlin sucked once more, and the orgasm rocked her. She released a keening wail, pushing herself on her tiptoes. Her hands moved from her pussy to clench in his hair, urging him to continue eating her. Back and forth she thrust to enjoy every second of the mind-numbing release.

His hands traced up her legs as he pushed himself to his feet. Before she could slide down from the crest, he positioned his cock at the entrance to her pussy and filled her, shoving so deep that she let out another cry.

"Put your legs around my hips." His voice was so thick now, it was barely recognizable.

Ella wrapped her legs around lean muscle and lowered her linked hands around his neck. By the goddesses, he was massively huge and seemed to grow with each push of his cock into her channel. He slammed her back and forth against the wall, unmindful of her physical comfort, but she liked it.

Mortals were too fragile. Ella had always craved raw, open sex. Nothing held back. Everything given. This man—this wizard—gave her everything she desired, everything she craved, and more.

Kevlin pumped furiously, his face buried in her neck. She felt his teeth against her skin and a slight twinge of pain as he bit her. One more slam against the wall, and he grew rigid, coming with a low, long groan which segued into short, jerky breaths.

Still holding her aloft, he lifted his head and fixed his gaze on her face. "I'd love to stay and play a little longer, but I'm afraid my father requires my presence." Slipping his cock out of her pussy, he lowered her feet to the floor. "Feel free to make use of the shower, but stay naked." He gave her a long, measured look that swept her from head to toe. "It'll save time when I get back."

He was gone before Ella could even summon up enough anger to throw something at his smug face.

"Hey! What about the handcuffs?" As she shouted the question, the metal bracelets opened and dropped to the floor followed by a low, throaty chuckle.

Ella's body hummed.

Amid a plush mound of blankets and silk sheets, Oriel lay so still and pale that Kevlin thought for a brief moment he was too late. Then his father stirred, opened his eyes, and held out one hand.

"Come, my son.

Moving forward, Kevlin took hold of the hand which used to hold his as a child. "How could a witch have caused this? You have no interaction with witches."

Oriel's lips pulled into a grimace. "I don't know. I only sense the presence of one. Here. Among us. I have instructed my counselors to investigate the matter and report back to you with their findings as I may not be—"

"Don't." Kevlin interrupted, holding up one hand. "I will not listen to this." He turned, presenting his back to his father. "You will survive this. We will discover the cause of—"

"Enough!" As weak as he was, Oriel's voice still rang with authority. "You must accept my fate."

Kevlin's shoulders sagged as the guilt wore heavily on his shoulders. His father lay dying while he enjoyed the pleasures of the flesh, the pleasures a witch had given him.

"Have you any word from your brother?"

"No." Kevlin practically bit out the word. If Ella's appearance hadn't caused his brother's disappearance, then he could only assume Devin had gotten himself into trouble—not a feat too difficult for his younger sibling.

Oriel let out a soft sigh and waved a hand toward the door. "I must rest. Leave me now."

Hesitation in every step, Kevlin walked to the door, then paused to look over his shoulder at the weakened form of his father.

"We will find the cause of this illness, Father. You will survive this."

Chapter 3

Damn. Still no magic. Ella paced around the perfectly circular living room, her hands fisted on her hips. Despite the wizard's command, she'd gotten dressed again, but now the silky material of her robe irritated her skin. She didn't question why, for the imprint of Kevlin's hands was still burned onto her flesh.

Her nipples tightened. Fuck. She needed to focus, to figure out a way out of this magical prison, but her mind remained stubbornly centered on the wizard who'd left her alone over an hour ago. And she wasn't a woman who was used to being left by any man. She always did the leaving, but then, she'd never fucked a wizard before.

"It was just a fuck, Ella." She felt the need to remind herself of the obvious. "Nothing more. He was just another guy." Who was incredibly magnificent in bed. Not that they'd actually made it to the bed. Her lips curved into a satisfied smile. Sweet Goddess, he'd taken her to heights she'd only dreamed about and had actually made her scream at the peak of orgasm.

She was definitely taking home some memories.

A noise, much like the tearing of paper, captured her attention, and she whirled around. The air split into two unequal halves, and Kevlin stepped through the gap, sealing it shut behind him.

Her mouth watered. He looked good enough to, well, do just about anything with. He'd changed into well-worn jeans and a loose cotton t-shirt which emphasized his muscles.

He swept a look up and down her clothed form. "I see you didn't listen to me."

The sound of his voice brought her gaze up to his face. For a moment, their eyes connected and held while the tension peaked. Heat splashed her cheeks and swelled within her, warming her from the inside out.

Without thinking, she walked toward him, eager to feel the hard skin beneath her palms.

Kevlin didn't look away, and as her hands connected with his shirt, his eyes darkened. Another step closer, and his hard cock bumped against her stomach.

"It's nice to see you missed me."

"You're not really seeing it, though, are you?"

The blatant invitation enticed her, but Ella didn't accept it. "How is your father?"

He winced as though the words caused him great pain. Taking hold of her wrists, he lowered her hands. "Not well. He believes a witch has caused this."

"Maybe he's right." She held up one hand before he could jump on her words. "Just hear me out first. What if a witch is involved, and my arrival gave him or her the perfect opportunity to harm your father? Is it possible that someone has been waiting to make such an attempt?"

"Anything's possible." Kevlin didn't look convinced.

"There's only one way to find out." She took a deep breath and plunged in. "You have to give me back my magic."

He took a step away from her. "No."

"It's the only way. You might be able to sense a witch, but you're never going to be able to get one to talk to you. However, if one of my own thinks I'm in trouble, they'll do what they can to help."

Kevlin began to shake his head then stopped. "What makes you so sure of that?"

Did she have to spell it out for him? "If you knew one of your wizard buddies was in trouble, wouldn't you help?"

"Perhaps. It would all depend upon the type of trouble."

Figures. "Let's assume it's dire. Life-threatening."

"Then possibly, yes, but I would have to consider the lives at stake."

Ella sighed and waved her hand in the air. "Okay, never mind. Forget the analogy. Just go with me on this. If a witch really has done this to your father, I can find out."

"And you would do this why?" Doubt colored his voice.

She couldn't blame him for not trusting her. Their union wasn't exactly written in the stars. "If I succeed, you send me home. And when I say send me home, I mean immediately after the mystery has been solved, not months later because you're tired of having sex with me."

His nostrils flared. "That's assuming I would tire of you."

Well, spoken like that, she could forgive his arrogance. "True, but it's possible I would grow weary of you. I wouldn't want to test it."

The wizard had the audacity to laugh. "You would not voluntarily leave my bed, Ella. I give you too much pleasure."

She held up one finger. "One time. That's it. You gave me pleasure once. Let's not make this into something it's not."

He caught hold of her waist and tugged her in until her breasts bumped against his chest. "So what is it exactly?"

"Survival." She inhaled the scent of his skin, an aromatic blend of spice and soap.

"So the sex we had earlier was a sacrifice?"

Damn, the guy was quick, and she doubted it had anything to do with magic. She tilted her head to one side as if considering his words. "Maybe not a sacrifice but definitely a chore."

The strike hit its mark. The wizard's silver eyes darkened to pewter. "For someone who is asking for assistance, you have an odd way of showing courtesy."

Her tongue moistened her lower lip. "Courtesy? Is that what you really want from me?"

His hand lowered, cupping her mound through the silk of her robe. "So, your magic for my father's life. Is that how it goes?"

A small flame began to burn in the pit of her stomach. "Not just my magic. A safe and secure return to my home."

"Done." Her robe disappeared the moment the word left his mouth, baring her skin to the coolness of the air, the heat of his gaze.

Fighting him didn't even cross her mind. Instead, Ella placed her palms against his chest and shoved him backwards, catching him off-guard. Without her magic, she had to physically tear his clothes off, and frustration made her grit her teeth.

"Allow me to help." His voice riddled with amusement, Kevlin disrobed within a matter of seconds.

Ella's breath caught in her throat as her hand closed around the thickness of his cock. Her fingers couldn't meet, and her temperature spiked. Definitely a better man than she'd had the pleasure of touching before.

She gave her fingers a tight squeeze, and a groan broke forth from the wizard's throat.

She had him right where she wanted him, naked and hard. With sinuous movements, she lowered herself to her knees and gripped the backs of his bare thighs. The crisp hairs scratched her palms, and the musky scent of his sex created a response between her thighs.

"Mmm. I love the way you smell." She rocked forward on her knees and gave his balls an experimental lick.

Kevlin released a throaty growl and grasped hold of her hair. "Careful."

"You don't really want me to be careful, do you?" Her tongue caressed the length of his cock from base to tip.

"Sweet Merlin." He moved his hips forward in silent invitation.

Lips pursed, she lightly sucked the taut skin and tongued the deep blue veins running the length of his cock. Pushing herself up higher, she took his glans into her mouth, twisting and turning her head in a corkscrew motion.

Kevlin jerked and dug his fingers into her shoulders, his approval loud and clear without saying a word.

Working her way down his cock, she took him all the way to the back of her throat, opening wider to accommodate his width. With her head moving and tongue stroking, she began to run her fingernails over and around his balls, lightly tickling, torturing.

Kevlin's hips moved slightly at first, just a simple rocking back and forth in time with each pull of her mouth. As her pace increased, he pumped faster, fucking her mouth in a desperate attempt to reach climax.

Ella grabbed his ass and created a suction cup with her mouth, sucking so hard her cheeks indented. She worked one finger between his thickly muscled ass and pushed it deep inside.

He made a gurgling noise in the back of his throat and threw his head back so hard, it banged against the wall. "Oh, yeah. Yeah. That's good."

The encouraging words spurred her on, and she intensified her moves, crooking her finger in his ass. He grunted and shifted his stance, shoving his cock even further into her mouth. She pulled back, but one of his hands cupped the back of her head, allowing little play room.

She gave him a light nip, and he cursed, dropping his hand. Ella went in for the kill, licking the palm of her hand before she began to furiously rub it up and down his shaft.

The sounds Kevlin made told her she was on the right path. He closed his eyes and his body grew taut. Ella closed her mouth around the head of cock just as a burst of hot juice shot out. He released a series of loud groans, and she swallowed every drop and milked his cock until it went limp in her mouth.

She drew back and licked her lips before pushing herself to her feet. Moisture trickled down her thighs, and she wedged one of his thighs against her pussy. "I'm guessing I did something right."

"I doubt you need me to verify that."

Kevlin's hands grasped her ass and shoved her down hard against his muscular leg. Holding tightly to her hips, he began to slide her back and forth over his thigh, rubbing her swollen clit with enough pressure to make her catch her breath.

Ella raised her hands and clenched his shoulders while she rode his leg. The pace took on a life of its own, and she moved so fast the world around her blurred. The thickness of his thigh and the press of his muscles against her throbbing clit sent her into a quick, hard orgasm.

Her muscles contracting, she gasped and continued to ride him straight into another release. Limp with satisfaction, every ounce of energy drained, she sagged against him. Feeling pleasantly sleepy, she rested her head against his chest.

"That was different." She managed to push the words past her lips.

Kevlin chuckled and kissed the top of her head. "You should sleep now. I doubt you're on the same time schedule in your world as here." Without giving her time to complain, he lifted her in his arms, cradled her against his bare chest, and carried her down a long, narrow hallway to a door at the end.

Her body craving the renewal of sleep, Ella curled against him. "You're probably right."

He turned the doorknob with one hand and crossed the carpeted floor to a massive circular bed which occupied the center of the bedroom. Placing her upon the thick comforter, he covered her with a lightweight blanket and leaned down to press a kiss against her forehead.

"Sleep. Your body needs to rest."

She didn't have time to argue, for she was already sliding into the vibrant imagery of her dreams.

Kevlin's muscles tingled as he left the bedroom. The witch slept peacefully in his bed, and his thoughts drove him mad with the memories of moments before. He shouldn't feel these things about the enemy, but he couldn't control himself around her.

Cursing his own weakness, he strode into the bathroom and turned the spray on full blast. He could have taken the easy way out to clean himself by magic, but right now, he needed the pummeling of the icy cold water.

Squirting soap into the palm of his hand, he lathered his body from head to toe, and his curses became more vibrant as his cock ignored the sluice of the bone-chilling water. Still standing straight, his thick member reminded him that the earlier sexual encounter hadn't been enough.

He hadn't fucked her, and now, with her several feet away from him, smelling of his scent and sex, he wanted to go to her, slide into her, bury his cock deep inside her until she cried out again.

His hand curled around his cock and began a slow stroke. He knew masturbating would be a lousy second to what his mind was showing him. Waking her was the only thought in his head. That and taking her.

"Fuck!" He shouted the word and turned the faucet off, bumping his forehead against the tiled wall. Stepping out of the shower, he didn't bother with a towel as he walked into the bedroom. His feet made damp imprints on the carpet as he watched Ella sleep.

He couldn't stand there forever, but the idea of walking around with a perpetual hard-on wasn't appealing, either. With a loud, long sigh, he damned himself to a night of no sleep, and he crawled into bed beside the witch, close to her soft, warm body. His cock nudged her ass, and he groaned.

Not the very best of ideas, but even as much of an ass as he could be, he wouldn't wake her. He'd seen the exhaustion on her face, and sleep what was she needed.

There was always tomorrow morning.

Warm kisses on her cheek woke Ella the next morning, and her lips curled into a smile. Still pleasantly sleepy, she rolled closer to the lips, as her hands curled into fists against broad muscles.

"It's time to wake up."

The deep rumble made her crack open one eye. "I've been deciding when to wake up for years now, but thanks for your help."

Kevlin pinched her ass, and she gave a squeak. "Don't forget who you're talking to, witch."

Her other eye opened. "If I had my magic—"

"What makes you think you don't?"

Excitement jangled her nerves, and she pushed herself up and shoved the hair out of her eyes. "I have my magic?"

Before he could respond, she directed a finger at a Ming vase atop a sleek black stand. The porcelain shattered, and invigorated, Ella leapt from the bed. "Excellent!"

Kevlin propped himself up on his elbows and glared at the broken pieces littering the carpet. "Do you have any idea how rare those vases are?"

She flung a saucy look over her shoulder halfway to the bathroom. "Just conjure another. Isn't that how you got the first one?"

He swung his legs over the side of the bed. "Actually, no. That was a trip to the Orient."

Finally able to choose something to wear besides the robe, Ella dressed herself in skin-fitting jeans and a snug black t-shirt. "This feels great."

"It looks even better."

His voice was close, but she hadn't noticed Kevlin's approach. Apparently, her senses weren't as strong as they ordinarily were. A sense of disappointed settled in the pit of her stomach. "You didn't return all of my abilities to me, did you?"

He lifted the heavy length of her hair away from her neck and pressed a kiss against her skin. "Is that a question you even have to ask? I couldn't risk your reneging on the deal."

Whirling around to find him several inches within her personal space, she glared up into his face. "Despite what you might think, witches have integrity. I always honor my word." Okay, not always, but the wizard didn't have to know that.

"I'm sure you do, but this was my insurance." Kevlin's arms slid around her waist and pulled her close.

Why didn't she resist him? Ella frowned and her hands flattened against his chest. "Your trust is overwhelming."

"I returned your magic, did I not?"

She looked down at her new attire. "That you did, but I'm guessing I still can't leave."

"That would be an accurate assumption, yes."

"Fine." She pushed away from him. "Then let's get started on finding your father's killer." Pursing her lips, she tapped one finger against her skin. "Do I have contact with the outside world?"

"No." He sauntered toward the foot of the bed, completely naked and impressively hard.

"Looks like you have something to take care of this morning. I'll leave you alone to handle it." Ella took two steps toward the bathroom before her legs refused to keep walking. Perhaps she could handle it for him. Hmmm. The idea had merit, but if she was to discover her fellow witch, she had to get started. After all, she wanted to return to Betony eventually, even if spending a few more days with the wizard had appeal. Angling a look over her shoulder, she slid a gaze up and down his strong, muscular body, expressing approval with the lift of one eyebrow. Oh, she could definitely spend a few more days with him.

Kevlin grinned at her. "Whatever you're thinking will have to wait. My father—"

"Needs you. I know. Tell him I'm working on it."

Her suggestion erased the smile from his face. "That would be difficult to do considering he doesn't know you're here. None of my family does."

Figured. "Why am I not surprised?"

"You should be thankful. I'm a nice wizard compared to my brothers."

Ella strolled to the dresser and held out her hand, palm up. A hairbrush appeared, and the sense of accomplishment made her frown. Outside of this world, she could stop time, change the weather, and fuck with other people's lives. And now, the little things gave her pleasure, much like a child getting a pat on the head.

She slammed the brush down without so much as one stroke. "The deal was my magic. There were no restrictions."

"There are always restrictions in my country. You will uphold your part of the deal, or I will renege on mine. And I might just see if I actually will get tired of you in my bed."

Whirling, Ella flung the brush at his head. He ducked expertly, caught the missile, and tossed it back to her. "I'll see you in ten minutes. In the meantime, I hope you make good use of your magic. I'd hate like hell to have to take it again."

"I bet." She didn't need to look over her shoulder to know he'd left her alone. "Bastard."

An incredibly sexy bastard, but a bastard nevertheless. Definitely doable. She wondered if he would consider a visit to Betony. The idea of having him powerless in her own country caused a smile to sweep across her face.

Chapter 4

One step into his father's bedchamber, Kevlin wished he hadn't answered the call, for surrounding Oriel stood three of his remaining brothers. With arms crossed and glowers on their faces, they aimed their fury at their oldest brother.

"So nice of you to join us." Ryder spoke first, which didn't surprise Kevlin because Ryder was always one to jump into the middle of any foray. "We sense a witch among us."

Shit. Time for some recon. "Father mentioned he believes a witch is responsible for his illness."

Ryder took a step toward him, his dark eyes narrowed to slits. "I sense a witch here now. You don't?"

Time to strike back. Kevlin glared at his younger brother. "Had I noticed a witch, do you not think I would have mentioned it?"

"Merlin only knows what you would mention, considering your lack of attention at our last meeting." The snide comment came from Jaden, the youngest of Oriel's sons.

Kevlin walked forward to stand on the opposite side of the bed from his brothers. "You needed me, Father?"

Oriel waved a hand, though the effort was feeble. "Jaden has intercepted a message from Devin."

"Devin? He is safe then?" Kevlin didn't have time to enjoy the moment of relief before Ryder spoke again.

"He's trapped between two worlds at present." Each word was practically spat across Oriel's bed.

Another silent curse reverberated in Kevlin's mind. He didn't need to ask which two worlds, but for the sake of remaining neutral, he did anyway. "Which worlds?"

"Betony and ours."

Kevlin rubbed one finger over his top lip. "How did he get there?" He didn't play stupid very well, and from the look on his brothers' faces, he saw they didn't believe it for a moment.

"Well, that was a question we thought you could answer. Several of our youngsters saw you taking a strange woman into your home recently." Ryder's lips curled into a snarl.

Kevlin's shoulders tensed. "She's not your concern."

"She's a fucking witch, isn't she?"

"Is this true?" Oriel coughed, his face paling.

Victor spoke up. The smallest of the brothers, he generally kept to himself and watched over their mother. So his words came as a surprise to all of them. "If you're harboring a witch, you have done us all an injustice. Bring her to us."

Kevlin stared at his brother for a long moment before shaking his head. "As I said, she is of no concern to you, and I do not answer to any of you."

"You answer to me," Oriel corrected.

"Not in this matter." Before anyone could respond, Kevlin waved one hand, and his body dissipated into thousands of molecules which arced out of Oriel's bed chamber.

He had to get to Ella. Fast.

"Oh, this is just beautiful," Ella muttered, massaging her temples. "Noelle, when I see you again, I'm going to kick your ass." The return of her magic had brought her more information than she really wanted. Information which could prove deadly.

"Shit, shit, shit!" She stomped one foot and whirled around. Had Kevlin been so kind as to give back all of her magic, she'd be gone. Instead, she was forced to await his arrival and, more than likely, his fury. By now, he had to have discovered where his brother was. The poor bastard was dangling between here and her home world, trapped, and it was only a matter of time before the witches of Betony picked up his trail. Could this get any worse?

Grumbling, she sat down in a lotus position in the center of the living room and tried to ignore the floating knickknacks. Closing her eyes, reaching deep down inside for answers, she focused harder than she ever had before, and the instant replay of the past twenty-four hours sent her senses whirling.

Walking down the long hallway between the classrooms and the courtyard, she'd been on her way to meet a fellow witch when the skies had torn open as if ripped in two by giant hands. She heard the screams of terrified witches and the rumbles of irritation from the council.

Ella's feet had flown out from under her, and before she could even think to save herself, she was descending through the air, spinning and whirling until she was nauseated. She remembered a hand reaching out to her—someone trying to save her perhaps. And then came the fierce, rending noise.

She'd caught a glance of black pants, heard a loud curse, and then Kevlin's arms had caught her.

She massaged her temples even more furiously. "Think, Ella, think. What was it about wizards and witches?" There was something she was supposed to remember. A spell, perhaps?

No, a conversation with Heart, the most lucid of their aunts. To enter a wizard's world meant… what? She tapped her forehead with one finger and cursed her memory.

Then a sick feeling curled low in the pit of her stomach before stretching outward until her limbs shook. She couldn't stand, and didn't want to stand, for the knowledge had returned.

A witch entering a Wizard Country by anything less than an invitation meant the death of the leader. It was survival of the fittest. If a leader could not protect his country, he was eliminated, regardless of whether the intrusion was his fault.

Bouncing to her feet, she began to pace. "Kevlin, where in the hell are you? I have to get out of here. Now."

The atmosphere grew thicker, and Ella swallowed her irritation. Did he have to make such a grand entrance? "Just get your ass here, will you?"

As the mist lifted, a hand manacled her wrist, and she looked up into cold, black eyes that didn't belong to Kevlin. "I know you were expecting my brother, but unfortunately, my father desires a word with you."

"Let her go, Ryder." Kevlin appeared next to the tall man who still held her.

"In due time."

Kevlin took a menacing step forward. "Do not test me, little brother. You have yet to best me."

Ryder dragged Ella closer to him. "True, but this time, it would appear I have the upper hand. This witch and I will be in father's bed-chamber, if you should desire to join us."

Ella tried to pull away, but the wizard was too strong. Damn all of these men. She snapped a spark which singed the sleeve of his shirt, and the wizard frowned down at her.

"Tell your woman to behave, Kevlin, or she may not make it to the tribunal."

Tribunal? No one had ever told her about a tribunal, and she doubted she'd get a fair hearing anywhere on this goddess-forsaken planet. A spark shot from her fingertips, and the wizard holding her barely managed to keep his toes safe.

His grip around her wrist tightened until his fingers dug into her skin. "It would appear I shall have to shackle her." The moment the wizard said the words, the manacles appeared, securing her hands and feet as if she were a slave girl going to market.

"Oh, come on. Do you really think I can't get out of these?" Ella scoffed.

Kevlin growled in the back of his throat and sent the chains winging across the room to smack against an antique apothecary table. "Release her, Ryder, or I shall be forced to take you apart piece by piece."

With a wry grin, Ryder hooked his arm through Ella's and back-stepped toward the vertical vortex. "Then you shall have to accompany me, and once we're in front of Father, you can explain why you felt it necessary to give this witch her magic while in our country."

"Fuck." Kevlin said as they disappeared. No matter how this would play out, it wasn't going to have a happy ending. And as much as he hated to admit it, he'd already grown a little fond of the mouthy witch.

So he had two choices, neither of which appealed to him. Save the witch and oppose his family, or back away. Damn. He'd never been one to run from a challenge.

"Here we go," he muttered before following his brother.

"You brought a witch to our home?" Oriel roared his displeasure and then coughed as the exertion winded him.

"I didn't bring her," Kevlin corrected. "She fell from the sky, and I just happened to catch her."

"Sounds like a bunch of bullshit if you ask me," Ryder said. From the moment Kevlin had arrived in their father's bed chamber, Ryder had taken up residence in the doorway, blocking Ella's escape route.

"It's not bullshit." Ella stepped toward the bed and the glowering wizard lying amongst the pile of blankets. "Look, I don't know much about Wizard Country, but I can tell you it isn't a place I would willingly come." She blew out a breath. "Unfortunately, I didn't have any say in the matter."

Oriel's eyebrows drew together. "Then how did you happen to arrive?"

Though doubt colored his voice, Ella chose to take the question as an open door. "Well, I have a cousin who is more than a little pissed at me, and she has never had a good sense of direction—or the ability to tell a transport spell from a flying one. In fact, if you want my opinion, she gives witches a bad name." She waved a hand in disregard before continuing. "At any rate, she sent me here as some form of punishment for sending her to Earth a few months back. Although, she really has no need to complain, considering she ended up with a guy hot enough to burn toast."

"Is anyone actually following this drivel?" Oriel wore a perplexed expression on his face.

Okay, she'd had just about enough of Father Time's nastiness. In fact, she'd just about decided it was time to make Kevlin keep his end of the deal. But first came the rest of the truth.

With a loud sigh, she spun around and faced Kevlin and his brother. "You wanted me to find out why your father is dying, who is doing this to him. Your father assumes it's a witch." She paused to nibble her lower lip. "I am that witch."

Kevlin shot forward just in time to catch Ella around the waist and drag her out of his brother's target area. He pushed her behind him, taking a fighting stance. "Don't even think about it." He directed the command at his brother, but Ryder was already advancing.

"She came here deliberately." Ryder practically growled the words. "The council will not stand for this."

"She didn't come here deliberately." Kevlin held one arm behind him to keep Ella from coming forward. "I know listening isn't one of your better qualities, but you might want to pay attention to this conversation, Ryder. Ella was sent here."

"Then her coven must have sent her on this—this—suicide mission."

Oriel pushed himself to a sitting position, managing a succession of several nods. "I agree with your brother, Kevlin."

"Now, hold on just a damned minute." Ella pushed her way around Kevlin. "Just because I'm a witch doesn't mean I'm a bad witch. Okay, I'll admit I haven't always been a good one. Naughty, yes, but I've never killed anyone or been the cause of anyone's decline in health. Believe it or not, guys, not all witches are bitches."

Ryder folded his arms, not at all convinced. "I say we let the council decide her fate."

"And while you're doing that, your father will die." Ella's words captured the eye of every man in the room. "That's right. The longer I stay in your country, the weaker your father will grow. Eventually, he will die. The only way to save his life is to send me back to my own world."

Kevlin's chest constricted. Send her back? The thought twisted his stomach into a knot. He didn't want her to go. *Yeah, try explaining that one to your family, Kev.* "Mother is a member of the council, and she isn't here. We can't hold a meeting without her."

Oriel glowered. "Fine. Then chain the witch in the dungeon. We'll send a messenger to your mother asking for her immediate return."

Ella pivoted slowly to face the wizard. "Are you prepared to die while you await your own brand of justice?"

Kevlin took hold of her arm. "It's best to just back off now."

She tossed him a saucy look. "I'm not the back-off sort."

"There's another way to save your life, Father." Ryder moved forward, his steps stealthy, controlled, causing Kevlin's muscles to tense.

"I'm listening."

"Ending her life should restore the balance to yours."

"You will not touch her!" Kevlin shouted, bringing all eyes to his face.

Ryder shook his head. "I might have known you'd find some use for even a witch." He slid a glance up and down Ella's body in an insulting manner. "Not that I can blame you. At least this one's a looker."

Ella retaliated with a fireball that neatly clipped the toe of Ryder's boot. He danced around for a second before extinguishing the flame, and when he looked up, his eyes were as stormy as a tornado sky.

"So you have a little magic you'd like to play with, do you?"

Kevlin inserted himself in between his brother and Ella. He held up one hand a scant inch away from Ryder's chest. "Don't. Ella is my responsibility. I'm the one who took her into my home, and I'm the one who will fix this."

"By making her your paramour?"

The sound of Jaden's voice had all heads turning. Kevlin noticed the arrow in his hand seconds before his younger brother sent it winging its way across their father's chamber. He caught it mid-air, barely managing to avoid its poisonous tip.

"Are you fucking insane?" Kevlin tossed the arrow to the floor and ground it under the heel of his boot. "We don't know for certain that her death would return Father's health."

Ella nudged his shoulder with her own. "Now you're talking about killing me, too? I have to say, things aren't looking too good for my team. Why don't you just send me back to Betony?"

"Without punishment for your crimes?" Ryder clicked his tongue. "That, my dear, will never happen."

"You know," Ella said, lifting one finger for emphasis, "I'm really starting to dislike you."

"As you should." Ryder's scathing glance raked her up and down. "Witches and wizards have never been on the best of terms, and a wizard with integrity would never demean himself or his family by sleeping with a witch."

Control slipping, Kevlin wrapped one arm around Ella's waist. He had to get her out of there before he snapped. He didn't know if leaving was more for the witch's safety or his brother's, but either way, it was the only option. For in a matter of minutes, his temper would get the best of him, and Ryder would take the brunt of his fury. Not that the idea didn't have its appealing aspects.

Apparently, his younger brother had forgotten what a good ass-kicking felt like. Kevlin would love to hang around and show him, but the sounds of booted feet in the hallway outside his father's bedchamber gave him his cue.

"We have to go." Holding Ella tightly to his side, he left the room, shimmering into a tiny ball of energy which traveled faster than the whisper of wind.

"Wait a second," Ella squeaked, scrambling for a hand hold.

"Just hold onto the sound of my voice," Kevlin instructed, guiding her through the air with the power of his mind. "I won't let you fall."

"Let's just hope your magic is better than my cousin's."

❧◈❧

The moment her feet touched land, Ella wanted to fall and kiss it. She'd never been particularly fond of flying, and this orbing thing wizards did definitely wasn't high on her list of things to do again.

Brushing her hands down the front of her t-shirt, she calmly walked across the vivid green grass. Everywhere she looked, all she saw was grass blowing in the wind and an eye-watering blue sky.

"Where in the hell are we?" Disgusted and more than a little ready for a fight, she whirled to face the wizard who was either her savior or her captor.

"Somewhere safe, for now. It will take my family a while to track us here. In the meantime, we have to get you home." As he spoke, angry clouds began to gather overhead. He shot a glance at the sky. "The sooner the better."

"Sounds like a plan. Just give me back all my magic, and I'll be happy to depart."

The look on Kevlin's face caused a sick feeling to settle in the pit of her stomach. She wasn't going to like his response. "Unfortunately, that's not within my capability."

"You mean you can't give me the power to leave?" He shook his head slowly, and she wanted to hit him. Hard. "So all of this time you've been fucking with me, making the deal with me, knowing you couldn't send me home?"

"I can't send you home. That's true. But I can take you home."

Ella gaped at him. "You can't take me all the way to Betony."

"I'm aware of that, but I can take you close enough to Betony to allow you to call for assistance. This way, everyone stays safe." A clap of thunder punctuated his words.

And he'd leave her. Just like that. She should have known better than to think there could be something between them. But for a moment, however brief, she'd started to believe the wizard actually felt something for her.

Cursing her own weak feminine traits, she squared her shoulders and gave an abrupt nod. "Great. Then let's get going."

"That's it?" His voice vibrated with fury.

"What else is there?" The look on his face told her the question wasn't what he was looking for, but it was too late to retract the words. She wasn't sure she wanted to anyway. She didn't owe this wizard anything.

"When you put it that way, absolutely nothing." He took hold of her arm, his fingers digging into her flesh hard enough to cause her to wince.

"Hey!" She flinched and peeled his fingers away. "What is your problem?"

Whirling around so that his back was to her, he cursed. "You. You're my problem. And you shouldn't be."

Forget it, Ella. Don't let him get to you. She walked around to stand in front of him. "Then the quicker we get going, the sooner you'll be rid of one problem."

He glowered at her. "Spoken like a true emotional female."

Her eyes narrowed. Emotional female? She'd never been called that in her life. The name didn't sit too well with her. "Do you not remember what happened the last time you provoked me?" She dropped a glance to his crotch before fixing her gaze on his face once more.

Something flared in his eyes, and her brain forgot to remind her to breathe. Apparently, his mind had taken him down a different memory lane, a more heated and sensual trip.

Before she could protest, Kevlin snagged a handful of her hair and swooped down to capture her lips with his. Storm clouds gathered overhead, and thunder rumbled in the distance, completely in tune with the mating of their mouths. A powerful, driving force pushed them together. Their hands moved across clothing, desperately pulling at the material until flesh was encountered.

The sky opened up, and rain poured down over them, soaking their bodies in a matter of seconds. Kevlin cupped the back of her head, his tongue dancing with hers. Catching the edge of her shirt, he ripped it away from her body and tossed the tattered remnants to the damp grass.

Ella arched against him, melding her body to his. He palmed her breasts and ran his thumbs over the peaked nipples. The silk of her bra chafed her skin, and, craving the feel of his warm hands, she reached behind her to unhook the band.

"Fuck!" Kevlin lifted his head and gritted his teeth. "We can't do this now."

"Sure we can. We've already started." She stood on her tiptoes and nipped his chin.

With a groan, he gripped her hands. "No. The storm. It's my family. They'll be here soon."

She dropped her head to his chest. "Damn."

He released her hands and stooped for her torn shirt, restored it to its original state, and handed it to her. "Here. You can dress on the way."

Holding her bra with one hand, Ella wrapped her arm around Kevlin's neck, absorbing the sound of his groans as her bare breasts crushed against his chest. "Are you sure we can't stay just a little bit longer?"

He buried his face in her hair. "I'm sure, unfortunately."

A loud crash gave the final warning, and as sparks littered the air, he began to whirl.

"We cannot allow her to return to her home," Ryder ground out, his eyes pinned to his father's pale face.

"Her return will save my life." Oriel shifted on the bed to roll to his back.

"She must be punished."

"Have you not already sent a garrison of wizards to take care of that?"

The grumpy tone of his father's voice didn't dissuade Ryder. "Yes, but they have not been instructed to kill her. Perhaps we should discuss this with the oracle. She would know better whether we should allow her to live."

Oriel seemed to consider the question for a long moment before he finally responded. "Perhaps, but from the look in your brother's eye, he shall protect her."

"Then he's a fool. That witch is his enemy, and if he's too stupid to see that, then he deserves punishment of his own."

"It's apparent you want to follow the witch."

Ryder curled his hands into fists. "What was Kevlin thinking? Putting a witch before his family!"

Pushing himself to a sitting position, Oriel propped the pillows up behind his head and managed a smile. "Sometimes, we cannot be blamed for our feelings."

"What?" Ryder's temper somersaulted before elevating. "Has the fever addled your brain? He's barely known the witch a day. Feelings are not part of this equation."

"I still remember when I met your mother."

"That's enough! I'm not listening to this. Kevlin's actions have nothing to do with emotions. His lack of loyalty guides him. That's why he no longer resides in the palace. It's that very side of him which is going to be the death of him."

"Ryder." His father's voice stopped him before Ryder's hand could close around the doorknob. "You will not harm your brother."

"Not intentionally, no."

"Hear me clearly." Oriel sounded stronger, more authoritative. "You will not harm your brother whether intentionally or unintentionally. That is my final word on the matter."

Squaring his shoulders, Ryder managed a brief nod before he tore open the door. He couldn't look back at his father, or the lie would be seen.

For whatever happened next, Kevlin would reap what he had sown. Their father's edict be damned.

"I feel her!" Heart, Ella's aunt, rushed toward her two sisters with her hands waving in the air. "Ella is near!"

Jazz sat up straight, peering up at her older sister. "Are you sure? I can't feel a thing."

"You can't find your ass in a windstorm," Emmie muttered, trying to rub the redness from her eyes. She looked down at the empty bottle of bourbon and gave a forlorn sigh.

Heart clasped her hands to her breasts. "She's stopped."

Her hair standing on end, Jazz linked and unlinked her fingers. "What do you mean she's stopped? Was she moving?"

"Yes, she was moving. That's how I felt her. She was moving closer to Betony. Now she's just hanging there."

"Hanging there?" Emmie pushed herself to her feet and glared up at the ceiling. "I can't feel a damned thing."

Heart harrumphed. "That's no surprise, considering how much you drank last night."

Emmie straightened her shoulders and closed one eye. "Ah, yes. There she is." In reality, she still couldn't feel anything, but she couldn't be one-upped by her sister.

Heart pointed upwards. "Great. Then bring her in."

Brows lowering into a deeper scowl, Emmie spun on her heel and practically stomped toward the door. "I'm not bringing her anywhere until I see who she's got with her."

Jazz gasped, leaving her secure position behind her older sister to snag hold of Emmie's arm. "She has someone with her? She can't bring anyone to Betony! That's against our law!"

Heart snorted. "Yes, well, we all know how good Ella is at obeying laws, don't we?"

"You do have a point." Jazz cast a worried glance toward the ceiling. "Regardless, you can't just leave her there, Emmie! You're the only one who can bring her in."

Bloody hell. "Well, I wouldn't have to if you weren't so addle-brained." Emmie massaged her temples. "And if you, Heart, weren't so inept."

Heart patted Jazz's shoulder. "Don't worry, dear. She's just hung over. You know how she gets."

Emmie cast a look over her shoulder in time to see her youngest sister's lip wobbling. "Oh, for goddess's sake, Jazz, if you start crying, I swear I'll—well, I don't know what I'll do, but it won't be pretty."

"Whatever you do, you might want to do it soon. I hear some rumbling coming down the hall." Heart jerked her head toward the door.

Could this day get any worse? If the Coven Council discovered Ella was hanging in mid-air with an unknown guest, there'd be more wailing from the older witches than when an elder passed onto another plane of existence.

"Okay. Fine. The two of you stay put. I'll go take a look." Hopefully, her magic would cooperate in spite of the vicious headache.

"Damn you, Ella," she muttered on her way out the door. "Whatever's going on had better be worth my time, or you'll be a gnat in some human's smelly shoe before this evening."

Chapter 5

"We're almost there," Ella announced as the lights of Betony came into view. She'd forgotten how pretty her homeland was from this distance. With the sparkle of the diamonds circling the sloping towers and the shimmering glow of the three moons, the city welcomed its residents.

Glittering molecules came together to shape Kevlin's muscular form. With his arm around her waist, he held her in mid-air, following the point of her finger. "So that's Betony."

She didn't like the tone. "That's my home." The elbow in his ribs offered her irritation.

"Easy. I didn't mean any disrespect."

The lie didn't appease her. "It's not my fault your father is dying, your brother is missing, and you're bouncing in the air here with me. You can blame that on my dimwitted cousin."

Kevlin turned her in his arms and framed her face with his hands. "Are you nervous?"

"You're outside a city of well over a thousand witches, and you're only one wizard. The odds aren't in your favor, and you're asking me if I'm nervous? You might want to grab a dose of reality."

He had the audacity to laugh and then to kiss her, his lips warm upon hers. "You think I should be scared?"

"I don't know. Do you think you can fight that many witches at one time?"

"Why should I fight them? I just delivered one of their sisters safe and sound."

"Oh, yeah, you're about to get a medal."

His hands dropped to cup her ass and draw her closer. "There's something else I'd rather have a hell of a lot more than a medal."

She welcomed the heat of his palms. "Unfortunately, that's going to have to wait. The welcoming committee just arrived."

The grumpy woman sailing towards them certainly didn't look like the welcoming committee. He shoved Ella behind him and gave the woman his full attention.

With gray hair in a haphazard bun, black robe, and matronly glasses sitting on the bridge of her nose, she looked more like a schoolteacher than the witch Kevlin knew her to be.

"Does she always look this annoyed?"

Ella's fingers bit into his arm. "Let's just say she's not enthusiastic about my free spirit."

"Get into a lot of trouble, do you?"

"Emmie!" Ella swept forward and engulfed the woman in a hug. "It's good to be home."

"Don't give me that bullshit." The snap of the woman's tone brought Kevlin closer which enabled her gaze to fix on his face, black, steely eyes. "You brought a wizard to our home? What in the hell were you thinking?"

"She didn't exactly bring me here," he corrected, reaching forward to take hold of Ella's hand. Not that she needed protection, but the woman's demeanor wasn't exactly reassuring.

"Emmie, this is Kevlin. Kevlin, my Aunt Emmie." Ella made the introductions with resignation in her voice. "And he's right. I didn't bring him here. He brought me here."

Emmie cracked her knuckles. "Oh, so he forced you to bring him to our home, did he? Wanting to scope out the enemy, were you, wizard? Well, let me show you how we treat our foes here."

She aimed her fingers toward Kevlin's chest, whiplashes of energy shooting from the tips. Ella shouted and zipped toward Kevlin, taking the full brunt of her aunt's fury.

The shock of the contact threw Ella's body into spasms. She cried out as Emmie stared in horror. Kevlin caught Ella before she could begin to plummet into the darkness below them.

Was she alive? Ella opened her eyes, but her blurry vision made her shut them quickly. Something warm and solid held her as her body floated in midair. Her head lolled back, and a hand cupped it and held it aloft.

Finally, her brain started to right itself. She opened her eyes once more, and Kevlin's face came into view.

"Where are we?" Her ass stung, but for the life of her, she couldn't remember what happened to make it hurt like that.

"I'm taking you back to my home."

Ella squirmed in his arms. "What? Wait. What in the hell is going on? Why is my ass on fire?" She tried to lean down and inspect her anatomy, but her vision hadn't fully cleared. All she could make out was a singed portion of her jeans.

Kevlin ignored her questions. If anything, he increased his forward speed, whipping through the air as if he'd sprouted a pair of wings. What had happened to that molecule-shifting stuff he did before?

Eyeing him suspiciously, she poked his shoulder. "Will you stop for a second and let me figure out what happened?" When he didn't slow down, she pinched his neck, finally capturing his attention.

He stopped, the abrupt cessation of movement jostling their bodies like kites in a windstorm. "What happened was your aunt almost killed you. There's no way I'm taking you back there."

Though the memory was vague, Ella caught glimpses of Aunt Emmie's angry face then a flash of sparks. Her brow furrowed. "She didn't mean to hurt me." One hand patted his chest while she sorted through images of the past few minutes. "In fact, she was trying to kill you." Her face cleared. "That's right. I saved your life."

Kevlin glared down into her upturned face. "Hardly. You put yourself in danger for nothing."

"You didn't have your magic."

"I wasn't in Betony. The loss only occurs when I'm within the city limits."

So apparently, her ass throbbed for nothing, and now, her side had begun to ache as well. "Next time, you could have warned me."

"There wasn't time."

"Then how about making some kind of effort to shove me out of the way. Jesus. This is going to leave some scars." She shifted in his arms to massage her tender flesh. "It's nice to know Aunt Emmie hasn't lost her touch."

"Yeah. It makes me feel better." Kevlin started to move again, his speed only slightly slower than a lightning strike.

"Will you wait a second? I'm not going anywhere with you. Taking me back to your home will only guarantee your father's death."

Kevlin paused in flight again, considering her words. "You're not going back to Betony."

"My aunt didn't mean to hurt me."

"My brothers are coming for you."

"Oh, well, that's a little tidbit of information you could have shared with me earlier." She scratched her nose. Definitely a damnable situation. Massaging her temples, she tried to think. Where could they go? They needed a safe place to think and to come up with a plan.

"Astara!"

He stared at her as if she'd taken leave of her senses. "What about it?"

"It's an uninhabited planet."

His jaw clenched. "I know that, but what has it got to do with anything?"

"Let's go there, at least long enough to gather our wits and avoid being targets." She tipped her head back to see the dimple in his chin. "Do you really think your brothers would try to kill me?"

"Do you really think your aunt intended to do me bodily harm?"

Nibbling her lower lip, Ella nodded. "Good point. Astara is twenty degrees right and four hundred below. We'll be safe there, at least until my aunts hunt us down."

"I'd lay odds my brothers will find us first."

"There's a cheery thought."

"Don't worry. I'll protect you."

"We're in my homeland now. I believe I can protect myself."

"Not if you keep making stupid mistakes, you can't," Kevlin scoffed.

Ella didn't appreciate the lecture. "Just keep driving. We can talk once we get there."

He shifted her in his arms. "Hang on tight."

Like she could do anything less. Or wanted to.

Astara was uninhabited for a reason. The planet left little to be desired by way of accommodations. Though it bore lush green vegetation and ice-cold springs, the sun bore down relentlessly, and the trees stood straight and tall, offering little shade. Fortunately, the less-than-welcoming atmosphere was no match for the combined magic of a witch and wizard.

In seconds, Kevlin constructed a ventilated stone shelter, dark enough to offer relief from the heat, and Ella increased the size of a particularly large oak, spreading its branches to create additional cool shade.

Kevlin held out his hand and allowed Ella to precede him into the cave. Cushy silk-covered pillows provided seating, which she sank down onto gratefully. "Okay, so now what?"

He sat down across from her. "This was your idea. I'm not accustomed to hiding out."

"Yeah, yeah, I'm sure you're used to confronting your problems head-on, but it sounds like we're in for a battle. Of course, there's always the option of just going our separate ways. I'm sure that would pacify our families somewhat."

Kevlin dropped his gaze for a second before pinning her face. "I doubt it. My family wants you dead."

"Oh, yeah. That would be a bit of a problem."

"I have another idea." The tone of his voice piqued her interest.

She drew her legs to one side, leaning forward. "I'm dying to hear it."

He followed her lean. "We could always disappear together."

Was he really saying what she thought he was saying? "And leave our families?"

One eyebrow lifted. "Would that be such a bad thing?"

"Yours might miss you." Ella didn't kid herself when it came to her family. The aunts would, no doubt, throw a celebration upon her permanent departure. Not that they didn't love her, but they didn't seem to appreciate her sense of adventure. Or her sense of humor.

"That sounds like you think your family wouldn't miss you."

The sympathy coating the words irritated her. "It's not a big deal."

"Didn't sound like it was."

She bit her razor-sharp tongue and tried to channel some of the great peacemakers on her planet, all to no avail. "Drop it, wizard."

His hand brushed her hair—when had he moved so close? She hadn't even heard him shift on the cushion much less sit down beside her. "You're very sensitive about that subject, aren't you?"

"So what you were saying about leaving, I don't think that would be such a good idea. In fact, I know it's not." Brushing an imaginary speck of dirt off the knee of her jeans, she pushed herself to her feet. "Just go home, Kevlin. I'll take my chances with your family."

He stood beside her, taking hold of her arm. "The hell you will. I'm not about to let you come face to face with my brothers. They don't exactly have your best interests in mind."

She made a feeble attempt to free her arm. In truth, the feel of his palm so hot against her skin made her hotter in other places. Closing her eyes, she inhaled his scent, so masculine and drugging. "I can take care of myself."

His fingers softened against her skin. "Fought many wizards, have you?"

Ella allowed herself to be pulled against his chest until his chin rested on top of her head. "What are you trying to do?" She had her answer even before he replied, for his hands had traveled around to cup her breasts.

"Since we're hiding out, I believe we can make better use of our time."

Melting against his chest, she leaned her head back against his shoulder. Kevlin's lips captured hers. What began as a stamp of possession segued into a gentle, searching kiss, an exploration. One hand cupping the back of her head, he pulled her under his spell, wrapping her in a cocoon of sensation as fiery as the flames of hell.

Hooking one leg behind his calf, Ella sucked lightly on his tongue and nibbled his lower lip. All thought escaped her as he grabbed her ass and pulled her closer. His cock nudged the apex of her thighs, and a gush of liquid warmth bathed her thighs.

He practically ripped the clothes from her body, baring her nudity to the cool interior of the stone shelter and the intensity of his gaze. For a long moment, he simply stared at her, his eyes covering her from head to toe. Her nipples pebbled. Her thighs quivered, and her breaths came in shallow pants. Goddess, she was close to an orgasm just from the power of his gaze.

Closing her eyes, she tipped her head back and thrust out her chest as she waited for that moment, that precious second, when he would touch her. When it came, his lips closing around one nipple, she cried out and took hold of his forearms to steady herself.

Kevlin switched his attention from one breast to the other, drawing the peak so far into his mouth that Ella released a low moan of pleasure and held his head in place. Tracing the aureole, his tongue swirled around each nipple and lapped the softness of her skin.

One hand burned its way down over her stomach until his fingers nested between the folds of her womanly flesh. His index finger caressed her clit in slow, measured strokes. Ella's fingers bit into his arms.

The orgasm built within her as every nerve in her body tingled and sang. His finger moved faster, stronger, and her breaths stuttered. He kissed her neck, urged her to let it build, and she dropped back onto the silken pillows.

In a cloudy haze of desire, she felt the push of his hard cock against her stomach, but she couldn't move enough to touch him. Her concentration centered around the pinpoint of pressure between her thighs. The walls of her pussy began to pulse, and heat splashed her skin as she warmed from the inside out.

Climbing higher and higher, she reached for the ultimate peak, and when it came, the orgasm hit hard. She bucked against his hand as she rode wave after wave of the perfect pleasure.

Going limp, she gave a low groan. "That's a good way to change the subject."

"It's just one of my many talents." He laughed in her ear, the husky sound only enhancing the tingles darting up and down her spine. He settled into the cushions and wrapped his arms around her.

Snuggling closer to him, she slid her hand lower and cupped him through the thick denim of his jeans. "You want to see one of mine?"

"Mmmm. I'd rather feel it."

"You'll have to take off these clothes."

The coy tone of her voice had his clothes gone faster than she could wink.

"You're fast when you want to be." One hand closed around the thickness of his cock.

"Yeah, well, feel free to take your time." He gritted his teeth and moved his hips in time with the stroke of her hand.

Her thumb stoked the head. "I could take you into my mouth, suck you, trace the long length of you with my tongue."

"Sounds like a plan," he muttered.

"But," she continued, dipping one hand into the dampness between her legs and drawing the liquid to his mouth. "I think fucking you sounds like a much better one."

She surprised him with a quick flip that tumbled them both across the piles of cushions. Taking his cock in her hand once more, she whisked her palm up and down its silky length with the lightest of touches, enough to make him groan and curse at the same time.

Then, straddling him, she sank down onto his rigid shaft. The walls of her pussy stretched to accommodate his width, and her breath lodged in her throat. He felt so good, so right, inside of her.

Kevlin gripped her hips and lifted her up before sliding her back down onto his cock. "Ride me," he instructed in a voice that sounded like a rusty nail.

"You mean like this?" She rocked forward, her knees dropping to the ground next to his hips.

His breath hissed out from between his teeth, and his fingers bit into her skin. "Fuck me." The command was unmistakable this time. Forceful. Compelling.

Ella threw back her head and laughed, riding the wave of power much as she rode him. He might be a wizard, but at the moment, she was the one in control. Her hands on his chest, she pushed upwards until only the tip of his cock remained at the opening of her pussy. Then she impaled herself on his length again.

He rose up off his back, his arms locking around her spine. Hips gyrating furiously, he buried his face between her breasts. His moans were like music, and Ella reveled in the sound.

She gathered his hair in her fists and held on. For now, she'd give him control. He shoved his cock deeper inside, and she gasped, shoving his face into her breasts. "Yes!" The one word became a litany. Over and over she encouraged him, telling him exactly what he was doing to her. For her.

Kevlin reared up and rolled over with her, pressing her back flat against the cushions. Taking hold of her legs, he draped her ankles over his shoulders, hitched her ass high in the air, and jutted his hips forward. The rhythm was as wild as the frantic beating of their hearts and as relentless as the sun beating down outside the shelter. And when they came, their cries bounced off the stone walls and echoed all around.

Ella dropped her head to his shoulder and drew in several gulps of breath. Damn. How in the hell had she gotten herself into this situation? For all of her bravado and desire for power, she'd gone and fallen in love with a wizard.

A fucking wizard. Well, the fucking part she didn't mind, but she didn't doubt her family was going to mind about the wizard part. Placing a kiss against his chest, she released a sigh.

Kevlin's hands cupped her ass. "What was that about?"

She pushed herself up using her hands on either side of his side. "You do realize this ends here, right? I mean, once I go my way, and you go yours, this is over."

He watched her without saying a word.

"There's absolutely no way this can continue. You're a wizard, and I'm a witch. There is no precedent for this, and furthermore, I doubt either your family or mine would ever agree to setting one."

"That's funny. I got the impression you had a wild streak. Guess I was wrong."

Her brow furrowed. He knew just what buttons to push. "There's a big difference between a wild streak and stupidity. My aunts I could probably convince. The entire coven would be another story."

His palm connected with her ass, and she yelped with the pleasure-pain. "Maybe you're thinking too much."

She couldn't read between the lines when he spoke, and that irritated her. Reading people was one of her better abilities. She pushed herself to a sitting position and drew her knees to her chest.

"We'd better get dressed. There's no sense putting off the inevitable."

Kevlin propped his hands behind his head. "What's the inevitable?"

"Our going our separate ways. Your family's continued attempts to kill me. My aunts' insistence on neutering you." His wince made her smile. "And don't think I'm kidding."

"Wouldn't dream of it." He yawned and closed his eyes. "There's no need to be in a hurry. I covered our tracks. We have plenty of time before the boom is lowered."

She poked him in the side, an action which caused his eyes to open. "You don't sound like you're even worried about the boom."

Kevlin gave her a grin which was more like a smirk. Ella debated whether or not to hit him but figured it might result in more trouble than the pleasure she'd get from it.

"Is that your only answer?"

Before he could respond, a loud crash sounded outside the entrance to the shelter, bringing both wizard and witch to their feet.

"I thought you said you covered our tracks," Ella accused.

Now clothed, Kevlin shot her a glare. "Did you hear me say I was infallible?"

"The tone of your voice said you were."

"Could we continue this conversation later once we know who are visitors are?"

He had a point, damn him. Ella took a fighting stance and waited.

"She almost killed our father. Did you really think we'd just let her walk away?" Ryder's words vibrated with fury as he walked into the shelter. His eyes burned with more malice, and the tension in his shoulders told Kevlin his brother hadn't come to talk.

"What happens to her isn't your decision." His stance just as threatening, Kevlin came face to face with his brother.

"Will you listen to yourself? You're putting a witch before your family."

"I would not allow you to hurt any woman."

Ryder's lips curled into a sneer. "Even if you weren't fucking that woman?"

Kevlin growled low in his throat and took another step which put him directly in his brother's personal space. "You're close to getting hurt."

"I doubt that."

"Let's rein in the testosterone for a moment and think about this like adults." Ella wedged her body in between the two forces of nature. "I didn't go to Wizard Country on my own. I mean, it's not the number one choice of vacation places for witches." Turning her attention to Kevlin, she thumped his chest. "And instead of flexing your muscles and attempting to defend my honor, shouldn't you be asking about your father's health?"

He wasn't particularly fond of being berated like a child, but Ella did have a point. Grudgingly, Kevlin addressed his brother. "How's Father?"

"Recovering." Ryder's voice was just as abrupt before he turned dark eyes on Ella's face. "And the reason for your arrival in our country means little. What matters is the ramifications of your visit. You almost killed our father."

"It's not like I took out a machete and tried to lop off his head," she groused. "Let's get some perspective here. My dumb-ass cousin made a mistake because she was trying to make a point. She's never been very good at transportation magic, and that's why I ended up smack dab in the middle of Bumfuck Country. Your father is healing and you found your brother. So instead of accusing me of being some wicked witch, why don't you consider the odds that a witch with an ounce of brain power would actually willingly, voluntarily take a vacation in your country!"

The last word ended on a shout that had both wizards staring at her.

She took a deep breath to regain some of her composure. "Now, if the two of you will excuse me, I'll return to Betony where I belong."

She disappeared before Kevlin could respond. "Damnit!"

Ryder folded his arms across his chest. "You should be glad she's gone."

"And you should mind your own damned business."

One of his brother's dark eyebrows rose. "You're starting to feel something for her, aren't you?"

"That's under the heading of none of your business." Kevlin whipped around, feeling nothing but emptiness. He couldn't track her.

"Something tells me you're about to do something incredibly stupid," Ryder drawled. "Like going after that witch."

The idea gelling in his mind, Kevlin smiled. "We do have some unfinished business."

"Think about what you could be throwing away. Do you really think Father will allow any type of union between the two of you?"

"Yeah, well, that's the great thing about being an adult, brother. We get to make our own decisions." Kevlin saluted him and vanished.

And hoped like hell his magic could get him inside the hallowed walls of Betony.

※※(♊)※※

Jazz gasped, one hand clasping her throat. "There's a wizard in our midst."

Heart stared at her, one eyebrow lifted. "You can actually feel a wizard?"

"No. No. I saw him. He's not dressed like a wizard, at least not the ones we've seen in our books, but I know he's one of them. He just looks, well, dangerous. Our male witches don't look dangerous." Jazz paused in her dissertation. "Do they?"

Ella rubbed her temples. Had Kevlin really been so stupid as to follow her to Betony? Her aunts would eat him for lunch. She turned and caught a flash of broad shoulders and dark hair. Her heart hammered underneath her breastbone.

"Is that your man?" Heart queried, coming forward to stand beside Ella.

"He's not my man." The words came out so quickly three sets of eyes turned to look at her. Heat crawled up her neck to suffuse her face. Damnit. Her aunt Emmie could spot a liar a mile away, and this close, there was no way Ella could escape her damning gaze.

"Well, glad to see you found something to keep yourself busy."

The snarkiness sent Ella's temper skyrocketing. "If any of you could keep Noelle in line better, I wouldn't be in this situation. So don't give me any bullshit."

"Ella! You can't blame your troubles on us." Heart's admonishment held just the right amount of self-righteous indignation to make Ella groan.

She held up one hand. "Okay, okay. You're right." Her head throbbed even more viciously. "I just need to talk to Kevlin and get him out of here before the council notices him."

"It's probably too late for that. A wizard can be felt by even the simplest of witches. No offense, Jazz." Heart patted her sister's arm.

"Then I have to move faster." Ella spun around and whizzed out the door, running right into Kevlin's chest. "You have to get out of here. The entire coven is going to be on your ass."

He took hold of her hand. "I can't leave without you."

"You got here without me."

"I was outside. Now I'm in. My magic doesn't work here, re-member?"

Why did he sound so smug? "If my aunts get hold of you, you'll leave here in minute particles." Curling her fingers around his, she tugged him down the long hallway toward the serenity chamber, a room all witches used to obtain peace. It had never worked for Ella, but then, she'd never been interested in peace. A piece, yes, but—she broke off that line of thinking and walked faster.

A group of voices blended together behind her, and she cursed. "You have no idea what you've done."

Kevlin surprised her by turning her in his arms and kissing her until breath became a scare commodity. "Then I suppose you'll just have to take me home."

"I'll take you outside Betony. That's as far as I'm going."

"Then we have a problem."

She stopped walking long enough to glare over her shoulder. "You are the problem."

"Granted, but I'm not returning home without you."

"I can't go back to Wizard Country with you."

He cupped her ass and lifted her to press his erection against her midsection. "Then let's take a detour."

"Are you even listening to yourself? We just met."

"Well, let's look at it this way. Your family wants me dead, and my family wants you dead. And I don't believe we've finished what we've started."

Ella pulled her hand free, holding it close to her breasts. "We haven't started anything. We've had sex. End of story."

He began to massage the soft globes beneath his palms. "Do you really think my brother is going to stop hunting you? One day, he'll catch you off Betony."

She hadn't thought of that. "Well, I don't need you to protect me."

"Maybe I need you to protect me. One day, one of your aunts could catch me out of the safety of my home environment." His lips turned upwards in a smile.

"Now, you're fucking with me."

"That idea has merits. So where does that door lead?" Kevlin jutted his chin toward the closed door.

"To the serenity chamber. There's a secret door inside which will help me get you out of here safe and sound."

"Weren't you listening? I said I'm not going without you."

"Now's not the time to get sentimental. So we've fucked a couple of times. That doesn't make us a happily-ever-after couple."

"So you're ready to walk away then?"

Shouldn't she want to walk away from a wizard? Hell, she should want to run, but it only took one look at those hands, at that mouth, to bring the sensual memories to the forefront. Yanking hold of his collar, she brought him close. "I don't have any idea what the hell I'm going to do with you, especially since we can't hide out forever."

"We're not hiding. We're just taking a vacation." He used her words against her as he picked her up into his arms.

"So where to then?"

"Not sure yet, but I've heard there's a little planet which has a really nice stone shelter."

"Your brother knows where it is."

"Yeah, but trust me, he won't be there."

"How can you be so sure?"

"I've kicked his ass before." Kevlin opened the door beside the wall lined with bookcases. "Clever."

"I don't know. He looked pretty formidable if you ask me."

"There'll come a time, but it won't be today. He'll regroup and try to talk my other brothers into joining him. In the meantime, we have some downtime."

Ella wrapped her legs around his waist. "I guess we'll have to think of something to do. Too bad I didn't bring a book."

Kevlin chuckled and lifted her higher. "I'm about to step outside this door. Don't forget to use your magic."

Emmie released a long sigh as she watched the couple sail away across the black sky. "There they go."

"Shouldn't we go after them?" Heart asked, standing beside her sister.

"She's having sex with a wizard. I doubt she wants or needs our help."

Jazz wrung her hands. "But he could hurt her!"

Emmie's lips twitched. "Let's face it, ladies. Ella can hold her own, and it's only fitting that she find a man who can handle her."

Heart smiled. "Then I would have to say mission accomplished."

"Indeed," Emmie replied.

About the Author:

Rachel is a multi-published author of fantasy and paranormal romances and romantic suspense. A freelance editor and non-fiction writer, Rachel is also a business consultant specializing in helping start-up companies. Making her home on the East Coast, she also runs a publishing company dedicated to historical romances.

For more information, you may visit Dawn's website at dawnrachel. com, *or you may read more about her at* moongladeeliteauthors.com.

Exes and Ahhs

❧⟨⟩☙

by Kate St. James

To My Reader:

I've always treasured stories about reunited lovers. There's just some-thing about all that emotional angst as the couple strives to overcome past mistakes and emerge stronger than before that tugs at my heart strings. Knowing how amazing the sex was between them—and could be again—ratchets the tension higher. In *Exes and Ahhhs*, Risa Haber and Eric Lange find themselves on such a journey. Please enter their world and enjoy the sweet sensations they generate.

This story is dedicated to my friend and critique partner, Brenda K. Jernigan, who patiently and quickly reads everything I write. Thank you, Brenda, for sticking by me all these years.

Chapter 1

Risa Haber swatted her business partner's hand. "Eric, get your nose out of my boobs."

"Can't help it, Risa. They smell delicious. The nipples are perfect—small and pink and puckered. Mmm." He glided his finger a hairbreadth away from one erect nipple. "I love how they peek out of the icing bra cups. You should wear bras like this all the time."

"You're impossible." Risa hip-bumped her ex-lover away from the demi-bra layer cake decorated with lavender frosting and sculpted marzipan breasts. However, in his usual flirtatious manner, Eric Lange continued to hover over her shoulder, over the sample erotic desserts lining the back room counter of her fledgling bakery and dessert catering company, over *everywhere*.

She fought a smile. The man didn't need any encouragement. At thirty-five and with a Peter Pan complex rivaling George Clooney's, Eric didn't know how *not* to flirt. But it didn't mean anything. She doubted it ever had.

Her responding banter probably sent him all the wrong messages, too. But she couldn't stop. Joking with Eric was a lot easier than battling the emotions she still felt for him—and which he, by his own admission when they'd broken up, couldn't reciprocate.

"You lost the right to vote on my lingerie choices after we split," she said lightly. "And of course the boobs smell delicious. I added extra ground almonds to the marzipan."

"Sheer brilliance."

Risa laughed and scooped more yellow frosting into her icing bag, then moved back to the second cake on the counter. Her hands shook. Damn it, with Eric's sexy blue eyes, his gym-honed body, and his cover-model sandy brown hair, he distracted her to no end. It didn't matter if he went bare-chested or, as on this sunny May afternoon, he wore a buttoned-down shirt and a tailored jacket to greet the dinner crowd at his Italian restaurant. Her attraction to him hadn't abated one iota.

Not that she'd ever let him know that. She could play lovers-to-friends-to-business-partners with the best of them.

He encroached on her space again, but she waved him off. "Move it, Lange. You're annoying me, and I need to finish icing this—"

"Cock?"

Her face heated. "—before Miss Fullbright arrives."

Steadying her hand, Risa frosted the ascot for the *On the Town* penis cake. She'd never before prepared erotic concoctions for a customer, but Elaine Fullbright wasn't a run-of-the-mill client. A former adult film star and retired publisher of female-pleasure-focused *V* magazine, Miss Fullbright had earned millions in the U.S. before returning home to raise eyebrows and stir headlines in the elegant harbor town of Victoria, British Columbia.

"She's paying me a mint to get these designs just right," Risa said without looking at Eric. "You should see the names on the guest list for her party. We're talking political and business figures, a Texas oil baron, and Hollywood types up the yin-yang. Miss Fullbright promised to mention my name loud and often. She even asked for brochures of my regular desserts to give her friends. If they like what they see, my catering business could take off."

"You mean, our catering business."

"No, *mine*. You're a silent partner, Eric. Sweet Sensations is mine." A fact he conveniently forgot when he dropped in three or four times a week to check how "they" were doing.

Tugging her lower lip between her teeth, Risa continued applying the icing to the oversized phallus lying on a blue frosting sheet cake. Sculpting the marzipan penis had been an exercise in laughter and humiliation because neither she nor her assistant Kyla possessed a recent memory of a real live penis on which to draw.

Undaunted, Risa and Kyla had worked late last Saturday night striving to produce an erect penis nicknamed Dick that would satisfy Miss Fullbright's needs. But the damn thing kept falling over. Three margaritas later, Risa brainstormed the design for the reclining *On the Town* penis featuring a plastic top hat perched jauntily on its pink marzipan "head." A walking stick and tiny martini glass with clear gel "gin" completed Dick's dashing ensemble.

Oh, please love Dick, Miss Fullbright. The campy mood of the dozen sample desserts achieved the lighthearted sensuality Risa's client had requested without appearing pornographic.

Happy with the ascot, she straightened. "Finished. What do you think?" She set aside the icing bag before wiping her hands on the rose bakery apron covering her tan slacks and white, short-sleeved blouse.

Eric pointed to the frosting bowls. "You need these?"

She shook her head.

"Good."

He poked a finger into the yellow icing. Risa's lips twitched. Four months of dating Eric had convinced her that men who reached their mid-thirties without marrying were basically overgrown boys. In the year since they'd kiboshed their romance and opened Sweet Sensations, he hadn't changed. He liked his food spicy, his cars flashy, and his women fast.

Too bad. At the ovary-shrinking age of thirty-two, Risa struggled with a biological clock that clanged louder than London's Big Ben. She longed to be *somebody's* mother, but not Eric's—or any other grown man's. She didn't want to coddle or scold him. She wanted to share a lifetime and make babies with him.

Well, not with *Eric* specifically. A man as sexy and fun-loving *as* Eric, but one who didn't sprint away from emotional commitment.

She stared, brow arched, at his icing-coated finger. "Do you mind?"

Sticking the finger in his mouth, he slowly licked the frosting. "Mmm, no."

Her breasts tingled. Thankfully, the chest-to-thigh apron provided an extra barrier to his probing gaze. He'd once sucked *her* fingers, her nipples, her sensitive clitoris with the same erotic absorption he employed with the icing. It wouldn't do if her body betrayed how easily he still aroused her.

She jabbed his arm. "I asked your opinion on the cake design, you dummy, not the icing."

Scooping more frosting onto his fingers, he cast the cake a cursory glance. "Nice tie."

"It's an ascot."

"Couldn't bring yourself to give him icing pubes, huh?"

"Pubes aren't very appetizing."

"I suppose that depends on the diner." He winked. "I like my nose tickled by the soft, female blonde variety myself."

Hot desire sped to the female blonde variety between her legs. She remembered. Ah, the things the man could do with his tongue. Ignoring her body's Pavlovian response to his teasing, she propped a hand on her hip.

"Get your mind out of the gutter, Lange, and tell me what you think of Dick."

With a glance at the closed swinging door separating them from Kyla and the bakery customers, he sucked icing from his finger so slowly that her mouth watered.

"Imitation is the sexiest form of flattery," he murmured.

Risa laughed. "What an ego! I did *not* model him after your—"

"Cock?"

She wished he'd stop saying that! "Sorry to burst your bubble, but my memory's a little fuzzy." *What a lie.* "I don't recall the size of your—"

"Co—?"

"*Prick.*" Hah, thought he'd had her again, huh?

He slapped his chest. "Risa, you wound me. At university, the girls called me Eric the Long. I was with you longer—get it?—than any of them. How can you not remember?"

She shrugged. "Guess it wasn't that memorable."

"Maybe we should arrange a viewing and refresh your memory."

"Maybe we shouldn't, and you could just fantasize that we did."

He grinned. "Believe me, Rees, I will."

Crud. She'd stepped right into that one.

He pushed his finger into the icing bowl and moved closer. "Want some?" His voice rolled low and acutely sensual as he lifted the frosting to her mouth.

Her breath hitched. He knew exactly what he was doing to her, damn it. Between the lingering aromas of this morning's baking, the scent of the finely ground almonds used in the marzipan, and Eric's electrifying nearness, her senses felt ready to burst.

"Uh, no thanks."

His finger inched closer. "You don't sound convinced."

She stepped back. "I said no."

He eyed her. "When we were together, you would have." He strode to the sink beside the big commercial dishwasher and swiped off the frosting with a wet cloth.

"Well, we aren't together anymore, are we?"

An aggrieved look tightened his face, but Risa didn't buy it. Eric would say or do darn near anything to get a woman into his bed—or *back* into it, as the case might be.

"I've been meaning to talk to you about that," he said.

She stacked the icing bowls and carried them to the sink. "About what?"

"Us."

Tension arced in her chest. "Not again." She dumped the bowls in the sink and rinsed them with the sprayer. On Valentine's Day, he'd surprised her with daisies—her favorites. Thinking he'd offered the pretty bouquet out of friendship, she'd been touched until he'd spouted a load of bullcrap about wanting her back. Since then, every few weeks, he instigated the *us* talk. But there was no *us*—just Eric and his overactive sex drive cruising for temporary action.

"Yes." He nodded. "Again."

She glanced at the clock above the ovens. "It's four-twenty. Miss Fullbright will arrive any minute."

"Kyla's up front. She'll buzz you."

Risa stopped spraying. "Yes, but I need to load the dishwasher, ditch my hairnet—"

"Please look at me, Risa."

She turned. Reading the false sincerity in his gaze, she crossed her arms and sighed.

"I've missed you," he said gruffly.

She rolled her eyes. "You see me all the time."

"Not in the way I want to. Or how I think you want to see me, either."

What she wanted was of no consequence. However, at the moment, with Peter and his Pan-shaft dreaming of the chase, he just thought it was.

"Eric, you always want what you can't have. Isn't it enough that I flirt with you?"

"I'm sick of flirting. I want more."

Her heart pinched. "You know, you say that. You might even believe it. But if we got back together, within two weeks max, I guarantee you'd change your mind."

His eyes lit up. "I'll take that wager."

"Huh?"

"Give me two weeks to prove you wrong."

Risa narrowed her gaze. Oh, she should. Give him two weeks of the raunchiest sex of his life, then sit back and watch the train wreck.

Softening her voice, she asked, "And what we would do with those two weeks, Eric?"

"Whatever you want. Dates, dinners, movies."

"Sex?"

He looked cornered. "If you want."

If *she* wanted? This was all about him and his physical urges.

The man needed to be taught a lesson.

And she was the woman for the job.

She stepped closer. "So if I want to, we could do this?" Placing a hand on his chest, she brushed a kiss across his mouth that left her lips burning.

His voice deepened. "Um, sure."

"And if I want to, I could do this?" She flicked her tongue into his ear then gently bit the fleshy lobe.

He groaned, and her panties moistened. *Oh, Eric. Too, too bad.*

"Or this?" Pulse racing, she lowered her hand to the front of his pants. Finding him hard—she swore he walked around with an erection half the time—she gripped his cock through the thin fabric of his summer trousers.

"God, Rees."

Stroking him, she whispered in his ear, "Or I could pull down your zipper, right here, and take you in my mouth."

His hips jerked.

"Do you remember my wet mouth on you? My hand fondling you?"

She swept down her fingers, cupping his balls "While I nibbled and sucked, and *sucked*."

His eyes shut, jaw tensing. "Kyla might come in."

"You'd like that, wouldn't you?" Risa whispered, smiling. "Me on my knees, another woman watching, maybe joining us."

"I only want you." But his cock jumped against her palm.

"Do you remember the first time you came inside me?" she asked, and he nodded.

She released his erection. "Well, cherish those memories, Eric, because it's never happening again."

"*Fuck*." His eyes snapped open.

"You think I'm giving you two weeks to break my heart again?" She kissed her fingertips and wiggled them at him. "Dream on." As she would. Sizzling fantasies of Eric on top of her, inside her, visited her every night.

"We don't have to sleep together. Just talk. Take walks. Play cards?"

She laughed at his hopeful expression. "You? Not having sex? Isn't that a little like asking Shaquille O'Neal *not* to sink a basket?"

"So we'll do the sex thing. Help me get you out of my system, Rees."

She smirked. "Oh, first he wants something real, now he wants me gone."

"Only if you want *me* gone, Angel."

She blinked. "Don't call me that."

"Why? Does it remind you too much of what we had together?" He skimmed a feathery trail of sensation along her cheek with strong fingers, weakening her knees and scooting traitorous hope to her heart. "We can be that close again."

"You've lost your mind."

His gaze probed hers with the tantalizing mix of tenderness and hunger reminiscent of his lovemaking, and her body reacted instantly—nipples stiffening, thighs buzzing.

"We ended too quickly, baby," he murmured. "We didn't get a chance to say good-bye how we both want to."

In bed. He read her too well.

"So your solution is sayonara sex?" she said as if the idea didn't appeal to her. But it did.

Oh, it did.

The sex part, anyway.

"I need you, Rees. One night, five days, two weeks—whatever you want. You name it."

"One night." Her eyes popped. *Crap,* had she just said that?

"See what happens when you go with your gut?" He grinned. "Or lower."

"I—But—"

"When?"

"What?"

"My night. If one is all I get, I want to make the most of it. But you're in charge. Say the time and place, and I'll be there."

She sucked in a breath. Glanced away. Ran her hand over her hot face. Looked at him.

The shop buzzer rang—her signal from Kyla. "Shit, Miss Fullbright's here!" She tore off her hairnet, fluffed her hair around her shoulders.

"Where are you showing her the samples?"

"It was supposed to be back here, for secrecy. But the place is a mess!" Due to her unprofessional tendency to lose track of time with Eric. "I'll have to show them up front." With the bakery customers watching—not what her client wanted. "Shit!"

"I'll help you carry out the trays."

"No." She untied her apron and slung it on a nearby hook. "Kyla can tidy while I wing an intro. You go. I don't want Miss Fullbright thinking—"

"That I was your inspiration?"

"Eric!" She ushered him to the rear service entrance.

"Only if you promise to call me about our night."

"Damn it, you can't hold me to that now."

He grasped her arm, mouth lowering to hers before she could utter a protest. Risa squeaked, and his tongue delved, seeking and far too easily coaxing a response.

Need peppering her body, she kissed him back with all the heat and yearning she'd closeted over the last year. *Yes. Yes, yes, yes.* How she wanted him. *Eric.*

Just as quickly, he broke the kiss. Traced a finger down her breast-bone, dipped it into her cleavage. Her skin burned.

"Why'd you do that?" she whispered.

"A little something to dream on until our night." His voice lowered. "It *will* happen, Rees. There's no backing down."

He slipped outside.

Risa squeezed shut her eyes, willing her heart to stop racing before she greeted her client. Crud, was *she* screwed. Because, no matter how much she might wish otherwise, she could no longer deny that she desperately wanted one last night with Eric, too.

Chapter 2

Eric pressed his palms again the tile shower wall, head bowed and erection straining as hot water pelted over his back and chest. His boner refused to die, a side effect of obsessing about Risa in the several hours since he'd left the bakery. He enjoyed the aching sensation, but enough was enough. He couldn't think, wouldn't sleep, until he spanked the bastard.

Gripping his cock, he pictured the yearning on her beautiful face when he'd said there was no backing down. The swell of her full tits beneath her blouse and prissy bakery apron. How her bare nipples peaked in his randy imagination when he brushed his fingers across them. Her long hair, pale as summer wheat in bright sunshine, cascading backward as she arched her neck, presenting her breasts to his mouth.

He stroked swiftly, his breathing picking up speed when the fantasy Risa appeared in the shower with him. She faced the wall, lifting her ass and spreading her legs, begging him to fuck her from behind. He covered her hands with his on the tile, their fingers twining as his heart thundered in his chest. She glanced over her shoulder, whispering his name, and he thrust inside her. Hot, slick, tight.

Risa.

Dropping a hand to her clit, he pinched and rubbed just enough to drive her insane. She cried out, bucking against him, his balls slapping her ass as he plunged in and out of her sweet pussy. His orgasm grabbed hold, and he slammed into her, coaxing her shuddering climax.

"Risa!" But she was gone.

Emptiness filled him. He opened his eyes and swore.

"Satisfied?" he asked his half-limp prick.

The damn thing twitched.

"I know how you feel," he muttered, rinsing his body clean.

He missed her. Not just the amazing sex, but *her*, Risa Haber, the determined, emotion-driven woman. Her admirable qualities kicked butt all over her premature talk of marriage that had instigated their breakup. The pride and excitement she felt for her work impressed the hell out of him, as did her devotion to her life's dreams, the way she stood up to him when he acted like an ass, even her stubborn refusal to believe he'd changed.

Screw their sham of a "friendship." The hollow sensation eating his gut wouldn't dissipate until they were a couple again—for good.

He jammed off the water and opened the glass shower door. The ringing of the phone carried from the adjoining bedroom. Slinging a towel around his hips, he dripped puddles onto the gleaming hardwood and grabbed the cordless from the nightstand.

"Yes?"

"Hi."

"Rees!" He grinned like an idiot.

She murmured in a low, throaty voice, "I know what you did."

"You do?" He whipped around. Had she been spying on him while he fantasized about her? But of course she wasn't there.

"Kyla told me. You cleaned the kitchen for me."

He chuckled. "Guilty." In more ways than one—his cock danced at the thought of Risa secretly watching him get off in the shower. "I snuck in after you went up front."

"But the service door locks when it closes."

"I have a key. The real estate agent gave us both one, remember?"

"Oh." Hesitation shadowed her tone. "Yeah."

"It wasn't a big deal." He'd wiped down counters, loaded the dishwasher, arranged the platters of sample desserts for maximum visual appeal. Second nature for a guy who'd worked in restaurants half his life.

"It's a big deal to me," Risa said. "I was so nervous when Lainey arrived—Miss Fullbright asked me to call her that. We chatted while Kyla ducked in the back to tidy. She returned within seconds with a confused look on her face, miming cleaning gestures behind Lainey's back and shaking her head that it wasn't her. I realized then what you'd done. Thank you, Eric."

"You're welcome." He dried himself one-handed, pecker thickening as the towel rasped his shower-warmed flesh and Risa's soft voice seduced his ear. When she didn't respond, he asked, "Is that the only reason you called?"

"No," she replied too quickly. "I wanted to tell you—Lainey loved the desserts! Especially Dick. She requested him for her birthday cake. Sixty candles, and she wants every one of them lit. So into the freezer he goes—until Friday night! Kyla and I will take everything we can prepare ahead of time to the party room in Lainey's mansion. It's in the Uplands—must be gorgeous. Mega-money lives there."

"Risa?"

"Lainey won't be around. She has a thing in Vancouver. But she'll return Saturday morning several hours before her guests arrive."

"Sounds good. Rees?"

"She's an amazing woman, Eric. Generous, easy to talk to. And she looks *fantastic*. Sure, she's gone under the knife a time or two, but—"

"*Risa!*"

She stopped babbling. "What?"

"*You* phoned me. I could be taking a wild stab in the dark, but I don't think you called to talk about Elaine Fullbright."

"You don't?"

He chuckled again. "No." Body dry, he dropped the towel to the hardwood and sopped up the shower puddles with a foot. His semi-woody bounced. "You're nervous about our night."

"Um, yeah. I'm not sure I want to go through with that, Eric."

"Oh, you *want* to." Whatever else had gone wrong between them, sex was never an issue.

"I don't trust you. But I think about you. All the time. I want you every night. It's making me crazy."

Lust rushed in. "Good."

"Maybe for you!"

He glanced down at his fully erect cock. *Yep.* He could wave a flag with the horny beast.

"Then why fight it? It's just one night." He smiled. "Unless you want those two weeks?"

"Eric…."

"One night it is." He knew when to cut his losses.

"The thing is, I'll be working non-stop until Lainey's party. But after that…."

He waited, erection growing stiffer by the second.

"I want you to surprise me."

His balls tightened. "Surprise you?"

"I don't want to plan the time or day. I need to feel like it's not my choice. Remember that time we…?"

Did he ever. His dick throbbed as erotic memories burned in his brain. Risa couldn't handle the responsibility of acknowledging what they *both* wanted, that their one night could possibly lead to more.

Well, okay. He'd surprise her, although not how she probably expected. And, while acting out her favorite fantasy, maybe he could finally achieve the beginnings of so much more.

Risa rolled over in bed, her body on fire. After all these months of flirting with Eric and satisfying herself solo, then nearly admitting to his face how much she still wanted him, a flood of sensual need had been released that refused to allow her one moment of uninterrupted sleep. It didn't help that she dressed in the lingerie he'd given her days before their split. The skimpy pink negligee caressed her overly sensitized flesh like the feather-light touch of his hands and mouth on her breasts, her tummy, her greedy pussy.

Before hanging up, he'd mumbled something about taking another shower. Was he jerking off, thinking of her, while she tossed and turned, depriving herself?

Images of his long, hard cock pumping into her hot opening burst into her mind, and she groaned.

"Screw it," she whispered.

Flipping onto her back, she slipped a hand inside the sheer panties, creaming instantly when she pushed one, then two fingers into her pussy. Thrust them in and out before sweeping her juices over her swollen clit. Then inside again. She wanted, *needed* the amazing sensations to last, but her climax began cresting. Damn it!

She pulled out her fingers, rolled onto her stomach, and buried her face in her pillow. Clenched her thighs together—which only increased her arousal. *Agh.*

Fisting her hands beneath the soft, down-filled pillow, she inhaled the lavender essential oil she'd dabbed onto the crisp cotton case in hopes the calming scent would help her claim sleep. What a joke!

She would not touch herself. *Would not.*

If she made herself come, her body wouldn't remain on full sexual alert as she wanted. Until Eric provided the mindless sex and pure fantasy she'd asked for.

She'd combust in his arms. Neat and efficient.

One night. Then they'd be done.

Eric parked a block from Risa's house and jogged stealthily through her quiet neighborhood, jacket hood covering his scalp and a black ski mask concealing his identity. When he reached the small bungalow, he pulled on his leather gloves and crept to her bedroom window.

It was open. Maybe two inches, just enough to flutter the gauzy curtains and let the cool midnight air trickle in through the locked screen. He could break the glass with a rock and slice the screen with his jack-knife, but if she mistook him for an intruder she'd probably dial 9-1-1 before he had a chance to crawl indoors—then wonk him on the head with one of the heavy, antique candlesticks she collected.

Clever girl. It was almost as if she'd anticipated his arrival and set a trap, testing to see if he'd honor her wishes and wait until after the party, or provide her animalistic-sex fantasy when it fucking well suited him.

His cock swelled.

That was now.

Resisting the temptation of the window, he stole around to the front of the house and located her spare key hidden in the fake bottom of a flower pot situated among the dozens of colorful blooms bordering her walkway. He slid the key into the lock, gingerly turned the knob, and cracked open the door.

Eric slipped into the house and toed off his shoes. The living room lay silent save for the grandfather clock ticking away the seconds until he sank into Risa's welcoming body. Excitement drilling him, he walked through the tranquil space and stopped outside her bedroom. Unless she'd had the door fixed, it would creak when he opened it, possibly waking her too soon.

Holding his breath, he twisted the knob. *No squeak.*

Air escaping through his teeth, he left the door open behind him.

His gaze drifted to Risa's sleeping form. As he waited for his eyes to adjust to the darkness, he rubbed his aroused cock through the thin fabric of his running pants.

Slowly, the night receded. She'd thrown off the feminine bed covers, exposing her sleeping on her back, one knee bent and her leg sprawled to reveal her bikini panties... as if she yearned for his touch. Her flimsy negligee parted in two pretty pink panels beneath her breasts. One hand rested on her flat tummy, the other lodged beneath her pillow.

Her head faced his direction, mouth open slightly, expression bliss-ful. A soft moan lifted from her lips, and he smiled. She always moaned when she dreamed about sex. Ah, the number of times he'd awakened and made tender love to her....

But she wouldn't want it tender this time. She'd want it raw, hard, fast. Primeval. Or, at least, he would give it to her that way.

With the thick carpet cushioning his steps, he padded to the bed and sat on the mattress. He gazed at her, but she didn't wake up.

Delicate shadows dusted the fragile skin beneath her eyes, speaking of her exhaustion. Yet her stiff nipples poked her negligee, lush tits rising and falling with her shallow breathing as she enjoyed her dream. Her shoulders shimmied, and she released another moan. "Ah...."

His cock hardened to granite.

He leaned over her, and her eyes shot open.

Clamping a gloved hand over her mouth, he whispered harshly, "Don't scream."

Chapter 3

Fear clawed Risa's throat. She struggled to sit, but he pushed her back down, snatching her hand from her stomach and shoving it up to join its twin beneath her pillow. He grabbed both wrists with one gloved hand. The position forced an arch to her spine and slid the lacy bodice of her negligee over her hard nipples. His shadowy gaze captured hers through the eye openings in his ski mask, and he winked.

Eric! Risa squirmed on the cool bed sheets, his name a muffle against the smooth leather glove pressing on her open mouth. She'd dreamt of him taking her like this. Had nearly left her front door unlocked, just in case.

But she didn't want him tonight! Forget efficient—this was too fast. Her body burned for his touch. It would be over all too soon.

"Surprised?" he murmured before tugging a lace-covered nipple into his mouth.

Ecstasy pulsed between her legs as his ski mask grazed her sensitive breasts and his firm lips sucked. He pulled his hand out from under her pillow and moved the glove off her face. His strong fingers replaced his lips on her aching nipple, tweaking and teasing while he plunged his tongue deep inside her mouth.

She lifted her knees and snapped her thighs together, wriggling against him. "Mmph."

His tongue plunged deeper.

"*Mmph!*"

He broke the kiss, gaze questioning in the speckling darkness as he slid his fingers from her breast to her panties. She batted them away before he reached her clit—she'd be putty in his talented hands, and he damn well knew it.

Pushing him off, she sat up. "Eric, you scared the shit out of me!"

He yanked off his ski mask and flicked on the low-wattage lamp. The navy cotton fabric of his jacket hood coiled around the back of his neck. "Christ, Rees, did I get the fantasy wrong? This isn't what you wanted?"

"No, no, you didn't get it wrong—"

"I didn't?" Relief flooded his blue eyes. His static-filled hair stuck up like a little boy's, and a pang of tenderness shot through her.

"I want the fantasy. I love the fantasy. Just not right now."

Frowning, he tugged off his gloves and lay them on the nightstand. "If you decide when, it's not a surprise."

"I know, but—"

"This *is* the fantasy you wanted?"

God help her. "Yes."

A sexy smile curved his mouth. He edged a finger beneath a ribbon shoulder strap of her flimsy top, and sensation spun through her nipples.

"But not tonight." She licked her lips. "I need to anticipate, to wonder *when* it will happen, a bit longer."

"Shh." He smoothed a hand over her shoulder, skating his fingers to the tie securing her negligee beneath her breasts. He tugged gently, but didn't undo the bow. Instead, he pushed his hand beneath the sheer panel draping her thigh, settled his warm palm on her hip, thumb brushing her equally sheer panties.

He gazed at them. "I like these." Husky lust drenched his voice, and her skin tingled.

"It's the set you gave me," she whispered.

"Ah." He looked up. "You wore it tonight. Were you dreaming of me?"

Her heart thudded. She nodded.

"Were you about to come in your dream?"

She closed her eyes briefly, admitting in a soft voice, "Yes."

He smiled. "I thought so." His thumb nudged one leg opening of her panties, explored her desire-dampened curls. Her pussy zinged. "Was your dream about *this* fantasy?"

"Eric." She turned her face away.

"*Risa.*"

"Yes."

Another slow, erotic smile. His thumb inched to her plump folds. He stroked her slickness, and she shivered.

"You want *this* fantasy, but not now. You demand the element of surprise, then decide you want to say when." His hand drifted away, then his voice lowered. Commanding, compelling, insatiably seductive. "I can't let you call all the shots, can I?"

He yanked her panties down her legs, and her rear jacked up on the bed.

"Eric!"

Without rising, he whisked her panties past her knees. "I could take you right now, and there's not a damn thing you could do about it." Jerked them to her ankles.

"I could scream." Her nipples jutted, taunting her.

"Yes." He grinned. "I definitely see that happening." He whipped off the panties and flung them aside.

"Eric, I can't. It's too soon."

He caressed her calves and her inner thighs. "Don't worry. This isn't our night, Rees. You can still enjoy your build-up."

He removed a condom from his jacket pocket, then unzipped the jacket and shrugged it off. Standing, he removed his T-shirt and running pants. He hadn't worn underwear, and his erection stood long, hard, and proud against his stomach. She stared at it as he moved to the foot of the bed, opened the condom packet, and rolled on the protection.

She asked, "If it's not our night, what is it, then?"

"A little something to take the edge off." He grabbed her ankles and dragged her down the bed, jostling a surprised gasp out of her. He raised her legs, spread them. "Do you want this?"

"Yes!"

With one swift stroke, he surged into her, pinning her legs to his chest with his strong arms. Her feet framed his face as he pumped hard and fast, one hand sweeping down to rub her clit.

"Ah, Rees, I've missed you so much."

She squeezed shut her eyes. "Don't say that."

"Don't say what? Nice things? I've missed fucking you. I've missed your tits, your hot pussy, missed eating you until you explode in my mouth. Is that better?"

"Oh, God." She grabbed the sheets as her orgasm slammed into her, her sex clenching and releasing as he rubbed and rubbed. "Oh, fuck. Oh, yes. Eric!"

He plunged deeper inside, then held himself motionless while the rippling sensations consumed her. "Take it, Rees. Take it all." He thrust again. *Hard.*

She cried out. "I can't. It's too much."

He stiffened. "You're in pain?"

"No. Too much pleasure."

He pulled out.

She opened her eyes, body quaking with sensual aftershocks. "You didn't come."

"I'm not complaining." A sexy smile spread over his face. He climbed on the bed and settled on his knees between her spread legs. "Scoot up," he whispered.

Risa backed up on her elbows until her head hit the soft feather pillows. Eric lowered onto his forearms and scooped her rear into his hands, murmuring, "Spread your knees."

Without thinking, she did as he asked. His head lowered to her open pussy. Her pulse zoomed. "I'm still too sensitive."

"I'll be gentle." He gazed at her wet, swollen folds. "I'll lick around it."

Her clit throbbed. He'd loved her like this so many times when they were dating, she knew exactly what she was in for. Pure heaven.

The cool, midnight spring air streamed in through the barely open window, rustling her frilly curtains. "You might want to close the window."

"For when you scream my name again?" He chuckled. "I don't think so."

He bent his head and lightly lapped her opening. Her juices flowed, and she moaned.

"God, Rees, I've missed eating you." He licked and lapped, circling around but not touching her swollen clit. "You taste so good."

The scent of her arousal flowed over them. His tongue swiped between her labia, and he gently chewed one outer lip. Her mind and body spun. She wove her fingers through his hair, swept them down his neck. Caressed his forehead, his closed eyelids, the soft, dark lashes.

Her heart squeezed, and tears pricked her eyes. She didn't want to, *couldn't* feel such strong emotion for him when she knew they had no future.

"Fuck me with your tongue," she commanded in a rough whisper. She'd rarely used the F-word to describe their lovemaking, but tonight she needed the arsenal of her base needs to prevent her from feeling like she was falling in love with him again.

That she'd never stopped loving him.

A sound something like a growl erupted from his throat and rolled into her pussy while he licked and lapped. He parted her with light fingers, then drove in his tongue. *Deep.*

Risa gasped. Her nipples ached as his tongue pushed into her again and again. He sucked her opening, thrust his tongue, then *finally* swept up his mouth to capture her clit, keeping her legs parted with his hands when her body demanded she wrap them around his head.

She panted, her climax barreling down on her. "Eric, Eric."

His head lifted, and she sat half-up, reaching down his hot skin for his strong, solid cock. "Eric, please," she begged when she didn't make contact.

"Please what?" He kissed her breast above the bow of her negligee. "Please fuck you? Or make love with you?"

Make love with me. "Please fuck me." Clutching his shoulders, she coaxed him up. "I don't care if the neighbors hear us—I want them to. I need you inside me. Now."

He smiled. Tugged the ribbon between her breasts. But instead of slipping open, the damn thing knotted. "Oops."

"Forget it." Risa curled her hand around his erection. "Get inside me."

"Patience," he murmured, sliding out of her grasp and reaching over the side of the bed.

"What are you doing?"

He lifted his running pants. After fumbling in the pocket, he sat up and flashed a tiny jackknife blade at her.

She stared. "What's that for?"

He sliced the knotted ribbon open. The freed lace slackened and skid over her breasts. Eric flicked the blade through the shoulder straps, neatly cutting them. He shoved the wrecked lingerie off her body. Only the remnants beneath her back remained.

Risa giggled. "You're resourceful."

"And inventive."

"I don't believe this." She grinned. "I'm screwing MacGyver."

He folded the jackknife and tossed it on her nightstand with his gloves. "No," he said as he lay on top of her. He gazed deep into her eyes. "You're screwing me."

Risa bit her bottom lip, battling her burgeoning emotions. "Will you buy me new lingerie to replace what you've ruined?"

"If you screw me again."

"Well, there *is* our night."

"Yes, there is." Keeping her gaze prisoner, he pushed his weight off her, then slid inside.

"*Ahh,*" she sighed when he sank as deep as his length allowed. *Eric.*

He grunted, pumping into her. Slid his hands under her rear and angled her pelvis so that his stiff penis stroked her G-spot. She was ready, so it didn't take much. Sensation scorched her from the inside out as her second orgasm gathered speed.

His breathing grew rapid. He let go of her rear, pulling her close and cradling her against his chest, whispering her name as he plunged in and out.

Risa locked her legs around his hips. His heart beat loudly against her breast, and love rushed through her, strong and clear. She couldn't have him guessing, so she whispered, "Fuck me, Eric. Fuck me hard."

His jaw tightened and his body thrust. He pinched her nipple, and her climax swept her. She released the tension in a long cry, and he went rigid as he pulsed inside her.

They lay there for several moments, her legs wrapped around him. She stroked the warm skin of his spine slick from the intensity of their lovemaking.

Finally, she unhooked her legs and settled them on either side of him.

He dropped a tender kiss to her lips and slipped from her body. Risa sat up in bed, sheets rumpled around her, watching in silence while he got rid of the condom and began dressing.

"You're leaving?" Her voice sounded small.

He tugged on his jacket over his T-shirt and running pants. "Isn't that part of the fantasy?" He reached to the nightstand for his gloves, ski mask, and jackknife. "I break into your house, screw you senseless, then leave again."

She nodded. "Through the window."

"My runners are in your entry. I'll get them some other time."

"Eric, this is silly. Just go get them. You can leave through the front door."
Don't go. Prove that you want more than sex from me. Prove it now.

He sat on the bed and caressed her hair tumbling in disarray over her shoulders. "I'm giving you your fantasy, Rees. All the way. I'll pick up my shoes at the bakery tomorrow."

She shook her head. "I'll send them to the restaurant."

He looked at her. "If that's what you want."

I want you. But her throat constricted, refusing to let the words pass.

He murmured, "Just be clear. This wasn't our night."

Good. Because she wasn't anywhere near finished with him.

She nodded. He didn't say another word. Just went to the window, unlocked the screen and lifted the glass fully open, then jabbed a leg over the sill. Her sexy intruder, on his way out.

"When will we finish what we started tonight?" she asked.

"What, and ruin the surprise?" A quick grin, and he was gone.

Risa got up and closed and locked the window. Padded naked to the entry and spotted his runners on the rush mat. A sigh escaped her as she bolted the front door.

If only, if only, she could lock up her heart.

Chapter 4

Eric sequestered himself in his office off the kitchen of Bella Fortuna, alternately staring into space and tapping his pen on the yellow pad where he supposedly brainstormed menus. Aside from an insane number of cartoon doodles, the last hour had produced a big fat bunch of nothing. Thoughts of making love with Risa last night consumed him.

He glanced at the lingerie-store box on the credenza. Man, he'd like nothing better than to pick up the phone and call her. Or forget the pre-liminaries and pop into the bakery unannounced like normal. Except, after last night, nothing about their situation remained normal. He'd tested the limits of their one-night agreement, and, considering she'd climaxed twice, she'd loved it. But did she want more?

A knock rapped at the door. Glad for the distraction, he turned in his chair. "Yes?"

Risa's assistant, Kyla Jackson, poked her head into the room. "Hey, Eric. Do you have a minute?"

"Kyla." He smiled, waving her in. "What brings you here?"

Kyla entered and closed the door, an infectious grin lighting her face. A brunette a bit taller and maybe three or four years younger than Risa, she had the most stunning green eyes he'd ever seen on a woman.

But he preferred blue.

She held out a bag marked with the Sweet Sensations logo. "From Risa."

"My runners?" Eric got up, accepting the bag. He peeked inside. Black Nikes. *Yep.* He set the bag on his desk. "Why didn't she have them delivered?" Like she'd said she would last night.

Kyla ran a hand down her jeans. "I had errands to run for the Full-bright party, so I offered to bring them." Her gaze flicked to the door. "I didn't mind."

Eric grinned. "Did you talk to Dante on your way in?"

"Who?"

He chuckled. "My new chef. All muscles, long hair, wears black-rimmed glasses. Don't give me that innocent look. I know you're into him."

Her eyes widened. "Risa told you?"

"No, I guessed. You should ask him out. I've noticed he's a little shy around women."

"That's what I like about him. He seems the no-talk, all-action type."

Eric laughed.

"So." Kyla plopped into the guest chair, purse on her lap. "What's with the runners?"

Eric hesitated. "What did she say?"

"That you left them at her place at some time or another." Kyla's green eyes speared him. "But, I dunno, Eric, Risa's way too organized to misplace something you might have left behind a year ago. And then she wants to courier them to you when you see each other nearly every day. What's going on? What did you do to her?"

He felt like he'd time-traveled back to the vice-principal's office in high school. His shirt collar constricted his throat as if the garment had shrunk two sizes. "Maybe you should ask her."

"She's remarkably mum today."

He propped a hip on his desk. "It's not my place to kiss and tell, Kyla."

"Ah ha!" She pointed at him. "I *knew* something happened between you two last night. Risa's acting so weird, pretending all her nervous energy is because of the party. But I knew it, I just knew it. You slept with her! Eric, how could you?"

"Well…."

"No, I don't want to hear the details."

"I wasn't planning on—"

"You know what she's like. Having sex means something to her."

He crossed his arms. "I didn't say we had sex."

"You don't have to. It's written all over your face. Hers, too." Kyla sprang off the chair. "Shit, Eric, I don't want to see her hurt again."

"I don't want that, either."

"She's like a big sister and a friend and a mentor to me, all rolled into one."

"Kyla, I won't hurt her. I'm giving her what she wants."

"What you *think* she wants."

He spread his hands. "It's all I have to go on. I care about her, and I'm sorry, but how much and what I plan to do about it is none of your business."

Rap-rap!

They both looked at the door. "Yeah?" Eric called, pushing off his desk.

Dante appeared, wearing his white chef's get-up. The rich scents of Mediterranean cooking drifted in with him, and his goofy chef's hat squished under the doorframe as his large body filled the space.

His gaze swept to Kyla, and her face turned pink. She fiddled with her hair, twisted her watch on her wrist, reached for her purse, tossed it back on the chair.

"Sorry to interrupt." Dante's complexion suddenly grew chalky for an olive-skinned guy living in a climate where the mercury seldom dipped below freezing. "For that chicken dish you asked me to update, I created some options to spice it up. Want to sample them?"

Eric nodded. "I'll be there in a flash."

Dante's gaze shifted to Kyla again. "Take your time."

The door closed, and Eric smiled at Risa's friend. "Flustered much?"

Kyla stuck out her tongue. "Shut up."

"Not so fun when the shoe's on your foot, is it?"

She jabbed a thumb into her jeans pocket, studying him. "You care about her?"

"I always have." And always would.

"Then why did you dump her? She had to quit her job."

As his pastry chef. "She didn't *have* to quit. She chose to."

"Because you dumped her."

Eric rubbed the side of his nose. "Our breakup was mutual."

Kyla's gaze narrowed. "Do you want her back?"

"Yes," he said without missing a beat.

Two seconds that felt more like an eternity passed. "I believe you," Kyla replied softly.

"Thanks. Although it's not like I need your permission to try to start things up with her again." No, he needed Risa's. Her permission, her eager compliance. *Her,* for all time.

Kyla's eyebrows arched. "You'd be surprised what my approval could get you."

Eric tipped his head. "Oh, yeah? So, tell me, is she acting like she regrets anything that might have happened last night?"

"It's not my place to *listen* and tell. Plus, she hasn't told me yet." Kyla grinned, and he chuckled.

"This approval thing," she said, "do you feel like playing Cupid?"

She jerked a thumb to the door, the focus of her thoughts clear. Dante. "That depends. Do you?"

Kyla returned from the bakery supply outlet as Risa handed a customer a pale pink bakery box of freshly baked croissants. Risa released a breath. Good, no Sweet Sensations bag concealing a black pair of Nikes lurked in her assistant's small armload of packages. Mission accomplished: Eric's runners were once more in his possession, and Risa hadn't needed to talk to or see him or otherwise run the risk of rehashing last night to get the job done.

She turned to a gray-haired employee transferring muffins from the rolling rack of baked goods into the display cases. "Marie, can you take over with the cash register? I'll finish unloading in a few minutes."

With a nod, Marie stepped over to serve the next customer.

"Thanks. Buzz us if you need us," Risa said before beckoning a finger at Kyla and mouthing, "Into the back."

Once the door had swung shut behind them, she asked her friend, "Was Eric surprised to see you? What did he say?"

Kyla grinned. "Honestly, you two, I feel like I'm passing notes between lovebirds in grade eight. Only, in yours and Eric's cases, it's parcels." She strolled to the rear of the kitchen redolent with the scent of banana-pecan bread dough and deposited her bags and purse on a square table near the exposed closet.

"What do you mean?" Risa asked.

Kyla hung up her jacket, then looped a bakery apron over her head. "The box with the scarlet wrapping is for you," she said as she tied the apron behind her back.

Risa blinked. "From Eric?"

"No, from Sasquatch. Yes, of course from Eric. Something he bought this morning, he said. He wanted to bring it over himself, but apparently you didn't want to see him again 'too quickly,' was the way he put it." Green eyes twinkling, she strode to the sink and pumped disinfectant soap onto her hands.

Risa picked up the gift-wrapped box bearing a gold sticker emblazoned with the name of a local, high-end lingerie store. Her replacement negligee? She gulped. "Uh, thanks."

Kyla rinsed and dried her hands. "You're not getting off that easy. Open it."

"Um, later." When she was *alone*.

"No way. You two got it on last night—that package is evidence."

Risa's fingers stiffened on the box. The foil wrapping scrunched. "Did Eric say that?"

"Like he needed to. Aside from how nervous you've acted all day, you both look equally guilty and perversely pleased with yourselves. So either you bongoed like monkeys on speed last night, or I'll volunteer myself as food for the fat, mooching seals at Oak Bay Marina."

Risa carried the package to the counter and set it on a clear space near the trays of cooling, erotically-shaped chocolate lollipops she'd prepared for the party. Her gaze drifted over the box again. *Her new lingerie.* Her tummy spun.

"Okay," she admitted, glancing at Kyla, who'd followed her. "Something did happen."

"Excellent! I guess working on Dick inspired you, huh?"

"I wouldn't say that." *Eric* had inspired her. She hadn't been able to resist his passionate enthusiasm for her masked-intruder fantasy. In fact, he'd quite exceeded her expectations.

Her thighs warmed at the memory, her nipples perking up just enough to tease and embarrass her. Flaunting high-beams in front of her assistant wasn't high on her list of priorities, she didn't care how many chocolate erections and red-tinged lip suckers surrounded them.

"Then what would you say?" Kyla prompted.

"That something might happen again. But I'm not sure when. He's supposed to, um, surprise me."

"Sounds fun. Like a hook-up? Or a second stab at a relationship?"

"A hook-up." That was all her heart could handle. "We're gearing up for sayonara sex."

Kyla laughed. "Now I've heard everything." She patted the box. "Open it."

The bakery buzzer sounded.

"Crap. Marie needs help. Guess that's me." Walking backward, Kyla said to Risa, "I want to know what's in there." She pushed through the door to the front, leaving Risa alone with her mystery gift.

Risa glanced at the box, pulse racing. She lifted one corner of the scarlet wrapping, and her fingers trembled.

"Shit," she whispered. What was wrong with her? Eric had sent her a replacement for something he'd damaged, not an engagement ring. Her life—and his plans for them—wouldn't change. He wanted one last night together, and so did she. He might not have even bought her the gift if she hadn't practically demanded it.

Quickly, she tore off the paper, opened the box, and peeled back the tissue.

"Oh!" A beautiful set of frothy baby dolls in shades of ivory, pear-green, and soft rose peeked up at her. She drew out the sexy top then the panties. Yes, this new set more than made up for Eric slicing her lingerie to pieces, although she'd loved it when he'd done that, too.

A store envelope nestled beneath the baby dolls, on top of more tissue. After laying the lingerie on the upturned box lid, Risa lifted the envelope and extracted a note.

Eric's angular handwriting sprawled on the fancy cream card:

Sorry I ruined your sexy sleepwear... Okay, not really. Here's the replacement set, as promised. Hope you like them. Eric.

P.S. Don't explore this box any further unless you're prepared to fulfill my fantasy.

His fantasy? Risa turned the card over.

It was blank.

Eric! How could he tease her like this and expect her *not* to satisfy her curiosity?

He'd known she'd dig to the bottom of the box, the nefarious man. Therefore, she was under no obligation to accept his terms.

Grinning at her cleverness, she lifted the next layer of tissue. A lavender demi-bra similar to the one she'd designed for Lainey Fullbright's boob cake curled around a flimsy lace thong.

Risa picked up the thong, and her face flamed. Correction—crotchless panties! Classy-looking, exquisite, lace crotchless panties, but still! She laughed. He had to be kidding.

Another envelope. She set aside the panties and opened the flap. Another note:

Nothing would please me more than the thought of you wearing these Saturday night while you're working the party. I want to think of you dressed to seduce as I await our night.

Love, Eric

Risa snorted. *Love?* He might have as well have signed the note *lust*. Cripes, she could see herself now, sporting crotchless underwear beneath her set of the skimpy French maid uniforms Lainey had ordered for Risa and the female members of her catering staff, while Eric did hedonistic things to himself back at his apartment as he fantasized about her and probably every other woman present at the Fullbright mansion Saturday night.

The man was depraved. Delusional. Nuts.

She stuffed his ridiculous gift back into the box and slammed it shut.

Risa took Eric's gift home after work and plunked the box on her dresser. She'd shown Kyla the baby dolls, but had managed to keep the bra and panties secret. Thank God. Kyla would have laughed herself silly, then pestered Risa to prove her sexual daring to Eric by wearing the Crotchless Wonders to the party.

Which would never happen. Risa had a professional reputation to build, and she wouldn't accomplish her goal by airing her muff in public.

Besides, she could *tell* him she'd wear them, and then not.

She half-expected Eric to phone to ask what she thought of his gifts, but he didn't. Neither did he show up at her house in the middle of the night, nor at the bakery the next day. She squelched her annoying disappointment and concentrated on prepping for Lainey's party. The catering uniforms arrived Thursday, French maid outfits for the girls and shirtless tuxedos for the guys. After choosing the dress with the longest hemline, Risa stored the rest in her catering van for distribution to the others. Exhausted, she left work early, asking Kyla to call her for further preparations at the bakery following a relaxing home break for them both.

Now, the French maid outfit lay on her bed where she and Eric had screwed their brains out Tuesday night. Risa nibbled a thumbnail as she gazed at the sexy ensemble complete with black fishnet thigh-highs. Her passion for naughty lingerie aside, her style was pretty conservative. If she needed to tart herself up for the party in two days, she'd better get used to it now.

Her gaze drifted to the gift box on her dresser, and a smile tugged her mouth. She could test out her new underwear at the same time. Eric would never have to know.

Risa stripped and tried on the bra. A perfect fit. Except the demi cups scooped so low that her nipples perched on two indentations in the stiff lace evidently designed to promote omnipresent areola erections. *Lift and salute.* Her smile widened.

She dressed in the black maid outfit and examined her reflection in her full-length mirror. Not bad! The bra displayed her cleavage, but the uniform's frilly white bodice covered her nipples as well as if she were wearing a sports bra.

Forsaking the fishnets for her first foray into slut-dom, she pulled on the Crotchless Wonders and pushed her feet into her gardening sandals at the back door. It hadn't rained in days, and her flowers were parched. She'd water them before strutting around the yard for practice.

Remembering her cell, she went outside. The warm afternoon sun bathed her arms and legs as she tossed the phone onto a chaise patio lounge, found the spray hose, and began watering. The breeze riffled her skirt, sweeping into the opening in the Wonders and washing her exposed flesh with incredibly pleasurable sensations, much like when Eric puffed soft breaths over her labia, driving her crazy with need before he plunged his hot tongue inside her.

She closed her eyes. Heat pulsed between her legs, and her nipples jutted in the sexy maid get-up while her mind swarmed with fantasies of Eric rushing into the yard, grabbing her around the waist, and taking her right there on the lawn.

Bzz-t! Bzz-t!

Her cell phone, set to vibrate, bounced on the vinyl lounge cushion. She jumped, cold water spraying her legs as adrenaline spiked up her heart rate. She turned off the hose. Grabbing the phone, she glimpsing the caller ID for Bella Fortuna.

"What are you wearing?" Eric asked when she answered. Her body tingled with the lingering arousal of her daydream, and his voice sounded intensely sensual against her ear.

"How did you know to call my cell?"

"I phoned the bakery. Marie said you and Kyla each went home to catch up on a few things. In your case, that usually means gardening, and you always take your cell with you."

Was she that predictable? "Well, you're right."

"Are you digging in the dirt? I always loved watching you do that. And helping. We always had a great time when I helped."

Risa smiled. "That's because we usually wound up making love."

"In the hammock."

"Or on the lounge." The same one she stood beside. The sun-toasted cushion nudged her bare calf.

"Or on a blanket on the grass."

Risa curved an arm around her waist, remembering. Tall cedar shrubs lined her high fence, and forty-year-old maples created a canopy near the rear of the small yard, providing a private haven for two people in love. Like she and Eric back then.

Before she'd stupidly opened her mouth about her aging ovaries and scared him off.

Sadness sprouted in her chest, but she tamped it down. She was beyond wanting Eric in her life that way.

She *was*.

"But, no, I'm not digging," she said. "I'm watering the flowerbeds."

"Wearing what?" he asked again.

A grin played around her mouth. "Nothing special."

"Huh. Did you get my present?"

"Yes."

"Will you do it?"

She bit her bottom lip.

"Oh-oh. You're quiet. I take it that means you've decided *not* to fulfill my fantasy. Rees, you naughty girl, I fulfilled yours."

His low voice shimmied desire through her Eric-addicted body. She brushed an imaginary speck off her short skirt. "You won't be at the party, Eric. What difference does it make if I wear the bra and panties or not?"

"So I can think of you wearing them."

"So I can get distracted *thinking* about you thinking about me wearing them?"

He laughed so quietly her nipples puckered. "What *are* you wearing then?"

"You're not going to give up, are you?"

"Nope."

She let out an exasperated-sounding breath—pure fiction. Protest though she might, she loved his erotic playfulness and persistence. "If you must know, Lainey ordered sexy outfits for the catering staff. I'm trying to get used to parading around dressed like a slutty French maid."

"Tell me more."

Why not? He deserved the torture. She murmured, "I'm wearing the bra and panties with my new maid outfit, Eric. Nothing on my legs, not even pantyhose."

A heavy moan of masculine appreciation met her ear. "Your back yard is very private."

"Yes, it is."

"If the restaurant were closer to your neighborhood, I'd race over there."

Longing strummed in her veins. Regret ached in her heart. "Eric, this can't be our night. I'm meeting Kyla at the bakery again as soon as she calls."

"But you're alone now?"

"Yes."

"When do your neighbors get home?"

"I'm not sure. I think Betty works afternoons this week, and Mr. Stanford's car wasn't in his driveway when I got home. Why?"

"Well, here I am holed up in my office. I have a meeting with a vendor soon and can't leave, much as I'd love to. You're busy preparing for Saturday's party, too busy to come see me."

And make love on his desk or under the stars out on the restaurant terrace, like they had so many times during the months she'd worked as his pastry chef and the dining room had emptied of staff and customers for the night.

"Eric, we can't keep having sex until 'our night.' It's supposed to be *one* night, not two or three."

For a long moment, he didn't respond. Then, "Do me a favor."

"What?"

"Put down your watering can."

"It's a hose. And it's already off."

"Then sit on one of your lounge chairs."

"Why?"

"Sit on a damn chair, Risa. Lean back in it."

Shaking her head at his suddenly abrupt tone, she sank onto the nearest lounger, one knee raised and her free hand resting on the resin chair arm. Her skirt rode up, and the sun-warmed vinyl toasted the backs of her thighs. *Mmm.*

"Spread your legs," Eric murmured in a deep, rich voice. "Lift your skirt for me. I want to imagine you feeling the warmth of the sun on your pussy."

Her breath caught. Closing her eyes, she spread both knees and balanced them on the armrests. Her skirt hiked up further, exposing her labia and opening to the caressing motions of the slight breeze. Blood rushed south, and her clit swelled.

"Are you on the lounger?" he asked softly.

She opened her eyes. "Yes."

"Tell me how it feels."

"*Amazing.*" The breeze kissed her pussy lips through the opening in her underwear, teased her mound through the pattern of the lace. She lifted her hips slightly, and her arousal mounted. She let her sandals slip off. With the backs of her knees resting against the chair arms, the sun-warmed cushion heated the sides of her bare feet. She curled her toes. As she rocked her rear back and forth on the toasty vinyl, the magical sensations built deep inside her without her once having to touch herself. Just thinking of her incredibly sexy man and listening to his low, husky voice drove her insane.

"Oh, Eric, I can't wait for our night."

"You don't have to, if you do what I say. Here, Rees. Now."

The bodice of her uniform brushed her erect nipples held captive by the demi-bra. She smiled at his insinuation. "Am I about to have one-sided cell-phone sex?" she asked. Another lovers' game from their past she was happy to repeat... this last time.

"The lock on my office door needs replacing, so my guess is, fuck, yes. If you're up for it. Because I sure am. Only I can't do anything about it at the moment. But you can. You can satisfy me with your breathless little sounds, Rees, as you come."

His sexy words burrowed through her. "But I want your hands on me. I want to touch you."

"I want that, too, angel. For now, though, slide your fingers between your legs for me. Are they there?"

"Yes." She stroked a finger into her slippery pussy. *Mmm.*

"How do you feel?"

"Wet." Her eyes drifted shut as she stroked her fingers in and out. "Like warm velvet. Smooth and creamy."

His low groan rumbled against her ear. "Fuck, Rees, I'm hard as granite. That's what hearing you does to me."

She swept her hot juices over her clit. One touch, and she began soaring. "I don't think I can talk while I do this," she panted.

"You don't have to. Just let me hear you breathing. Angel, hearing your passionate noises when we're making love is the sexiest thing in the world."

She stroked her clit faster and faster. "I love fucking you, Eric."

"I love every move you make, Angel."

Angel.

"Do me another favor," he said.

"Anything." To keep him murmuring carnal words. Spurring her on.

"Put down the phone between your legs. I want to hear your fingers moving in and out of your pussy, over your clit. I want to imagine I'm fingering you when you come."

Risa moaned. At any other time, his request might have sounded ridiculous. However, right now, the raw eroticism of the images he described had her hips bucking against her hand.

She put the phone on speaker and lay it between her spread knees. Following his instructions, she rubbed her swollen clit.

His voice lifted quietly from the cushion, "Fuck, Rees, *yes,* I hear you. It's like I'm there with you, feeling your heat, your slick cunt. Like

I'm licking you, fucking you. I love it."

She gasped. Her orgasm shot down her spine, sweeping her limbs. She pushed her head back against the lounge chair as the exquisite waves flooded her and her pussy convulsed.

"Yes, Rees, yes, baby, keep it going. I love hearing you like this. I love—"

"Oh, my God," she cried.

The pounding in her ears drowned out his voice as she slammed her fingers inside her, picturing Eric's face over hers, ecstasy tightening his features as he came, their bodies slick, hearts beating in a unison she'd never experienced with any other man.

Only her man.

Only Eric.

Chapter 5

The things he did for Risa….

With a grimace at his reflection, Eric re-capped the shaving cream and exited the service-staff washroom off the massive, state-of-the-art kitchen in Elaine Fullbright's opulent party room. Ahem, make that party *floor*. From what he'd glimpsed in the twenty minutes since Kyla had admitted him through the deliveries area, the "party room" occupied the majority of the three-story mansion's basement. Raucous Seventies music and blurs of conversation drifted from the main gathering space, and wide hallways boasted alcoves filled with leafy plants, velvet-covered benches, and sculptures of nude couples in interesting positions. Marble and gold accents abounded. He'd noticed a door proclaiming an indoor swimming pool and sauna, too.

Must be nice. The indoor pool, at any rate. Admittedly, Eric knew zip about interior decorating. However, as much as he liked Lainey Fullbright and admired her business acumen, her over-the-top surroundings reminded him of a sex-starved bimbo with too much cash on her hands indulging her every whim.

He hung the bag containing his street clothes and personal effects in one of several small lockers outside the washroom, then entered the kitchen. After pushing through the milling catering staff of bare-chested guys and French-maid-uniformed women, he reached Kyla. He waited until she finished giving instructions to two waiters, then he tapped her shoulder.

She turned and grinned. "Hey, you clean up nice!"

He glanced down at his just-shaved chest. "My nipples look naked." Tight black pants constructed of a shiny fabric his torturer had called "sateen" straddled his pelvis. Stiff white shirt cuffs without benefit of sleeves banded his wrists, and a black bow-tie cinched his throat. "I feel like a prissy show dog."

Kyla chuckled. "Well, you look like a Chippendale's dancer." She poked his chest. "Nice pecs. Miss Fullbright's guests will love you."

He didn't give a rip about the guests. "As long as *Risa* appreciates it."

"How can she not? God, I'm glad you were home when I called. You're helping us out of a major bind, Eric. What's better, you'll get to see Risa tonight. Now you really owe me." Kyla's eyebrows wiggled.

"I know, I know. You want that date with Dante."

Her grin widened. "You got it."

Eric glanced around the kitchen. "Where is she?"

"Risa? In the butler's pantry, supervising the creation of the Sinful Sundaes. The banana 'heads' require last-minute carving, so they don't go soft."

Eric laughed.

"Good. That's what we want—a smile. You can worry about Risa later. For now, I need you to get to work." She picked up a serving platter from the stainless steel island and pushed it into his hands.

Eric gazed at the tray. "Ah, the chocolate penis suckers."

"The older women love them. But only when the guys deliver them." Kyla nudged his bare back. "Go."

Eric balanced the silver tray high on one hand like his father had taught him and turned toward the marble-floored hallway. He passed two senior citizens making out beneath a gilt-framed movie poster of *Lay Me in St. Louis*. Raising an eyebrow at the display, he strode into the humongous party room. He didn't get more than ten feet in when a group of well-preserved older women in sparkly evening dresses swarmed him. Several different perfumes billowed, stinging his nostrils. He struggled not to cough.

"Oh, look!" a curvy bleached-blonde exclaimed. "Fresh meat!"

Another blonde beamed. "And more chocolate cocks!"

A voluptuous redhead elbowed them. "Out of my way, you withered old hags. I missed this tray the last time through." Her ring-laden fingers darted toward Eric's abs.

He smiled. "Now, now, ladies, there's enough for everyone."

The women tittered. Lowering his tray, Eric reprimanded the redhead in husky tones, "No grabbing—me or the suckers."

She pouted. "Spoilsport."

He extended the tray, and she selected a lollipop. After the others had made their choices, he proceeded to the next group, where a slender blonde laughed gaily. Hey, was that Goldie?

He didn't get a chance to find out. Lainey Fullbright, sweeping past him on the arm of a heavyset gentleman, stopped dead in her tracks. She and her companion turned. "Eric? Darling, whatever are you doing here?"

Before he could reply, his swarm of admirers descended.

"We discovered him, Lainey." The redhead brandished her sucker.

"Oh, but I already know him. Eric has a delightful little Italian restaurant downtown, a few blocks from the harbor. Don't you remember, Viv? Bella Fortuna. We dined there when you visited last year."

Viv clapped a hand to her chest. Her ample breasts jiggled, navy dress sequins flashing. "Oh, yes, I loved that place. Your chocolate mousse is divine."

"The sweet girl catering my party tonight worked for Eric then," Lainey said.

"Risa was my pastry chef," he elaborated.

Eyes innocent, Viv stroked her tongue languidly over her lollipop. "She made my cock?"

The women laughed, and Lainey's gentleman friend shook his head and grinned.

"Viv, dear, you need to get out more often." Lainey flourished a hand at Eric, then gestured around the circle of women. "Eric, these are my friends from the old days. Viv Va-Voom, Glori-Asking-For-It, and Boom-Boom Barbie." She rubbed her male companion's shoulder. "And this is Fred Buckham, from Texas. You've heard of Buckham Oil?" She snuggled beneath the man's arm. "That's Fred."

Fred shook Eric's hand with a hearty hello and a welcoming smile. Nice guy.

Lainey patted Eric's bare forearm. "Don't tell me you had to take a second job? I hope there's no trouble at Bella Fortuna. Why, I'd be happy to invest in such a promising venture."

Eric chuckled. "Thanks, but there's no trouble. The restaurant is going great guns. A couple of Risa's waiters called in sick tonight, so when I heard she was short-staffed—"

"Well, we certainly can't say that about *you*," Viv remarked. Her bold gaze dropped to his crotch. "Honey, those slacks leave nothing to the imagination."

Her cohorts chortled, looking Eric up and down. *Way* down.

Shit, if Risa ogled him like that, he'd go hard in an instant.

"Uh, Eric?" The cautionary note in Lainey's voice diverted her friends' attention. "Does Risa know you're here?"

The back of his neck chilled. "Not yet. Why?" He hadn't seen or talked to her since their sexy phone escapade Thursday afternoon.

"She does now. By the doors. She's staring at you."

Eric glanced over his shoulder. Sure enough, Risa stood at the entrance to the party room, startled surprise widening her eyes and a tray of the Sinful Sundaes wobbling in her hands. Her sexy French maid outfit clung to her curves, displaying the creamy skin of her cleavage and accentuating her long legs. Her blonde hair framed her beautiful face in a frothy, fuck-me cloud.

Her eyebrows plunged, and all evidence of fuck-me vanished. "Get over here!" she mouthed, shoving her tray at another server.

"Looks like you're in trouble," Viv sing-songed.

Gloria snickered. "Maybe he'll get a spanking."

"Only if he's lucky!" Barbie chimed, and they all laughed.

Shit. Double shit. He hadn't wanted to blindside Risa like this.

He looked at Lainey. "The boss calls. Glad to meet you all. Next time you visit Bella Fortuna, dessert's on me." Winking, he handed Viv the tray of chocolate erections. "Enjoy."

"Oh, yum."

"Go get her, tiger," Barbie said as he turned.

"Don't let her 'sucker' you, now." Gloria giggled.

"Take your lickings like a man!"

Risa couldn't believe her eyes. Eric Lange, owner of one of the city's trendiest restaurants, half-dressed like her twenty-something waiters, and cavorting with the woman she desperately needed to impress tonight with her professionalism, hard work, and creativity—and flirting with that woman's former porn-movie pals?

What the man wouldn't do to surprise her!

She crossed her arms, which resulted in the unfortunate effect of thrusting up her breasts and deepening her cleavage in the French maid outfit. But, oh, she was pissed off.

As Eric neared her, he lifted a hand. "I can explain."

"You shaved your chest!" Her voice emerged more strident than she'd intended. Even with the Rolling Stones' old disco song *Beast of Burden* thumping throughout the large room, the heads of several guests turned, including that of a prominent local businessman.

Risa sucked in a breath. *Calm down. These are your future clients.*

"Kyla asked me to shave it," he said. "So I'd fit in with the young guys."

He looked incredible. The perfect combination of rugged handsomeness, lean muscle, and trim hips, in pants that showcased his, um, attributes in a manner that put her other waiters to shame.

Not that she *wanted* to notice.

She frowned. "Kyla?"

"She called me at the restaurant a little while ago. Said you'd lost two waiters to the flu." Eric pointed behind her. "There she is. In the hall. You can ask her."

Turning, Risa spied Kyla issuing instructions to another bare-chested waiter she didn't recognize.

"Follow me," she commanded Eric in hushed tones.

His footsteps echoed behind her on the gold-veined marble floor. Catching Kyla's eye, Risa crooked a finger, and her assistant sent Mystery Waiter into the party room with a tray of Saucy Little Tarts.

Risa pulled Kyla and the ex-love-of-her-life into an alcove featuring a giant blowup of *V* magazine's first cover.

"Shit, you found him," Kyla murmured. "I was hoping to get to you first."

"So you did call him?"

Kyla nodded. "I tried our regular backups, but no one was available on such short notice. Eric sprung to mind." Guilt flitted over her face. "Jeremy, too—the guy with the tarts. He's my new neighbor. You were so busy, I thought you'd appreciate my initiative."

"I do. But, Kyla, *Eric?*"

"What's wrong with Eric?"

Risa's face warmed. "Nothing." And therein lay the problem. With a lifetime of experience backing him up, professionally Eric was a welcome addition to tonight's catering staff. However, personally, his presence would unnerve her.

Worse, both he and Kyla knew it.

Kyla's gaze skipped down Risa's uniform. "Hey, I didn't notice before, did you add fabric to the hem of your skirt? I see a stitch line."

"Uh, maybe a couple of inches."

Kyla laughed. "More like three or four."

Eric studied her legs. "Your stockings look different than Kyla's and the other girls', too."

The skin of her inner thighs tingled. Risa shifted her weight to her other spiked heel. "No, they don't."

"Yes, they do!" Kyla smacked her arm. "The rest of us are wearing thigh-highs. The pattern of your fishnet is smaller than ours, and the tops of your legs don't show."

Risa planted a hand on her hip. "I'm in charge. I wanted to look more demure." If Kyla knew what she'd substituted the thigh-highs *with*, she'd die of humiliation.

Eric shook his head, his gaze hot and brimming with masculine appreciation. "Angel, you could strap on a chastity belt outside that get-up and still not look demure."

Her nipples tightened. Darn demi-bra.

"In fact, you'd look kind of wild," Kyla teased.

"All right, all right." Risa held up her hands. "Kyla, thank you for stepping up to the plate when we needed it. Only, next time, please pass the names by me first."

"Sure thing."

"And, Eric, I guess I should thank you, too."

"Yeah, you should. Bella Fortuna was packed when I left. But when you need me, honey, you know I'll jump."

She'd have him jumping from the electric jolting of a cattle prod if he wasn't careful.

"Thank you," she said in a voice that would have done Eva Braun proud. "Now get back to work. The sundaes are melting."

"Can't have those bananas going flaccid," Kyla chirped.

Risa ignored her. After glancing around to ensure no party guests mingled nearby, she instructed Eric, "Let Lainey's girlfriends ogle you all they want. When they do it to the young guys, it creeps me out. And plug Sweet Sensations whenever possible. Maybe we'll salvage some decent P.R. from this party yet."

Eric smiled. "Aw, Angel, you know the only woman I want ogling me is you."

Rolling her eyes, she turned and marched to the kitchen. Eric's mellow chuckle trailed her. Despite her irritation, a smile tweaked her lips.

If he knew what he was missing, he wouldn't let her out of his sight.

Over the next three hours, Eric worked his ass off delivering desserts and flirting with women older than his mother. He hadn't intended to become the party boy-toy for the post-menopausal set, however, as the booze flowed, Lainey's film career friends developed into his personal entourage, introducing him to their friends, who introduced him to theirs. He quickly discovered that the more time he spent charming the women, the easier it became to pimp Risa's catering division, which led to increased exposure for the bakery. Although he never did get a chance to scope out the Hollywood attendees, by the time his break arrived, he'd garnered several promises from wealthy locals to drop into Sweet Sensations and sample Risa's daily fare.

While on break, he dug his cell phone out of his locker and called his assistant manager at Bella Fortuna for a re-cap of the night's business. As he secured the locker again, he glimpsed Risa whirling around and practically running from the tiny room.

"Hey, Rees!"

High-tailing it, she glanced back. "I forgot to do something."

No kidding. Like, say, pay him one scrap of attention since their conversation with Kyla.

He bolted down the hall after her, in the opposite direction of the party room. She hurried around a corner.

"Rees!"

"I'm on my break!"

"Where are you going?"

"For a cigarette."

He laughed. "You don't smoke."

"Maybe I should start."

Taking the corner, he nearly collided with a wall of huge, leafy plants. "Risa?"

The leaves of the two largest plants rustled. Frowning, he parted their tangled branches to reveal a deep and very private alcove.

"It's like a jungle in here. What is this?"

Risa's back was to him as she used one of the keys dangling from her retractable wrist band to lock a small cabinet sunk into the black-painted wall to his left. Leopard-print hangings of various sizes draped all three walls. A zebra-striped bench flanked the rear wall, and water trickled over rocks in a small fountain atop a vine-shaped pedestal to his right. The same music playing in the party room drifted from concealed speakers, the female singer sounding orgasmic as she oohed and told her baby how much she loved to love him.

"Lainey told me about it." Facing him, Risa popped a hard candy she must have retrieved from the cabinet into her mouth. She set the wrapper on a built-in wall shelf, also painted black. The candy's berry flavor scented the air. "She said I could use it as my private break room."

God love that Lainey.

Stepping between the plants, Eric entered the hideaway. The leaves of the tropical plants rustled, once more forming a wall behind him.

Risa smoothed her uniform skirt. "What are you doing?"

"Pretending I'm taking up smoking. What are *you* doing?"

Her gaze skipped away. "Avoiding you."

"Why? Risa, all I've done tonight is try and help you."

"I know, but—Oh, if you must know, it's your chest." Her hand jerked.

Eric glanced down. "Well, it's not like I looked like an ape-man before, but, yeah, I'm not sure how I feel about the shaving, either."

She pushed back her hair from her temples in a gesture of frustration, unintentionally creating the slightly messy, just-been-loved look he adored. "I didn't say I didn't like it."

"Huh?"

She blew out a breath. "Maybe I like it too much."

He smiled. "Rees, if I'd known that, I would have shaved it while we were dating."

"No, I like the natural look, too. But this is different. Novel." Her hand lifted toward him. However, unlike when Viv Va-Voom had nearly stabbed his stomach with her dagger-like fingernails, he didn't mind. At *all*.

As if suddenly realizing what she'd done, Risa pulled back her hand.

Stepping closer, Eric clasped her hand and placed it, palm flat, against his bare chest. Her pinky finger grazed his right nipple, and it puckered.

The rhythm of her breathing tightened. She gazed at his chest with her mouth parted. "It feels smooth, but not effeminate, like how some of the guys at your gym look."

"That's right, we used to work out together there sometimes. I miss that." He raised her hand to his mouth and placed a tender kiss on her fingertips. "I miss you."

His chest literally ached with the love he felt for this woman. Two days ago, on the phone, when her passionate declaration of climax had reached his ears, he'd told her. *Idiot.*

Had she heard him? Believed him? Had he scared her off?

Her gaze met his. "Eric, I've been thinking…." Her voice shook.

"So have I. Thinking, dreaming, fantasizing about being inside you again." This time, he wouldn't screw up.

Her fingers twitched against his lips. While the singer's voice oohed over the speakers, he slid Risa's hand to his bare shoulder, murmuring, "Listen. She's enjoying herself."

Risa licked her lips. "Donna Summer."

He chuckled. "What?"

"The singer. It's Donna Summer. Lainey showed me her play list."

"Nice to know. But I was thinking more along the lines of how *you* sounded on the phone the other day, way sexier than Donna Summer. And now, your maid uniform. I imagined how hot you'd look wearing it, and I'm definitely not disappointed. You look amazing, Rees. You *are* amazing." He curved his hands around her waist, half-whispering, "Did you wear them?"

"I need to get back," she replied with an utter lack of conviction.

He unlatched her tiny cell phone clipped to her waist and transferred the gadget to the wall shelf. "Our break just started."

"I'm, um, not really scheduled for a break right now," she admitted in a soft voice.

"Well, you should be. You deserve one." As he brushed a kiss across her mouth, he tasted the rich, ripe flavor of spring berries. His throat tightened. "*Did you?*" he repeated, voice hoarse.

"Eric...."

"You want me to check, don't you? Naughty girl." Whipping her around so her gorgeous ass faced him, he slipped one hand beneath her altered skirt. "Oh, baby, you *did*."

Chapter 6

"Looks like you're not the only one capable of surprises," she murmured.

Eric's cock ached. From the lust spearing him head to toe. From the need to take her *now*, hard and fast, as she screamed her passion for anyone walking past their private hideaway to overhear. From the damn-fucking-too-tight stripper/waiter pants.

"No, I'm certainly not," he agreed. One arm wrapped around her waist, his hand still beneath her skirt, he pushed a finger into her pussy from behind and ran his thumb along the fancy lace opening of the crotchless panties framing her downy outer lips. Letting out a small gasp, she planted her hands on the wall shelf and pressed back against his hand. Her wetness lubed his finger.

"Someone might see us," she whispered.

"Not if we're quiet."

"I don't want to do this." Her eyes fluttered shut as she sighed.

"You sure about that?" Eric slid his finger out of her moist heat and up to her already swollen clit.

"Um." She crunched the berry-flavored candy. "Not really."

"That's my girl," he murmured. But he released her.

She turned, blue gaze yearning, her dewy mouth parted. "Want to see?" she whispered, vulnerability softening her voice and features.

"Oh, yeah," he returned in equally hushed tones.

A sultry smile tipped her mouth. "Sit on the bench."

His dick practically saluted. He backed up to the zebra-striped bench, tried sitting—and winced. "Can't. Not in these pants when I have a monster erection."

Her eyes growing heavy-lidded, she stepped away from the wall of tropical plants, deeper into the alcove. Slowly, with her back to the dense leaves, she lifted her skirt. However, before he caught more than a glimpse of her stocking tops, she lowered the skirt again.

"It's okay," he murmured. "No one can see us through those plants. I wouldn't have known you were in here if I hadn't run after you."

She glanced over her shoulder, her golden hair flowing with her movements. Her breasts rose as she drew in a breath, and the frilly white front of her French-maid outfit expanded, displaying her magnificent cleavage. Then she looked at him again, and, gathering her skirt in both hands, hoisted it up, exposing herself from the waist down.

A groan escaped him. "You're beautiful." He strove to keep his voice quiet, but it was damn difficult when the sight of her made him want to growl. The black, mini-skirt-like garter belt he'd given her when they were a couple barely covered his latest, and perhaps last, gift. "Is that why you added fabric to your skirt? So you could wear the panties?"

"And not feel like the madam of the Slut-Whore Catering Company?" She nodded.

He smiled. "That's why you wore the garter belt, too. To cover yourself better."

She inhaled deeply, eyes closing for a moment. "Yes. I had to buy new stockings. The fishnets that came with the uniforms didn't reach to the garters."

"I like it." He waved a hand. "Turn around."

With the skirt bunched at her waist, she turned slowly on her spiked heels.

"Bend forward a little."

She hesitated.

"Please."

Her back tensed as she held her breath. Another moment later, she bowed forward as if she were dusting a priceless vase in a parlor. Her pussy peeked through the gap in her panties.

Eric moaned quietly. "More."

She parted her legs. Her ass lifted higher, revealing her dusky-pink inner lips.

He rubbed his erection through his pants. Just once. "God, Rees, I'd love to fuck you."

"You'd have to be quick," she whispered, completely surprising him.

"You mean it?" He unzipped his pants, nearly tearing off the button.

The slacks were so tight, he hadn't worn briefs, and his cock leapt from the slippery confines of the shiny fabric.

Straightening, she faced him, and her skirt dropped to cover her again. "Can you sit down?" she whispered.

"Hell, yes." He yanked his pants to his knees and sat on the bench, cock straining.

"Crap," she murmured in a voice as tender as if she'd said she loved him. "Do you have a condom?"

Fuck! His jaw clenched. "No."

A mischievous smile curved her mouth. "Aw."

Eric chuckled. "Tease."

She stepped toward him. "We can't do it without one. My uniform would get messy."

He nodded, realizing that she meant after they finished and he pulled out.

She sank onto her knees on the hard—and no doubt cold and uncomfortable—floor. Her hand hovered inches from his stiff cock, her mouth not much farther.

"I wonder what we could do instead?"

"You could suck me," he murmured.

"Hmm, there's an idea." She ran her hand along his upper thigh.

His nuts almost climbed inside himself with the need to feel her hot mouth on him. From this vantage point, him sitting, her kneeling, he glimpsed her tits beneath her uniform top. The shape of her bra exposed her rigid nipples. He'd love to taste them.

"You wore the bra, too. *Rees.*"

As her hand curled around his cock, she smiled. "I figured, in for an inch, in for nine."

"Well, maybe not nine."

Her gaze swept his cock. "Okay, eight-and-a-half." Stroking him, she lowered her head. Her thick blonde hair fell forward, grazing his thighs, and her candy-slick mouth closed over the swollen tip of his dick. His breath whistled out through his teeth.

"Shh," she whispered before firming her lips around him.

Her tongue and hands worked quickly, and the thrill of discovery with her on her knees when only he knew what secrets lay beneath her skirt drove his excitement higher as she licked and sucked. Faster and faster. Squeezing, releasing. Teeth grazing, tongue soothing. The Donna Summer orgasm-fest ended, and the rhythm of an old Barry White song he had no trouble identifying with filled his ears. *Can't Get Enough of Your Love, Babe.*

Closing his eyes and weaving his fingers through her hair, Eric leaned back his head. He couldn't possibly get enough, never would get enough of Risa. Her smile brightened his day, her intelligence challenged him, her friendship and belief in him bolstered him.

He pumped his hips, increasing the friction of her hand and mouth. Suddenly, she pulled away. His eyes snapped open, his vision unfocused. "Wha—?"

She'd stood and grabbed her cell from the shelf. She pressed a finger to her lips as her gaze pleaded with him to stay quiet. Drunken voices carried from the hall, muffling the water rippling in the small fountain. Barry White continued his serenade—surely they were safe. Eric would curse himself to hell and back if his need for her compromised her authority with her staff or ruined her chances to promote Sweet Sensations.

Rising silently, he stuffed his woody into his pants. A guy in the hall guffawed at another guy's stupid joke. Erection deflating, Eric zipped up.

The concern creasing Risa's forehead spoke volumes.

"Don't worry," he mouthed, wiggling his fingers at her to pass him the phone.

She did, mouthing back, "I have to go."

Nodding, he scanned the text message:

Whr r u? Client wnts Dick.

Risa and Kyla's nickname for Lainey's birthday cake.

Sez she wnts 2 blow him out.

A grin tugged his mouth. When he glanced up, Risa rolled her eyes, but her lips twitched.

He released a breath. For a second, he'd thought she regretted what they'd done.

He held up a hand. They stood motionless until the boisterous partiers continued in the direction of the pool and sauna room.

Lowering his hand, he whispered, "I think we're safe."

Worry shadowed her gaze. "Can you check?"

He nodded. After handing her the cell, he stepped out between the plants and peeked both directions. "All's clear," he whispered over his shoulder.

Risa exited the alcove, her key bracelet on her wrist again. She crunched another berry candy—eradicating the taste of him from her mouth?

"Visit a bathroom or something," she murmured. "Just don't come with me. If anyone finds out...."

"They won't."

"Just do what I ask, Eric." Irritation sharpened her tone.

"Hey, what's with the attitude?" he whispered.

"We nearly got caught."

"We were nowhere close to getting caught."

"We were close enough." She glanced around. Their portion of the hall remained clear. Hands stiffening, she stepped away. "I'm sorry, Eric, but you bring out a side of me I'm not too happy about. Keep your distance for the rest of the night, okay?"

"Whatever you say, boss." He turned toward the pool room.

"Where are you going?"

"To see if our drunk guests need something." Like rescuing from steaming themselves into lobsters. Another server had informed him that the pool was locked for safety, but the sauna featured a separate entrance once inside the main doors.

"All right, but hurry back to Lainey's girlfriends. They love you."

Wasn't that the truth?

Eric's lips thinned.

At least someone did.

Risa operated on an overabundance of nervous energy for the rest of the night, focusing on nothing but supervising her staff and networking for Sweet Sensations. She rarely saw Eric. He would try to catch her eye, but she would look away, embarrassment—and excitement—brimming when she thought about what they'd done. The sight of him in that damn waiter's outfit had eliminated what little common sense she possessed these days. Never mind that an aura of campy sexual titillation hovered over the party, because if they *had* gotten caught, her reputation as a serious businesswoman would lie in ruins right now. What had she been thinking?

As one a.m. approached and the party petered out, she released most of her staff. Those remaining attacked cleanup with fervor, aside from Eric, who'd disappeared.

Kyla noticed the tension between them. "What's up with you and Eric?" she asked while helping Risa load the catering van in the small pool of light at the rear doors of the mansion.

The ocean breeze fluttered Risa's hair into her eyes. She brushed away the strands and concentrated on adjusting a stack of plastic supply boxes. "Nothing."

Kyla eyed her. "Well, remember he only came here tonight because I asked him to. And he's been a great help. He really cares about you, Risa."

"Does he?" Or did he get off on how easily she lost her head around him? Thursday in her back yard, tonight in the alcove, last Tuesday in her bedroom. At the rate they were going, their "one night" would last fifty years.

Dusting off her hands, she changed the subject. "Are you heading home?"

"Are you kidding? Lainey said we could keep the uniforms, so we stragglers are meeting the others at the clubs before they close. Hey, do you want to come? You could bring Eric."

"Thanks, but I shouldn't." God only knew what trouble she'd get into bumping and grinding with the man on a crowded dance floor. "You guys have fun." She closed the van doors.

"Aw, Risa, you never know where a night of letting loose might lead. Live a little."

Risa arched her eyebrows. That was the problem. She'd been living it up *too* much. If she didn't watch out, her heart would pay the price. Already, her feelings for Eric felt dangerously close to re-morphing into love. "We'll see."

"Do more than 'see.' Go for it! Have you hooked up with him again?"

"Not yet."

"Maybe you will tonight." Kyla's eyebrows wiggled.

"I don't know," Risa said as they re-entered the mansion. For days now, she'd considered kiboshing the whole sayonara-sex thing. Because, honestly, what was the point? She needed to get her crap together and decide what she *really* wanted. More erotic fun with Eric? Or the chance to move on and eventually find a man who shared her dreams of a home and children? "I need to check the kitchen. Make sure we packed everything."

"Sounds good. I'll see if my clubbing pals have left—" Kyla stopped short. "Shit, can I have your keys? I forgot mine in the van."

Risa glanced at her. "You did?"

Kyla nodded, slapping her forehead. "I put them on the passenger seat before we began piling in the stuff. Sorry! I'm such a bonehead."

"That's okay." Risa passed her the key bracelet. "I'll check the party room first."

"Great. I'll find you." Kyla scampered out the doors.

Risa headed for the main gathering space, then thought better of it and detoured to the kitchen, which passed her inspection. A cleaning service would scour the mansion's lower floor tomorrow and Monday, but it wasn't in her to leave the place a mess.

In the hall again, she turned toward the party room. The absence of voices and music hung heavily in the air, and the tapping of her heels echoed on the marble floor. Behind her, the delivery doors clanged open and shut. Expecting Kyla, she glanced back. Instead, Eric strode toward her, past the pool room and their secret alcove. Risa's heart tripped. The sateen pants practically shrink-wrapped his hips, drawing her gaze to his impressive bulge. Her fingers itched to smooth her hands over his shaved chest, to unbutton his slacks and finish what they'd started.

"Good, you haven't left yet," he said as he reached her. "We need to talk."

"I know." Damn it, he was so handsome—and a genuinely nice guy. Easy to talk to and joke with, always willing to lend her a hand, miraculously appearing when she needed him most. Not just tonight, but so many other times in their past, offering advice, lively discussions, and good, healthy, *non*-sexual fun and laughter.

She'd miss him. Both in her bed and out of it.

"Is anyone else still here?" he asked.

"I don't think so. We'd hear them in this silence."

He nodded. "Rees, what we did tonight, you wanted it as much as I did."

She sighed and crossed her arms. "I know that, too."

"Then why give me the evil eye the rest of the party? Kyla noticed. So did Lainey's friend, Viv. She had too much to drink and started blabbing about recruiting other guests to encourage us to make up. I had to agree to escort her back to her hotel to get her to shut up. She had the limo service driver take the scenic route. It was a nightmare."

So that was where he'd gone. Risa curled her hair behind an ear. "Eric, thank you. I promise we'll talk, but not tonight. Kyla's returning any second with my keys, and I just want to lock up and go home."

His head tipped. "Kyla's not coming back."

"Yes, she is. Didn't you see her?"

He nodded. "She just left."

"In her car?" Risa frowned.

"No, the van. She said that Jeremy guy borrowed her car, so if I could drive you home, she'd park the van at her building for the night and catch a ride from another friend to the clubs."

Risa's jaw dropped. "Well, thanks for consulting me! She has my keys!"

"Rees, you keep a spare under that pot of bright red flowers on your walk way."

The key he'd used to "break into" her house Tuesday night and screw her senseless. She hadn't thought straight since.

"Not *my* keys—Lainey's. To this floor. Kyla and I were the only ones here tonight with sets." Risa swept her hands over her suddenly hot face. "Kyla said hers were in the van, so she took mine to get them. Damn it, I can't lock the deadbolts without them. I'll kill her!"

Risa marched to the doors. Eric's voice trailed her. "It's no use. She's gone."

Risa whirled around. "Isn't that hunky-dory? Eric, Lainey gave her regular household staff the weekend off, and two hours ago she and Fred Buckham flew to Hawaii on his private jet. The rest of the house is secure, but I'm responsible for this floor."

He spread his hands. "Call her security service. She must have left the number."

"No way. They'll alert her, and then she'll think I'm brain dead."

"Everyone makes mistakes, Rees." Looking far too accepting of that idea, he strolled toward her.

"But I don't like to admit mine! That's what Kyla's banking on."

"Huh?"

Risa whipped her cell phone off the Velcro loop at her waist and speed-dialed the demon she called a friend. Kyla's cheerful message immediately transferred her to voice-mail.

Gritting her teeth, Risa slapped shut the cell. "She's not answering."

"Leave a message."

"Like that would help. Kyla's a smart girl. She knows what she's doing."

Eric turned up his hands. "Which is?"

"Trapping me in this house all night with you."

Chapter 7

Eric shifted his weight to his other foot. "Oops."

"*Oops?*" Risa's gaze narrowed. "Eric, you didn't have anything to do with this, did you?"

"After your reaction to almost *not* getting caught in the alcove? Not a chance." Although, he had to admit, Kyla's screw-up amounted to one hell of a creative surprise.

"Then what's with the 'oops?'" Annoyance rode off her in waves.

"Um, Kyla and I have—I guess you could say we sort of have a deal."

Risa jammed her hands on her hips. Her cell phone snagged the skirt of her sexy outfit, and the hem bounced. Unfortunately, not high enough to expose her garter and panties.

"What deal?" Her voice echoed off the wide hallway walls.

"That she'd talk me up to you if I got her a date with Dante."

"Dante?"

"My new chef. Making off with your keys must be Kyla's way of thinking she's helping me out." Shit, he'd better get his ass in gear and score her that date.

Risa flung up her hands. "I feel like I'm in high school!"

He laughed. "Not to be blunt, but you're acting like it, too."

She glared at him. "Thanks a lot. I've been working like a dog all week, and now, because of your deal with Kyla, I'm stuck here with you and your shaved chest!"

Eric swallowed a chuckle. Stepping to within a few inches of her, he brushed her arm. "Technically, you haven't been working *all* week. We've played a lot as well." A light blush kissed her cheeks. He skated his hand down her arm and dislodged the cell from her grip. "Call Kyla again. Leave a message this time. Tell her how unhappy you are.

Eventually, she'll call back. Meanwhile, I can think of countless ways to pass the time."

Her eyes closed. "You're trying to seduce me *now?*"

"Mm-hm."

Her eyes flew back open. "Eric, you're free to leave. I don't need a babysitter."

"Now you're making me sound like a pervert. I babysat my cousins all the time when I was a teenager, and I never once tried to seduce any of them."

The barest hint of a smile curved her lips. "I'm serious. You can go."

He flipped open her cell. "All right. What club did Kyla mention? If she doesn't answer her phone, I'll track her down."

Risa shook her head. "She didn't say."

"Well, there can't be more than a dozen of them. Or, if you insist on playing security guard, I could hang around, help you get comfortable." Sucking in his abs, he reached into the waistband of his pants and extracted a key from an inside pocket. Dangling the key at her, he winked. "Come on, Rees, aren't you the least bit curious to find out why Viv gave this to me?"

❧⟨✿⟩❧

She was hopeless. Utterly spineless when it came to resisting Eric Lange. She could have said, "Nope, not curious at all," and sent him on a goose chase after Kyla before collapsing in one of the wing-backed chairs placed throughout the hallway, where she could have stayed comatose until her assistant returned or the Sunday cleaning crew—equipped with their own keys—discovered her. But, no, instead she'd succumbed to Eric's bait, leaving a terse message on Kyla's cell, locking the delivery doors from inside, then following him to the party room, gaze glued to his muscular butt, which she knew from experience was *very* bite-able. Gently, of course. More of a nibble, really.

Agh! She whipped her gaze to his naked shoulders, but the view remained as aggravatingly divine.

"Eric, I'm exhausted. Tell me that key leads to a bedroom, or you're fired."

He chuckled. "You can't fire me. I'm your partner."

"*Silent* partner."

"Tut-tut, Rees, if you're not gonna be nice, why should I show you the bed?"

She blinked. "There's a bed?"

He nodded. "There's more than one."

"Where?" She glanced around the dimly lit room. Posters of Lainey's movies and *V* magazine covers competed for wall space with the campy decorations Viv Va-Voom and Lainey's other acting biddies had supplied. A couple of wing-backed chairs and several velvet-covered benches clustered the east wall on either side of the wet bar, but not one bed beckoned.

"Over here." Eric led her to the far side of the bar. An inflatable penis stuck out of the wall—she hadn't noticed the novelty when partiers packed the room. And damn it if Eric didn't point out a hidden door camouflaged with the same ivory paint used throughout the floor.

Risa yanked off the penis, revealing a shiny brass doorknob. "Try the key," she half-whispered, feeling like a trespasser.

"I already know the key works." Eric unlocked the door and pushed it open.

"How?" She tossed the penis onto the bar.

"Viv wanted to show me the rooms. Lainey gave her a key years ago."

Rooms? As in plural? "And now Viv wants you to have it?"

He shook his head. "She asked me to stuff it back into her bra. Giving her a thrill by tucking it in my pants instead seemed a wiser option."

"Ew. The bra thing, not your pants."

Eric laughed. "Tell me about it. Then, when we reached her hotel, she created such a commotion about kissing me goodbye that I forgot to give it back."

Risa's stomach soured. "You kissed her?"

"Don't worry, she wanted me to pucker up, but I only let her kiss my cheek."

"I'm not worried."

"Funny, you look it." Palming the key, he shepherded her into a short hallway with two doors on either side.

Holy crap, he *had* meant plural. "Was Lainey running a brothel in here?"

He laughed again. "As far as I know, not for profit."

"Oh, for charity?"

Chuckling, he opened the first door on the right. "Three bedrooms and one bathroom. In case, during one of Lainey's wild parties, anyone feels the need to spread the love."

"*Ewww.*" But curiosity had her slipping into the small bedroom decorated in an Arabian Nights theme. A round bed covered with a satin spread in an ornate pattern of gold, ivory, and scarlet crowded one corner. Several satin pillows in vivid jewel colors formed a soft headboard, a dark walnut dresser flanked the nearest wall, and a glass-topped nightstand on an elephant-shaped base boasted a scarlet bowl of condoms. *Naturally.*

"It's not vulgar when you think about it." Eric placed the key on the dresser, then sat on the bed and bounced the mattress as if testing its firmness. "Each bed gets fresh sheets before every party, and more are in the dressers along with freshly laundered costumes. There's a hamper and loads of towels in the bathroom. It's like a mini, luxury theme hotel. Unused tonight, by the way, aside from Viv's private tour."

Risa snickered. "I'm sure she showed it to you because of its real estate value."

A grin split his face. "No, you're right, she wanted me. How could she not?" Clearly mocking the concept, he sprawled on the bed with one knee raised like a *V* centerfold model.

His bulge appeared to inflate. Risa's nipples tightened, and her muff warmed. Because her ridiculous underwear continually allowed little rushes of air to caress her flesh beneath her uniform, her labia tingled with arousal.

"Want to check out the other rooms?"

Risa ripped her gaze from his crotch. Had he caught her staring? "What are the themes?"

"Seventies kitsch—complete with a waterbed. The third I can only describe as Valentine's Day Gone Berserk."

She shook her head. "This room is fine. Are there robes in the bathroom?"

"I counted half a dozen."

"Good." She'd sleep in slave-girl satin after a wonderfully long hot shower. "I'll take this room. If you want to stay, you can have one of the others. Oh, and I'll leave another message for Kyla, so she knows where to find us."

Eric grinned. "You're thinking all wrong." He patted the bed. "Come, sit by me."

"Why?"

"Angel, how we can waste this opportunity? This is our night."

Eric had never met a woman so determined *not* to have a good time. "Risa, it's perfect," he said from outside the bathroom. "A fantasy setting. We can really let go."

Shuffling noises that sounded an awful lot like pacing filtered through the door. When she didn't reply, a vague sense of insult sifted through him. A few hours ago, she'd enthusiastically given him a blowjob just off the main hallway. Now, his sexy inspiration to get them through the rest of a long night met with her sudden need to hide in the can.

"This can't be our night," she finally answered, uncertainty threading her tone.

"Sure it can. The party's over. Isn't that what you wanted? To get your business out of the way so we could screw like bunnies?"

"Maybe I've re-thought things. Maybe I want something else now."

Leaning against the door, he smiled. "Hey, if you're not into sayonara sex, neither am I. I'd love to start dating you again, you know that." Hell, he wanted more than dating. How many times over the last three months had he tried talking to her about his hopes for their future? A billion?

Every single time, she'd shot him down.

The pacing noises ceased. "Give me a second," she said.

"Then I can come in?"

"No. Um, wait in the bedroom. I have something to say, but I need to think first. I'll be there in a minute." Her voice sounded strange.

"Okay." Frowning, Eric returned to the Arabian Nights room. He took off his shoes and the chokehold bowtie, then sat on the bed. Several minutes passed. Shaking his head, he padded in sock-clad feet to outside the bathroom again. Risa's pacing noises had resumed.

"Risa?"

"I said one second!"

He gawked. "What the hell is going on?"

The door whipped open. A stricken expression pinched her face. "I lose my head around you. You ask me to wear crotchless underwear to a professional function—"

"A damn *casual* professional function."

"—and I do. You follow me into the jungle alcove, and next thing I know I'm so horny for you, I could scream."

He lifted his eyebrows. "That's a problem?"

"Yes. It is. Because this whole 'one night' thing is a joke. We could screw for hours, and next time you came into the bakery I'd want you all over again."

He smiled. "Like I said, that's a problem?'

She shouldered past him into the hall. "Yes, it is, for me. I can't keep having sex with you, Eric. If we do this tonight, you have to understand, there's no screwing around."

"This *can't* be our night if we *don't* screw around, Rees," he teased in an attempt to eradicate her foul mood.

"You know what I mean. Afterward." She crossed the hall to the Arabian Nights room.

"So you *do* want sayonara sex?"

She turned in the doorway. "I want—I *need* more than goodbye sex with you, Eric. I need to really say goodbye."

His chest caved as if he'd been struck with a wrecking ball.

"I want to buy your share of Sweet Sensations," she continued as a vice grip clamped his heart. "I've thought about this for days, and there's no other option. When you're around, I do things I shouldn't. Now that we're having sex again, it's getting worse. This last week—ah, these last five days—nothing I do makes sense anymore."

"Angel, preparing for this party has put you under a lot of stress."

She shook her head. "Stress I could handle if I were sole owner. If I didn't feel like I'm indebted to you, Eric."

He touched her arm. "You're not."

"Yes, I am. I couldn't have built the business without you. Without your faith and your financial support, I wouldn't have even gotten it off the ground. But now, with the contacts I've made through Lainey and the way the bakery has blossomed over the last year, I don't need your backing anymore. In all honesty, I haven't for months." She looked away.

"But you didn't want to say goodbye before now?" Acid chewed his stomach.

She looked at him. Nodded. "I know it's not fair to you, and I'm sorry. I should have realized our messing around would come to no good."

"Risa, honey, don't say that."

Pain filled her beautiful blue eyes. "It's true. Eric, I want this last night with you. I do. I want to remember everything we've shared. But then you have to agree to stay out of my life. No more dropping into the bakery whenever the spirit moves you. No more tempting me to have sex in public places, for God's sake. No more *all* of it."

He stared at her, disbelief congealing in his veins. A break? Yeah, he could see that. Selling her his share of the biz—okay, she needed to be her own boss. But curtailing all contact? Decimating their friendship? How could she think either of them would survive that?

"So this really is goodbye," he murmured.

"Yes," she whispered. "I'm sorry."

He drew in a breath, lowered his head to hers. "Then we're not going to screw, Rees. We're making love."

Chapter 8

Risa felt glued to the spot as Eric's mouth met hers and his hand curved around the back of her neck, fingers twisting in her hair. Intense need and desire and a bittersweet yearning swelled within her. She loved him. Oh, *how* she loved him. But it wasn't healthy love. It swallowed her whole. Even after a year without them making love, their dalliances of this last week had consumed her all over again.

A passionate whimper rose in her throat. His hand swept from her neck to her jaw, skipping over her diamond stud earring before he cupped her face with both hands, lips moving tenderly on her mouth, demanding nothing, offering everything... honest emotion, heart-stirring sensations, a timeless soul-connection... incredibly tempting and dangerous to her peace of mind.

But she couldn't pull away. She needed him closer.

She wrapped her arms around his naked shoulders, squeezing him tight. Her nipples hardened against the frilly bodice of her uniform, and the heat of his bare chest seeped through the fabric, arousing her further. He must have removed his shoes and bowtie while she hid in the bathroom agonizing over what to say to him. However, his shirt cuffs remained on his wrists, grazing her chin as his hands continued to hold her face captive.

His tongue flicked along her lips, and she parted her mouth. His kiss was slow and languid, as if he were branding this memory in his mind forever.

As she was.

Another rush of need crested, and the kiss deepened. Risa clutched at him, whispering, "Eric, the bed," but he surprised her by walking her backward until they stood in the hall again.

His hands ran down to her waist, then her bottom. Breaking the kiss, he lifted her into his arms and turned to the second door on the right.

"Seventies kitsch?" Risa murmured. She had no desire to make love on a sloshing waterbed, but right now she'd be hard-pressed to deny him anything.

He shook his head. "Valentine's Day Gone Berserk." He lowered a hand to the doorknob. She tilted in his arms, and he released the knob to cradle her again. "Can you open the door?"

Nodding, she reached down and turned the knob. Eric pushed open the door with his hip. As he carried her into the small room, she snuggled deeper against his chest. No other guy had ever attempted to carry her over a threshold. The romance of the moment knocked flat any lingering reluctance.

She gazed around the room at the white lacquer dresser and nightstand, and a heart-shaped bed with mountains of white satin heart pillows clustered at the top. Cupid-infested wallpaper assaulted her vision, and giggles bubbled inside her. "Now I know what you meant by berserk."

Eric laid her on the quilted, red satin bed cover. "I know it's corny, but I'm corny over *you*. I love you, Risa. I thought that would change after we broke up, but it hasn't."

Hot tears pricked her eyes. "Oh, Eric."

He lifted a hand. "I won't say it again. I know you don't believe me. But this room—corny as it is—*this* is how I feel about you. I'd gladly make a fool of myself for you, Angel."

Her throat tightened. She didn't know what to say.

Leaving her on the bed, he selected a black felt pen out of a tray next to the condom bowl and fat red cherub lamp adorning the nightstand. For the first time, she noticed the felt hearts and initials drawn on the dresser.

Eric knelt in front of the middle drawer on the right. Glancing back, he said, "Don't say no. Let me have this."

Throat cramming with emotion, she nodded.

He uncapped the marker, and the tangy scent of felt ink saturated the air as the pen squeaked over an empty space on the white lacquer. *E.L + R.H.* After hesitating a couple of seconds, he wrote beneath their initials, *Forever.*

Risa's heart fluttered.

He rose and set the marker on the dresser, then chose a spray bottle from an assortment and squirted the contents around the room.

The sickly-sweet scent of cotton candy infiltrated the small space. Eric's face screwed up. "Shit, I thought roses, maybe cinnamon."

Risa laughed. "I love it." *I love you.*

She'd never tell him. She couldn't risk getting sucked into his world again only to suffer the inevitable pain and heartache when he realized he wasn't ready to settle down. That he might never be.

Instead, she swung her legs over the curved side of the bed and kicked off her spiked heels. "I want to make love with you, Eric."

She stood. Less than four feet separated them, and he quickly crossed the distance while she detached her cell from her waist and set it on the nightstand.

As she strained to reach her back zipper, he shook his head, murmuring, "Let me."

She nodded. The scent of aloe shaving cream lingered on his chest, and she savored the clean aroma mingling with his masculine essence and the ultra-sweet air freshener while she smoothed her hands over his well-defined pecs. The pounding of his heart reverberating loudly beneath her palms, he reached behind her and easily unzipped her uniform. He pushed the bodice off her shoulders with exquisite slowness, revealing the demi-bra showcasing her erect nipples.

His gaze flew over her breasts, and she shivered with a fresh burst of desire.

His gaze returned to hers. He stripped off her uniform until it pooled at her feet. She stepped out of the garment and toed it aside, her bra, garter belt, panties, and fishnet stockings her only remaining clothing.

"You look like a goddess," he whispered.

She smiled. "You're the only man I would ever wear crotchless underwear for. They make me feel depraved and more than a little silly."

He chuckled. "Angel, on you, they're so sexy."

"Believe what you will," she teased as she undid the buttons on his shirt cuffs and tossed the novelties onto her crumpled uniform. Their foreplay in the jungle alcove had alerted her that he wasn't wearing underwear, but now the outline of his long, stiff cock beneath the shiny waiter pants proclaimed again that undeniable and very delicious fact.

"That can't be comfortable," Risa murmured, unbuttoning the pants and carefully sliding down the zipper. He drew in a breath, eyes closing briefly, and she grinned.

As she peeled off the pants, his erection emerged to stand against his stomach. Reaching his feet, she instructed him to step out of each pants leg before she tugged off his socks.

Her heart raced. She finally had him where she'd wanted him for twelve long, lonely months—completely naked. An erotic feast for her eyes and hands and lips.

Kneeling at his feet, she glanced up to catch him watching her with a hooded gaze. His hands tangled in her hair again, making her feel desirable. And wanted. Again, his eyes closed, and she caressed his strong legs and the backs of his thighs as his coarse leg hair tickled her palms. When her hands neared his erection, his tensing leg muscles betrayed his need.

Smiling, she fondled his balls and they constricted in her palms. Slid her fingers up the length of his warm cock, massaged the hollow beneath the swollen head with her thumb, relished the play of sensuality on his handsome face as her strokes grew bolder and his hips pumped.

He groaned, eyes opening. "It's time to undress you, Risa."

She shook her head. "We have unfinished business."

Still on her knees, she gripped his cock and slurped the head into her mouth. Thrust her hand up and down, then took him into her throat as deep as she could, loving his hot, salty taste. His moan sounded like it climbed up from his balls, and her excitement drove higher.

He urged her lips off him, gasping with raw pleasure when she sucked hard on the tip before letting it pop from her mouth.

"I love what you're doing, baby, but I need more." He coaxed her off her knees. The bed bumped the backs of her legs as she stood.

He cradled her face and gazed into her eyes, his blue irises expanding as the inky pupils zeroed in on her soul. He kissed her oh-so-gently. Then again, with pure carnal want.

Oh, she loved how he combed his fingers through her hair. The waves fluffed over her naked shoulders and instigated a rush of speckling sensation along her skin. Her pussy ached for his touch, the lace of the opening in her panties against her flesh escalating the gotta-have-it intensity building inside her. Desire had her slick and ready, clit budding and pulsing, breasts heavy. While his tongue tangled with hers and she massaged his penis with a lighter touch, he rubbed her exposed nipples with his thumbs, and need sailed through her body.

Lowering his head, he sucked one nipple, and his lips collided with the rigid bra cup. He unclasped the bra and removed it. Immediately, his gaze dropped to the slight red chafing beneath her nipples.

"Fuck, Rees, I'm sorry. I didn't realize the bra would hurt you."

She shook her head. "It doesn't feel bad. A little sore maybe, but worth it to see the look on your face when you realized I'd worn my new lingerie tonight."

"Well, I feel awful."

His erection stirred against her belly, and she grinned. "I can tell."

"I'm gonna make it up to you."

His heated gaze assured her that he meant in a most sensual manner. She wriggled her shoulders.

Eric smiled. Stepping away, he dragged the quilted cover off the bed, revealing scarlet satin sheets cinching the heart-shaped mattress. He settled his hands at her waist and gently moved her so she sat on the curved edge of the heart. The satin cooled the backs of her thighs and erotically tickled her pussy. Her wet lips dampened the slippery fabric. Good thing he'd mentioned that more clean sheets resided in the dressers or her Suzy Homemaker tendencies would have her stripping the bed to avoid stains.

He sank onto the mattress beside her and licked the chafed undersides of her nipples. They spun into tight peaks, and want burrowed deep inside her. When the sensations grew overwhelming, she leaned her head back. Groaning, he rested her on the mattress, one hand supporting her spine, and continued swirling his hot tongue over her breasts. His other hand danced down her tummy, and her pussy clenched in anticipation. His mouth traveled up again. While they kissed, he unsnapped her garters with familiar expertise, and the fishnets drooped on her thighs.

He moved off the bed and knelt, then urged her legs apart with his hands. Her clit tingled. She felt so spread. Exposed and vulnerable. And damn sexy.

"You're glistening, Rees," he whispered, sliding a finger between her inner and outer labia.

She moaned. She wanted, no, *craved* him inside her. However, she wouldn't deny him the pleasure of exploring her vagina like he'd always loved to do.

"You're so wet and slick," he whispered, parting her inner lips with his fingers. He rolled the sensitive folds between his index fingers and thumbs, then gently tugged on them.

"*Eric.*" She jogged her hips up and down.

He tugged again before planting his mouth on her hot opening and thrusting his tongue inside her.

Risa released a cry of primal gratification. His tongue swarmed in, out, and around her vagina while he played with her labia and swollen clit. Then his thumb sank into her, pumping rapidly while his fingers caressed the cleft of her behind. His thumb massaged her G-spot as his lips latched onto her clitoris. She cried out again, a long, low, husky keening that rolled through her body. The strong waves of her orgasm pulsated.

Struggling to catch her breath, she swept her hair off her face. "Oh, God, Eric, I'm sorry. I wanted us to come together."

He climbed onto the bed and kissed her lightly on her breastbone. "Like I made that a possibility. I love how responsive you are with me, Rees."

"I've never come that fast with anyone else."

"Good." He smiled. "It's a testament to my talent."

It was a testament to how she felt about him. With the handful of other men she'd slept with before he'd entered her life, if she'd managed one teensy climax per encounter, she'd felt ecstatic. But she trusted Eric so completely that she had no difficulty letting go in bed.

She trusted him. Her heart crashed into her ribs. Had she ever stopped? Had she forced herself into denial these last several months?

Not wanting him to guess the nature of her thoughts, she faked a giggle. "Yes, you are. My talented booty call."

Expression grim, he studied her. Oh, crap, had she hurt him? "Eric."

His sexy smile returned. "Stay still," he whispered, then removed her fishnets and garter belt.

"Panties?" She reached down to shuck them off, but he shook his head.

"I want to fuck you while you're wearing them."

Tears burned behind her eyes. She blinked, swallowing the sudden lump in her throat. Her flippant remark *had* hurt him. Sometimes she was a class-A idiot.

Turning, he retrieved a condom and ripped it open. "Let me put it on for you," she half-whispered.

"Too late." He faced her again with the task half-completed.

Risa propped herself on her elbows. "You're more than a booty call," she murmured.

"You sure about that?" He finished rolling on the condom.

"Of course."

"Because I've been told that I have a very fine booty." He slapped his ass.

She didn't smile. "Eric, I'm sorry."

"Shh. Risa, I don't want to talk. If this is our last night making love, I don't want anything ruining it."

"I've ruined it already."

"No, you haven't. I'm too sensitive. Must be that time of the month."

Now she did smile. "Oh?"

"Pansy Man Syndrome. But have no fear. That wimp is gone." He grabbed her legs and arranged them so her knees arched and her feet gripped the mattress. "Get ready, Rees. Because I'm gonna fuck you hard."

Just how she liked it. His frank language sparked her arousal.

Pressing her knees further apart with his hands, he positioned his long cock at her entrance. However, in direct contrast to his words, he pushed in only the head.

Flattening the top of her panties and mound with his palm, he slid the first few inches of his erection in and out.

Risa remained propped on her elbows. Her breasts ached, and she arched her back. He clamped her hips with his hands, continuing his slow, steady thrusting. His gaze riveted on the gap in her panties.

She moaned. "Eric, stop teasing me."

"I can't help it. You have the most beautiful pussy, Rees. Look… where we're joined. I could fuck you like this all night."

"It's not enough for me."

"That's the beauty of it." His gaze lifted, and he smiled. "I know I'm driving you crazy."

"Eric!" She panted.

He held her hips. "I know you want me to do this." He slammed his cock home, and pleasure coursed through her body. Her elbows skidded on the slippery sheets, collapsing her onto the mattress. "But instead I'll do this." More short, tortuous thrusts. "Until—" Long and hard. *Yes.* "I can't—" Shallow and rapid. *No!* "Take it any more." He plunged deep.

"Ah!" She clenched her inner muscles around his thrusting cock.

His breathing roughened as he pumped. The tension tightened in her clit, and soon the fluttering beginnings of her second orgasm rushed in. He must have read the signs, because he pulled out, quickly lifted her hips, and yanked off her panties.

The sensations drifted away. "Eric, damn it."

"Sweet Jesus, I need you bare to me, Rees. God help me, I love you."

He got on the bed, pulling her up with him to the small satin pillows. Their mouths fused, his hands running over her breasts while she clutched his strong shoulders. He tumbled them over so she sat astride him. She lifted her hips and guided his cock inside. She couldn't say the words she knew he wanted to hear. He always said he loved her while they were making love. How many other woman had he spoken those same words to over the last year? Would tell in the coming months, when they were no longer together?

Don't be a fool, Risa. You know he means it.

Ignoring her conscience, she squeezed her eyes shut. Focused on the sensations building in her body and rode him for all she was worth.

She did, and the love and sincerity shining in his blue gaze nearly killed her.

"I love you, too," she whispered, then came apart in his arms.

Eric cuddled his love beneath the red satin sheets.

"Angel, that was amazing." He traced a finger along her collarbone, then kissed her shoulder peeking from the covers she'd drawn up while he'd shed the condom "I love you so much. When you said it back, it blew me away."

She tugged in a breath. "Eric, I…." Her voice trailed off, eyes brimming with confusion.

"What?" he prodded gently.

Breaking his gaze, she shook her head. "Nothing."

"Risa, honey, you can't pretend you didn't say it."

"I know I did. But it's not something I'm prepared to discuss right now."

He tried to smile. "That sounds ominous."

"I'm sorry. I don't mean it to."

"Well, not to pry, but when will we discuss it?"

She gazed at the ceiling. "This is supposed to be our last night."

"After you finally admitted you love me? I don't think so." He rubbed her arm.

Silence descended, and tension permeated the small bedroom. For several moments, she didn't reply. Then, with a breezy, "Let's take a shower," she threw off the sheets and sprang out of bed. "See if we can get you primed for round two." Her smile wobbled.

He sat up. "Risa, we're talking about this."

"No, we're not," she sing-songed, sashaying nude from the room.

Eric ground his teeth. *Damn it.* What would it take to get through to her? She loved him, he loved her—a pretty simple equation. But she remained determined to complicate the issue.

Was she testing him? If so, he hoped he'd pass.

He joined her in the bathroom. Rewarding him with a broad smile, she opened the shower door and reached for the tap.

"Risa! Eric! Where are you guys?" a muffled voice carried from the party room.

Risa's face whitened. "Kyla's here! Crud! I forgot to call her again." She grabbed a robe from the multiple hooks and jammed her arms into the sleeves.

"She doesn't know about these rooms," Eric whispered. "If we're quiet, she might leave."

"Are you nuts? I practically threatened to disown her if she didn't come get me. She won't leave until she finds us."

"Reee-saa! Yoo-hoo! Risa, darlink!"

"Eric." Risa's hand flicked. "Get a robe."

He rolled his eyes. "You'll use any excuse to get away from me, won't you?"

"What? I'm hardly responsible for Kyla showing up at this precise moment."

"Yeah, but I'll bet you're nowhere near as disappointed as you're *not* pretending to be."

"For God's sake, Eric, just get a robe." Tying her belt, she swept into the hall.

He snagged the nearest robe, muttering, "Eric, sit. Eric, stay. Eric, come boy. Good boy. No, no, Eric, not *that. Bad* boy." He was her freaking lap dog.

She wanted him out of her life? Not a problem. Because he was damn sick and tired of Risa "I Need To Feel Like It's Not My Choice" Haber treating his heart and his honest intentions like a beat-up soccer ball.

Chapter 9

Eric picked up the ringing telephone. "Bella Fortuna, Eric Lange."

"It's me."

"Risa." Straightening in his desk chair, he gazed out the multi-paned window onto the restaurant terrace. Tourists and staffers from the nearby provincial parliament buildings dominated the mid-week lunch crowd clustered at the sunshine-strewn tables. The first rainless afternoon since Sunday had brought them out in full force. "What can I do for you?"

Awkwardness imbued her long silence. Scratching an eyelid, he counted the dried raindrops on the glass and waited. She needed something? Then she'd better make it damn clear. He was done guessing.

She replied in a thick-sounding voice, "I know I hurt you."

He frowned. Had she been crying? "Don't worry about it."

"I thought you'd call."

"You asked me not to." They hadn't spoken to or seen one another since he stalked out of the Fullbright mansion in the middle of Saturday night wearing nothing but the bathrobe filched from Lainey's secret bathroom. Kyla's surprised gaze had held sympathy for him as he'd passed. As for Risa, he hadn't a clue, because he hadn't looked back. "Doesn't 'I need you out of my life' include no phone calls?"

"I wanted to make sure you're all right."

"I am." As much as could be a guy coming to terms with the very real possibility of a future devoid of the love of his life. He paused. "Are you okay?"

"I will be."

Good, she was having a rough time of it, as well. Call him an asshole, he knew he shouldn't twist the guilt screws too much, yet, perversely, he didn't want to make their separation easy on her, either.

"But we still have things to discuss," she added.

"Like what?" His chest itched—the damn hair growing back.

"Visiting the lawyer about drawing up papers."

"For...?" *Go ahead, say it.*

"Eric, you know why. Selling me your half of Sweet Sensations. I was hoping you'd step in with the lawyer. I've talked to a real estate agent and discussed the situation with our accountant. I think I have a decent grasp of the market, our assets and liabilities."

He grunted. "The only liability *I* have is that I'm in love with you, and you're too stubborn or freaked out or whatever is the going trend these days to give us a chance."

"Damn it, I'm not trying to make this difficult."

"Then why not send me an email?"

She hesitated. "I wanted to hear your voice."

"Risa, be fair." He rolled back his chair. "You can't demand I get out of your life, then claim you miss the sound of my voice. I said it nine days ago, and I'll say it again now—you want me gone, I'm gone."

There was the joke of it. When he'd blithely spoken those words last Tuesday in the bakery, he hadn't believed their relationship would arrive at this painful impasse.

Life certainly was one fucking surprise after another.

"Okay, you're right, I'm sorry," she said. "We still need to deal with the sale of the business, though."

"I'll *give* you the freaking business."

"Eric, no. I have to pay fair value."

His fingers ached from gripping the receiver. "Don't worry, you'll have your damn papers." *Woof-woof!*

"When?"

"When I'm good and ready." Scowling, he slammed down the phone.

Deal with that.

Risa lay curled in a ball on her living room couch, trying to focus on the images flickering across her TV screen. Her head swam, and she moaned. Darn flu. At least she'd stopped barfing sometime around three a.m. Thank heaven, because her stomach had nothing left to offer the Great Porcelain God in her bathroom.

A light knock rapped on her front door a few feet away, and she glanced up, tummy cramping. Head weighing as heavy as a tub of nails, she wrapped her arms around the old sweatshirt covering her sore middle.

"Kyla?" The name scraped from her raw throat.

"No. It's Eric."

Silly heart leaping, she closed her eyes. *Aw, crap.* He'd brought her the papers *now?* Five days had passed since he'd hung up on her, and, while she couldn't fault him for his anger, she'd wanted to be at her best when she faced him again.

She licked her dry lips. "I'm sick. I can't answer the door."

The knob jostled. "It's not locked."

"It isn't?" Wonderful. On top of everything else, she'd left her house unsecured all night.

"Risa, I know you're not feeling well. Kyla told me."

Clutching her blanket around her shoulders, she swung her legs off the couch. *Urrrg.* Her head sank back onto the cushions. Tears seeped from her eyes. "Damn it. Why'd she do that?"

"Because she knows I care about you. Even if you don't want to accept it, she knows."

"She's *my* friend. She's supposed to be on my side." After forgiving Kyla for trapping her at Lainey's with Eric, Risa hadn't imagined her assistant would betray her again.

"She's on both our sides," Eric said through the door. "Don't be stubborn, Risa. She only called me because she can't check in on you herself until after the bakery closes. I brought you some of Dante's minestrone soup. You don't want to miss it. It's amazing."

A tiny rumble of hunger raised a white flag in her stomach. "Do you have the papers?" she asked in emotional self-defense.

"Not on me. I'm holding the soup."

"But you have them?"

"In the car."

"All right. You can come in."

The door opened. As Eric entered, looking handsome and sexy, tanned and healthy in a sky-blue golf shirt and khakis, she tried to stand. A wave of lightheadedness had her sagging onto the couch again.

She gestured him to the sofa. "Promise you don't want anything from me?"

"Yeah, like I want to make love to you now. You look a mess." Smiling, he sat beside her on the couch and set the covered soup container on the coffee table. He sniffed her hair. "No offense, but you've smelled better, too."

She laughed weakly. "I meant, you won't try talking me out of my decision, will you?"

Sadness flickered in his blue eyes. He rubbed the blanket covering her arm. "No. Let me take care of you, Risa. An hour, tops, then I'll go."

"You'll catch the bug," she protested.

He shrugged. "It's going around. If I have to catch it, it might as well be from you."

Too weak to resist him, she nodded. He turned her spine toward him and massaged her shoulders through the thick blanket. Her eyes fluttered shut as his body warmth flooded her.

Oh, Eric. If only she could open herself up to trusting him again. Or was that trusting herself? Having the faith that she wouldn't repeat her biological-clock screw-up. To know deep in her heart that she wanted him for *him,* not the children he might give her.

"That feels incredible," she murmured, allowing his gentle ministrations to relieve her aches. The flavorful aroma of the minestrone soup lifted from the coffee table. Her tummy grumbled. "I'm definitely hungry."

"Good," he replied, voice soft. "You're on the road to recovery, then."

He eased away and peeled the lid off the container, then unwrapped the plastic spoon and passed it to her. As she dipped the spoon into the bowl, he tore open a packet of salted crackers and crushed them into the broth.

She smiled. "You remembered."

"That you junk your soup full of crackers? It's one of your lovelier quirks."

Her smile stretched. She sipped the soup, and the rich medley of broth-softened vegetables and pasta soothed her empty stomach. "I might actually keep this down. Thank you. It tastes fantastic."

"You're welcome," he murmured above the quiet TV.

While she ate, he retreated into silence. Not wanting the mood to grow uncomfortable, she asked, "Did Dante tell you about his date with Kyla?"

He chuckled. "No. We're guys."

Risa smiled. "It was a disaster."

His eyebrows lifted. "That's good?"

"Not usually. However, in this case, it's pretty funny. Dante's old girlfriend heard about the date—don't ask me how. She showed up at the restaurant, threw Dante's wine in his face, then hexed him."

Eric laughed. "What?"

"Cursed his love life for all eternity. Apparently, she dabbles in some sort of witchcraft."

He laughed again. "Poor Dante."

"Kyla still likes him, though," Risa said. "She wants to try again."

"Well, she'll have to ask him herself this time. My days of playing Cupid are over."

Because of her?

She dared not ask.

She pushed aside the bowl. "I think I'm done. I don't want to rush things."

"How do you feel?"

"A bit better." She swiped her hands through her stringy hair. "I must look a fright. I need a shower, but I don't think I can stand long enough to take one."

"Don't then."

"Hm?"

"Lie here and relax." He helped her into a reclining position on the couch, then disappeared down the hall. Seconds later, the gurgle of running water carried from her bathroom. A scent drifted to the living room. Rose petals?

Risa forced herself off the sofa, blanket dragging behind her on the carpet Linus-style. Entering the bathroom, she blinked. Eric had retrieved her radio-alarm/CD player from her bedroom and plugged it in on the counter. The tropical rain CD she woke to every morning streamed from the small machine while the tub filled with fragrant water.

She whispered, "You drew me a bath."

"That's right." Moving behind her, he slipped the blanket off her shoulders and chucked it into the hall. "You're having a nice, hot soak, and then I'm putting you to bed." He closed the door, and steam misted the small room.

The idea sounded so appealing, she didn't balk. "Where did you find the bath beads? I thought I ran out."

"Right here." He patted his pants pocket. "I bought them on the way over. And before you get the wrong idea, I didn't bring them to seduce you." He smiled.

When they were dating, the rose-scented bath beads paired with candles flickering from several of her antique candelabras had often coaxed them into slow, sensual bathtub lovemaking. "Well, yes, because we've already established that I stink," Risa joked.

He chuckled. "Lift your arms."

"I can undress myself."

"This isn't sexual, Risa. I want to take care of you."

Her heart panged. Well, okay. He'd seen her in all her glory countless times, so what did it matter?

She raised her arms, and he tugged up the sweatshirt. She hadn't thought to wear a bra, and her breasts bounced as her top popped off her head. The bathroom air puckered her nipples. Eric's gaze lowered to her breasts, and pleasure gleamed in his eyes.

"Sorry." He glanced away. "Old habits."

"I'm not wearing panties, either," she warned him.

"Got it. Uh, maybe you should do the sweats, then."

She nodded. A wave of nausea rolled over her. *Oh, God, don't puke now.* She shoved her thumbs into the waistband of her sweats and scooted the baggy pants down. An invisible fist grabbed her insides, and her temples throbbed. Shaking, she hugged her bare arms. Her sweats remained lodged above her knees.

"Sit on the toilet lid," Eric murmured, spreading a towel across it. He looked at her. "In case it's cold."

A sweet, achy sensation blossomed in her chest. She plopped unceremoniously onto the commode. Eric knelt on the linoleum, then removed her socks and stripped off the grubby sweats. After stuffing the dirty clothes into her laundry hamper, he faced her.

"Need help getting into the tub?" he asked.

"Yes. I'm sorry."

"Don't be. That's why I'm here."

He held her hand while she climbed gingerly into the tub. The water enveloped her nakedness to her waist, and she shivered.

"Too hot?"

She shook her head. "Just getting used it." Still clasping his hand, she leaned against the curved back of the tub and slipped into the rose-scented water. When the heavenly warmth swam over her breasts, she released his hand and sighed. "This feels so good." She dragged her fingers through her greasy, half-wet hair.

"Pass the shampoo," he murmured. "Let me wash your hair for you."

She smiled. "I'll feel like a little kid."

"You don't look like one." He winked.

Attempting a grin, Risa handed him the shampoo. He placed the bottle on the floor. After getting a plastic cup from her vanity, he scooped hot water over her head until the excess dripped from her hair.

"Close your eyes."

When she did, he applied a healthy dollop of shampoo and gently massaged her scalp. Her skin tingled.

His fingers wove through her hair, the wet strands plastering her back and shoulders. "Keep your eyes shut," he whispered, pouring more water over her head.

Suds trickled down her face. Within seconds, a soft towel dabbed away the soap, and she smiled, eyes closed. "You're good at this."

"You bet. Warren Beatty has nothing on me."

Laughing, she slit open one eye.

"*Shampoo*," he elaborated. "The old movie. He played a hairdresser who had sex with his customers."

"And here I figured you for more of a car-chase guy."

"It was on cable last summer. I was bored, so I watched it."

"You? Bored?" She opened both eyes.

He nodded. "Lonely, too. Contrary to popular belief, I didn't bed half the eligible population of Victoria after we split."

She pursed her lips. "We'd better not go there."

"Agreed." He snapped his fingers. "Conditioner."

She passed him the bottle. As he squirted conditioner onto his palm, her gaze drifted to the erection tenting his khakis. Evidently, nursing her through her illness was literally hard on him. That he chose to follow through with the task spoke to his generous nature.

Or maybe he thrived on self-torture.

He finger-combed the conditioner through her hair, then rinsed the strands clean. Risa leaned against the tub again. Without asking her permission, Eric stood and grabbed the soap and washcloth. Crouching outside the tub, he soaked the cloth in the fragrant water. While birds chirped and rain pattered leaves on her CD, he lathered the cloth and glided it over her upper chest. The washcloth skated between her breasts... and desire rippled between her legs. Not the response she'd expected, considering her fever of the last twenty-four hours.

She must be getting better.

Eric's gaze looked unfocussed as he slid the washcloth under the water and over her tummy, scrubbing down her nearest thigh and up her raised knee. Massaging and cleaning everywhere, except over her nipples and between her legs.

The cloth slid down her tummy again, and she moaned. "Eric, please."

Sensuality clouded his gaze as it drifted up. "Hm?"

"Between my legs," she whispered.

He shook his head. "I should leave the private areas to you."

She lifted her hips, and the water sloshed. "I want you to."

A smiled curved his mouth. "Do you now?"

"I think my health depends on it."

"Well, in that case."

He slipped the washcloth beneath the rose-scented water. She closed her eyes and relished the gently arousing sensations. The cloth skidded over her sensitive folds, then drifted away. His hand replaced it, finger questing for her hot button. The water splashed, and she groaned. His fingers moved, pinching, rolling. Quickly, her climax crested.

When she'd caught her breath, she opened her eyes. Desire but also a heavy sorrowfulness slackened his features.

"I'm sorry," she whispered. "It wasn't fair to ask you."

He dragged the washcloth out of the tub and wrung it out. After placing it on a tub corner, he settled his hand on her tummy beneath the water.

Without glancing at her face, he murmured, "I always dreamed of seeing you swollen with my child."

Risa's chest ached. She didn't breathe a word.

"The whole marriage-and-family thing—you never hid what you wanted out of life, Rees. Regardless of how I reacted at the time, that's a good thing." He gazed at her. "But it scared me. I fell for you so fast. I couldn't believe it was happening to me, of all people."

"Wh-what was happening?"

"Love. Real love. And wanting what you did—marriage and children. I'd never experienced that sense of urgency and rightness with any other woman in my life. I thought I was crazy with lust, that it would wear off over time. I didn't trust my instincts, so I drove you away." He smiled sadly. "What can I say? I was a coward."

Silent tears trickled down her cheeks. "Why are you telling me this now?"

"Because." He swiped his thumb across her parted lips, brushed away her salty tears with a gentle touch. "You're sick, and I have you trapped in the tub. I figured you might finally listen." He rubbed her arm. "Whatever else happens between us, I hope we can become friends some day. Not to socialize with—I couldn't handle the pretense. But when you start seeing the guy you'll eventually marry and have those kids you want so much, if I see you in Beacon Hill Park with your family, Rees, I don't want to feel like I have to turn and walk away. I want to say hello and feel truly happy for you."

"Oh, God." She sobbed. "Eric."

"I know I shouldn't dump this on you when you're not feeling well. But, Angel, I want you to find that guy and go after the life you deserve."

Unable to speak, she covered her mouth with shaky fingers.

He got up and placed a fluffy towel on the toilet lid. "Soak as long as you need to. Then I'm putting you to bed."

The door closed behind him, leaving her cold and alone. She hugged her knees to her chest and let the tears flow.

Chapter 10

Several hours later, Risa woke from a deep sleep feeling like she'd finally re-entered the land of the living. Eric had allowed her plenty of privacy following their talk in the bathroom, and she'd emerged from her emotional watershed to discover he'd changed her bed linens and prepared a hot, lemon flu remedy for her to drink that had zonked her out. Sounds of him moving around her house had lulled her as she'd drifted off. Was he still here?

Her robe sprawled across the foot of the bed. Getting up, she tugged it on over her PJs and headed to the living room. The *TV Guide* lay open on the coffee table, but the house sat eerily silent, Eric nowhere in sight.

Chest pinching, she went to the bathroom and brushed her teeth. As her gaze drifted to the tub, her throat sealed shut. She'd really hurt him, and she wouldn't blame him if he *did* turn his back when he saw her in the park someday.

Sighing, she finished her bathroom regime and wandered to the kitchen. Eric must have opened the window overlooking her back yard. Birdsong cheered the fresh air streaming in.

She placed the kettle on the stove to boil. After collecting a mug, she sat at her dining table, and her heart rammed her ribs. A key resided atop a large manila envelope beside a sheet of notepaper. Mouth dry, she unfolded the note.

My Dearest Risa,
The legal documents for your purchase of Sweet Sensations *are enclosed. Please don't argue with me about the price. I won't accept any more.*
Here's to seeing you with your family in Beacon Hill Park some day.
All my best,
Eric.

Her chest squeezed. The key had to belong to the bakery. All these months, he hadn't relinquished it. Now, it suddenly signified the last nail in the coffin of their relationship. She couldn't pick it up.

Tears burned her eyes. A moment later, the ringing doorbell shot up her heart rate. She hurried into the living room. Kyla stood in the doorway.

"Oh. It's you."

"Is that any way to greet the person who ran herself ragged for you all day? Look, I brought banana bread. Eat some." She held out a foil-wrapped bundle.

"Sorry." Risa accepted the banana loaf. "Thank you."

The kettle shrieked from the kitchen. Knowing Kyla would accompany her, Risa turned.

"Eric said he'd drop by this morning," Kyla said. "Did he?"

Nodding, Risa placed the banana bread on a cutting board and retrieved the kettle. Kyla found a knife and sliced thick chunks of the spicy bread onto small plates.

Once they each sat at the table with their mugs of tea and banana bread slices, Kyla asked, "So how did it go?"

Risa tapped the manila envelope. "Looks like I got what I wanted."

"His share of the bakery?"

"Yes. And him out of my life." The finality of the words thudded in her ears.

Kyla pulled out the papers and scanned them. "Wow. He's practically giving it to you."

"I told him not to! Let me see that." Risa grabbed the contract. "Three dollars?"

"I also saw something in there about applicable taxes and legal fees."

"Crap. Why would he do this?"

Kyla scratched her cheek. She sipped her tea, then glanced up. "Risa, you know I love you, right? So, when I say this, it comes from the heart."

Risa looked at her friend sideways. "Okay."

"You're an idiot."

"Excuse me?"

"You know that bone that covers your brain?"

"My skull?"

"You should get it measured. I'll bet it's ten inches thick."

Risa snorted. "What?"

"You have the chance of a lifetime sitting right in front of you, and you're too big a fool to grab it."

Risa shoved the papers into the envelope, scrunching them. "He only did this to force me into contacting him again."

Kyla shook her head. "He did it because he loves you, and he's run out of ways to show you. He did it because he wants you to succeed. Because he can't handle not being a part of your life in *some* way, for God's sake. If you're too dense to realize that you and Eric are meant to be together, then at least accept this from him. Let the man have his crumbs."

Risa leaned back in her chair. "Sheesh. Give it to me with both barrels, why don't you?"

"Someone has to! Apparently, Eric is too much of a gentleman. Risa, don't you ever wonder how you snapped up Elaine Fullbright's business?"

"Sure. She loved my desserts at Bella Fortuna, so when she needed a caterer she contacted the restaurant and learned I'd opened Sweet Sensations."

Kyla snickered. "Who told you that?"

The hairs on Risa's nape prickled. "No one. But when I called Eric all excited about the party—"

"He let you believe what you assumed."

Risa hesitated. "Why would he?"

"So you wouldn't accuse him of interfering in your business, like you're fond of doing."

"I wouldn't have said that."

"Yes, you would have. Risa, Lainey has all the money and connections in the world. The Empress Hotel is widely known, and their Afternoon Tea goodies are divine. With those sorts of resources at Lainey's fingertips, why would she deal with a newbie?"

"Because she needed someone willing to create Dick."

"She could have ordered erotic cakes off the Internet and had them delivered overnight."

"Because I gave her a great price."

"She invited Hollywood bigwigs to the party. Do you honestly believe she was concerned about cost?"

"Because my staff was willing to dress half-naked?"

Kyla grinned. "Nope."

Risa dropped her head into her hands. "My thick skull hurts. Just tell me."

Kyla's voice softened. "Risa, every step Eric has taken in the last year has been to help or support you in some way. Lainey's party was no different. He heard the scoop through his restaurant connections. *He* approached *her* and convinced her to give you a chance."

Risa glanced at her. "How do you know that?"

"I told you, he and I had a deal. I wouldn't agree to talk him up to you unless he spilled his guts. So he did." She patted Risa's hand. "Honey, he's good for you. Granted, I didn't know either of you before the bakery opened, so I can't compare how you are with him now to how you were with him then. However, I can say, these last couple of weeks since you began sleeping with him again—I haven't seen you so full of life since you hired me."

"You haven't?"

Kyla shook her head. "Do you love him?"

"Yes." She bit her lip.

"Then what's the problem?"

"I'm afraid I'll say or do something to break us up again."

Kyla laughed softly. She snatched the envelope and waved it. "You already have. He deserves better, Risa. He deserves you."

Risa tented her hands over her nose. "God, I'm such an idiot."

"Yes, you are. The good news is you have nothing to lose from this point, and everything to gain."

Eric stepped out of the shower and cinched a towel around his waist. Scrubbing his hair dry with a second towel, he strode into his bedroom lit only by the nightstand lamp. He sank onto the mattress, and paper crumpled beneath his ass. *What the hell?*

Standing, he turned. During his sojourn beneath the hot spray, a large manila envelope had miraculously appeared on his bed, the same envelope he'd left at Risa's three days ago, according to the law office address in the upper left corner.

"That was quick," he mumbled, drying his arms and chest before chucking the second towel to the floor. Her illness was definitely behind her. How had she delivered the contract? Using her key? Which, he noted with another glance at the bed, she hadn't returned.

"What a chicken." She could have called or announced her presence, allowed him time to finish his nightly shower routine, then faced him like the strong, independent woman he knew her to be. But, no, similar to a year ago when his insecurities had chased her out of his arms, she was too great a coward.

Grunting, he sat on the bed again and opened the envelope flap. He stuck in a hand to pull out the contract, but his fingers met with a tattered mess.

"What the fuck?" Holding the envelope upside down, he shook the shredded contents onto his bedspread. Disappointment dropped like a rock in his stomach. "Aw, Risa, couldn't you accept this one thing from me?"

"Yes," her soft voice murmured from the far end of the room. "Although not on those terms."

He whipped his head to the doorway. She stood there barefoot, holding a glass of red wine in each hand. The hallway light cast a glow behind her, illuminating her cream-colored dress and creating a sexy aura around her golden hair. Her blue eyes twinkled.

Clenching the envelope, Eric rose. "What's going on?"

"I'm not signing the papers."

"Well, yeah, that'd be a little difficult to do, seeing as they're in a million pieces." He tossed the envelope onto the nightstand. "What's with the wine?"

Strolling toward him, she smiled. "I'd hoped we could celebrate."

"That you're not signing the contract?" he asked as she sipped from one glass before placing both on his dresser.

"I'd love to sign a legal document with you, Eric. Just not that one." Her gaze drifted over the towel wrapped around his waist. "I like what you're wearing."

His cock stirred beneath the terry fabric. He ignored the uncontrollable physical response. "What do you want, Risa?"

"You," she whispered, reaching him and settling her hands on his hips over the towel.

Her fingers grazed his naked abdomen, and his erection surged. *Shit.* "I don't want to be your booty call, Rees."

"You're not." Her gaze searched his, her blue irises large, iridescent, and brimming with what looked an awful lot like unabashed love.

The air evaporated from his lungs.

"Why three dollars?" she asked. "On the contract."

He sucked in a breath. "For three little words."

"I love you."

He shook his head. "I know, I'm a romantic sap."

She chuckled. "No. *I. Love. You.*" She swept a hand over the prickly hairs sprouting on his pecs. "You shaved your chest for me. You convinced Lainey to hire me. You went into business with me when you could have walked away completely. You were at the bakery almost every day, encouraging me, asking for nothing in return."

"Other than the chance to date you again."

"Which I insisted on misinterpreting as nothing more than you wanting to sleep with me. But you weren't after sex, were you, Eric? Not *only* sex," she added, smiling. "Sleeping together was all you thought I'd agree to."

He swallowed. "Right."

Regret filled her eyes. "I'm sorry I was such a lunatic. I was afraid I'd go off on another baby-making rant and scare you away again."

"*Was* afraid?" Eric prompted. For the first time since she'd entered the room, he allowed himself to touch her. A quick brush across her forearm wrinkled her soft dress sleeve.

She nodded. "As in not any more. Not in any way, shape or form. Don't get me wrong. I'd still like a family someday, if you do. It's a decision we should make together, though, and definitely not on some imaginary, anxiety-ridden schedule. I'm only thirty-two. I have a good ten years before my ovaries begin rotting away."

He laughed. "I want a family, too."

"Don't say that to appease me."

"I wouldn't."

"Because I love *you*, Eric. I love making love with you. I love hanging out with you. That's all I want for our whole lives. Anything else is icing on the cake." She winked. "A bit of bakery humor."

"God." He closed his eyes briefly. "I love you, Risa."

She kissed him. "Good. Because I don't want to buy Sweet Sensations from you. I'd like to run it and Bella Fortuna together, if that's what you want."

He caressed her arms. "I'd love nothing better, except for you to marry me."

A beautiful smile blossomed on her face. "Well, Mr. Lange, that's exactly the sort of legal contract I'd *adore* signing with you."

"Are you saying yes, then? Will you marry me, Rees? I realize I'm not dressed for a proposal—"

"I'd marry you in a flash." She untied his towel and flung it onto the floor. "And I think your outfit is perfect." Her hand curved around his hard cock.

He pulled her into his arms, kissing her deeply, savoring the taste of red wine on her tongue. "We have to get you out of this dress."

"It's a wrap dress," she murmured between kisses. "Pull the sash."

He tugged the long sash at her waist, and, unlike a little over two weeks ago when he'd had to slice her knotted negligee ribbon with a jackknife, the dress front parted effortlessly. She stepped back, undid a tiny, inner sash, and peeled off the sleeves. The dress dropped to puddle at her feet.

A moment later, she'd shed her bra and panties. They fell back on the bed, the shredded contract crunching under their hot bodies.

Eric flipped them over so she lay beneath him. Cradling her, he covered her face with kisses before reaching into the nightstand. Once he'd protected them, she grasped his cock, positioning it at her entrance, and he slid inside her with one sure stroke. Her breathless moans spurred his excitement, and he pumped until they both reached the precipice. Then he stilled.

She kissed him lightly. "Is something wrong?"

"No." Emotion clogged his throat, thickening his voice. "Everything is incredibly right."

Remaining deep inside her, he brushed her hair off her face and gazed into her desire-hazed eyes. "Say it again, Risa," he whispered. "Say you'll marry me."

Tiny tears glimmered on iridescent blue. "I want to marry you more than anything. I love you, Eric."

"I love you." As they resumed their sensual rhythm, he hugged her tight. "Ah, Angel, you're the best surprise of my life."

About the Author:

Kate St. James lives in the Pacific Northwest with her husband and two sons. When she's not trying to whip her disobedient muse into submission, you can find her chasing her dog in the hills above an azure lake, ignoring the smoke alarms blaring from the kitchen, or endlessly renovating her house. Visit Kate on the web at www.katestjames.com.

The Spy's Surrender

by Juliet Burns

To My Reader:

From the age of 12 I've been fascinated with anything British, and especially the Regency era. As a teen, I spent my summers reading Jane Austen, the Bronte sisters, and Barbara Cartland. Last summer I watched the BBC America *Sharpe* mini-series starring the yummy Sean Bean, and was inspired to write about a British major fighting against Napoleon. Major Ambrose Delacourt is a veteran soldier; strong, sexy, and… about to meet his match! Enjoy!

Chapter 1

Never seek to tell thy love,
Love that never told can be;
For the gentle wind doth move
Silently, invisibly.
William Blake

Outside Paris, March, 1812

Leaves crunched underfoot as he darted through the dense thicket of trees at Havenwood Manor. His makeshift sword was drawn and ready for battle and John ran by his side. The savory scent of woodsmoke ushered in the first crisp autumn day. The grounds were his Sherwood Forest and his older brother was Little John, of course. The gamekeeper's cottage was their hideout—

No, it was just a dream. He was a major in the army now, and John was Viscount Pembrook.

Ambrose blinked away the fever-induced haze. A prison guard was yelling at him in French to get up. As they dragged him out of a farmer's cart, the sword wound in his side made him double over in agony. The iron binding his wrists chafed. He looked up at the building they were entering and his gut clenched.

La Force.

Instinctively he fought, striking the guard in the stomach with his chained fists. But the guard struck his skull with the butt of a rifle and sent him into blissful oblivion again.

When he came to, it was dark and cold and a stench filled his nostrils. His head ached and his throat was parched.

Had he been out wenching last night? He was shivering. Where was his coat? He'd been sent down from Cambridge and rather than face his father, he'd headed for London. He must have cast up his accounts in a dark alley somewhere and passed out—

No, Cambridge had been more than a decade ago.

A large rodent scuttled across his boot and Ambrose kicked at it. He opened his eyes and tried to sit up. Shooting pain in his ribs and head made him decide to wait a bit. Heavy iron rattled around his wrists.

Bloody hell, now he remembered where he was.

He'd been caught behind enemy lines. It was the devil's own luck he'd not been carrying a packet of letters this time, and because he'd been dressed in uniform, they couldn't honorably execute him as a spy.

But could he escape La Force?

He must. As soon as his damned head quit pounding….

He awoke when his cage door opened. A torch blinded him for a moment and he covered his eyes.

"Get up, ye English bastard," a guard commanded in guttural French.

How long had he been in this dank hellhole? Ten days? A fortnight? Thanks to this fever, he'd lost track of time.

"I said get up!" Rough hands hauled him to his feet and dragged him from his cell.

Had he been ransomed, at last? Had John forgiven him, then? They'd been close as boys, but other than the terse note informing him of their father's death, John had never written to him. Finally Ambrose had quit sending letters.

Another beefy guard gripped his other arm and they dragged him ever upward along a dark passageway, through a heavy wooden door and out into the cold night. The fresh air cleared his head a bit and he spied a coach and four waiting in the street. Relief filled him. He was going home! The thought almost brought tears to his eyes.

But why would the French conduct a prisoner release at night?

"Hurry up!" A guard shoved him toward the carriage and he finally noticed the guards wore rough worker's clothes instead of uniforms. And they carried pistols, not sabers or rifles.

A cold chill slithered down his spine.

"I am—" He had no voice at first and cleared his throat. "I am Major Lord Ambrose Delacourt, of the 7th Brigade, Infantry." And newly recruited "exploring officer", but he sure as hell wouldn't mention that. "If you inform my superior—"

"Shut up and get in!" They grabbed his arms and tried to force him into the coach, but he managed to cuff one in the jaw with his fists. He tried to grab a pistol, but the other guard knocked him to the ground. Though he struggled with all his strength, they overpowered him. As soon as the carriage door closed the horses were whipped to a gallop.

Ambrose remained alert, waiting for the burly men to relax their vigilance, but an hour passed and their hold never slackened. The windows were covered but he smelled country air, not the sea. Wherever they were taking him, it wasn't to England.

At last the carriage slowed to a stop and the guards dragged him out of the carriage and down a muddy drive to a coal chute behind a grand chateau. What the bloody hell was happening?

This was his last chance to get away. While the guard's attention was on opening the trap door, Ambrose reached once more for one of the pistols at their waists. As his hands closed around the gun, he felt the cold metal of the other guard's pistol push against his skull and heard the click of the hammer being cocked.

He froze.

And they shoved him down the steep stone stairs and he plunged into darkness.

He never knew when the fall ended and the beatings began. The two "guards" took turns with their fists or whips, pausing only long enough for his jailor, an elegantly dressed Frenchman, to question him.

"What is the number of English troops? What are the regiment positions? What is your code name??

Ambrose refused to answer all questions.

But he hated it more when he was whipped in silence. The Frenchman would challenge him, "If you scream, I'll give you cheese with your bread." Or sometimes, "How many strokes can you take before screaming today, Major?"

The sick bastard would lick his lips with relish at the sight of every newly raised welt.

After they left him, he'd lay huddled in his cell, shivering, drifting in and out of consciousness. He was a madman's captive. And reality was settling into his frozen bones. If he didn't escape soon, he wasn't going to make it.

Chapter 2

"I have procured a love slave for you, Madame Mystère," the Marquis de Séréville announced from behind her.

Eva hid her nervousness with a coy smile. "But I thought *you* would fill that role, my lord."

The other guests chortled. After a fine supper, they'd all assembled in the drawing room for the night's entertainment. The marquis was renowned for hosting depraved house parties that lasted days at his chateau in the country outside Paris. A dozen gentlemen and their mistresses lounged around the opulent room on chaises, sofas, and pillows. Some mistresses already undressing, fondling, sucking....

"I intend to fill many holes, eh, roles, *ma chérie*." As the ladies and gentleman snickered, the Marquis snapped his fingers and a British prisoner was hauled in, barely standing.

It was him. Her quarry, delivered into her hands with the greatest of ease. Almost too easily.

The Marquis was watching her closely for a reaction. Did he suspect her? Surely not. She'd received his invitation days before her orders had arrived.

With a malicious smile, the marquis reached around her, placed a hand at the swell of her breast above her bodice. "I wish to watch you dominate him first. I've heard it is a specialty of yours."

Eva studied the shackled, bloodied man. He held his chin high, his expression giving away nothing. It was true she'd had a unique arrangement with a certain gentleman a few years ago. Still, she must be wicked indeed to be so aroused at the sight of this Englishman with his wrists chained behind him.

The British officer—what she could see of him beneath the disheveled hair and filthy beard—hardly looked in any condition to pleasure even the most innocent virgin, much less an experienced courtesan such as herself.

"How did you acquire an officer? Did you buy him from the prison before he could be ransomed?"

"He is a spy." The marquis kissed down her neck, his fingers tilting her chin. "Caught behind enemy lines."

"*Vraiment*? But he wears a uniform, *non*?"

The marquis raised his head. "I had no idea you were so learned in the ways of espionage, my dear."

Merde. Had she just given herself away? She flipped open her fan, held it to her face and half-turned to peek at him, fluttering her lashes.

"I'm learned in the ways of many things, my lord. Where would a talented courtesan be without spying on her competition?"

"*Touché,* Madame," the marquis murmured with a sly smile.

She lowered her fan and brought her lace handkerchief to her nose.

"But there's a disgusting odor about him, *monsieur*." She mustn't appear too eager to interact with the Englishman.

With a wave of his hand the marquis commanded two footmen to bring a ewer of water, scented soap, and towels.

"Strip him."

The air hummed with anticipation as the footmen ripped at the spy's soiled and tattered uniform until he was full naked.

A hush fell over the room.

Whether it was at the soldier's magnificently honed body or the multitude of welts and bruises he'd sustained she couldn't guess.

Both made her tremble.

After the servants had washed him, Eva stepped close to the prisoner and gave his impressive male parts a lengthy perusal.

"Very well. As my slave, he must be taught to obey me. Remove his shackles."

"But, *ma chérie*, what if he attacks you?"

Eva shrugged. "He seems a docile enough beast."

She circled around the Englishman, noting his muscular arms, thick thighs, and taut buttocks. After more than a month of deprivation, was he healthy enough to endure tonight?

His thick mahogany locks were now washed and pulled away from his face, curling around his ears and dripping onto his broad shoulders.

Coming full circle, Eva made herself look up into his eyes. Defiance. Disgust. Daring. If only she'd been as confident during her years as someone else's property. This man had casually withstood her examination without uttering a word. He controlled himself too well, she feared, to ever be dominated. Admirable, but extremely dangerous.

She reached down and encircled his flaccid organ, stroking its magnificent length and rubbing her thumb along the tip.

"With such extraordinary attributes, he will serve me very well indeed, my lord," she purred as she coaxed his splendid cock to rise.

The prisoner's dark brown eyes flared and blazed in fury as he hardened. He could hate her if he wished. She would do what she must.

Though the top of her head just reached his shoulder, she kept her gaze locked on his as she released his cock and cupped his bollocks, which overflowed her palm. Soft brown hair protected them as she rolled each sac between her fingers, and then grabbed his thick shaft again and tugged.

"Do you know how to pleasure a woman, slave?"

He didn't answer, but his intelligent eyes heated and he raised an arrogant brow.

"The English only know how to rut," Monsieur le Comte de Chambeau called out, slurring his words. Everyone laughed.

"If he refuses to answer, perhaps we should flog him." With an eager quiver in his voice, the marquis stepped over to a table where various sex toys and whips had been laid out and picked up a leather tawse. He pulled it through his hand as he moved behind the prisoner.

Stifling her revulsion, she laid a finger to her jaw and circled the prisoner once again. Judging from the raw stripes across his back, he'd suffered enough whippings.

"'Twould be a shame to soil such a handsome rug with dirty English blood, my lord. I have other means of inspiring obedience." She moved to the sideboard, poured two glasses of cognac, and returned to press the snifter's rim against her new slave's mouth. "*Buvez.*"

When he flattened his lips, refusing to drink, she smiled and drained her own snifter.

"There, you see? Now, if the liquor is poisoned, we shall both die, or experience the 'little death' together, *oui?*" She pressed the cup to his lips again.

After a moment of hesitation, he opened his mouth and drank. Mesmerized by the line of his throat as he swallowed and by his chiseled lips, glistening with wine, she met his challenging gaze, unprepared for the punch of desire low in her belly. Eva needed to regain control the only way she knew how.

Slowly, seductively, she began to strip.

The cognac burned as it hit Ambrose's empty stomach. He was thirsty, weak. The fire's warmth seemed far away as he shivered and fought to stay on his feet. The sword wound in his side throbbed. He gauged the strength of the two brawny footmen hovering by the door. In his condition, he couldn't hope to fight them. Playing the whore's slave was his best chance of escape.

And damned if Madame Mystère didn't arouse him as she dropped her bejeweled skirts and began unpinning the bodice.

He knew her, of course, if only by reputation. The famous Parisian courtesan was rumored to own more jewels than all of Prinny's mistresses combined and to have once entertained Napoleon himself.

But he hadn't expected her to be so young, so… innocent looking. The stunning beauty with moonglow hair and big blue eyes could've passed for a debutante in any ballroom in London. Except for those thick, lush lips. He'd never seen lips such as hers. They tempted a man to press his mouth to them. They promised ecstasy.

By the time she stepped out of her crinolines and removed her corset, Ambrose, against his will, was entranced. Long, shapely legs, a tiny waist and large, plump breasts showed through a thin, gauzy chemise. She'd made removing one's clothes an art, even while her light eyes remained as cold as a Prussian morning. He'd make them burn and plead before he was done with her. And show her how it felt to be brought to passion while strangers watched.

How long since he'd had a woman? He'd been on the Peninsula three years. An officer did not press his needs on the camp followers. There had been one widowed *señora*, but she'd turned into a watering pot halfway through his lovemaking. What man of honor could have finished then? Surely that was the reason his cock betrayed him now.

Loosening the ties of her chemise, Madame pulled it off her pale shoulders and retreated to a red divan. She lay on her side to offer an eyeful of her slender legs encased in white silk, and a tempting glimpse of her bountiful breasts.

"Kneel before me, slave." Her tone was harsh. Commanding.

Every bone in his body rebelled. He couldn't force himself to obey. No woman had ever ordered Ambrose Delacourt.

His captor remained beside him, watching him with an intensity that soured his stomach. He must endeavor to forget the bastard's presence. And the rest of the depraved audience.

"Perhaps he's a buggerboy." The Frenchman ran a hand over Ambrose's chest and pinched his nipple. "Do you like men, Major?"

Ambrose twisted away, straining at his manacles. He braced himself for a blow, but the madman merely smiled, showing perfectly white teeth.

"Don't worry, Major. We'll find plenty of uses for your cock before the weekend is over." De Séréville palmed his own rod until a small wet spot appeared on the placket of his satin breeches.

Clamping his jaw, Ambrose looked away. This situation must be suffered. What kind of fool allowed his pride to prevent what might be his only chance for escape? Willing himself to relax, to play the game, he dropped to one knee, ignoring the sharp stitch in his side.

"I am your humble slave, my lady."

"Oh, bravo!" The marquis applauded then nodded to his servants, who produced a key and unlocked the iron cuffs.

As Ambrose rubbed his raw wrists, flexing his fists against the tingling in his deadened arms, he stared into Madame Mystere's ice blue eyes. They sparkled like the diamonds at her throat.

"This should be a most entertaining night." The marquis sighed and settled into a leather wing chair. He motioned for a young maid to come to him and sit in his lap, then began fondling the girl's breasts.

Ambrose thought he saw the courtesan flinch at the sight of the young maid being abused. But when she looked down at him, her expression was brittle.

"Lower your eyes, slave, and remove my stockings!" She lifted a leg to him.

He grasped her warm leg, his calluses catching on the silk. As he reached beneath her chemise to untie her garter, his hands trembled.

Her skin was soft and hot to the touch where he caressed the inside of her thigh. Slowly he drew her stocking down and her musky woman's scent drifted to his nostrils.

She stroked his flagging member with her foot, caressing with her toes until it once again stood at attention. How mortifying. He risked a quick glance at her. A small smile hovered around her lush, ruby lips.

He'd played boudoir games with a particularly feisty opera dancer once, but his inclinations had never included feet. Yet watching Mystere's dainty silk-clad toes rubbing his cock shot a rush of blood straight to his groin.

"Pay attention, slave!" She gripped his hair and tugged his head back to look at her. "You will answer, 'Yes, mistress.' to my commands."

The marquis chuckled wickedly. "We should find the dog a collar."

Ambrose ground his teeth. He'd be damned if this Parisian whore would best him. He raised a brow and smiled. "Yes, mistress," he drawled.

She grabbed a glass of wine and sipped as he removed her other stocking. When he'd completed the task she held the cup to his lips and bid him drink the rest. It seemed a kindness until she muttered, "Perhaps that will loosen up his provincial English reserve."

The devil! She was a cold-hearted whore.

But for a thin layer of batiste, she lay naked. He sucked in a breath as she grabbed its hem, raised it to her stomach and bent one knee. The blondest fleece he'd ever seen crowned her pink nether lips.

"Lick me, slave."

Ambrose bent to the task. Her moist flesh was softer than silk on his tongue. There were worse tortures than this. He dug his fingers into her creamy thighs, spread her wide, and set to complying with eager lips, swirling his tongue through every crevice, around every fold. Soon her musky juices flowed, and her fingers played in his hair. She even lifted her hips as he delved his tongue deep inside her. The only thing missing was a chorus of soft sighs.

Once upon a time in his misspent youth, he'd prided himself on enticing the sweetest sounds from a woman. The room echoed with the moans of contented couples. Yet Madame Mystère remained surprisingly quiet.

What was her real name?

He raised his gaze and found her watching him intently, her expression unreadable except for her eyes. In their depths he spied... confusion.

But they soon chilled again. "I did not give you leave to stop, slave," she spat.

Vowing to force a moan from her, he buried his nose in her yellow curls and renewed his efforts. His cock pulsed with need. The wound in his side, his bruised and aching body, all faded in his driving hunger to plunge into her tight passage. Whether Madame commanded him to or not, he would take her.

With his fingers he exposed her swollen pleasure button and used his teeth to capture it, stroking it with his tongue before he began suckling her in earnest.

She jerked her hips, and then clenched her fists in his hair, but still no sound escaped her. As he inserted a finger, then two, and mimicked what his cock would soon be doing, he glanced again at her face. Her eyes were closed. He reached up and slid her chemise off one breast and lightly teased the rose-pink nipple. Soon he was caressing her magnificent breast and rubbing his thumb over its hardened peak.

Her breathing became more and more labored and she clamped her thighs around his head as he alternately licked and suckled her, working his fingers faster and faster.

She bucked and then stiffened. Now was the moment! He rose up, lay over her, and sunk his cock in to the hilt. Ripples of pleasure gripped him and he squeezed his eyes shut to gain control. But his body was too far gone. He dropped his head to her breast as he pushed into her again.

At last, she gasped. It was enough to send him over. Finesse abandoned, he drove onto her hard and fast before crying out and shooting his seed into her like an untried schoolboy. With a final violent push he strained and stiffened while the most powerful orgasm in his memory rolled through him.

He lay on her as the tidal wave of pleasure ebbed, weak as a newborn. The release left him sated, but exhausted, trembling. He was still inside her, still hard. He meant to rise, get off, but he couldn't find the energy. His eyelids grew heavy. And he knew no more.

What was the matter with her?

Eva blinked and disentangled her fingers from the Englishman's curly brown locks. His breath tickled her nipple and his rough beard scratched her skin.

Since when did she cradle a man's head against her bosom? Only in her earliest years of training had she allowed a climax to make her forget her surroundings. Allowed? There'd been no allowing just now, only surrendering to a power greater than her will.

The old count had taught her many things, chief among them how to determine what she wanted from men and how to use her beauty to get it. But the importance of remaining in control had been his most valuable lesson.

She glanced over at the marquis, hoping he'd been too absorbed by his own coupling to notice her abandonment.

He had the maid on her knees before him, his spunk on her face, and his cock softening. But his sharp gaze was fixed on Eva.

Merde. She squirmed and pushed at the Englishman.

But he didn't budge.

His head lay on her breast, his dark lashes fringed against high cheekbones, flushed with fever. A fine sheen of sweat beaded his brow.

"Get up!" She pushed at his heavy weight again.

When he still didn't stir she brushed the hair from his face. He was burning hot! How had he found the strength to perform?

Rien!

Her plan would not be put into effect this night.

Chapter 3

"Perhaps your maid could tend him, Madame."

De Séréville had summoned Eva to his study as the physician was leaving. Why would he suggest such a thing? Was he playing a dangerous game of cat and mouse?

"Nurse the Englishman, my lord? Marie is more suited to styling hair than tending sickbeds."

"I would consider it a personal favor. My maid is squeamish with blood, and my footmen were hired more for causing injuries than nursing them." He ran the back of his hand down her cheek. "I daresay she can be trusted to tell you if he speaks of war matters in the night? You are Napoleon's favorite, are you not?"

Eva searched the marquis' face. She could tell nothing from his eyes. She dared not trust him, but perhaps this would afford her the chance to speak with the spy in private.

"Very well. If you insist. I'll have her check on him after I retire. Will that do?"

"*Oui. Merci.*" He clicked his heels, took her hand, and brought it to his wet lips.

An hour later, the halls were deserted as Eva entered the upper bedchamber dressed in her maid's thick black gown and oversized mobcap. The room was cold, the fireplace empty and the Englishman thrashed about, threatening to reopen his wound. His sheets were soaked. If the fever reached his lungs he wouldn't last the night.

Perhaps that would be merciful.

Certainly, it would be safer for her. She could leave tomorrow and report to Wellesley that his spy had perished, taking his secrets with him.

But what a waste. Such a courageous, handsome officer. Such a talented mouth and tongue….

No! How could she let her thoughts stray to that?

She lit the coals, then took the servants' staircase to fetch clean bed linens and willow bark tea, scurrying back to the room lest another servant recognize her. After changing the bedding, she strode to the basin and wrung out a cloth.

The moment the cool rag touched his forehead, he seemed to calm. As she pressed it to his temple, she studied him. The high cheekbones and Roman nose, even the masculine shape of his lips spoke of an aristocratic ancestry.

She ran her palm down his distinguished jaw, and he pushed into her hand and mumbled something. Though she leaned closer, he only muttered something about Little John and Sherwood. Were they code names?

His voice was low and gravelly. When he'd grinned and answered her earlier, she'd been shocked at his deep dimples and even deeper voice.

Russet hair covered the area between his flat brown nipples. She ran the wet cloth over the hard muscles and down his concave stomach. His chest burned beneath her fingers, yet he was a powerful presence, even in illness. She pictured him as he might have dressed on the streets of London before the war.

He'd wear a tailor-made satin coat, broad at the shoulders and nipped at the waist, and a starched white cravat tied expertly round his neck. And on his head, a tall beaver hat he would sweep off as he smiled and bowed to the ladies of the English *ton*.

When she'd traveled to London as a child, Eva had peered from her carriage and gazed with envy at the gentlemen and ladies strolling down the sidewalk with their canes and parasols, eating ices, and buying ribbons. At the time, they'd seemed to enjoy a freedom she would never achieve.

She'd earned that freedom now. But at what cost?

Eva poured the tea, sat beside the English officer, and forced a sip down his throat. He mumbled something again, and she bent to listen. But it was only more disjointed mumbling, and again, the name John.

She alternated between cold cloths and the tea until he finally grew still. She dozed off in the chair until the major's raspy wheezing awoke her. He was shivering uncontrollably. Jumping up, she added more coals to the fire and pulled the counterpane back over his shaking body. She rubbed his arms and legs until her muscles screamed for rest, but still he shivered. Finally, she slipped next to him beneath the blankets, sharing her own heat.

Sometime close to dawn, she raised her head and looked at him. He was staring at her, his eyes fevered and full of anguish. Was he suffering pain from his injuries? Or did he, too, harbor deep regrets? He'd find no absolution from her.

The past two years she'd hoped to find a measure of redemption by using her body for a greater good. But this mission might very well condemn her to hell if she wasn't already damned. Her orders were to rescue the major if possible. But under no circumstances reveal her identity to the French.

If she couldn't save him, she must poison him.

Eva fingered the gold locket around her neck. Even to prevent a mad Corsican from conquering the world, could she murder an innocent man?

Ambrose opened his eyes to sunshine pouring through a lavishly dressed window. Where had he billeted last night? Why couldn't he remember making the acquaintance of his host? And why the devil was he naked?

Throwing off the duvet, he tried to swing his legs over and sit up, but a sharp pain wrenched his side and one of his ankles was chained to the bedpost. Despair weighted his chest as he remembered last night. It had not been a wicked dream.

Yet as he squinted at the bright sunlight, his heart lifted. He'd not seen daylight in weeks. Nor lain in a soft bed. And his body felt rather replete for all its aches and pains. He touched the dressing on his side. Someone had stitched and bound his wound.

The veteran soldier in him automatically assessed his surroundings. Upper bedchamber, smallish, but not the attic. Perhaps there'd be a handy tree outside the window. No clothes, no weapons. Nothing to jig the lock on this blasted leg iron.

Footsteps outside his door sent him flying back under the covers. As the key turned in the lock and the knob rattled, he closed his eyes and faked sleep.

The rustle of a skirt came close to the bed followed by separate, lighter footsteps and the clank of a tea tray, and then a heavier set of boots. Ambrose breathed in the reviving aroma of coffee and his stomach gurgled.

"*Merci.* You may go."

It was her. Madame Mystère.

The lighter footsteps—a maid presumably—faded toward the door.

"Madame, you claimed your maid to be no nurse, yet she has wrought a miracle. He is a glorious specimen of manhood, is he not?" The Marquis de Séréville gave a long sigh. "I've ordered a servant to shave him. I wish to see his face clearly when we use him tonight."

A soft hand landed on his forehead. "Unfortunately, he's still feverish. Perhaps by tomorrow night…"

But he wasn't feverish. Slightly weak, perhaps, but except for his wound, he felt remarkably well.

"I have plans for him this evening," the marquis said. "If he's not well by tonight, he's of no further use to me."

Madame Mystère gave a throaty chuckle. "You are more impatient than a child at *Noël*. I think I should be insulted," she purred. "I don't have the proper equipment to compete with a man."

"*Chérie*," the marquis said huskily. "I can provide any sort of equipment you wish to use."

Lord. Good thing his stomach was empty.

"We want him able to withstand your equipment, don't we?"

"He served you well enough last night with a fever." An edge had come into his captor's voice. "Perhaps, too well?"

A tense moment of silence passed. Ambrose wondered what he was hinting at. The Madame's skirts swished toward the window.

"Perhaps the food will revive him."

"Just so he's able to perform. Or I'll return him to La Force for execution."

"Does Henri Clarke know you keep a spy at your party?"

The whore seemed to be challenging her lover. But why? Was this a game between them?

"My dear, Napoleon's minister of war has much more to worry over than one British prisoner."

After several seconds of charged silence, she answered, "As you say, Julian."

Ambrose heard the marquis' boots step to the door. "Do you join us for *Vingt et un* this afternoon?"

"Card games bore me. I require a nap before this evening's entertainment."

The marquis answered, "But of course." Then the door opened and clicked shut.

The mattress dipped at his hip and he breathed in the courtesan's alluring scent.

"Listen carefully, we haven't got much time," she said urgently at his ear, her breath tickling his neck.

Ambrose opened his eyes and beheld a woman poles apart from the night before. The sultry courtesan had been transformed into a proper lady, dressed for a walk in the park or perhaps sitting at her escritoire writing letters. The sunlight framed her head and reflected off her perfectly pinned hair. Her yellow silk morning gown seemed to glow. A golden locket lay nestled in the delicious cleavage peeping above her bodice.

He'd have to watch his step around this stunning chameleon. "Much time for wh—"

She scowled and clamped her hand over his mouth. "Speak quietly. He might be listening at the door."

Why would she warn him, except to establish herself as his confidant? Best to play the harmless rogue until he knew more. He grabbed her hand and kissed the palm before she snatched it away.

"Make up your mind. Do you wish me to speak or to listen?" He grinned.

"Pay attention." As she glanced anxiously at the door, he grabbed the sides of her head and kissed her full on the lips.

But he'd barely begun to taste her before she struggled violently and shoved away, wiping her mouth with her hand.

"Don't *ever* do that again!"

Ambrose blinked. Rather a fierce reaction to a simple kiss. He sat up, leaned back against the pillows, and cleared his throat. "I don't suppose you could hunt up some clothes for me, could you, darling?"

"I am not your darling," she muttered between her teeth. "This is not a game. And—"

"Was it you who fetched a doctor to sew me up?" He pressed a palm to the bandage. "Making sure your slave stays in good health?"

Her eyes flared in anger and her lips compressed. "I think I preferred you on your knees, weak with fever. At least then you did not interrupt me."

One of her white blonde curls had come loose in her effort to avoid his kiss. In different circumstances, he would have dug his fingers in, pulled out every pin, and then spread her fair locks across his pillow.

"What is it you wanted to say?"

She dropped onto the edge of the bed again and placed a hand on his chest.

"You are called *The Wolf*?"

Nothing else she could have said would have shocked him as much. He could only hope he'd recovered quickly enough.

"I beg your pardon?"

"That is your code name, is it not?"

Bloody hell! "Madame, I have no idea—"

"I work for Wellesley, same as you. I was sent to rescue you, you fool."

He stared at her. A secret agent working for Wellesley as a courtesan? If it were true, it was bloody brilliant. But she'd been too smooth last night. And why not simply unlock him now? He couldn't take a chance that she might be a double agent.

"Well, you may be babbling nonsense, but I certainly wouldn't be opposed to a rescue. So, if you'll just unlock this thing," he shook his chained leg, "and scare me up some breeches, you can call me anything you like."

She folded her arms across her chest and shook her head.

"You can't leave now. It was all arranged for last night, but you fell unconscious." Pushing off the bed, she paced to the table and began pouring coffee.

He still had pertinent information on French troop positions. And if she were a double agent, Wellesley must be informed. But first he should eat.

"How inconsiderate of me. Is there bacon under that silver dome? I'm devilish hungry."

Absently, she lifted the dome, grabbed the tray and brought it to him. He could almost see the cogs turning in her brain as she dropped beside him and set the tray on his lap. Her knuckles brushed his privates through the muslin sheet and she—

By God, she snatched her hand back as if she'd been bitten. After boldly grabbing him last night. Which act was false? Or were they both?

"Eat up. You'll need your strength for tonight."

"I thought you were going to—" he leaned close and whispered in her ear, "—help me escape." Like a ravenous dog, he set to eating the bread, cheese and a thin broth.

"Not now. He'd know I assisted you and my position would be revealed."

"You could always come with me," Ambrose offered, swallowing a mouthful of coffee. He was thoroughly intrigued. Was she friend or foe?

"I can't. Even now he probably watches from a spy hole. Whatever the marquis has planned must be endured tonight." She uttered the words as if they were her personal mantra. Who was she? What had led her to the life she now lived? He had to know more before he could decide whether to trust her.

He'd begin by introducing himself. He cleared his throat. "It occurs to me, despite our rather... intimate activities last night, we've never been properly introduced." Though he couldn't stand, he bowed as best he could from the bed. "Major Ambrose Delacourt, seventh brigade, Infantry, at your service. And, you are?"

She just looked at him, her big blue eyes turning glacial. "You may call me mistress tonight, as you certainly *will* be at my service."

As she continued to stare at him, memories of last night rocked him. His cock began to swell and his pulse sped up. Once he'd gotten past her first command, he'd enjoyed "servicing" her.

She drew in a deep breath and heat flared in her eyes, and he knew she was remembering the carnal pleasure they'd shared.

"Well, m'dear. As much as I'd love to have another go, if you'll just sneak me a key and some clothes, I'll disappear without worrying your pretty head about it."

"I'm afraid that's not possible. You must wait until after everyone retires to their rooms," she said softly. "There will be a horse waiting for you behind the carriage house. What were you doing so far behind enemy lines?"

The abrupt change of subject caught him off guard. So, she *had* been sent to lull him into disclosing some vital information.

"A rather stupid wager, I'm afraid. I made a bet with my Sergeant that I could pinch a bottle of brandy from the Frenchie's camp. And how would it look to my troops if—"

"Do you take me for a fool?" Coffee sloshed over the rim of his porcelain cup as she jumped off the bed. "Did you discover the information you went exploring for before you were caught?"

"I beg your pardon?" Did she expect him to simply blurt out numbers and locations? "I'll admit, sneaking across enemy lines for brandy is a bit stupid, but I'd hardly call a wager a—-"

"*Mon Dieu*," she growled under her breath and dropped beside him again. "Think, Major. How would I know your code name unless I am on your side? I've been eavesdropping on secret conversations and sneaking into my paramours' desks for almost two years."

For a moment she made horrible, agonizing sense. What if—no! He shook himself. He couldn't risk believing her. More likely she was a double agent. Either way, he couldn't take the chance.

"After you went missing, word spread that you'd deserted."

He sat up. "Deserted?" What rot was this?

"Arthur knew better, of course, and asked me to keep my ears open for word of you. He was most impressed when you saved Lieutenant Pomeroy's life. When I—"

"Pardon, but did you just refer to *Colonel* Lord Wellesley as *Arthur*?" And how the devil did she know about Pomeroy?

She gave him a quelling look. "When I heard de Séréville was boasting of a special diversion at his party, I feared, with his reputation for deviant pleasures, that the entertainment might include English prisoners." She shrugged. "You're not the first."

Ambrose became aware his mouth was hanging open and clamped it shut. He didn't believe a word of her preposterous story. He couldn't. She was obviously as mad as King George.

"I hadn't much time to prepare. Did you reveal any sensitive information under torture?"

Indignant, he straightened his spine. "No. Does *Arthur* speak to you in your dreams, or does he come to you in person?"

"What? How could—oh! You still don't believe me!" Her eyes flared in fury, and then slowly cooled to their usual frosty blue. "Do you think it wise to mock me, Major?" Her voice had turned low and chilling. "When I stand between you and certain death?"

Just his luck. The only one who might help him escape was completely addle-brained.

"You're exactly right, Madame. I apologize."

She stared at him a moment then stood.

"Don't forget. Behind the mews. I'll endeavor to make sure you're not locked in irons." Then she picked up her skirts and marched to the door. She reached for the doorknob but looked back. "I was going to try to keep de Séréville from you tonight. But perhaps I'll let him have at you."

With that she opened the door and closed it quietly behind her.

Ambrose listened to her footsteps fade down the hallway, then shoved the tray aside, grabbed the hairpin he'd stolen from her, and went to work picking the lock at his ankle.

The stubborn man could rot in hell!

As Marie undressed her, Eva fumed over the major's asinine refusal to see the truth. Did he think women in general too stupid or weak for espionage? Or was it her in particular?

After reminding her loyal maid of their escape plan should the worst happen, Eva dismissed her, flopped onto the bed and hugged a pillow. Perhaps the witless Englishman had done her a favor. Rather than tonight's events souring her stomach, she would take great pleasure in calling him a dog and ordering him to lick her slippers. In watching the marquis humble and abuse him.

No, that wasn't true.

Turning over, she stared at the burgundy silk half-canopy above her. She'd always been honest with herself at least. She'd take no pleasure in what the marquis would do. Nor in the sight of the major's hard, muscular body exploited.

She untied her chemise, closed her eyes, and let her mind remember Major Delacourt's dark eyes smiling at her after he kissed her palm. And how they'd burned with desire after she brushed against his surprisingly hard member. She envisioned him as he held her head and pressed his lips to hers.

Thinking of him thrusting into her last night, she began touching herself. She pictured him lying naked and chained to that bed, his tanned skin so masculine against the white sheets, vulnerable to her touch, weak with desire for her, she would straddle his hips....

She finally achieved a small, disappointing orgasm, a pale imitation of the devastating climax she'd experienced last night with his hands and mouth claiming her body.

Fear gripped her. Satisfying herself had been her only diversion these last few years. If she couldn't—was she now to be denied even that small recreation?

Calm down, Eva, a voice of reason reminded her. *You are merely exhausted.*

She'd been up all night tending the aggravating man. As if to confirm her diagnosis, an unladylike yawn escaped her.

No, she would not see him violated. But nor could she allow him to take control of her body as he had last night. Not even if he were to call her by her real name and kiss her tenderly, as a husband might....

She stood in her country villa surrounded by a lovely garden with a fountain at its center. In the distance sheep grazed on vibrant green hillsides and she smiled at the sure knowledge that her children played somewhere close by. As she gazed out her kitchen window, she spied her husband just returning from his ride, home to her and their children. He came through the door, picked her up, swung her around, and kissed her long and hard with all the true love in his heart....

But this time, in the familiar dream her love had a face. Major Delacourt.

Eva awoke to a blood-curdling scream followed by muffled hysterical sobs.

Mon Dieu! What had happened?

She rose, tied her wrapper and hurried from her room toward the sound of a maid's frightful weeping.

As she rounded the corner in the hall, she saw the major braced at the staircase landing in nothing but ill-fitting breeches. His back was to her, but she could see he held a terrified, half-dressed footman in front of him, a shaving knife held against the man's throat. On the other side of the hallway, a maid wailed behind her hands.

The marquis stood halfway down the stairs, his right arm extended, pointing a pistol at Ambrose and the footman. His smile was icy.

"Go ahead, Major. Think you I care if you kill a servant?" He pulled back the hammer as he mounted the stairs.

With no time for second thoughts, Eva grabbed a large china vase of fresh flowers from a hall table and raced up behind Ambrose. In a flash she lifted it high and brought it crashing down on his head.

He recoiled, wavered on his feet, and looked back at her with pure loathing just before his eyes rolled back in his head and he dropped to the floor.

The footman scrambled out of the way as the marquis lowered his pistol.

"What a quick thinker you are, Madame." His gaze drifted to the broken ceramic shards along the landing and his mouth tugged down a little moue of disappointment. "But, *chérie,* the footman could have been replaced."

Chapter 4

Ambrose raised his head and winced. His skull ached like the very devil! He yanked at the ropes binding his wrists and ankles to chair in a dark, windowless room. He'd been right not to trust that whore. Rescue him, indeed.

How long had he been out?

As his eyes adjusted to the dark he deduced he was in a small dressing room. A moment later the door opened and a timid maid approached carrying a candle and a glass of water.

"The lady who saved my Jean Paul, she bid me bring you this," she said in French. Averting her gaze from his nakedness, she held the glass to his lips.

The clear liquid tempted him, made him aware of his parched mouth. But he turned his head and let it dribble down his chest. Madame Mystère had been toying with him. There'd be no horse waiting. His next attempt at escape must succeed. If the whore knew his code name, what else did she know? How many Englishman would die because of her?

With an impatient huff, the maid called out and a manservant appeared beside her. The footman grabbed Ambrose's hair and held his head back while the maid pinched his nose. No matter how vigorously he fought, he finally had no choice but to open his mouth for air. She poured the liquid down his throat, nearly drowning him.

Goddamn it! He coughed and sputtered and spit, but it did no good. He'd ingested some of it. Whatever it was.

As he cursed and flailed, the couple scurried from the room, leaving him in darkness again.

He must keep his wits about him. He had to get word to Wellesley that he was feeding information to the enemy through a sly courtesan pretending to be an ally. The marquis might be depraved, but the Madame was evil.

An hour later, he was still alive. He just wasn't sure death wasn't preferable.

Eva sat beside the marquis counting the moments until this mission was complete. She'd hosted many naughty assemblies at her townhome. What made the Marquis de Séréville's seem so malevolent? Never before had she grown disgusted watching Paris' crème de la crème debauch themselves. Usually she felt a rush of power at the wicked secrets revealed by society's leaders and stored them away for later use.

But tonight a deep uneasiness descended over her.

She was no better than them. Since the age of sixteen she'd survived—no, thrived by taking advantage of men's weaknesses. She'd chosen her lovers from among the wealthiest of men and never examined how her actions might hurt others.

Until a strange little man had approached her. Offering a way to make amends and, perhaps, a difference. She'd proved her loyalty to England by memorizing information from papers in her paramour's desk, and giving the information to the milliner spy. From that day on she'd felt a new sense of purpose and control.

But she had no control over the events here. The turmoil she felt now reminded her of her terrifying childhood. Of her father's perfidy. And of the uncertainty of her future.

A high-pitched yelp drew her attention back to the stage. The marquis had announced that in honor of their English captive, the theme of tonight's charades would be Britain's most famous playwright. Eva had already been subjected to *Measure For Measure*, where two men had measured the length of their pricks by using a woman's throat, and a depraved version of a scene from *Two Gentlemen From Verona* where one of the women portrayed Julia dressed as a boy. Wearing a buckled on dildo, 'Julia' took 'Sylvia' in the mouth while a gentleman playing Valentine took her from behind.

At the moment, one of the guests' paramours was dressed as a milkmaid and bent over a bale of hay while a "farmer" ploughed into her from behind. Her breasts bounced with each thrust and she squealed again when the man slapped her buttocks.

The audience cheered him on and called out their guesses as to which Shakespearean play the scene represented.

"*Love's Labours Lost.*"

"*All's Well That Ends Well.*"

The "farmer" spewed his milk over the maid's reddened buttocks and shouted, "That was just *As You Like It*, wench!"

The audience cheered as curtains closed on servants clearing the stage and setting up new backdrops. Whores scantily dressed as sixteenth century wenches carried in trays with more wine to whet the thirst of the guests.

The marquis stood to appoint the next players. Immaculately dressed in snowy lace and deep purple satin, he raised his arms to quiet the crowd.

"And now we come to the moment you've all been waiting for. The *pièces de résistance.*" He turned to Eva and offered his arm. "*Ma chérie*, if you'll follow me. It is our turn."

The crowd applauded and Eva rose and smiled and followed de Séréville to the anteroom next door to change into a costume. She'd agreed to play a scene with him. Nothing less than she'd expected. But where was Major Delacourt?

"He is even more handsome clean-shaven, is he not?" The marquis stepped aside and gestured to the major, who was gagged and tied to a chair.

With an evil smirk, De Séréville approached his prisoner. He ran a hand down the major's jaw and Ambrose jerked away from his touch.

The charming rogue from this morning was gone. His naked body gleamed with sweat, and his cock stood proudly erect, a deep purple hue at the tip. He fidgeted and fought his bindings and when he looked up and noticed her, his glassy eyes filled with hate, and his rod twitched in eagerness.

This was no ordinary fever.

She turned to de Séréville. "What have you given him?"

"It is a special herb I obtained from the Orient. He should be torturously stiff all night."

Mon Dieu! If she still believed in God, she would have prayed. Even once the Englishman found release, he'd be in agony most of the night. The needs of his body would war with his natural inhibitions. He might be capable of anything. Could tonight break his spirit?

Events were spinning further out of her control. She couldn't protect him.

She wished she had a pistol at this moment. To hell with her identity. She would shoot the marquis between the eyes, slash the ropes binding the major and put him on a fast horse to Calais.

She swallowed the lump in her throat. "And what is to be our performance?"

"You shall play Kate, the shrew." The marquis waved a hand at Marie who held a thin bodice, skirt and stomacher in the style of three centuries before. "You are adept at role playing, are you not, Mystère?"

Eva searched his face for a hint of double meaning, but she could see nothing in his expression except heated anticipation.

"The major shall play your suitor, Petruchio."

A servant placed a jaunty cap with a feather on the major's head.

"And I shall play your dear father, Baptista, who despairs of ever taming his naughty Kate." The marquis smiled evilly.

Marie began helping her undress.

"I have explained to the spy that tonight you are his love slave. A settling of debts, so to speak." Keeping his gaze on her, the marquis snapped his fingers and the same two brawny footmen from last night freed Ambrose, grabbed him by the arms and lifted him to his feet. The servants dressed him in a quilted doublet without a shirt and a pair of Venetian breeches.

"I shall enjoy watching Petruchio tame you."

Dread choked her. Eva fought to keep her expression composed as Marie lifted off her dress and pinned on the Elizabethan costume.

"I see. And what if I do not wish to be tamed? Suppose I box his ears as proud Kate did?"

The marquis narrowed his eyes. "I'm counting on it."

She mustn't let de Séréville see her fear. She schooled her features to indifference. But why was she not indifferent? What was it about this Englishman? Why did she care? *Merde!* She must not care. That would lead to insanity.

She attempted a coy smile. "It sounds exciting. But I see no need for a feverish prisoner to be involved. I doubt he is strong enough to tame me. I would be tamed by a virile man like you, my lord."

She moved close to the marquis. As it had perhaps hundreds of times, her body performed mechanically. She watched her hand lift to his chest as if it belonged to someone else. And in a way, it did.

The marquis grabbed her wrist. "Ah, *chérie*. Where do you go while you're seducing men? Back to Austria, perhaps?"

A chill snaked through her veins. "*Pardon*? I am right here."

"*Non*. Your body stays, but your mind wanders. I see it in your eyes." Her stomach clenched. "*Non*."

"*Oui*, Eva."

He'd called her Eva. She froze but said nothing.

"Did you ever wonder how I escaped Madame Guillotine during The Terror? I lived in Milan during the revolution. There was a scandalous rumor at that time that the Conte di Cabrissi had taken a famous young girl as his mistress."

He knew her past. He knew who she used to be! Alarm swirled through her. What else did he know about her?

"How... interesting, I'm sure." Eva turned and smoothed her hair. She made eye contact with her maid and gave her the sign to return to Paris and oversee their escape. She spun back to face de Séréville, meeting his hard gray eyes with a haughty glare. "But, what has that to do with us now? I played your game last night, Julian, but these tawdry theatricals grow tiresome. I'll participate in tonight's charade on one condition."

She held her breath.

He flashed a cunning smile. "I live to fulfill your desire, Madame."

"Having a stiff cock at my disposal the entire night excites me. Leave the prisoner with me all night to amuse myself as I may."

"That's impossible, Madame!" he barked. "Eh, that is, I would fear for your safety."

"You may watch from your little holes if you must, post guards at the door, or chain him." She paused. "I would hate Monsieur Clarke to discover you kept a British spy for your own amusement."

The Marquis' eyes narrowed and glittered with fury, promising retribution for her threat. "But of course you must have him to yourself tonight, *chérie*. After you've entertained my other guests, you may do with him what you will."

At his nod, the footmen dragged Ambrose to the door, untied the gag, and then tossed him out onto the stage.

Gripping her arm, the marquis pulled Eva out into the little theater.

She began a familiar chant she'd repeated in her mind as a child when her father beat her.

This must be endured. This must be endured.

A small frame with a straw mattress had been placed on stage along with the same merchant's backdrop from *Two Gentlemen From Verona*. Glasses clinked as the curtains drew apart and the light from dozens of torches lining the front of the stage blinded her. The small orchestra began to play and applause broke out.

"Petruchio, I give you my vicious, ill-tempered daughter. I bid you do what you must to tame her."

The marquis shoved her into the major and before she realized his intent, Ambrose caught her wrists behind her and pulled her firmly against him.

"Kiss me, Kate! We will be married on Sunday," he quoted from the play. His eyes wild with anger and lust, he lowered his mouth to hers.

Panicked, she turned her head and struggled, which rubbed her breasts against his bare chest.

"Ahhh, that's right," he whispered in her ear. "The magnificent Madame Mystère doesn't allow anyone to kiss her mouth." He clamped her jaw with his free hand and forced her lips to his.

Eva willed her mind to float away. But his touch became light, nibbling one corner of her mouth, then the other. His sensuous lips teased hers, sending a tingling through her nerves. His tongue licked at the seam of her mouth, coaxing, playing. She felt every stroke as if her lips were the harp strings and his tongue the nimble fingers.

She'd never been kissed so tenderly before. Had allowed no man's lips to touch hers since the count. And even him only in the beginning when she'd been too afraid to tell him no.

He changed the angle of his head and dropped a soft kiss under her ear and down her throat, which set the hair along her arms and nape to rise.

Slowly he brought his mouth to her lips, gazing into her eyes as he took possession. She belonged to him, he seemed to be saying, and this time she didn't fight him.

His kiss was filled with desperation, moving his mouth over hers, suckling at her tongue and generous in giving his. Yet she felt a measure of restraint as he cupped her face in his palms and explored the inside of her mouth.

A part of her noticed her hands had been freed and she now gripped his shoulders. His muscles bunched and corded beneath her palms. He angled his head, his mouth never leaving hers, and splayed his hands across her back, squeezing her to him. With a little groan, he rubbed his chest against her tightened nipples. A sharp ache and a gush of warmth between her thighs made her push her hips against him.

"Petruchio, who tames whom?" The marquis clamped a hand on the major's shoulder.

Bellowing a curse, Major Delacourt shoved her away. He reached up and yanked the feathered cap from his head. "Remove your clothes and kneel at my feet, wife."

Stunned, Eva blinked. For a moment, she'd forgotten they had an audience, or that Ambrose had been given an herb to make him rage with lust. His kiss had seemed real. And she had opened to him, returned his kisses.

Before she could decide what to do, Ambrose reached out, ripped her bodice down the middle and off her shoulders. Her breasts were exposed to the audience who hollered and clapped in approval.

She raised her hands to cover herself, but Madame Mystère would never react so.

The major stared at her breasts, his breathing hitched, and his eyes glazed over.

"They are so beautiful, so creamy and full." He reached out and cupped them in his hands, squeezing them together, thumbing her sensitive tips. "Your nipples are the palest pink, blushing just for me."

He pulled on them gently and rolled them between his fingers. The combination of his husky words and the sensation of his calloused hands on her tender skin made rational thought difficult.

Still holding them, kneading them, he lowered his head and licked each pointed nub, making her gasp in pleasure. He chose one and took it into his mouth, suckling and nibbling until she speared her fingers into his hair and tried to pull him off. He left it shiny wet, then blew on it.

Eva closed her eyes and tried to regain her usual reserve, but he went directly to the other, giving it the same reverent concentration. Her knees weakened as her body thrummed in rhythm with his suckling.

He withdrew and straightened, shivering. His eyes rolled back in his head and his hips jerked forward.

"Oh, God. I need...." When he opened his eyes, they blazed in fury. "On your knees!"

Should she comply? But no. The marquis would be more pleased if the taming was not so easy. She reached up and boxed the major's ears, thumbed her nose and flounced away.

"You shall be punished for that, shrew!" The major caught her arm, spun her around and dragged her to the bed.

The marquis called out, "Spank her, Petruchio!"

She struggled, but only a little as the major pulled her over his lap and flipped up her skirt, exposing her bare bottom.

Stealing herself for the blow, she focused on the wooden floor and the hairy warmth of the major's thigh beneath her palms.

Smack!

He hit her bottom hard with his bare hand.

The slap hurt and humiliated her. The guests applauded and encouraged him with obscene shouts. She should pretend to struggle and yell, but she couldn't summon her usual acting skills.

He spanked her bottom hard again. Real tears stung her eyes and she bit her lip. Where was her usual *ennui* with such role playing?

Another twack. Ow! Eva's shame simmered into fury. How dare he treat her so when she was risking herself to save him!

But his next blow was a mere tap and he began kneading her backside, slipping a finger along her crevice and dipping it into her passage which was surprisingly wet.

"Spread your legs."

The hard length beneath her stomach twitched and hardened more as she complied. His ragged breathing stopped a moment as he scooped up her moisture and used it to massage the tight ring of her anus.

"Do you take men here, wench?" He eased his thumb in and she tried not to squirm, willed herself to remain impassive. But his touch, his scent, the need in his deep voice kept her spirit present.

"Or only here?" His fingers traveled back down to swirl in her heat and press down on her little kernel. He slipped one finger in, and then another, pumping and massaging, his thumb still inserted above and she cried out and lifted herself to him, overcome with the need to feel him inside her.

His hands left her suddenly. He pushed her off his lap to her knees.

"Tonight, *you* kneel before *me*." Anger tinged his voice. His hands trembled as he tried to unbuttoned the flap of his Venetians. Finally he ripped them open and palmed his painfully swollen rod, touching the glistening tip to her lips. He grabbed her hair and pushed in as she opened to him. A long groan escaped his lips as she swirled her tongue down his length and sucked him in.

His penis tasted strong and sweet, its slick skin loose over an inflexible core. It was too long to take it all without gagging, so she clasped a hand around the base and pumped him while she tongued his little hole, then closed her lips around the tip and suckled.

With a strangled cry, he scooped her up under her arms, turned and threw her on the bed. He shoved her skirt up to her waist, lay over her and spread her thighs with his knees. But he didn't just take her. With beads of sweat on his brow and upper lip, he looked into her eyes.

"You want my cock, whore?" Desperate need edged his voice.

"I do. I want you, Major."

He squeezed his eyes closed. "No, I am Ambrose," he rasped.

"Take your release in me, Ambrose."

The words had barely left her mouth before he plunged into her. Her body sighed in fulfillment. As if her channel had craved him, longed to be filled and stretched by him again, she felt complete. She clasped him to her, wanting to protect him, to ease his distress.

He pumped his hips once, twice. The third time he cried out, his head thrown back, the veins in his neck straining. He shuddered and collapsed on top of her, his arms coming round her to hold her close.

Eva lay still, sliding her hands under his doublet to run them over his damp back. She looked over and saw the marquis had moved off stage, pumping into the backside of a courtesan bent over a chair. He dug his nails into her fleshy bottom and grunted with each thrust until he came.

The crowd was breaking into couples or threesomes and moving out of the theater to find their beds.

Slowly, the stage candles were extinguished and the curtain closed, leaving them in shadows.

The major breathed harshly against Eva's shoulder, his body relaxed. But she knew his release was only a brief respite. Soon, the hunger would claim him again.

Chapter 5

His nose buried in her neck, Ambrose dragged a harsh breath into his lungs, reeling with the potent sweet scent of her.

The power of his release left him weak, boneless, finally at rest. But shame filled his soul. Never had he treated a woman so. Even if she were a traitor and a whore, he was a gentleman. *Had been a gentleman.* If nothing else, he was still an officer in His Majesty's service, damn it.

But he'd been on fire for hours, and a mad rage had swept over him, uncontrollable. It had turned him into a brutal, mindless, walking cock-stand. And there'd been witnesses. An audience of drunken, debauched French nobles. God, what had he done? That monster wasn't him.

And more peculiar, she had allowed it. Even now, she soothed him with her soft hands. Goose bumps formed on his skin and he shivered. "Are you hurt? Did I hurt you?"

"No. I am well."

He stirred, lifted off her, sliding out of her warmth. He couldn't look at her as he sat up and ran a hand through his hair.

"My apologies, Madame. I was not myself." He'd ripped the buttons off his breeches, for God's sake! What the hell had they forced down his gullet?

"Ambrose." Her voice sounded hesitant, worried, yet he liked hearing his name on her lips. She sat up and adjusted her skirt, fumbling with the remnants of her bodice. "If I hadn't bashed you over the head this afternoon, de Séréville would have shot that footman without remorse. You must believe me."

"Must I? And your reason for giving me that bloody potion?"

"That was not I. I knew nothing of that until I saw you tonight."

Could that be true? How could he believe anything she said? He stood, holding his breeches together.

"It doesn't matter now. It's over."

"*Mon Dieu*, if only that were true."

"What do you mean?"

But already his body began to burn again. As he turned to look at her a sizzling white heat pulsed through his veins and shot into his hardening cock. No. He would control it this time. He closed his eyes and pictured the icy streets of London, drifts of snow on the lawns of Havenwood, the freezing rain in Portugal. But he only flared hotter.

"Damn you to hell, I will not be reduced to a bloody sex fiend again!" He strode off the stage. He had to get away from this madhouse. Back to the peninsula and the honesty of a battle fought with rifle and sword.

"Ambrose!"

He heard her footsteps behind him and spun to challenge her. "If you are who you say, help me escape now!"

God help him, she'd wrapped herself in the bedding and pale blond locks of her hair fell from her elaborate coiffure. A fire swept through him, making his body tremble with lust. He wanted her again. She looked mouth-watering, as if she'd just risen from a satisfying tumble. He clamped his teeth together. But she hadn't been satisfied, had she? He'd given more pleasure to tavern maids when he was sixteen.

He turned and opened the changing room door. The marquis stood there, lazing against a hall table, his legs crossed at the ankle.

Two oversized footmen grabbed Ambrose's arms. He ducked away from one servant's hold and landed a right hook in the other one's jaw. But a beefy fist hit his wound and pain shot up his torso. He fell to one knee.

"*Arrêtez!*" The courtesan clamped a hand on the footman's arm to stop another blow. With the bedclothes slipping off one shoulder, she moved close to the marquis, who now held a pistol aimed at Ambrose.

"Julian. The shrew was properly tamed, was she not?" Her voice was sultry, placating.

"*Oui*, Madame. I was most entertained."

Ambrose steeled against the throbbing of his wound and got to his feet.

"I suppose I must keep my word or you'll go tattling to that twit, Clarke." He pouted, sauntered over to Ambrose, and ran his pale hand down his chest. When he tried to grab his genitals Ambrose knocked his hand away and drew back his fist, but the footmen grabbed him again.

"Until tomorrow night, Major." The marquis smoothed back Ambrose's hair and caressed his jaw.

"I'll see you in hell, you sick bastard."

The courtesan glared at the servants and ordered them in French to take the prisoner to her room. They looked to the marquis, and at his nod they dragged him away.

When Ambrose glanced back, he saw Madame Mystère whispering with the marquis, and then she kissed him. Damn it! Why did that make his gut roil?

All the while they climbed the staircase, his fever rose. The need raged more potent than before. His vision blurred, his body perspired, and his cock swelled and ached in hunger.

The guards shoved him into a large blue bedchamber before taking their posts on the other side of the door.

A moment later Madame strolled in and closed the door on them. She turned and smiled at him, then moved to light a candelabra on the mantle above a crackling fire.

"I can help you through the worst of the herb's effects."

"If you will not help me escape, leave me be."

He strode to the window and pulled back the heavy drapes. Three floors up. Overlooking the formal gardens. No tree or trellis in sight. No ledge to climb to the roof.

"You'll be more comfortable out of that ill-fitting costume." She closed the distance between them, tugging the tight doublet off his shoulders.

Trembling to hold himself in check, he let her pull his arms from the sleeves and stepped out of his torn breeches. As she helped him undress, the sheet slipped from her body. The sight of her voluptuous curves in the faint candlelight drove him to the brink of control.

He wanted—

He needed—

No. He'd be damned first.

He clenched his fist until he broke skin to keep from grabbing his cock and bringing himself to completion in front of her.

"Get out," he ordered through gritted teeth.

Her light blue eyes were filled with worry. Her lips were red and swollen. "I can help you."

"I said leave me. I don't want you here!" His hands shook. In his madness, he'd told himself Madame deserved whatever he did to her. But the truth was, a part of him had enjoyed the rough coupling. The herbed brew had merely unleashed those tendencies. Vivid images of her kneeling before him, her lips closed around him, made his knees weak and his rod burn with need.

She pressed her body to his, running her palms down his shoulders and chest and further down, closing her fingers around his throbbing shaft.

"You need me, Ambrose."

"No," he groaned, shaking his head, unable to keep from pushing his erection into her hand.

"It's all right," she whispered into his jaw and stroked her hand along his length. "Every man has needs." She slid a hand to his buttocks and cupped his cheek, squeezing in rhythm to her stroke.

How many men had she said that to? How many had she pleasured this way?

His rod leaked and she rubbed her thumb over the engorged tip, smearing the stalk with his clear fluid. He twitched in agonized pleasure.

While she increased the speed of her pumping, her other hand slid between his buttocks and pressed a finger against his anus.

"Oh God," he cried out. Resentment warred with relentless need.

"Don't fight it. Let go."

Closing his eyes, he pushed into her hand. When her finger entered his anus, he shouted and exploded in her hand, discharging against her stomach. Colored lights burst behind his eyes, and as she kept stroking him, a series of smaller spasms rocked him.

"Enough!" He grabbed her wrist and flung it away. Staggering back, he dropped onto the edge of the bed and doubled over. "How long?"

"Perhaps a little longer until the next time," she said softly. "Lie back and rest while you can. We can't leave until everyone sleeps."

His body shuddered in a powerful aftershock. Elbows on knees, he buried his head in his hands. Once he could breathe normally, he looked up, but averted his gaze when he saw her cleaning his seed off her stomach and breasts.

Loathing filled him. For her, and her part in this. But mostly for himself. Weariness crept over him and he laid back and rolled to his side.

Julian François Antoine Bichoté, the Marquis de Séréville, closed his eyes and came hard into his hand as he watched the whore push her finger into the English spy's hole. How delicious. He only wished he could have seen the major's face and watch his milk spew out. But catching the expression of concern on the courtesan's face was worth missing the spy's.

This spyhole—ah, the irony of the double entendre—was hidden in the wall above the bed. Perhaps he should move to the fireplace eyehole. Maybe later. For now, this afforded the best view of the room.

Julian had planned to bugger the spy himself tonight, but the bitch had him by the balls. Henri Clarke was a bureaucrat with no imagination or tolerance for deviant pleasures. He'd never understand that protocol would never win this war.

The marquis could simply kill her before she could return to Paris, but he wanted to see her publicly branded a spy and sentenced to the guillotine.

Ah, well. The waiting would only make taking the rugged Englishman that much more satisfying. Sometimes pleasure was found more in drawing out the moment. In the meantime, he could anticipate the next performance.

He wanted to watch as Eva was violated and abused. He wanted her spirit and body broken. He wanted to see if the Major could get past her defenses.

For four years Madame Mystère had ruled the Parisian demimonde with poise and confidence. Nothing touched her. Even when offered *carte blanche* by some of the most powerful men of France, she'd never shown a weakness for anyone.

Until last night.

In the past year or so, she'd had no protector and her guest list had become curiously more political in nature. Julian had set out to investigate everything about her, especially when Napoleon's ministers had become her prime companions.

He'd hardly believed what he'd read in the intelligence report. The famous little girl from Salzburg all grown up. And with the Austrian armies pressing south into Italy, it seemed clear where Eva's loyalties lay. But Julian had to be sure.

The moment he'd seen the British officer lying wounded in La Force, his gut had told him the Viscount's brother, a well-connected peer, might prove useful.

Using British prisoners at his chateau was fun, but a lord of the realm? Would British intelligence risk their secret weapon to rescue him?

Julian leaned back in his chair and waited for the next round. Would the spy take her violently again? Would she allow it? Would he tell her his secrets? Would she? It was all so delightfully amusing. If only he could hear more than muffled words.

But watching was entertaining enough. For now.

And once Eva proved she was a traitor, he would have his fun before seeing them both executed as spies.

Ambrose gasped for breath. Soaking wet, he flung the covers off. Burning. Shooting pains in his groin. His bollocks were on fire and his staff so hard, the head touched his stomach. He grabbed it to stroke himself, but the pain was too much. Goddamn, bloody, fucking hell! He'd lain here as long as he could stand it.

The clinking of porcelain and a splash of water pouring jerked his attention across the room.

She was there, wringing out a cloth into a china basin. It had taken only slightly longer this time. The candles were not much shorter. The fire flickered behind her and silhouetted her form. She'd donned a demure lounging robe, combed her hair and braided it down her back. It reached to just above the curve of her petite, heart-shaped bottom.

"Why the bloody hell are you still here?" He got up and began pacing, running his fingers through his hair.

"You are my mission," she murmured as she approached him with a wet cloth.

"You persist in your story?"

She placed the damp linen over his mouth. "Not so loud. I don't know how much he hears."

When she moved the cool cloth onto his cheek, he grabbed her wrist and held it. "Why do you do this?"

"Is it so incredible to you that a woman could be a spy?"

"It's not your gender which makes me doubt you, Madame. If you were in my position, would you risk believing a Parisian whore?"

Did he detect a flinch at his words? Perhaps she was telling the truth. Had this potion made his wits go begging? Or could he trust his instinct to believe her? Either way, she was the key to getting out of here. But the officer in him abhorred his predicament. He didn't want to need her.

"Believe what you will." She pitched the cloth to the floor. "I already spent one night sponging you off."

A foggy memory emerged of waking from a nightmare to find himself in her arms. The way she'd held him then, her expression anxious. Now she glanced down at his engorged, inflamed rod.

"Of course last night there was a small difference."

"Small? Perhaps your eyesight is failing you, madam."

He raised a brow, but his lips twitched. Even as his body burned with need, he felt a mad urge to grin. There'd been a time in his life when a charming smile and a witty rejoinder had been all he'd needed to make women of every class his for the taking. How long ago that seemed now.

"I was referring to your missing beard, of course, Major."

"You called me Ambrose before." Their gazes met and held and her smile faded. "Tell me your real name."

She hesitated. "Eva. Sit down." She gestured to the bed. "I have something that will help."

"Nothing will bloody help," he growled. He must escape, but not in this condition. He could barely walk without doubling over. He stalked back to the bed and sat. A spasm of fire shot to his groin, and the need to sheath himself in her overwhelmed him.

Bloody hell, here it came again. He grimaced as his cock pulsed and throbbed for attention. His bollocks were bursting into flames.

She turned as if to move away.

"Where are you going?" Hating the tinge of desperation in his voice, he grabbed her robe and yanked her into his arms. He wanted her, damn it. Her parted lips were mere inches from his.

"Earlier you wished me gone."

"I've changed my mind." He took her mouth in a crushing kiss and shoved the robe off her shoulder to cup her breast. Was he a lout to use her? He didn't know anymore. His rational self had crumpled under the crippling needs of his body. Trailing frantic kisses down her jaw and neck, he cupped her bottom with his free hand, pushing her against his raging need.

She climbed on his lap and straddled him. Grabbing his rod, she positioned it at her entrance and impaled herself.

"Ah, God, you feel so good." He gently bit her shoulder and squeezed her breast, plucking at the nipple. His heels dug into the carpet as she slammed down onto him again and again. His balls tightened as his cock was ready to shoot.

"Wait." He grabbed her hips to stop her movement but she made a little simpering sound and wouldn't be slowed. "Stop, damn it, I can't hold back."

She rose and fell once more and, jaw clenched, he shuddered his release.

Eyes closed, she kept moving, seeking her own end, but she eventually stilled, breathing heavily, unsatisfied.

Frustrated, he reached up and stroked her cheek. Blond tendrils of hair hung in wisps about her face. Her beauty was entrancing, ageless. He ran his thumb along her bottom lip and looked up into her eyes. Gently, he tucked a strand of hair behind her ear and slid his hand around her neck to pull her to him.

For a brief moment she allowed him to close the distance between their mouths. But she stopped, opening her eyes and jerking back. She pushed off him, but he caught her hand.

"Tell me your full name."

Her courtesan's mask back in place, she fluttered her lashes and gave him a coy smile. "Allow a woman a little mystery, sir."

Playing the coquette, now, was she? But he'd glimpsed the true woman behind her act. How had she ended up a courtesan? "You are young to be so practiced at artifice."

"I am three and twenty."

He looked down at her delicate hand in his. "Definitely too young."

"And your age, Major?"

"I am nine and twenty. An old soldier, past his prime."

"No."

He met her intense gaze. Her blue eyes no longer resembled chips of ice. The heat he felt as she stared at him matched the burning in his gut.

"You're a skilled warrior, brave. Strong. Most men would have broken after all you've endured."

His heart squeezed at the admiration in her voice. "My skills have gone begging tonight."

She tugged her hand away and straightened her robe. "That's for the best, I think."

"Why would you say such?"

"Life is less complicated when I keep a professional distance." She put words to action, moved to her dressing table and sat. Picking up a brush, she smoothed her mussed hair back into place.

"I see. And I am a complication in your professional career."

"Yes." She spoke the word as if she were agreeing to another cup of tea.

He pushed off the bed, poured himself a glass of water and gulped it down, then stalked behind the privacy screen and relieved himself. Why did that vex him so? He knew what she was. Even if she were Wellesley's agent, she was also a famous courtesan. But twenty-three. How many men had she aligned herself with in her career? Damn it, why should he care? He grabbed a towel from the screen and wrapped it around his waist as he stepped from behind it.

To hell if it was ungentlemanly to ask. And to hell if he shouldn't care.

"How many?"

Her hands stilled in the act of rubbing in some sort of lotion. She stood, taking a glass bottle with her as she moved to the bedside.

"Surprisingly, in eight years, only four."

"Eight years? Eight years ago you were but fifteen! My God." His concern about her legion of lovers was forgotten. His stomach turned at the thought of a young girl's loss of innocence. "Were you fleeing The Revolution? Had you no family, no friends to turn to?"

"Were there not girls that age in the brothels you've patronized?"

"Well, I-I suppose, but I've never—How the devil did you—" He shoved a hand through his hair, cursing his stupidity in ever raising the subject. "Never mind."

She giggled. A musical sound so girlish and innocent he looked up in astonishment.

"You have a beautiful laugh."

Of course, her smile vanished. She set the bottle of perfume or whatever it was on the table beside the bed.

A loud thud followed by a rash of giggling somewhere down the hallway reminded Ambrose of his need to escape once the house quieted. He wouldn't be caught a second time. But, was the marquis watching their every move?

"Does the marquis really watch through spy holes?" He moved to the fireplace and began searching the portrait above it for any sign of a puncture.

"Perhaps he watches, perhaps not. But even if you managed to find and cover the holes, it might only provoke him from spectator to participant." She sat on the bed and crossed her legs. "When the time comes, I have a plan. Until then, we must endure."

Endure? That was hardly an endorsement of his skills. His pride pricked by her words, he left off searching the wall and swung around.

"You need not *endure* my attentions, Madame." As if his wrath triggered the herb, a spasm of pain shot through his groin. He grimaced and tensed as a firestorm pulsed through his body and down to his cock.

"It has begun again, Major?"

"Go to hell."

"I can help ease your discomfort."

"No. I'm quite capable of taking care of this myself."

"Come lie on the bed and I promise you'll feel better soon."

He strode to her, grabbed her arm and pulled her off the bed toward the door. By God, he'd redeem himself and hear no more talk of endurance from her.

"You should learn to take no for an answer, woman."

Chapter 6

With his face creased in pain, and his knuckles white from clenching, Eva wished her careless words back. Truly, she'd not meant them as he took them. Stubborn man! Stubborn, strong, honorable, arousing man.

"Don't be so proud."

He stopped in his tracks and spun to face her. "My pride is all I have left!"

Something she'd yielded long ago. "And what will it take to keep your precious pride intact?"

His expression softened, his dark eyes heated and flared as his gaze roamed down her body.

"Surrender yourself to me."

Mon Dieu. What purpose could be served by this? To save his pride? And what of her hard-won detachment? Was it worth sacrificing? And was that all that she would lose? Yet the stubborn set of jaw told her he would throw her out if she didn't agree. She straightened her shoulders and took a deep breath.

"Very well."

Without hesitation, he flung off the towel, took her hand and pulled her to the bed.

Like a dried, thirsting plant, Eva drank in his long, lean frame made perfect by the prominent muscles in his arms and abdomen. The nicks and scars, the bruises and unruly hair only served to make him more potently masculine. His member jutted out from its nest of brown curls, sore and angry-looking, pointing to the ceiling. She could almost see it pulsing with each swing of his hips.

"I—I have something to soothe your discomfort, if you'll allow me." Was that her voice? So hesitant and beseeching?

"What is it?"

In answer, she took the bottle from the bedside table and pulled the stopper out. "It's only scented oil. If you'll lie back, I'll show you."

He studied the contents of the bottle and inhaled, then raised his dark eyes to hers. "It has your fragrance."

"It's my own special mixture. Lilies with a trace of honey."

With a narrow-eyed wariness he sat on the edge of the bed, lay back, and crossed his arms under his head. His clenched fists and jaw were the only signs of his inner turmoil.

Moving between his legs, she started to pour the oil onto his rod.

"Unbraid your hair." His eyes burned into hers.

"Why?"

In answer, he merely raised that arrogant brow and stared at her. Had she ever thought to command this magnificent warrior? What a fool she'd been.

While he watched with a glint of approval, she pulled her braid over her shoulder, untied the strip of cloth and loosened her hair.

"Now take off your robe."

Feeling like a vulnerable virgin—which was clearly ridiculous—she stepped back to untie the sash on her robe and shrugged out of it.

"The shift and stockings as well." His voice was low and husky.

She could sense his gaze caressing her as she untied her garters and rolled down her stockings. Her hands trembled. As she lifted the chemise over her head, her nipples tightened under his intense stare.

"Satisfied, my liege?"

He nodded. "You may proceed."

"Tell me if I cause you pain." She poured a generous amount of the scented oil onto his rod and smoothed it around with a light touch of her fingers, then gently gripped him and began stroking.

He sat up and caught her wrist.

"Is that too painful?"

"No. It helps."

He released her wrist and relaxed a little. She stroked him again and he moaned.

"Straddle my hips. I want you in my arms."

As she climbed on, setting her knees on either side of his hips, he circled his arms around her and lay back down, pulling her with him. Her hair cascaded around them, enclosing them in a private world more intimate than bed curtains. The oil spilled onto his chest and he rolled them over, holding himself up on elbow and knee.

"Pour some onto my hand." He held out his palm expectantly.

"What do you—

"That was the bargain. Do it or leave me be!" His mouth was a grim line.

She obeyed.

He slid his hand down between them and cupped her mound, moving his fingers through her curls and around her outer lips, caressing and massaging, building the pleasure in her with the expert touch of an experienced lover. Yet she strived for detachment.

He stared at her lips and she knew he intended to kiss her.

A profound longing came over her to surrender to his will entirely. Let someone else be in control. Someone strong, yet trustworthy, who wouldn't betray her, but would care for her. She closed her eyes and pushed the feeling down, back into the dark void where her heart had once been.

"Give in to me, Eva," he commanded hoarsely as he captured her lips.

The need in his voice broke her resistance. Helpless, incredulous, she let go and opened to him, consumed by the need to, for once, hold nothing back. His mouth moved over hers as if he could never kiss her enough, sweeping his tongue in and setting off sparks of fire in her belly.

From her mouth he traveled to her throat, her collarbone, and the swell of her breast. He smoothed his hand down her shoulder to her breast and gently cupped and caressed, lifting the tip for his gentle suckling.

As he took her nipple she plunged her fingers into his soft brown hair trying to stifle her cry. His hands and mouth moved lower, trailing open-mouthed kisses down to her stomach and below, nuzzling into her curls. With a groan he clamped a hand on her thigh to open her and licked and nibbled around her slit. Two fingers slid in slow and gentle, rotating inside her passage to press her most sensitive spot.

She whimpered.

His fingers spun a torturous web of delight, increasing the pressure. Her hips rose, silently asking for what she needed, but his mouth only suckled harder.

She gripped his shoulders, pulling, tugging, desperate to have him inside her.

"Now," she moaned.

"No." He caught her wrist. "You surrendered to me, remember?" As he suckled he slipped another finger inside and worked it in a rhythm set to drive her wild, then abruptly removed it. Unrelenting, he looked up at her. "You must trust me to bring you pleasure." His voice sounded strained, raspy.

She shook her head, squeezing her eyes closed. No one had ever made her feel so vulnerable.

"Open your eyes. Look at me."

Against her will she looked into his eyes. She saw hunger there, and curiosity, and a tortured desire. He held her gaze, seeming to search her soul. "It's Ambrose Delacourt you're making love to. Do you trust me?"

She wanted to look away. To force her emotions back where they'd resided comfortably for years. But it was too late. Like that night so long ago when she'd lost her innocence, she would never be the person she once was.

"Yes, Ambrose. Make love to me."

A flicker of satisfaction crossed his face as he rose up and plunged into her. Digging his fingers into her hair, he kissed her as tenderly as his thrusts were rough.

"Do you feel me inside you?" he whispered against her lips.

Oh yes. He was hard and solid, more than filling her, punching the very depths of her with each thrust.

"No. Don't close your eyes." He cradled her face, kissing the corners of her mouth, the tip of her nose, the hollow of her cheek. "Say my name again."

She wanted to beat his chest and command him to get on with it. The sexual act was too intimate this way. Too much. It was more than physical pleasure. It was sharing a part of her soul.

He stilled. "Say my name."

A strangled moan escaped. "Ambro—ahh." Before she'd finished he thrust hard into her, then stilled.

"Again."

Tears slid down her temples. "Please, Ambrose. I surrender. I am yours!"

He began a steady pumping, moving his hips to create the perfect friction she needed to feel him to her depths. The pressure and the need in her built, straining for release. Colors seemed more vibrant, texture more alive, every breath and rustle a symphony of their lovemaking. She hugged him to her and gulped in air. Her emotions felt raw.

"Yes. Sigh for me, my Eva." He kissed her, his lips conveying a chasm of yearning.

Freeing her face, he circled his arm beneath her hips and held her while he thrust into her, faster and faster, his trembling breath the only sign he was not in control.

"I can't wait." His face contorted. "Now, Eva. Come with me."

Digging her nails into his shoulders, Eva squeezed her eyes closed as a surge of exquisite joy exploded inside her. As if a string on her harp had been wound too tight and finally snapped. Only instead of a sharp sting, there was aching bliss. Only Ambrose, holding her in his arms and calling her name as he surged one last time and poured himself into her.

For a moment they lay quiet, breathing deep. Then with his hands cupping her bottom, he rolled to his back, taking her with him. She rested her head on his heaving chest and nuzzled into his dark curling hair, luxuriating for the moment, laying atop him in boneless contentment.

His hot breath fluttered her hair and his hands roamed softly over her. She started to move off him, but he tightened his arms.

"No. Stay. I'm still deep inside you." His cock moved. "Do you feel me?"

"*Ja*," she breathed the word on a sigh, then stilled. She'd spoken in her native language.

"Ah, my beautiful Eva." He brushed the hair from her face. "*Mir etwas Ale holen.*"

She raised her head and looked at him. "You want me to bring you ale?"

He grinned. "It's the only thing I know how to say in German. You're Prussian?"

What did it matter if he knew? "*Nein.* I was born in Salzburg."

"Yet you speak perfect French. When did you leave Austria?"

She was so accustomed to keeping her past a secret she didn't hesitate to deflect his question with one of her own. "You are fluent in French as well, *monsieur.* Did you learn your German phrase in the army?"

His gaze drifted to the silk canopy above them and his smiled widened. "No. From my brother. He toured the continent before the war, lucky devil."

"You have other siblings?"

"No, only John. Or, Pembrook, as he's called now. He's become the new viscount since I was last home."

So, Ambrose was a viscount's son. She had assumed he was of that class. A pang of regret ached in her chest. But at least she'd had this one night.

"Your father died while you were fighting?" She brushed the damp hair from his forehead, her fingers lingering in his mahogany strands. "I'm sorry."

"Don't be. We were… at odds most of my life." He still caressed her back, his palms gliding down her spine.

Reveling in his casual touch Eva lay her head back on his chest, her eyelids growing heavy. "Are all fathers resentful of their children, then? Can a man not feel love for his child as a mother does?"

His hands stilled a moment, and then moved up to stroke her hair. "I believe some can. My lieutenant's stories of home are filled with the joys of fatherhood."

Her heavy lids closed on images of a soldier cradling a babe lovingly in his arms. A soldier who looked much like Ambrose.

Fierce heat scorched her back. A soft mouth delved into her neck as a rough hand slid along her hip and waist, around to her stomach and up to play with her nipples. A low growl rumbled from his chest and a hard length pushed against her buttocks. Ambrose. His touch and his need caused a spasm of rapture between her thighs. She squeezed them together, covered his hand with hers and pushed back against his erection.

A tortured moan reverberated against her back.

"Eva?"

In answer she lifted a knee and reached behind her to guide him in. With a strangled cry he pushed his long, hot hardness into her. Both their juices from earlier ensured a smooth entry, and Eva gasped as pleasure shot through her with each driving thrust. Her hand drifted lower and she caressed his sac, squeezing just hard enough to make the pain pleasurable.

"Oh God!" The grip tightened on the hand he held beneath the pillow. He hugged her to him and his kisses spread to her shoulder and ear as he clutched her hip and moved in her.

The intensity low in her belly coiled with each forceful motion. Then his fingers traveled from her hip to play between her thighs. She cried out and bucked her hips, so close.

He rolled her to her stomach, grasped the back of one knee and slid it up. His breathing labored, his sweat-dampened hips slapped her buttocks as she felt his thumb push into her anus. It broke through her tight hole and pushed all the way in and his strokes quickened. One last hard drive sent her spiraling into bliss at the same time he cried out.

They both sank onto the mattress. After a moment he pushed off the bed and padded to the washstand. She heard water splashing and he returned with the wet cloth.

"Roll over, darling. And brace yourself. This might be a bit cold."

With a soft touch, he spread her legs and washed her sticky thighs and folds. The look of tenderness on his face as he cleaned her broke her composure. No man had ever done so for her, nor behaved in such a gentlemanlike manner. Hot tears stung her eyes.

"Ahhh, my sweet." His hands smelled of soap as he framed her face and kissed her eyes, wiping away her tears. He climbed in beside her, gathered her into his arms and kissed her tenderly. As tenderly as the man in her dreams.

He stroked her hair and back.

"Eva," he breathed out her name, then lifted her chin with a finger and bent close to kiss her. His lips were sweet and exploring, then powerful and commanding. The heat from his body enveloped her as he wrapped his arms around her.

She'd never felt so treasured, so safe.

He gently kissed her temple, her cheek, and then placed another soft kiss on her lips, gazing at her.

"You are not his mistress, are you?" It wasn't a question.

"No. I attended this party only for you."

"For me," he repeated, running a hand down her hair, tenderly playing with the strands. "Because you work for Wellesley? And your mission is to rescue me?"

He cupped her breast tenderly and lowered his head to kiss just above her nipple.

She tried to control her breathing. "*Ja.*"

"Hmm…" He nuzzled between her breasts.

What did that mean? He still thought her a traitor?

"Tell me everything now. How you came to live in Paris. How you came to be a courtesan."

She stiffened and tried to push out of his arms.

"No." He held tight. "You must trust me. I will never betray you."

As she stared into his determined brown eyes, her defenses crumbled. She was weary of hiding her past, of trusting no one. Detachment had kept her sane all these years. But now it seemed like a giant wall keeping her imprisoned alone.

"I am Eva Werner. As a child, I toured Europe playing the harp for kings and Emperors."

Ambrose stilled. Shock reverberated down his spine. He vaguely recalled the girl. His mother had taken him to hear the prodigy play once in London. He'd been fifteen and longed to be anywhere else. But once the young harpist began plucking the strings he'd become spellbound. He ran his palm down her arm and twined his fingers with hers.

"My father took full advantage of my looks by dressing me in diaphanous white robes with gold trim to match my harp."

Ambrose had no recollection of the father and not much of the child. His adolescent mind had centered mostly on wine and a certain tavern maid back then. But the music. That he remembered.

"As I grew older, crowds no longer cared if a half grown woman could play so well. I didn't know we were deep in debt. That my father had lived extravagantly for years. So, what other value had I to him?"

Eva stared at the canopy above the bed. Her tear-filled eyes wrenched Ambrose's gut.

"He sold me to an Italian count four times my age for five hundred pounds." Eva squeezed her eyes closed, her fists clenched.

"The bastard!" He remembered her words about a father's love. Good God. By all that was holy, how could a man do such a thing? "Ah, my darling."

He turned Eva's face toward him to kiss her, but she twisted away.

"You must hear the truth. After Franco died, I *chose* to continue. I came to Paris already the mistress of another man."

"So, you've had four lovers. I've bedded countless women. Yet you've risked everything—your very life!—to rescue me. And how many other lives have you saved by gathering information for Wellesley?"

Luminous sapphire eyes stared up at him. "You believe me?"

He realized somewhere in the night, his suspicions had dissolved. He didn't know when or why, but he believed her. He tightened his arms around her.

"I do." Why did those words sound more like a promise than a mere answer?

"Ambrose. I must tell you one more thing."

His breathing stopped. Her voice sounded dead.

"My mission was to rescue you if I could. And if I couldn't... to kill you. There is poison in my locket."

He grinned. "I suspected as much. Is that all?"

She rose up on her elbow. "You knew? But I—I can't do it."

Her plump breasts dangled before his eyes and he couldn't think for a moment. Was there anything more appealing than a woman's comforting breasts? No, *this* woman's comforting breasts. Unable to resist, he reached for them, pushing them together to bury his face against them, kissing the hollow between.

"It's all right, my love." Her soft flesh muffled his words. "I understood the risks before I joined British intelligence."

"We should—" She threw her head back and moaned as he suckled a nipple. "Ambrose..." She said his name on a sigh, breathy and languid.

"Yes, my darling," he mumbled against the rounded swell of her breast. It was still dark. But he had no concept of the time. They'd taken his watch, a gift from his grandfather, in prison. But all that mattered now was getting to England alive. With Eva.

"The house has quieted. We must make our escape now. I want you away from here. Safe."

She pushed him away and sat up. "I can't leave with you. My deception would be exposed. But you're right. You must go."

Without a backward glance she rose from the bed, grabbed her robe from the floor, and slipped her arms in. Ambrose shoved off the bed and moved behind her.

"You think to continue working for Wellesley in Paris? I can't let you. The marquis is bound to suspect you once I escape. It's too dangerous."

She threw a contemptuous glare over her shoulder. "Obviously sentiment has affected your reasoning. You have no say in my life."

His heart froze, as if someone had thrown him into the icy Thames. Was he a fool to care for her? Or was it simple gratitude he felt for relieving his cock? Perhaps the constant sexual release *had* given him a false sense of intimacy. He'd believed they were making love. But that was exactly the art in which she was trained, to make men believe themselves in love. And that she returned those feelings.

She moved across the room, not bothering to belt her robe. Her pale, smooth body was the most perfect woman's form he'd ever beheld. Large, round breasts, slim waist and legs, a supple, rounded tummy. She was utterly luscious.

And utterly confounding. Pliant and passionate one moment, cold and unfeeling the next. He'd have sworn the intimacy they'd shared was real. Was she that fine of an actress?

Perhaps so.

She flung open the armoire and turned to him.

"Come stand behind this door and dress." She grabbed a pair of black breeches and a rough woolen shirt. "Take these."

He stepped into the armoire and hastily donned the breeches. No. He refused to doubt his gut instinct. He'd seen something in her eyes tonight. Something good and true.

She moved with a sensuous grace to her dressing table, draped the gold locket around her neck, and belted the robe. Making her way back to him, she slipped a dagger into his hand.

"Take this."

He stood a moment, stunned that she would give him a weapon. But he finished dressing, debating his next move.

One thing was certain.

He wouldn't leave her behind.

She stood waiting at the door. "You must wrestle with me and tie me to the chair or bed."

He approached her, hardening his heart as he did before battle. When she looked down to pull off her sash, he grabbed her hair and held the blade to her throat. "Make no sound or I will slice open your throat."

Chapter 7

All was quiet when Ambrose ordered Eva to open the bedchamber door. The sconces remained lit, yet no footmen stood guard. Had they been ordered away? Or was it sheer luck that they'd abandoned their post? A feeling that this was too easy nagged at his gut.

Scanning the shadows for the guards, Ambrose kept his grip on Eva's hair and held the knife loosely at her throat as they stole down the servant's stairs.

"Which way?" he whispered.

She pointed and walked stiffly in front of him.

He said nothing more until they passed through the kitchen and reached the outer door. Something was wrong. Why hadn't the marquis chained him as he had the night before? Had the bastard fallen asleep or did he still watch? Without the blasted herb he might have thought of all this earlier. Still, he had to escape.

"Leave me tied in an empty stall. A stable boy should rouse soon enough and set me free."

"No. You're coming with me."

She raised her brows and regarded him as if he were a simpleton. But she didn't fight him as he pushed her before him to the mews, ducking past the carriage house and dodging from hedge to hedge.

Once they made it to the stables Ambrose lowered the dagger from her throat. He swallowed as a hulking figure emerged from the shadows, leading a horse.

"All is in readiness, my lady," the man said in French.

"*Merci*, Pierre." Eva approached the horse and stroked its muzzle, murmuring to it. "His name is Zeus." She turned back to Ambrose. "He will carry you to Calais with little rest if you ask him to. My only request is that you leave him in caring hands."

"He's a magnificent animal. But you shall ride him. I'll choose another." He moved to enter the stable, but she grabbed his arm.

"Don't be foolish. None can carry you so fast, nor so far. He's already saddled. You will find food, money, and papers in his bags. Now go."

He turned to her, his stomach aching. This could still be an elaborate ploy. He might yet be proved a fool. But at this moment he bloody well didn't care. He grabbed her shoulders and ducked his head to take her mouth, kissing her with a desperation he'd never thought to feel for any woman.

Her arms stole around his neck and she opened to him with unrestrained passion. His cock hardened and his chest heated, filled to bursting with emotion. But this was not the return of the herb-induced lust.

"Eva." He murmured her name as he raised his head.

She shoved him away. "Pierre will bind me. Now go."

Gritting his teeth, he tried to tell himself she was a courtesan. And a spy. She could well take care of herself. Had managed for years without him. Why then, was he loath to leave her? He took her hands in his.

"You must come with me."

"Ah, oui? And what would I do then?" She sneered and yanked her hands back. "Give up my beautiful home and my comfortable bed and become a camp follower? Service all your men? Do not insult me." Picking up the full skirts of her robe, she spun on her heel. "Goodbye, Major."

Calling for Pierre, she stalked into the stables.

Whether she spoke with true disdain, or sheer bravado, he debated throwing her over his shoulder and carrying her off. But she had made her choice. With a final glance in her direction, he mounted and kicked the stallion to a gallop.

Eva welcomed the darkness inside the stables as she listened to Zeus' heavy hooves galloping away. Her usual detachment had abandoned her. She swiped the tears from her cheeks, felt her way to a post, and leaned her trembling body against it. This was her first rescue mission. It would be perfectly normal for nerves to kick in. Surely this wild panic was common for even an experienced spy.

She jumped as someone clapped behind her. Applause from an audience of one.

"Quite a performance, Madame," the marquis mocked. "Even *I* believed you had no wish to go with him. Almost."

Julian! Merde, how much had he heard? How much did he know? She steeled herself for the performance of her life.

"My lord." Pulling a hankie from her pocket she slowly turned to face him and sniffed delicately. Did he notice her shaking hands?

"I've been foolish, I know. But surely every woman is allowed to be swayed by a handsome man once in her life?"

"*Chérie*, I had no idea you were a romantic."

She forced a coquettish smile. "Did you not?" She fingered the locket beneath her robe and looked up at him from under her lashes. "Then why allow him to leave now?"

His pace unhurried, the marquis took her elbow and guided her out of the stables. "Testing your loyalty, of course."

Panic filled her, blurring her vision, pounding against her ribs. He knew. *He knew!*

"The Englishman knew nothing, my lord."

She shrugged as she strolled out of the mews with him, still toying with her jewelry. She had no more time to waste and no more chances to squander. As discreetly as possible, she dumped the poisonous powder from the locket over her breasts. "If it is the money, I will pay whatever his brother would have ransomed him for, *oui*?"

He smiled and raised a brow. "But Madame, what kind of patriot would I be to let a British spy escape?"

Did he mean her or Ambrose? Or both of them? In a rising panic, she glanced around the stables.

"Where is my coachman?"

They rounded the corner and she saw Pierre sprawled in the mud, his throat slit. A scream almost escaped her.

Terror singed her veins. This was it. She would die this day. But as long as Ambrose got away—

A shot rang out from a distance and a horse squealed in pain. Horrible anguish engulfed her.

"Ambrose!"

Eva picked up her skirts and raced into the lane behind the mews. On the horizon appeared the silhouette of a man with a pistol aimed down the lane.

"No," she whispered. The man, the lane, her entire world seemed to bend and distort. Hot tears spilled down her cheeks.

Brutal hands gripped her arms. "Did you think yourself more clever than I? You should have kept to whoring, Eva, and left spying to those infinitely more proficient."

The marquis dragged her toward the chateau. The carriage house and then the garden passed by in a blur. Her arm throbbed where his long fingers dug as he yanked her inside and up the curving staircase. But her mind was numb.

"I let you have the handsome Englishman to yourself last night. Now it's my turn." He hauled her through a bedchamber door and shoved her so hard she stumbled to her knees.

Ambrose! She hugged her churning stomach. What had she done?

The marquis made a tsking sound as he crouched before her.

"Look at your tears." He flicked a finger over her cheek. "You cry for a foolish Englishman? Do you imagine he cared for you simply because he offered to take you with him? Of course, he wouldn't leave a woman behind. Chivalry was likely beaten into him in those proper English schools. But a viscount's son and a whore? Really, Eva." He shook his head. "He had a delicious body, I'll grant you. But his sort isn't for you."

His debasing speech reminded her of her father, every time she'd dared to enjoy her celebrity as a child, to make a friend or be happy. It touched upon the passive defiance she now realized had been key to her endurance all these years.

With that realization, her spirit rallied. The need for cool-headed thinking replaced numbness. If the marquis had suspected her, he might have been feeding her false information. She must survive to warn Wellesley.

"Come, now." Pain jolted her as he yanked her up by her hair. "We must ready you for your punishment."

A cold chill prickled her skin as she looked around the chamber. It had been turned into a playground for sexual deviants. There was a padded bench with iron cuffs attached to each side, and one entire wall held riding crops, whips and other instruments of torture. On a table lay dildos of ivory, leather, and wood. Her only hope of escape depended on the poison she'd spread over her breasts. Surely, he would kiss her there, eventually.

As he shoved her toward his great mahogany bed, two footmen yanked off her robe and tied her wrists and ankles to each bedpost.

"Have you read any of the works of the Marquis de Sade, *chérie*?" De Séréville sat beside her, pulled her hair over one shoulder, then smoothed the strands down over one breast.

Raising her chin, she stared at the purple velvet canopy while his pale hands crawled over her. He squeezed her nipples hard and licked inside her ear.

"I've been waiting for this a long time." He chuckled. "After I have a little fun, I shall expose you as a traitor of France. Oh yes. I know all about your midnight rendezvous with Wellesley's lackey. Not very wise of you to meet him yourself, Madame. You never know who might be watching."

She held her tongue and didn't allow even a flicker of expression to betray her.

"What shall I use first?" He moved to the table and picked up a small leather ball and a strip of rawhide. "Open wide, *mon amour*."

With a tiny smile he pinched her nose until she gasped for breath, then popped the ball between her teeth and tied the leather around her head to hold it in place.

Panic seized her as she tried to breathe slowly through her nose.

"He never took your tight back hole last night. I kept waiting." Leisurely, he selected an ivory dildo and a jar of white cream.

Eva had used such toys but rarely, and even then she'd more often been the provider than the recipient.

"I must say, I was greatly disappointed by your performance."

Her body shook with terror at what he retrieved next: a riding crop.

"Your lovemaking was so tender," he sneered the word. "So tame. Where was the imagination? The brutality?"

Barking orders for the guards to wait outside the door, the marquis set the crop next to her on the bed and began to prime her anus with the cream. "We'll take care of that now, shall we?"

Even as she twisted her wrists in the ropes, she reached for her shield of detachment, trying to will her thoughts to her make-believe country house. But the image brought no solace. She could only picture Ambrose, how he'd managed to look elegant even in coarse, ill-fitting clothes, his brown locks disheveled and his jaw shadowed in bruises.

How his dark eyes had pleaded with her to go with him! And she'd let him leave without her.

As if he knew she thought of Ambrose, the marquis murmured his encouragement as he fingered both her openings. Finally, her eyes closed, she shamefully moved her hips for more. Then, with exquisite slowness, he worked the ivory dildo into her anus until she grimaced and squirmed. She opened her eyes, unable to sustain the pretense that it was Ambrose's touch. Silently, she willed him to suckle her breasts soon.

Wiping his hands, de Séréville began to undress. "I was going to whip your milky white skin first, but after watching you with the Englishman all night, I'm impatient to take you." He smiled cruelly. "But after that, the naughty whore shall have a flogging."

Ambrose had galloped right into a trap.

The question was: who had laid it?

A twig snapped above him, but Ambrose remained still, feigning unconsciousness. When Zeus had been shot from beneath him, he'd flown over the stallion's head and landed hard in this marshy ditch. The wind had been knocked from his lungs, and his wound had ripped open, but at least the mud and grass had saved his bloody neck.

Inside his sleeve he gripped the dagger, waiting for his enemy to come closer.

The squish of heavy boots in the muck signaled the assassin had found him. Had he come to finish the job, or take him prisoner again? Only a truly bungling marksman would have shot the horse by mistake. Ambrose could only assume the marquis still wanted him alive.

As a hand grasped his shoulder and tried to roll him over, Ambrose opened his eyes and plunged his dagger up through the man's heart.

The man grunted, his eyes wide in shock just before he collapsed on top of Ambrose.

Ambrose shoved him off and scrambled out of the ditch, shaking. After gulping a few uneven breaths, he returned to the assassin and pulled the knife from his chest. He took the pistol from his coat pocket and rummaged for shot and powder bag. After reloading it he exchanged clothes, slipping on the assassin's boots and hat as well.

If the marquis had a man waiting to shoot Ambrose, de Séréville must know Eva had helped Ambrose escape. What would that fiend do to her? He must get there in time to stop whatever perverted retribution the marquis intended. Tamping down horrific images, Ambrose raced back to the chateau.

The dawn had given way to morning now, but the sun still rested low on the horizon. His hat pulled down to hide his face, Ambrose barged through the outer door into the kitchen.

"Is that you, Gustav?" A plump older woman looked up and squinted as he entered. The housekeeper, he presumed. A cook and a scullery maid also sat at a rough-planked table eating bread.

"Oui," he responded as he shuffled past them to the narrow servant's staircase. The housekeeper's eye's widened in fright, but she said not a word.

The mouth-watering aroma of sausage and coddled eggs reminded his stomach his last meal had been almost twenty four hours ago. But at least the bloody potion seemed to have finally left his body in peace.

Before entering the main floor, he drew his pistol. The chateau was quiet, most of the guests still abed after a night of drink and depravity. But he couldn't assume the marquis would be asleep. Where would he have taken Eva?

He headed for the main staircase, his muddied boots leaving an easy trail for any pursuers. His side throbbed, and he fought against pain and exhaustion. At the landing, he glanced down the hall from under the hat's wide brim. The same henchmen who'd enjoyed pounding him the past weeks stood sentry at the farthest door.

Hiding the pistol behind his thigh, he strode toward them.

"Ou est l'Anglais?" the shorter guard called to him, snapping to attention as Ambrose approached.

"Il est mort," Ambrose muttered, continuing toward them.

"Arrêtez!" Both guards drew their swords.

Ambrose cocked the hammer on the pistol, brought it up and aimed it at them. "Leave now and I'll let you live."

One scowled, while the other gave him a pitying look as they charged him. Ambrose drew out the knife and, praying his aim was true, threw the dagger at one henchman while he fired the pistol at the larger man.

The hulking guard stopped in his tracks and fell to his knees. The dagger pierced the other guard just below his right shoulder. He dropped his sword and clutched his arm.

Ambrose grabbed the sword and stuck the tip of the blade to the guard's stomach.

"Say your prayers." Remembering the days and nights of brutal beatings he'd suffered at his hands, Ambrose ran him through.

The pistol shot would alert the entire household. He hadn't much time. Grabbing up the other sword and retrieving the dagger, he kicked open the door and raced into the room, only to stop short.

The marquis lay over Eva in the bed, naked, his mouth on her breast.

"Get away from her, you sick bastard!"

Chapter 8

The marquis smiled and wrapped his hands around Eva's throat.

"I can snap her neck before you reach me with that sword, monsieur."

Eva's eyes were wide. She whimpered around the gag in her mouth. By God, Ambrose would kill the demented monster!

But he couldn't risk Eva's life. And he had no doubt the marquis was capable of breaking her neck while she lay tied and helpless. His arms were thin but sinewy, more than strong enough to perform the deed.

"Drop the sword or her death will be on your hands," de Séréville threatened. He slid his fingers down through Eva's blonde curls and began probing between her thighs.

Ambrose noticed the ivory phallus. Anger burned through his veins. But he coldly considered his options.

Already a footman with pistol drawn had reached the doorway behind him. Ambrose calculated the odds of wrestling the pistol from the footman and shooting the marquis before he could kill Eva. A risk he couldn't afford. He tossed the sword across the room.

The dagger tingled in his boot.

"A wise decision, Major." De Séréville nodded to the footman. "Wait outside. I'll call you if I need you." He focused his manic gleam on Ambrose. "I told you I'd plug your arse before this was over. Strip off your clothes and join us."

Ambrose yanked off his coat and ripped his shirt over his head. "You want me, you son of a bitch, come and take me!" He reached for the buttons of his breeches.

Wiping his sweaty brow, the marquis eyed him suspiciously. "Don't think to fight me. My servant won't hesitate to shoot at my command." His gaze dropped to Ambrose's crotch and he licked his lips. "You will suck my cock for me now, Englishman." He slithered off the bed, stalked to Ambrose. "On your knees!"

As if to comply, Ambrose dropped to one knee, slipped the dagger from his boot and brought it to the madman's throat.

"Call your servant off. Tell him to have your two fastest horses saddled."

The marquis stared at him, his eyes wild. But no words emerged from his open lips. He began shaking convulsively and spittle formed at the corners of his mouth. His hands shook as he tried to grab Ambrose's shoulders.

"Bitch… poisoned…"

He gasped his last breath and dropped to the floor, his eyes seeing nothing.

"May God damn you to hell, de Séréville."

Ambrose raced to Eva, untied her gag, and sliced the ropes at her wrists and ankles. She removed the phallus and sat up. A strangled sound escaped her throat, and her body trembled.

"I thought you were dead."

"Ah, my darling. I shouldn't have left you."

Ambrose wrapped her in his arms. She cared for him! Tender emotions threatened to unman him. He swallowed the hard lump in his throat, pushing aside sentiment. "Come. We must dress quickly."

Stepping out of his arms, she headed for the sitting room. But she wouldn't look at him as she retrieved her robe. She'd drawn into herself, as if she were no longer in the room.

"He knew about me. I can't be sure how long I've been fed false information."

"Good God." Ambrose scooped up the shirt and coat and followed her. "We must inform the war office immediately."

"*Oui*," Eva agreed. She tugged open the armoire and began pulling out satin waistcoats and breeches. She glanced back at him, but in her eyes he saw no hint of affection. Only a dull flatness. It must be the horror of committing murder.

"I have hidden money and false papers just outside Paris. And last night I sent my maid ahead to close up the house and send my trunks on."

"Excellent." He was glad to see she would not be stubborn about this. As he bent to retrieve the sword, he glanced back at the dead body. By God, she'd killed a marquis! She must have spread the poison on her body, knowing what he would do to her. Her past had made her capable of doing whatever must be done. She was a woman like no other, brave and strong. His heart exploded as if cannon ball had hit him in the chest. Somehow this courtesan had broken through his rogue's armor and found a place there.

Eva returned to the bedchamber, dressed as a man. She'd tied loose-fitting breeches up below her breasts, wore large boots, and her hair was pinned up under a tricorn hat.

Settling a black felt hat on his head, he took Eva's hand and moved to the hall door. He instructed her to call to the footman, and then when the servant opened the door, Ambrose aimed the dagger at his throat. Eva grabbed his pistol and trained it on him while Ambrose tied him up and gagged him. If the earlier pistol shot had awakened any of the other guests, they hadn't been disturbed enough to leave their rooms to investigate.

With Eva's hand firmly in his grasp, they raced down the servants' staircase to the kitchen.

The kitchen was clean and deserted, and Ambrose realized it was Sunday morning and the servants must have left to attend church services. They encountered no opposition as they ran to the stables and saddled two sturdy geldings.

After an hour of hard riding, they came to a crossroads. The main highway. The morning was cold and foggy, and the horses blew steam from their nostrils. Ambrose turned south to Calais, but Eva reined in her gelding.

Eva dug her nails into her palm, her heart breaking. It was time. She would never see him again.

"This must be goodbye, Major. I'm returning to Italy," she called to him, glad her voice held no hint of emotion.

"What?" He glowered and cut his horse around to face her. "Don't be ridiculous. You'll come with me to London."

His stallion pranced beneath him but he controlled it with the skill of a man born to privilege. Eventually he would return to that life.

If he survived the war.

And she? Her dreams had never been meant to come true. Would she sit by the hearth and embroider? Or watercolor? Even playing the harp for the ton would seem ludicrous while she knew Ambrose risked his life for king and country. Perhaps she could still use her skills somehow to help defeat Napoleon.

"Did you hear me, Eva? I won't let you go again."

She sniffed, determined to hide her feelings. She must convince him to leave her.

"Do you think because I surrendered my body out of pity last night that you may command me at will?"

His dark eyes flashed, his nostrils flared.

"Pity?"

He kicked his horse to move beside hers. She jumped when he grabbed the reins from her grasp and led both horses down the embankment and into the forest.

Eva didn't fight him. She felt frozen inside at the thought of losing him. Even now, with his dark hair plastered with mud, and his face drawn, she longed to be with him. He was so beautiful to her. So precious. She would never forget the joy that had leapt into her heart when he'd burst into the marquis' bedchamber, alive! When had she come to love him? How could she feel so strongly for someone in such a short time?

How could she not? He was an honorable man. Intelligent, strong, caring. Her emotions had unraveled the moment he'd raised that arrogant brow and grinned at her.

He halted once they were well hidden from the road, dismounted and tied the horses to a trunk. Advancing on her, he reached up and dragged her off the saddle and into his arms.

"If what we shared last night was pity," his voice rumbled with anger, "than grant me mercy once more."

He lowered his head to capture her mouth.

She cried out as his possessive lips moved over hers, giving heat and strength. His powerful arms circled her, gripped her waist, and lifted her against him.

No mortal could have resisted the need in his kiss, the want in his touch. She ran her fingers through his hair, and he tugged her breeches to her ankles. She kicked them off along with the boots.

"Is pity what you feel for me now?" He moaned into her mouth as he slid a hand under her shirt.

When he cupped her breast, she whimpered. When he squeezed her bottom, she pushed her stomach into his erection. She felt the rough bark of a tree at her back as his fingers fumbled with his breeches.

Her leg lifted to his hip and circled his waist and then he was there, pressing into her entrance. He gasped as he pushed into her and their eyes met.

"You're mine." His deep, husky voice, so dear to her, sent an ache to her chest.

She gripped him tightly around the neck. It might be foolish to linger here, where they might be found, but one last time, she wanted to feel him, know him.

He kissed her as he bent his knees and pushed up into her again and again. He felt so good moving inside her, filling her. His lips traveled down her throat and he pulled at the top button on her shirt while she nuzzled into his neck. She exploded as his mouth settled over hers and he pushed hard into her one last time. A hoarse cry escaped his throat as he stiffened. Then, lowering her feet to the floor, he dropped his forehead to hers, gasping.

One arm supported her bottom, the other held her around the waist. His chest rose and fell. He opened his eyes and looked into hers.

"I love you."

Her stomach clenched to hear him say those words to her. Slowly, as she regained her breath, she straightened her clothes, and moved out of his embrace.

"We must not linger here. They will find the marquis' body and come after us."

"Have you nothing else to say?"

Even if it destroyed what was left of her soul, she must portray indifference.

"Did you hear me, Eva? I love you. I want to marry you—"

"Ambrose." She pulled on the breeches and sat on a fallen log to tug on the boots, stalling for time to harden her heart. "Do you know how many men have fallen in love with me over the years? With my beauty? My body? You weren't the first. And you won't be the last. I comforted you. You're grateful. Let us not misunderstand what happened between us."

He came up behind her and dug his fingers into her hair, pulled her head back and kissed her. She struggled for a moment, then her body turned to him and her trembling lips surrendered to his kisses. As he fell to his knees, her hands came around his neck and she whimpered and kissed him back, stroking his jaw.

He broke the kiss and said hoarsely, "I love *you*, Eva Werner. Not your beauty or your body. But your bravery. Your strength. Your fortitude to carry on, after such horrendous betrayals. You risked your life for a country not your own and for a man who was a stranger to you.

"But it is not just admiration. It's a feeling, here." He took her hand and thumped it against his heart. "I've fancied myself in love before. But never have I wanted to give my life for a woman, thought of no one but her, wanted to be faithful only to her."

Her heart stopped. She tried to convince herself her feelings for him were only momentary passion. But the breathless trembling of her body denied the lie. Oh, how she loved him! She'd barely survived watching him leave her once. How would she be able to let him go again?

"No!" She pushed against his hard chest but he didn't move. "Such devotion is misplaced. Do you think your brother, the viscount and his noble wife will welcome a French courtesan into their home? Into their family?"

"You are more a war hero than I, my love." He shook his head. "In my youth, I was a wastrel. A womanizer who drank and gambled his life away. Wealth, privilege, education, all was squandered in my selfishness. My father finally gave me an ultimatum: take the commission he'd purchased, or starve." He grimaced, derision twisting his beautiful mouth. "The worst of it is, joining the army was the making of me. But I still cursed my father till the day he died."

He ran the back of his knuckles down her cheek. "If my past has made me who I am, then yours has made you into the courageous woman you are."

Her vision blurred as tears filled her eyes. She used the excuse of wiping her eyes to drop her gaze.

He took her hand. "Let's start over, Eva. Together. We can make of our lives whatever we wish."

Tears streamed down her face as she shook her head.

He tightened his arms around her. "If we have both sinned, then let us be each other's redemption."

Eva squeezed her eyes closed. "I cannot have children, Ambrose."

"Ah, Eva." He kissed her forehead. "If you want children, there are orphans aplenty we can care for and love. As for me, you are all I need."

Her body would no longer hold in the pain. If his arms hadn't been holding her she might have collapsed. He scooped her up and cradled her in his lap.

While she sobbed quietly against his shoulder he ran his hands up and down her arms and back, comforting her as he would a child. "Hush now, it's all right. I'm here, my darling."

Once her sobs abated he pressed a handkerchief into her hands. "Our love can bring us both the peace we seek, Eva."

"Ambrose." She threw her arms around his neck, hugging him fiercely. "I do love you, I do!"

He grinned. "Of course you do, my darling." He gripped her head and kissed her deeply, taking her mouth on a sensual exploration of love.

Eva basked in his love and acceptance, running her hands through his hair, down his shoulders, then cradled his face.

"I am your love slave, sir. Command me."

"And I am yours. I love you, Eva. Marry me, darling. Surrender to me and torture me no more."

She smiled, love and peace welling up inside her. "I surrender."

About the Author:

Having had the good luck to be born in Texas, Juliet can't imagine living anywhere else. She's lucky to share her life with a supportive husband, three rambunctious children, and a sweet golden retriever. She likes to think her emotional nature—sometimes referred to as moodiness by those closest to her—has found the perfect outlet in writing passionate stories late at night after the house gets quiet. Juliet loves reading romance novels and believes they have the power to change lives with their eternal message of love and hope. She'd love to hear from readers. You can contact her by visiting her website www.julietburns.com.

Men you've been dreaming about!

Secrets

Satisfy your desire for more.

*F*eel the wild adventure, fierce passion and the power of love in every **Secrets** Collection story. Red Sage Publishing's romance authors create richly crafted, sexy, sensual, novella-length stories. Each one is just the right length for reading after a long and hectic day.

Each volume in the **Secrets** Collection has four diverse, ultra-sexy, romantic novellas brimming with adventure, passion and love. More adventurous tales for the adventurous reader. The **Secrets** Collection are a glorious mix of romance genre; numerous historical settings, contemporary, paranormal, science fiction and suspense. We are always looking for new adventures.

Reader response to the **Secrets** volumes has been great! Here's just a small sample:

> *"I loved the variety of settings. Four completely wonderful time periods, give you four completely wonderful reads."*

> *"Each story was a page-turning tale I hated to put down."*

> *"I love **Secrets**! When is the next volume coming out? This one was Hot! Loved the heroes!"*

Secrets have won raves and awards. We could go on, but why don't you find out for yourself—order your set of **Secrets** today! See the back for details.

Secrets, Volume 1

A Lady's Quest by Bonnie Hamre
Widowed Lady Antonia Blair-Sutworth searches for a
lover to save her from the handsome Duke of Suther-
land. The "auditions" may be shocking but utterly
tantalizing.

The Spinner's Dream by Alice Gaines
A seductive fantasy that leaves every woman wishing
for her own private love slave, desperate and running
for his life.

The Proposal by Ivy Landon
This tale is a walk on the wild side of love. *The
Proposal* will taunt you, tease you, and shock you. A
contemporary erotica for the adventurous woman.

The Gift by Jeanie LeGendre
Immerse yourself in this historic tale of exotic seduction, bondage and a concubine's
surrender to the Sultan's desire. Can Alessandra live the life and give the gift the
Sultan demands of her?

Secrets, Volume 2

Surrogate Lover by Doreen DeSalvo
Adrian Ross is a surrogate sex therapist who has all
the answers and control. He thought he'd seen and
done it all, but he'd never met Sarah.

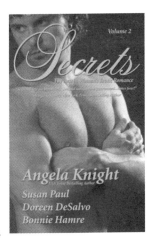

Snowbound by Bonnie Hamre
A delicious, sensuous regency tale. The marriage-shy
Earl of Howden is teased and tortured by his own
desires and finds there is a woman who can equal his
overpowering sensuality.

Roarke's Prisoner by Angela Knight
Elise, a starship captain, remembers the eager animal
submission she'd known before at her captor's hands
and refuses to become his toy again. However, she has
no idea of the delights he's planned for her this time.

Savage Garden by Susan Paul
Raine's been captured by a mysterious and dangerous revolutionary leader in
Mexico. At first her only concern is survival, but she quickly finds lush erotic nights
in her captor's arms.

Winner of the Fallot Literary Award for Fiction!

Secrets, Volume 3

The Spy Who Loved Me by Jeanie Cesarini
Undercover FBI agent Paige Ellison's sexual appetites
rise to new levels when she works with leading man
Christopher Sharp, the cunning agent who uses all his
training to capture her body and heart.

The Barbarian by Ann Jacobs
Lady Brianna vows not to surrender to the barbaric
Giles, Earl of Harrow. He must use sexual arts
learned in the infidels' harem to conquer his bride. A
word of caution—this is not for the faint of heart.

Blood and Kisses by Angela Knight
A vampire assassin is after Beryl St. Cloud. Her only
hope lies with Decker, another vampire and ex-merce-
nary. Broke, she offers herself as payment for his services. Will his seductive powers
take her very soul?

Love Undercover by B.J. McCall
Amanda Forbes is the bait in a strip joint sting operation. While she performs, fellow
detective "Cowboy" Cooper gets to watch. Though he excites her, she must fight the
temptation to surrender to the passion.

Winner of the 1997 Under the Covers Readers Favorite Award

Secrets, Volume 4

An Act of Love by Jeanie Cesarini
Shelby Moran's past left her terrified of sex. International film star Jason Gage must gently coach the young
starlet in the ways of love. He wants more than an act—
he wants Shelby to feel true passion in his arms.

Enslaved by Desirée Lindsey
Lord Nicholas Summer's air of danger, dark passions,
and irresistible charm have brought Lady Crystal's
long-hidden desires to the surface. Will he be able to
give her the one thing she desires before it's too late?

The Bodyguard by Betsy Morgan & Susan Paul
Kaki York is a bodyguard, but watching the wild,
erotic romps of her client's sexual conquests on the
security cameras is getting to her—and her partner, the ruggedly handsome James
Kulick. Can she resist his insistent desire to have her?

The Love Slave by Emma Holly
A woman's ultimate fantasy. For one year, Princess Lily will be attended to by three
delicious men of her choice. While she delights in playing with the first two, it's the
reluctant Grae, with his powerful chest, black eyes and hair, that stirs her desires.

Secrets, Volume 5

Beneath Two Moons by Sandy Fraser
Step into the future and find Conor, rough and masculine like frontiermen of old, on the prowl for a new conquest. In his sights, Dr. Eva Kelsey. She got away before, but this time Conor makes sure she begs for more.

Insatiable by Chevon Gael
Marcus Remington photographs beautiful models for a living, but it's Ashlyn Fraser, a young exec having some glamour shots done, who has stolen his heart. It's up to Marcus to help her discover her inner sexual self.

Strictly Business by Shannon Hollis
Elizabeth Forrester knows it's tough enough for a woman to make it to the top in the corporate world. Garrett Hill, the most beautiful man in Silicon Valley, has to come along to stir up her wildest fantasies. Dare she give in to both their desires?

Alias Smith and Jones by B.J. McCall
Meredith Collins finds herself stranded at the airport. A handsome stranger by the name of Smith offers her sanctuary for the evening and she finds those mesmerizing, green-flecked eyes hard to resist. Are they to be just two ships passing in the night?

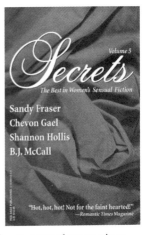

Secrets, Volume 6

Flint's Fuse by Sandy Fraser
Dana Madison's father has her "kidnapped" for her own safety. Flint, the tall, dark and dangerous mercenary, is hired for the job. But just which one is the prisoner—Dana will try *anything* to get away.

Love's Prisoner by MaryJanice Davidson
Trapped in an elevator, Jeannie Lawrence experienced unwilling rapture at Michael Windham's hands. She never expected the devilishly handsome man to show back up in her life—or turn out to be a werewolf!

The Education of Miss Felicity Wells by Alice Gaines
Felicity Wells wants to be sure she'll satisfy her soon-to-be husband but she needs a teacher. Dr. Marcus Slade, an experienced lover, agrees to take her on as a student, but can he stop short of taking her completely?

A Candidate for the Kiss by Angela Knight
Working on a story, reporter Dana Ivory stumbles onto a more amazing one—a sexy, secret agent who happens to be a vampire. She wants her story but Gabriel Archer wants more from her than just sex and blood.

Secrets, Volume 7

Amelia's Innocence by Julia Welles
Amelia didn't know her father bet her in a card game with Captain Quentin Hawke, so honor demands a compromise—three days of erotic foreplay, leaving her virginity and future intact.

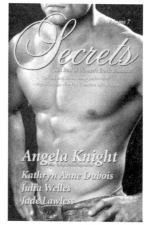

The Woman of His Dreams by Jade Lawless
From the day artist Gray Avonaco moves in next door, Joanna Morgan is plagued by provocative dreams. But what she believes is unrequited lust, Gray sees as another chance to be with the woman he loves. He must persuade her that even death can't stop true love.

Surrender by Kathryn Anne Dubois
Free-spirited Lady Johanna wants no part of the binding strictures society imposes with her marriage to the powerful Duke. She doesn't know the dark Duke wants sensual adventure, and sexual satisfaction.

Kissing the Hunter by Angela Knight
Navy Seal Logan McLean hunts the vampires who murdered his wife. Virginia Hart is a sexy vampire searching for her lost soul-mate only to find him in a man determined to kill her. She must convince him all vampires aren't created equally.

Winner of the Venus Book Club Best Book of the Year

Secrets, Volume 8

Taming Kate by Jeanie Cesarini
Kathryn Roman inherits a legal brothel. Little does this city girl know the town wants her to be their new madam so they've charged Trey Holliday, one very dominant cowboy, with taming her.

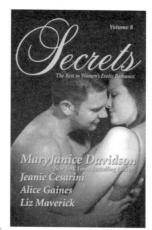

Jared's Wolf by MaryJanice Davidson
Jared Rocke will do anything to avenge his sister's death, but ends up attracted to Moira Wolfbauer, the she-wolf sworn to protect her pack. Joining forces to stop a killer, they learn love defies all boundaries.

My Champion, My Lover by Alice Gaines
Celeste Broder is a woman committed for having a sexy appetite. Mayor Robert Albright may be her champion— if she can convince him her freedom will mean they can indulge their appetites together.

Kiss or Kill by Liz Maverick
In this post-apocalyptic world, Camille Kazinsky's military career rides on her ability to make a choice—whether the robo called Meat should live or die. Can he prove he's human enough to live, man enough… to make her feel like a woman.

Winner of the Venus Book Club Best Book of the Year

Secrets, Volume 9

Wild For You by Kathryn Anne Dubois
When college intern, Georgie, gets captured by a
Congo wildman, she discovers this specimen of male
virility has never seen a woman. The research possibilities are endless!

Wanted by Kimberly Dean
FBI Special Agent Jeff Reno wants Danielle Carver.
There's her body, brains—and that charge of treason
on her head. Dani goes on the run, but the sexy Fed is
hot on her trail.

Secluded by Lisa Marie Rice
Nicholas Lee's wealth and power came with a price—
his enemies will kill anyone he loves. When Isabelle
steals his heart, Nicholas secludes her in his palace for a lifetime of desire in only a
few days.

Flights of Fantasy by Bonnie Hamre
Chloe taught others to see the realities of life but she's never shared the intimate
world of her sensual yearnings. Given the chance, will she be woman enough to
fulfill her most secret erotic fantasy?

Secrets, Volume 10

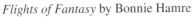

Private Eyes by Dominique Sinclair
When a mystery man captivates P.I. Nicolla Black
during a stakeout, she discovers her no-seduction rule
bending under the pressure of long denied passion.
She agrees to the seduction, but he demands her total
surrender.

The Ruination of Lady Jane by Bonnie Hamre
To avoid her upcoming marriage, Lady Jane Ponson-
by-Maitland flees into the arms of Havyn Attercliffe.
She begs him to ruin her rather than turn her over to
her odious fiancé.

Code Name: Kiss by Jeanie Cesarini
Agent Lily Justiss is on a mission to defend her country
against terrorists that requires giving up her virginity as a sex slave. As her master
takes her body, desire for her commanding officer Seth Blackthorn fuels her mind.

The Sacrifice by Kathryn Anne Dubois
Lady Anastasia Bedovier is days from taking her vows as a Nun. Before she denies
her sensuality forever, she wants to experience pleasure. Count Maxwell is the perfect man to initiate her into erotic delight.

Secrets, Volume 11

Masquerade by Jennifer Probst
Hailey Ashton is determined to free herself from her
sexual restrictions. Four nights of erotic pleasures
without revealing her identity. A chance to explore her
secret desires without the fear of unmasking.

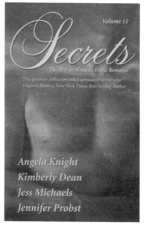

Ancient Pleasures by Jess Michaels
Isabella Winslow is obsessed with finding out what
caused her husband's death, but trapped in an Egyp-
tian concubine's tomb with a sexy American raider,
succumbing to the mummy's sensual curse takes over.

Manhunt by Kimberly Dean
Framed for murder, Michael Tucker takes Taryn
Swanson hostage—the one woman who can clear him.
Despite the evidence against him, the attraction is strong. Tucker resorts to uncon-
ventional, yet effective methods of persuasion to change the sexy ADA's mind.

Wake Me by Angela Knight
Chloe Hart received a sexy painting of a sleeping knight. Radolf of Varik has been
trapped there for centuries, cursed by a witch. His only hope is to visit the dreams of
women and make one of them fall in love with him so she can free him with a kiss.

Secrets, Volume 12

Good Girl Gone Bad by Dominique Sinclair
Setting out to do research for an article, nothing could
have prepared Reagan for Luke, or his offer to teach
her everything she needs to know about sex. Licen-
tious pleasures, forbidden desires… inspiring the best
writing she's ever done.

Aphrodite's Passion by Jess Michaels
When Selena flees Victorian London before her evil
stepchildren can institutionalize her for hysteria,
Gavin is asked to bring her back home. But when he
finds her living on the island of Cyprus, his need to
have her begins to block out every other impulse.

White Heat by Leigh Wyndfield
Raine is hiding in an icehouse in the middle of nowhere from one of the scariest men
in the universes. Walker escaped from a burning prison. Imagine their surprise when
they find out they have the same man to blame for their miseries. Passion, revenge
and love are in their future.

Summer Lightning by Saskia Walker
Sculptress Sally is enjoying an idyllic getaway on a secluded cove when she spots a
gorgeous man walking naked on the beach. When Julian finds an attractive woman
shacked up in his cove, he has to check her out. But what will he do when he finds
she's secretly been using him as a model?

Secrets, Volume 13

Out of Control by Rachelle Chase
Astrid's world revolves around her business and she's
hoping to pick up wealthy Erik Santos as a client. He's
hoping to pick up something entirely different. Will
she give in to the seductive pull of his proposition?

Hawkmoor by Amber Green
Shape-shifters answer to Darien as he acts in the name
of long-missing Lady Hawkmoor, their ruler. When
she unexpectedly surfaces, Darien must deal with a
scrappy individual whose wary eyes hold the other half
of his soul, but who has the power to destroy his world.

Lessons in Pleasure by Charlotte Featherstone
A wicked bargain has Lily vowing never to yield to the
demands of the rake she once loved and lost. Unfortunately, Damian, the Earl of St.
Croix, or Saint as he is infamously known, will not take 'no' for an answer.

In the Heat of the Night by Calista Fox
Haunted by a curse, Molina fears she won't live to see her 30th birthday. Nick, her for-
mer bodyguard, is re-hired to protect her from the fatal accidents that plague her family.
Will his passion and love be enough to convince Molina they have a future together?

Secrets, Volume 14

Soul Kisses by Angela Knight
Beth's been kidnapped by Joaquin Ramirez, a sadistic
vampire. Handsome vampire cousins, Morgan and
Garret Axton, come to her rescue. Can she find happiness with two vampires?

Temptation in Time by Alexa Aames
Ariana escaped the Middle Ages after stealing a kiss
of magic from sexy sorcerer, Marcus de Grey. When
he brings her back, they begin a battle of wills and a
sexual odyssey that could spell disaster for them both.

Ailis and the Beast by Jennifer Barlowe
When Ailis agreed to be her village's sacrifice to the
mysterious Beast she was prepared to sacrifice her vir-
tue, and possibly her life. But some things aren't what they seem. Ailis and the Beast
are about to discover the greatest sacrifice may be the human heart.

Night Heat by Leigh Wynfield
When Rip Bowhite leads a revolt on the prison planet, he ends up struggling to
survive against monsters that rule the night. Jemma, the prison's Healer, won't allow
herself to be distracted by the instant attraction she feels for Rip. As the stakes are
raised and death draws near, love seems doomed in the heat of the night.

Secrets, Volume 15

Simon Says by Jane Thompson
Simon Campbell is a newspaper columnist who panders to male fantasies. Georgina Kennedy is a respectable librarian. On the surface, these two have nothing in common... but don't judge a book by its cover.

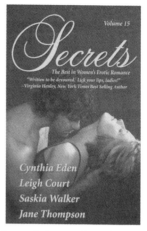

Bite of the Wolf by Cynthia Eden
Gareth Morlet, alpha werewolf, has finally found his mate. All he has to do is convince Trinity to join with him, to give in to the pleasure of a werewolf's mating, and then she will be his... forever.

Falling for Trouble by Saskia Walker
With 48 hours to clear her brother's name, Sonia Harmond finds help from irresistible bad boy, Oliver Eaglestone. When the erotic tension between them hits fever pitch, securing evidence to thwart an international arms dealer isn't the only danger they face.

The Disciplinarian by Leigh Court
Headstrong Clarissa Babcock is sent for instruction in proper wifely obedience. Disciplinarian Jared Ashworth uses the tools of seduction to show her how to control a demanding husband, but her beauty, spirit, and uninhibited passion make Jared hunger to keep her—and their darkly erotic nights—all for himself!

Secrets, Volume 16

Never Enough by Cynthia Eden
Abby McGill has been playing with fire. Bad-boy Jake taught her the true meaning of desire, but she knows she has to end her relationship with him. But Jake isn't about to let the woman he wants walk away from him.

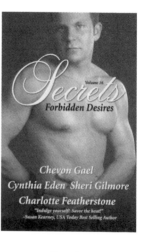

Bunko by Sheri Gilmoore
Tu Tran must decide between Jack, who promises to share every aspect of his life with her, or Dev, who hides behind a mask and only offers nights of erotic sex. Will she gamble on the man who can see behind her own mask and expose her true desires?

Hide and Seek by Chevon Gael
Kyle DeLaurier ditches his trophy-fiance in favor of a tropical paradise full of tall, tanned, topless females.
Private eye, Darcy McLeod, is on the trail of this runaway groom. Together they sizzle while playing Hide and Seek with their true identities.

Seduction of the Muse by Charlotte Featherstone
He's the Dark Lord, the mysterious author who pens the erotic tales of an innocent woman's seduction. She is his muse, the woman he watches from the dark shadows, the woman whose dreams he invades at night.

Secrets, Volume 17

Rock Hard Candy by Kathy Kaye
Jessica Hennessy, descendent of a Voodoo priestess, decides it's time for the man of her dreams. A dose of her ancestor's aphrodisiac slipped into the gooey center of her homemade bon bons ought to do the trick.

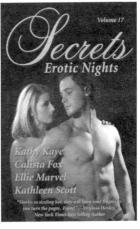

Fatal Error by Kathleen Scott
Jesse Storm must make amends to humanity by destroying the software he helped design that's taken the government hostage. But he must also protect the woman he's loved in secret for nearly a decade.

Birthday by Ellie Marvel
Jasmine Templeton's been celibate long enough. Will a wild night at a hot new club with her two best friends ease the ache or just make it worse? Considering one is Charlie and she's been having strange notions about their relationship of late... It's definitely a birthday neither she nor Charlie will ever forget.

Intimate Rendezvous by Calista Fox
A thief causes trouble at Cassandra Kensington's nightclub and sexy P.I. Dean Hewitt arrives to help. One look at her sends his blood boiling, despite the fact that his keen instincts have him questioning the legitimacy of her business.

Secrets, Volume 18

Lone Wolf Three by Rae Monet
Planetary politics and squabbling drain former rebel leader Taban Zias. But his anger quickly turns to desire when he meets, Lakota Blackson. She's Taban's perfect mate—now if he can just convince her.

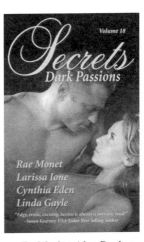

Flesh to Fantasy by Larissa Ione
Kelsa Bradshaw is a loner happily immersed in a world of virtual reality. Trent Jordan is a paramedic who experiences the harsh realities of life. When their worlds collide in an erotic eruption can Trent convince Kelsa to turn the fantasy into something real?

Heart Full of Stars by Linda Gayle
Singer Fanta Rae finds herself stranded on a lonely Mars outpost with the first human male she's seen in years. Ex-Marine Alex Decker lost his family and guilt drove him into isolation, but when alien assassins come to enslave Fanta, she and Decker come together to fight for their lives.

The Wolf's Mate by Cynthia Eden
When Michael Morlet finds "Kat" Hardy fighting for her life, he instantly recognizes her as the mate he's been seeking all of his life, but someone's trying to kill her. With danger stalking them, will Kat trust him enough to become his mate?

Secrets, Volume 19

Affliction by Elisa Adams
Holly Aronson finally believes she's safe with sweet Andrew. But when his life long friend, Shane, arrives, events begin to spiral out of control. She's inexplicably drawn to Shane. As she runs for her life, which one will protect her?

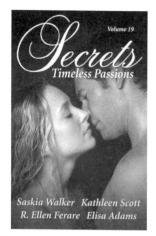

Falling Stars by Kathleen Scott
Daria is both a Primon fighter pilot and a Primon princess. As a deadly new enemy faces appears, she must choose between her duty to the fleet and the desperate need to forge an alliance through her marriage to the enemy's General Raven.

Toy in the Attic by R. Ellen Ferare
Gabrielle discovers a life-sized statue of a nude man. Her unexpected roommate reveals himself to be a talented lover caught by a witch's curse. Can she help him break free of the spell that holds him, without losing her heart along the way?

What You Wish For by Saskia Walker
Lucy Chambers is renovating her historic house. As her dreams about a stranger become more intense, she wishes he were with her. Two hundred years in the past, the man wishes for companionship. Suddenly they find themselves together—in his time.

Secrets, Volume 20

The Subject by Amber Green
One week Tyler is a game designer, signing the deal of her life. The next, she's running for her life. Who can she trust? Certainly not sexy, mysterious Esau, who keeps showing up after the hoo-hah hits the fan!

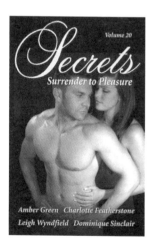

Surrender by Dominique Sinclair
Agent Madeline Carter is in too deep. She's slipped into Sebastian Maiocco's life to investigate his Sicilian mafia family. He unearths desires Madeline's unable to deny, conflicting the duty that honors her. Madeline must surrender to Sebastian or risk being exposed, leaving her target for a ruthless clan.

Stasis by Leigh Wyndfield
Morgann Right's Commanding Officer's been drugged with Stasis, turning him into a living statue she's forced to take care of for ten long days. As her hands tend to him, she sees her CO in a totally different light. She wants him and, while she can tell he wants her, touching him intimately might come back to haunt them both.

A Woman's Pleasure by Charlotte Featherstone
Widowed Isabella, Lady Langdon is yearning to discover all the pleasures denied her in her marriage, she finds herself falling hard for the magnetic charms of the mysterious and exotic Julian Gresham—a man skilled in pleasures of the flesh.

Secrets, Volume 21

Caged Wolf by Cynthia Eden
Alerac La Morte has been drugged and kidnapped. He realizes his captor, Madison Langley, is actually his destined mate, but she hates his kind. Will Alerac convince her he's not the monster she thinks?

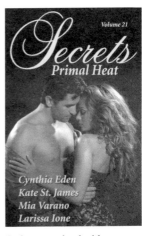

Wet Dreams by Larissa Ione
Injured and on the run, agent Brent Logan needs a miracle. What he gets is a boat owned by Marina Summers. Pursued by killers, ravaged by a storm, and plagued by engine troubles, they can do little but spend their final hours immersed in sensual pleasure.

Good Vibrations by Kate St. James
Lexi O'Brien vows to swear off sex while she attends grad school, so when her favorite out-of-town customer asks her out, she decides to indulge in an erotic fling. Little does she realize Gage Templeton is moving home, to her city, and has no intention of settling for a short-term affair..

Virgin of the Amazon by Mia Varano
Librarian Anna Winter gets lost on the Amazon and stumbles upon a tribe whose shaman wants a pale-skinned virgin to deflower. British adventurer Coop Daventry, the tribe's self-styled chief, wants to save her, but which man poses a greater threat?

Secrets, Volume 22

Heat by Ellie Marvel
Mild-mannered alien Tarkin is in heat and the only compatible female is a Terran. He courts her the old fashioned Terran way. Because if he can't seduce her before his cycle ends, he won't get a second chance.

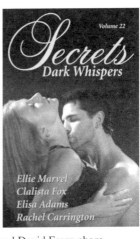

Breathless by Rachel Carrington
Lark Hogan is a martial arts expert seeking vengeance for the death of her sister. She seeks help from Zac, a mercenary wizard. Confronting a common enemy, they battle their own demons as well as their powerful attraction, and will fight to the death to protect what they've found.

Midnight Rendezvous by Calista Fox
From New York to Cabo to Paris to Tokyo, Cat Hewitt and David Essex share decadent midnight rendezvous. But when the real world presses in on their erotic fantasies, and Cat's life is in danger, will their whirlwind romance stand a chance?

Birthday Wish by Elisa Adams
Anna Kelly had many goals before turning 30 and only one is left—to spend one night with sexy Dean Harrison. When Dean asks her what she wants for her birthday, she grabs at the opportunity to ask him for an experience she'll never forget.

Secrets, Volume 23

The Sex Slave by Roxi Romano
Jaci Coe needs a hero and the hard bodied man in
black meets all the criteria. Opportunistic Jaci takes
advantage of Lazarus Stone's commandingly protective nature, but together, they learn how to live free...
and love freely.

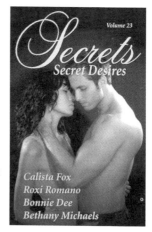

Forever My Love by Calista Fox
Professor Aja Woods is a 16th century witch... only
she doesn't know it. Christian St. James, her vampire
lover, has watched over her spirit for 500 years. When
her powers are recovered, so too are her memories of
Christian—and the love they once shared.

Reflection of Beauty by Bonnie Dee
Artist Christine Dawson is commissioned to paint a portrait of wealthy recluse, Eric
Leroux. It's up to her to reach the heart of this physically and emotionally scarred
man. Can love rescue Eric from isolation and restore his life?

Educating Eva by Bethany Lynn
Eva Blakely attends the infamous Ivy Hill houseparty to gather research for her book
Mating Rituals of the Human Male. But when she enlists the help of research "speci-
men" and notorious rake, Aidan Worthington, she gets some unexpected results.

Secrets, Volume 24

Hot on Her Heels by Mia Varano
Private investigator Jack Slater dons a g-string to
investigate the Lollipop Lounge, a male strip club.
He's not sure if the club's sexy owner, Vivica Steele,
is involved in the scam, but Jack figures he's just the
Lollipop to sweeten her life.

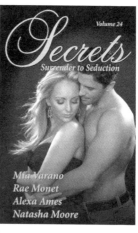

Shadow Wolf by Rae Monet
A half-breed Lupine challenges a high-ranking
Solarian Wolf Warrior. When Dia Nahiutras tries to
steal Roark D'Reincolt's wolf, does she get an enemy
forever or a mate for life?

Bad to the Bone by Natasha Moore
At her class reunion, Annie Shane sheds her good girl
reputation through one wild weekend with Luke Kendall. But Luke is done playing
the field and wants to settle down. What would a bad girl do?

War God by Alexa Ames
Estella Eaton, a lovely graduate student, is the unwitting carrier of the essence of
Aphrodite. But Ares, god of war, the ultimate alpha male, knows the truth and becomes obsessed with Estelle, pursuing her relentlessly. Can her modern sensibilities
and his ancient power coexist, or will their battle of wills destroy what matters most?

Secrets, Volume 25

Blood Hunt by Cynthia Eden
Vampiress Nema Alexander has a taste for bad boys.
Slade Brion has just been charged with tracking her
down. He won't stop until he catches her, and Nema
won't stop until she claims him, forever.

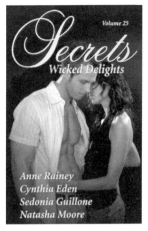

Scandalous Behavior by Anne Rainey
Tess Marley wants to take a walk on the wild side.
Who better to teach her about carnal pleasures than
her intriguing boss, Kevin Haines? But Tess makes
a major miscalculation when she crosses the line
between lust and love.

Enter the Hero by Sedonia Guillone
Kass and Lian are sentenced to sex slavery in the Con-
federation's pleasure district. Forced to make love for an audience, their hearts are
with each other while their bodies are on display. Now, in the midst of sexual slavery,
they have one more chance to escape to Paradise.

Up to No Good by Natasha Moore
Former syndicated columnist Simon "Mac" MacKenzie hides a tragic secret. When
freelance writer Alison Chandler tracks him down, he knows she's up to no good. Is
their attraction merely a distraction or the key to surviving their war of wills?

Secrets, Volume 26

Secret Rendezvous by Calista Fox
McCarthy Portman has seen enough happily-
ever-afters to long for one of her own, but when her
renowned matchmaking software pairs her with the
wild and wicked Josh Kensington, everything she's
always believed about love is turned upside down.

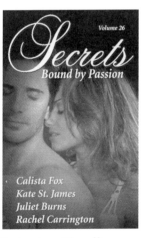

Enchanted Spell by Rachel Carrington
Witches and wizards don't mix. Every magical being
knows that. Yet, when a little mischievous magic
thrusts Ella and Kevlin together, they do so much
more than mix—they combust.

Exes and Ahhhs by Kate St. James
Former lovers Risa Haber and Eric Lange are partners
in a catering business, but Eric can't seem to remain a silent partner. Risa offers one
night of carnal delights if he'll sell her his share then disappear forever.

The Spy's Surrender by Juliet Burns
The famous courtesan Eva Werner is England's secret weapon against Napoleon. Her
orders are to attend a sadistic marquis' depraved house party and rescue a British spy
being held prisoner. As the weekend orgy begins, she's forced to make the spy her
love slave for the marquis' pleasure. But who is slave and who is master?

The Forever Kiss
by Angela Knight

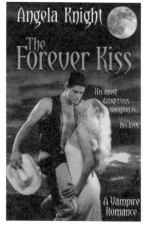

Listen to what reviewers say:

"*The Forever Kiss* flows well with good characters and an interesting plot. … If you enjoy vampires and a lot of hot sex, you are sure to enjoy *The Forever Kiss*."

—*The Best Reviews*

"Battling vampires, a protective ghost and the ever present battle of good and evil keep excellent pace with the erotic delights in Angela Knight's *The Forever Kiss*—a book that absolutely bites with refreshing paranormal humor." **4½ Stars, Top Pick**

—*Romantic Times BOOKclub*

"I found *The Forever Kiss* to be an exceptionally written, refreshing book. … I really enjoyed this book by Angela Knight. … 5 angels!"

—*Fallen Angel Reviews*

"*The Forever Kiss* is the first single title released from Red Sage and if this is any indication of what we can expect, it won't be the last. … The love scenes are hot enough to give a vampire a sunburn and the fight scenes will have you cheering for the good guys."

—*Really Bad Barb Reviews*

In *The Forever Kiss*:

For years, Valerie Chase has been haunted by dreams of a Texas Ranger she knows only as "Cowboy." As a child, he rescued her from the nightmare vampires who murdered her parents. As an adult, she still dreams of him—but now he's her seductive lover in nights of erotic pleasure.

Yet "Cowboy" is more than a dream—he's the real Cade McKinnon—and a vampire! For years, he's protected Valerie from Edward Ridgemont, the sadistic vampire who turned him. Now, Ridgmont wants Valerie for his own and Cade is the only one who can protect her.

When Val finds herself abducted by her handsome dream man, she's appalled to discover he's one of the vampires she fears. Now, caught in a web of fear and passion, she and Cade must learn to trust each other, even as an immortal monster stalks their every move.

Their only hope of survival is… *The Forever Kiss*.

Romantic Times Best Erotic Novel of the Year

Check out our hot eBook titles available online at eRedSage.com!

Visit the site regularly as we're always adding new eBook titles.

Here's just some of what you'll find:

A Christmas Cara by Bethany Michaels

A Damsel in Distress by Brenda Williamson

Blood Game by Rae Monet

Fires Within by Roxana Blaze

Forbidden Fruit by Anne Rainey

High Voltage by Calista Fox

Master of the Elements by Alice Gaines

One Wish by Calista Fox

Quinn's Curse by Natasha Moore

Rock My World by Caitlyn Willows

The Doctor Next Door by Catherine Berlin

Unclaimed by Nathalie Gray

It's not just reviewers raving about *Secrets*. See what readers have to say:

"When are you coming out with a new Volume? I want a new one next month!" via email from a reader.

"I loved the hot, wet sex without vulgar words being used to make it exciting." after *Volume 1*

"I loved the blend of sensuality and sexual intensity—HOT!" after *Volume 2*

"The best thing about *Secrets* is they're hot and brief! The least thing is you do not have enough of them!" after *Volume 3*

"I have been extremely satisfied with *Secrets*, keep up the good writing." after *Volume 4*

"Stories have plot and characters to support the erotica. They would be good strong stories without the heat." after *Volume 5*

"*Secrets* really knows how to push the envelop better than anyone else." after *Volume 6*

"These are the best sensual stories I have ever read!" after *Volume 7*

"I love, love, love the *Secrets* stories. I now have all of them, please have more books come out each year." after *Volume 8*

"These are the perfect sensual romance stories!" after *Volume 9*

"What I love about *Secrets Volume 10* is how I couldn't put it down!" after *Volume 10*

"All of the *Secrets* volumes are terrific! I have read all of them up to *Secrets Volume 11*. Please keep them coming! I will read every one you make!" after *Volume 11*

Finally, the men you've been dreaming about!

Give the Gift of Spicy Romantic Fiction

Don't want to wait? You can place a retail price ($12.99) order for any of the *Secrets* volumes from the following:

① online at **eRedSage.com**

② **Waldenbooks, Borders, and Books-a-Million Stores**

③ **Amazon.com** or **BarnesandNoble.com**

④ or buy them at your local bookstore or online book source.

Bookstores: Please contact Baker & Taylor Distributors, Ingram Book Distributor, or Red Sage Publishing, Inc. for bookstore sales.

Order by title or ISBN #:

Vol. 1: 0-9648942-0-3
ISBN #13 978-0-9648942-0-4

Vol. 2: 0-9648942-1-1
ISBN #13 978-0-9648942-1-1

Vol. 3: 0-9648942-2-X
ISBN #13 978-0-9648942-2-8

Vol. 4: 0-9648942-4-6
ISBN #13 978-0-9648942-4-2

Vol. 5: 0-9648942-5-4
ISBN #13 978-0-9648942-5-9

Vol. 6: 0-9648942-6-2
ISBN #13 978-0-9648942-6-6

Vol. 7: 0-9648942-7-0
ISBN #13 978-0-9648942-7-3

Vol. 8: 0-9648942-8-9
ISBN #13 978-0-9648942-9-7

Vol. 9: 0-9648942-9-7
ISBN #13 978-0-9648942-9-7

Vol. 10: 0-9754516-0-X
ISBN #13 978-0-9754516-0-1

Vol. 11: 0-9754516-1-8
ISBN #13 978-0-9754516-1-8

Vol. 12: 0-9754516-2-6
ISBN #13 978-0-9754516-2-5

Vol. 13: 0-9754516-3-4
ISBN #13 978-0-9754516-3-2

Vol. 14: 0-9754516-4-2
ISBN #13 978-0-9754516-4-9

Vol. 15: 0-9754516-5-0
ISBN #13 978-0-9754516-5-6

Vol. 16: 0-9754516-6-9
ISBN #13 978-0-9754516-6-3

Vol. 17: 0-9754516-7-7
ISBN #13 978-0-9754516-7-0

Vol. 18: 0-9754516-8-5
ISBN #13 978-0-9754516-8-7

Vol. 19: 0-9754516-9-3
ISBN #13 978-0-9754516-9-4

Vol. 20: 1-60310-000-8
ISBN #13 978-1-60310-000-7

Vol. 21: 1-60310-001-6
ISBN #13 978-1-60310-001-4

Vol. 22: 1-60310-002-4
ISBN #13 978-1-60310-002-1

Vol. 23: 1-60310-164-0
ISBN #13 978-1-60310-164-6

Vol. 24: 1-60310-165-9
ISBN #13 978-1-60310-165-3

Vol. 25: 1-60310-005-9
ISBN #13 978-1-60310-005-2

Vol. 26: 1-60310-006-7
ISBN #13 978-1-60310-006-9

The Forever Kiss:
0-9648942-3-8
ISBN #13
978-0-9648942-3-5 ($14.00)

Red Sage Publishing Order Form:
(Orders shipped in two to three days of receipt.)

Each volume of *Secrets* retails for $12.99, but you can get it direct via mail order for only $10.99 each. The novel *The Forever Kiss* retails for $14.00, but by direct mail order, you only pay $12.00. Use the order form below to place your direct mail order. Fill in the quantity you want for each book on the blanks beside the title.

_____ *Secrets* Volume 1	_____ *Secrets* Volume 10	_____ *Secrets* Volume 19
_____ *Secrets* Volume 2	_____ *Secrets* Volume 11	_____ *Secrets* Volume 20
_____ *Secrets* Volume 3	_____ *Secrets* Volume 12	_____ *Secrets* Volume 21
_____ *Secrets* Volume 4	_____ *Secrets* Volume 13	_____ *Secrets* Volume 22
_____ *Secrets* Volume 5	_____ *Secrets* Volume 14	_____ *Secrets* Volume 23
_____ *Secrets* Volume 6	_____ *Secrets* Volume 15	_____ *Secrets* Volume 24
_____ *Secrets* Volume 7	_____ *Secrets* Volume 16	_____ *Secrets* Volume 25
_____ *Secrets* Volume 8	_____ *Secrets* Volume 17	_____ *Secrets* Volume 26
_____ *Secrets* Volume 9	_____ *Secrets* Volume 18	_____ *The Forever Kiss*

Total _____ *Secrets* Volumes @ **$10.99 each = $**_____

Total _____ *The Forever Kiss* @ **$12.00 each = $**_____

Shipping & handling (in the U.S.) $_____

US Priority Mail: UPS insured:
1–2 books .... $ 5.50   1–4 books $16.00
3–5 books .... $11.50   5–9 books $25.00
6–9 books .... $14.50   10–26 books $29.00
10–15 books $19.00
16–26 books .... $27.00   SUBTOTAL $_____

Florida 6% sales tax (if delivered in FL) $_____

TOTAL AMOUNT ENCLOSED $_____

Your personal information is kept private and not shared with anyone.

Name: (please print) _____

Address: (no P.O. Boxes) _____

City/State/Zip: _____

Phone or email: (only regarding order if necessary) _____

You can order direct from **eRedSage.com** and use a credit card or you can use this form to send in your mail order with a check. Please make check payable to **Red Sage Publishing**. Check must be drawn on a U.S. bank in U.S. dollars. Mail your check and order form to:

Red Sage Publishing, Inc. Department S26 P.O. Box 4844 Seminole, FL 33775